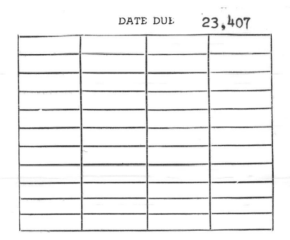

MOSCOW RULES

MOSCOW

RULES

Robert Moss

VILLARD BOOKS NEW YORK

Grateful acknowledgment is made to the following for permission to reprint previously published material:

Nouvelles Editions (Paris): Excerpts from lyrics written by Marina Vlady (as recorded by Vladimir Vissotsky). Translation made with permission of the publisher.

Viking Penguin Inc.: Excerpt from a ballad by Aleksandr Galich. Galich, a dramatist who turned to satirical writing after the death of Stalin and achieved enormous popularity in *Samizdat*, left the Soviet Union in 1974 and died in Paris in 1978. Reprinted from *To Build a Castle: My Life as a Dissenter* by Vladimir Kostantinovich Bukovskii. Copyright © 1977 Novelpress S.a.r.l. This translation reprinted by permission of Viking Press Inc. Copyright © Viking Penguin Inc. 1978.

CONTENTS

The mouse dreams dreams that would terrify the cat.
—OLD ARMENIAN PROVERB

MOSCOW
RULES

PROLOGUE:

GOGOL
BOULEVARD

Insurrection is a machine that makes no noise.
—TROTSKY

He looked crowded behind his desk, like a racehorse confined in a narrow stall. He was very tall, and powerfully built, and his eyes were the gray of Baltic waters, surrendering nothing of their depths. He seemed young to be wearing the shoulder boards of a Soviet major-general with his khaki uniform. Those who were close to him—and there were not many—called him Sasha. Others called him Alexander Sergeyovich or, more formally, General Preobrazhensky.

He had reached the bottom of the stack of papers on his desk, going through them with the clipped exactitude of an automatic sheet-feeder. He initialed the last report, on army discipline in the Leningrad military district, and stared up at the pale yellow wall across the room. That was where the portrait of the last General Secretary had hung. It was taken down when he died, and the painters were sent round to touch up the faded oblong that was left underneath, so that no trace of the past remained. The authorities were meticulous about things like that.

There was no portrait of the current General Secretary in Preobrazhensky's office. To judge from the reports leaking out from Kuntsevo, where the best cardiac specialists available to the Kremlin clinic were gathered around his bedside, this was a sensible economy; it wouldn't have hung for long. In its place was the standard icon of Lenin and an old photograph of the Defense Minister, thick and jowly even when it was taken.

There were no books, no mementoes, not even a plaque from one of the Warsaw Pact divisions. You could have scoured that office for clues to the character of the man who occupied it, and learned solely that he was important enough to have a window overlooking Frunze Street, a direct line to the Chief of Staff, a small room at the back with a shower, a bed, and a row of hangers for his dress uniforms. There was only one oddity: among the uniforms was a civilian suit, a neat gray wool-and-polyester blend made in Canada for Brooks Brothers of New York.

Sasha's secretary, an army major, came in with a fresh stack of reports and requisitions, mostly addressed to the Chief of Staff, Marshal Zotov. The Marshal was not overly fond of paperwork. It fell to Preobrazhensky, as his personal assistant, to relieve Zotov of the tedium. Sasha drafted most of the orders that were issued over the Marshal's signature. Sometimes, to spare his boss the burden of handling the documents, Sasha would sign them himself and scrawl *p/p* where Zotov's autograph was supposed to appear. In Russian, these initials signified that the Chief of Staff had signed the original, which was assumed to be locked away in a safe somewhere.

Preobrazhensky swore softly under his breath as he leafed through one of the new reports. It contained a psychiatric evaluation of an army commander he had come to know well when they served together against the Afghan guerrillas. The general had been relieved of his duties and hauled off to the notorious Serbsky psychiatric institute, where dissidents were passed off as lunatics or actually driven insane. The evidence of the general's psychosis was that he had failed to accept the necessity of ordering his troops to fire on unarmed strikers during the labor troubles at the giant auto factory in Togliatti.

The report recommended intensified medication. Treatments were scheduled to begin in two days' time. One of the drugs specified was aminazin. Sasha was familiar with its effects. It replaced memory with a yawning black hole and eroded all the cognitive functions. After being treated with aminazin, even a Nobel laureate for literature would have trouble scanning the headlines of his hometown paper. The treatment prescribed for General Pavel Leybutin would transform him into a grinning vegetable. Then the people who had authorized it would be able to show him to the world to demonstrate that he had disobeyed not because of principle, but because he was off his head.

Sasha scribbled a request to delay the new treatment for a period of one week so that the high command could pursue a further investigation of the general's "anti-Soviet activities" in his former military district. At the bottom, he put the letters p/p and his own signature. It was irregular, of course, for the General Staff to try to interfere in this way. Leybutin was now the property of the Committee for State Security. But all Preobrazhensky needed was to hold things up for a while.

A week will be plenty of time, Sasha told himself. *If the bitches agree.* His long surname sprawled across the paper like an arctic horizon. He called in his secretary and handed him the memo.

"Ilya, give me a cigarette."

The major raised his eyebrows. In the months he had worked for General Preobrazhensky, he had never seen him smoke. He fished out a pack of coarse Russian cigarettes, and started making apologies for the brand.

"Just give me a light." Impatient, Sasha got up from the desk and stood next to his secretary, towering over him.

The major was nervous, and his first match sputtered out. Sasha took the box from him and lit the cigarette himself.

"See that report gets processed immediately," he instructed his aide.

Sasha started to prowl between desk and window. Seven floors below him, along the narrow strip of Frunze Street, a line of black staff cars snaked in front of the main entrance to the General Staff building, with its massive Grecian portico. Over to the right, the solid concrete bulk of the building that housed the stacks of the Lenin Library blocked out the domes of the Kremlin. To the left, Sasha could make out the star-shaped Arbatskaya metro station, constructed from polished red stone, and, beyond it, the surge of traffic and the double row of ugly tower blocks—the Dentures of Moscow, some wit had called them—along Kalinin Prospekt. Out of sight, under the leafless maples of Gogol Boulevard, pensioners were sitting in twos and threes on the benches, playing chess for a rouble in the thin light of autumn, watching the cars whizz by on either side, toward Kalinin Prospekt or the river.

Preobrazhensky kept circling back to the lone black telephone on his desk, an old-fashioned rotary model with a row of buttons underneath.

There should be word, he told himself. He pictured the General Secretary under the scalpel in the bright modern clinic hidden away in the birch woods behind what had once been Stalin's hunting lodge. The man hadn't made a public appearance in weeks. That had at least spared the people the embarrassment of listening to him wheezing his way through a speech, losing his place, garbling and jumbling the text until any sense was lost. Moscow was buzzing with rumors. In the beer-bars, you could hear people whispering that the General Secretary was already dead "They" were keeping the body on ice until they agreed on who was going to take over. Sasha knew better. It was actually the other way around. This time, the men who were bent on sharing the succession weren't waiting for the doctors to pronounce the General Secretary dead before they started dividing up the spoils.

The phone shrilled. The flashing light indicated that the call had come through on his direct outside line. He let it ring a second time before lifting the receiver.

"Sasha?" The voice at the other end was a full, rich baritone, the voice of a man who is always ready to burst into song and probably does not sing too badly.

"Yes, Feliks."

"Sasha, it's time. Bangladesh!" The caller sounded positively elated, possibly a little drunk.

"What?"

"Yes, there's more trouble in Bangladesh," the caller amplified. He added: "Not only that, but it's nearly four o'clock and you haven't bought me a drink yet. The sooner we get out of our offices, the better."

"You're right," Preobrazhensky replied, adopting the same bantering tone. "I'll try to think up a new alibi for Lydochka."

"*Ty chto mumu yebyosh?*" the caller goaded him. "Why are you fucking a cow?" This was his favorite invitation to proceed with the drinking. "Let's get to it."

"All right," Sasha laughed. "*Nalivay!*"

Preobrazhensky hung up, took a deep drag on the last of his cigarette, and mashed the butt into the plain glass ashtray beside the phone. His face was empty of expression.

He did not call his friend Kolya over at the Aquarium—military intelligence headquarters—to ask for an update on Bangladesh. He was indifferent to whether one strongman had ousted another in that corner of South Asia. The message he had just received had nothing to do with *that* Bangladesh.

He did call his wife, to tell her not to expect him for dinner. No, he could not say when he would be home; he would probably have to spend the night at the office because of something that had blown up. Lydia went through the motions of complaining. She always did. But he knew she would think nothing of it; it had happened often enough before. Certainly, the dialogue would sound natural enough to anyone from the Committee—the office euphemism for the KGB—who happened to be listening in.

Sasha did not use the black telephone for his next call. Instead, he opened his safe. Inside was a special device that he had had installed only three days before by a military technician. It connected him to the residence of the commander of the special forces brigade at Kavrov, a smoky industrial city on the railroad east of Moscow. When Sasha lifted the handset, Olga—General Zaytsev's wife—answered at once. There was a slight quaver in her voice, but Sasha knew the woman. She was doggedly loyal, a peasant at heart, like her husband. She would play her role.

"I've been trying to reach Fedya," Preobrazhensky lied to her. "If you happen to talk to him before I do, please tell him Sasha called. Tell him the meeting we arranged cannot take place because our friend must leave immediately for Bangladesh." He stressed the last word, the unfamiliar one, to make sure she got it right.

She did not ask him to repeat anything. As soon as he was finished, she hung up, without formalities.

Sasha's third call, on the black phone, was to the special forces base at Kavrov. All messages in and out of the base—by phone, telex, or cable—were monitored by the KGB.

It took several minutes before Zaytsev was brought to the phone. He was breathing heavily, as if he had been putting himself through punishing physical exercises. Sasha could picture the man, bull-necked, broad-chested, sweating his way around the brutal obstacle course that ran through the pine forests, his arms swinging evenly, like pistons, reminding his recruits that he asked nothing of them he was not prepared to do himself.

When he spoke to Zaytsev, Sasha was clipped and formal. His tone was that of higher authority dealing with a subordinate. Both men held the rank of major-general, but Sasha was the right arm of the Chief of Staff, and Zaytsev was just a brigade commander, a position held by colonels in most branches of the army. Listening in on the conversation, you would not have suspected that these men were friends.

"The Chief of Staff wishes to know how the preparations for the exercises are coming along," Sasha began.

"Comrade General," Zaytsev responded equally stiffly, in his low, gravelly voice, "everything is proceeding in accordance with standing orders. You can inform Comrade Marshal that he will be able to attend the exercises at the appointed time, one week from today."

"Good. I am sure you understand that the Marshal is extremely concerned that the maneuvers are executed without a hitch, one week from today." Sasha repeated Zaytsev's phrase to be sure that the KGB monitors did not fail to grasp it. They were sometimes a little slow on the uptake.

There was a curt exchange about transport arrangements, and then Preobrazhensky hung up abruptly. Another light on his phone had flashed on.

He punched the button and said, "Yes, Comrade Marshal."

"Get in here immediately," Marshal Zotov growled. "We have a visitor. A friend from the Committee."

As Sasha marched along a corridor the width of a railway car, spotlessly clean under unremitting fluorescent lights, he tried to think of a reason why the KGB had called on the Chief of Staff—any reason except the one he feared most. He had not found a satisfactory answer by the time he reached the door to the Marshal's office. The door was massive, like the man sitting behind it, oak covered with padded black leather designed to shut out eavesdroppers. The leather was deceptively soft to the touch, like the seat of an old studded chesterfield.

The Marshal's adjutant threw open the door, and Sasha's whole body tensed as if he had just walked into an ambush. Marshal Zotov sat at his desk, his huge arms folded across his chest. His expression suggested he was trying to prevent himself from committing an act of violence with them.

Lolling in an armchair on the far side of the room, his face turned toward the window, was a man of medium height with the blue tabs of the KGB on his uniform and a colonel's badges of rank. He affected not to have noticed the new arrival.

Sasha had seen this man only once before, in the bar of the Bega restaurant at the Moscow Hippodrome, where successful gamblers drank to their wins and others to obliterate their losses. But the colonel's face was etched on his memory, the lines traced in acid.

It was an unremarkable face, undistinguished by any signs of more than average intelligence. The eyes were small and bright and hard, like a jackdaw's. The features did not seem big enough for the pendulous head; they might have been molded from moist putty. The ears were large, but fitted tightly against the cranium, as if the man had spent most of his life pressed up against keyholes. It was an ageless kind of face, but Sasha knew the man was over sixty. It was not a face to inspire fear, under normal circumstances, just a mildly unpleasant reaction. It was a face that, in a different society, might have belonged to the night clerk at the kind of flophouse where they rent rooms by the hour.

But for Sasha, this ordinary-looking man was the human symbol of tragedies that had misshapen his youth, deprived him of the possibility of a normal life, and set him on a course that, in the space of twenty-four hours, would end in something almost beyond imagining, an event that would convulse all of Russia—or in the squalor of his own arrest and execution. As he watched Colonel Topchy, Preobrazhensky was certain that, at that moment, the man was a lethal weapon pointed at *him.* Knotted inside, his adrenaline pumping, the young general still betrayed no outward emotion.

Marshal Zotov made the introductions.

"Oh yes, General Preobrazhensky. Assigned to the General Staff for *Special* Missions." As Topchy recited Sasha's official title, he made no effort to conceal the edge of sarcasm in his voice. "You have developed quite a reputation in the Third Directorate." The Third Directorate of the KGB—Topchy's section—was charged with spying on the armed forces. It was Topchy's men who listened in on Sasha's phone calls. Their power was such that there was nothing incongruous about Topchy, nominally a colonel, dropping in on the Chief of Staff.

"Colonel Topchy is here on some very delicate business," the Marshal explained.

Sasha scanned the Marshal's face for guidance. Had there been a leak? Had the operation he had set in motion with his phone call to Zaytsev's house already been betrayed?

The Marshal looked confident enough behind his desk, a commanding physical presence, magnificently ugly.

"Our friends from the Committee"—Zotov's sideways glance at Topchy was less than friendly—"have nominated a new chief for the special unit at Kavrov. A careful and *sober* man, we are told."

Topchy's department had "special units," or *otdeli*, attached to military commands throughout the Soviet Bloc. Zaytsev's command, the Spetsnaz brigade at Kavrov, rated its own KGB section. A curious incident had taken place at Kavrov a couple of weeks before. The head of the KGB unit responsible for keeping tabs on Zaytsev's men had broken his neck, apparently in a fall from the tower that was used for parachute training. The circumstances looked fishy; the KGB man was no kind of athlete. At the same time, he had earned a considerable reputation as a *zakhleba*, a guzzler. And the autopsy showed he had consumed more than a liter of vodka before the accident. The provisional verdict was accidental death while under the influence of alcohol. Topchy's presence in the Marshal's office suggested that the Third Directorate was not satisfied with this conclusion. The appointment of a new chief for the KGB section at Kavrov was, after all, a routine business. It did not require a meeting with the Chief of Staff, or even his assistant.

The drift of the conversation served to deepen Sasha's suspicions. Colonel Topchy wasted little time talking about Kavrov. When he turned to Sasha, you could hear him working the gears. His manner, at first cold and sarcastic, became exaggeratedly cordial. He complimented Preobrazhensky on his work and on past assignments, dwelling on the time Sasha had spent in the United States on intelligence missions. He threw out some odd, offhanded questions about Sasha's opinions about the Americans. Sasha began to feel that the KGB man was less interested in what had happened to his spy in Kavrov than in feeling both of them out. There was a treacherous undertow in his words, most forceful when he was most agreeable on the surface.

Marshal Zotov gave it precisely a quarter of an hour, counting off the minutes on his wall clock. Then he rose from his desk—topped with green baize and bristling with model tanks and planes, trophies from Warsaw Pact armies—as if to dismiss his visitors. With his massive shoulders and heavy jowls, propping himself up on his fists, Zotov looked rather like the old mastiff he kept at his dacha in the Silver Forest.

"I'm leaving early," he told Sasha, as Colonel Topchy handed the young general some standard forms relating to the transfer of the new KGB section chief to Kavrov. "I won't be back until late tomorrow," the Marshal added. "I have been summoned to attend a special extended meeting of the Politburo. So I rely on you to hold the fort."

The Marshal avoided looking at Sasha as he said this.

Topchy smiled and nodded, as if to indicate that he, too, was in on the secret of the Politburo meeting.

Sasha knew—because a man had called him with the code word *Bangladesh*—what was on the agenda for the Politburo session. They had pronounced the General Secretary dead, and were going to pick a new one. He wondered whether the doctors had already shut off the life-support systems in that secluded ward among the white birches, or whether that would come later.

Sasha left the Marshal's office first. Topchy lingered for a moment. He made sure that Sasha was still within earshot when he remarked to Zotov, "You know, of course, that some people criticized you for appointing your son-in-law to such a senior post on the General Staff."

Zotov scowled, and the KGB man quickly added, "Of course, they were wrong. Preobrazhensky is an exceptional officer." Again, there was that cutting edge of irony in his voice.

"Oh, yes, exceptional," Marshal Zotov grunted, ignoring the innuendos, impatient to be rid of his KGB guest.

This exchange convinced Sasha that the danger was imminent, and that Topchy's main motivation for visiting General Staff headquarters that afternoon was to play cat-and-mouse with them before coming in for the kill. Topchy was no stranger to killing. Now Sasha felt certain that Topchy was amusing himself, while awaiting his moment to return to the building with an order to take him to Lefortovo prison.

As he hurried back to his own office, Sasha brooded over the apparently disconnected remarks that the KGB man had thrown out in the Marshal's office. The questions about New York and the Americans, seemingly casual, made him most uneasy. In his own room, he threw open the window, despite the chill in the air and the noise of the traffic on the left side of the building, facing Gogol Boulevard. There was a wide-meshed net tacked to the window frame, as in many of the offices in the building. It was not meant to keep bugs out, but to catch documents that might get caught up and blown away by a sudden breeze. This was a rational precaution; only a handful of generals and marshals rated air conditioning, and in the depth of summer, many of the windows were opened to get relief from the stifling heat. Sasha stared out through the mesh of the net, almost wide enough to stick a hand through, and suddenly he realized the point of the KGB man's questions about America. For an instant his stomach clenched up inside like a fist.

He went to the safe, unlocked it, and took out his pistol and one of the boxes of ammunition he kept on the same shelf. The pistol was a P-6 with a built-in silencer, like the ones the Spetsnaz commandos used. Methodically, he fitted in the magazine, tested the weight of the gun in his palm for a moment, then slipped it into his pocket and closed the door of the safe.

Whatever the night held for him, it was not going to end Topchy's way.

1.

DISCOVERIES

I love my country, but with a strange love: my
reason cannot fathom it.
—LERMONTOV, "MY COUNTRY"

1 It had begun a quarter of a century before, with an accident on the fifth-floor landing of the featureless gray apartment block where he lived with his mother and grandmother. He had just turned sixteen, though he looked older. It was a Saturday, and he had been sent to fetch groceries from the local *gastronom*, whose big glass windows were filled with dusty plastic replicas of cuts of meat and with pyramids of blue-and-silver cans of caviar. When he got home, his grandmother did not let him leave immediately, but sniffed at everything, as usual, complaining that the sour cream was no longer thick and fat, the way it used to be, and that the beef looked and smelled as if it had been left lying around for days for the flies to inspect.

Finally released, Sasha went racing down the stairs that spiraled around the elevator shaft, his boots slung over his shoulder, worried he was going to be late for his hockey game. He could see the metal roof of the elevator cage in the shaft two floors down. Either it wasn't working, he thought, or else repairmen were moving their equipment in. Most of the tenants complained of leaks; there were buckets and basins all over the place. The building committee had been trying for months to get something done.

Sasha was already over six feet tall, not stocky but tightly knit, a hard man to stop on the hockey rink. He swung down onto the fifth-floor landing at the same moment that a stooped, angular man came out of the lift, cradling a pile of books. Sasha swerved to avoid him, but the older man shuffled sideways in the same direction, so they became tangled up in each other's legs. Both they and the books went flying.

Sasha was up again in an instant, red-faced, muttering apologies as he helped the older man to his feet. He could see now that the stranger was at least fifty. Sasha could feel the man's bones, close to the skin. They seemed loose and brittle, like a wounded bird's. The stranger's hair and his wispy beard had once been reddish. His eyes were an indeterminate color, between hazel and slate, blinking up through the little round glasses he was trying to hook up over the bridge of his nose.

Instead of blustering, as Sasha expected, the stranger peered at him thoughtfully.

"I hope I didn't hurt you," Sasha said.

"It's nothing, it's nothing." The stranger set about collecting his books, handling them as gently as old parchment.

"Here, let me help you," Sasha volunteered. He noticed that most of the books were works of history. Some were in French and other foreign languages Sasha did not recognize.

He followed the man to the open door of his apartment, and paused at the threshold. Books rose in teetering piles high above the windowsill, blanketed the narrow, iron-framed bed against the wall, burst out of an old glass-fronted cabinet, the kind you couldn't find anymore.

"Give those here," the stranger said sharply, rushing to take charge of Sasha's cargo, as if frightened that the boy might deface his precious books. His hands were shaking as he reached out, and Sasha saw that his fingers were stained a deep tawny yellow, all the way to the joints. He started wheezing, and then a noise rose out of his chest that was more like a creaking door than a cough. He lunged for the table and stuck a butt in his mouth. The room began to stink with the smoke. It was not an ordinary cigarette, but some awful black shag.

"Old habits," the man muttered, conscious of the boy's attention.

Sasha turned to leave, but the stranger called out, "Wait a minute. You live here, I suppose?"

Sasha nodded.

"Well, we must make proper introductions. I am Arkady Borisovich Levin." He stuck out his hand, and Sasha took it. There was surprising force in the old man's grip. The boy looked at him with increased curiosity. He knew only one other Jewish family in the building. The son, Yuli, had been one of his classmates until all the rumors began to circulate about how the Jews were plotting to murder the father of the country, Great Stalin. Then, every recess, the other boys had started beating up Yuli in the schoolyard. They broke his nose, and his glasses, but he kept coming to class every day. Sasha didn't join in the beatings, but he stopped walking to school with Yuli. Like the others, he was filled with rage and terror at the thought that the Jews were trying to kill the country's leader. What would happen to them all without Stalin? But Stalin died anyway, and life went on as before. Now Stalin's name was no longer mentioned in school, and Yuli was left alone.

Levin was looking at him expectantly.

"Preobrazhensky," the boy said formally. "Alexander Sergeyovich."

His seriousness must have seemed comic to Levin, who gave a lopsided smile that did not completely mask his ruined teeth. The man was a shambles, Sasha thought, with his bones sticking out and his collapsing lungs and his broken teeth. But there was a mystery about Levin that attracted him, not to mention the books. That disheveled library, whose musty, mothballed odor mingled with the reek of Levin's *makhorka*, seemed tantalizing and illicit.

"Preobrazhensky?" Levin was frowning now as he repeated the name. "There is something—" he started muttering to himself, and went rummaging among his books. He went from one carton to another, blowing dust off the old bindings. Sasha hesitated. If he waited any longer, he was sure to be late for the game.

Levin emerged with an ancient tome. The covers were cracked, but it had marbled endpapers and the pages were gilded with gold leaf, not just at the top but down the side as well. Sasha had never seen such a book.

"Here, here." Levin was holding it open at one of the plates, which showed an officer with a curling moustache in a bottle-green jacket, reviewing a line of soldiers. "Your namesakes. The Preobrazhensky Guards. The household regiment of Peter the Great. But I expect you know all about that."

"I know a bit," Sasha said cautiously. He stared at the picture. Shave off the moustache and the officer, with his arrogant good looks, strongly resembled the photographs of his father in the apartment upstairs.

"With a name like that, I suppose your father is a soldier," Levin suggested.

Sasha's face clouded. "My father is dead," he explained. "He was killed fighting the Germans."

"I'm sorry." The professor watched him with an odd expression, a mixture of cunning and alarm. Sasha began to distrust him. Levin said, "I'm sure your father was a very brave man."

"He was a Hero of the Soviet Union," Sasha announced proudly.

"Ah. Was he killed in Russia?"

"My father was killed in the front line in Germany at the end of the war."

Levin took off his glasses and rubbed his eyes. He let his hand linger across his brows. It trembled violently, like a shade in an open window caught by the wind.

"Is something wrong?" Sasha asked.

"No. That is—" He slapped his hand flat on the writing table, as if to subdue it. "You must forgive me. It's just—there were so many good people who died. It was a time of madness."

Sasha started to warm to him again. Obviously the professor had also lost people close to him during the war, perhaps his entire family.

"Well, it was nice to meet you," Sasha said politely, turning to leave.

"Stay for a minute. Do you know the name of your father's unit?"

"He was in the artillery." Sasha began to recount the story of how his father won the star of a Hero of the Soviet Union. His grandmother never tired of telling it. His father was a captain commanding a battery of antitank guns on the borders of East Prussia, when a Panzer column mounted a desperate counterattack. When the lead tank opened fire, every man in the battery was killed or disabled except Captain Preobrazhensky. Alone, he managed to aim and fire one of the guns. But he had to lean in close to the armored shield to see through the sights, while reaching across to jerk the firing cord at the same time. He was unable to back away to escape the recoil of the gun. Each time he fired, the shield scraped across the side of his face like a blunt razor. Blood streaming down his face, numbed to the pain of the lacerations, he kept on firing until eight of the enemy tanks were knocked out. From a trench in the rear of his position, a high officer from the General Staff watched the battle through a periscope. Afterward, he had Sasha's father, swathed in bandages, brought to him from the field hospital and pinned the coveted star on his chest.

Sasha's voice rose as he told the story. Levin fidgeted and patched together another rough cigarette from a wad of shag. He looked tortured, as if he were sharing the pain of Sasha's father.

"And you," Levin resumed his questions. "You were born before the war?"

"At the end of it," Sasha corrected him. "I never knew my father." He stared at the worn carpet on the floor. Why did he have the feeling that Levin knew more about his father than he did?

"Preobrazhensky. That name—" Levin began. Then he paused, seeming to twist his thought in midsentence. "—is a responsibility." The detached phrase was almost lost in a new coughing fit.

"Were you in the army?" Sasha asked him.

"I was engaged in Party work," Levin said quickly. "Then at the university. I was—I *am*," he corrected himself, "a professor of history."

"Oh." Sasha's tone betrayed his disappointment. Party work and the practice of history. Now, there was a good combination for you. At school, history was his least favorite subject. He preferred languages, for which he had a flair, and mathematics, which was neutral and exact. History was all learned by rote. You memorized dates and formulas, and rehearsed them like a catechism. For a while, when he was younger, Sasha had found it reassuring. All of history was moving inexorably toward the triumph of socialism, his teacher insisted, and Stalin was the incarnation of the socialist idea. History was something certain; you could lean on it, like the trunk of a sturdy oak.

But without warning, the timber split. Overnight Stalin shrank to the stature of a petty tyrant and the female history teacher set them new lines to learn. This was the same fat cow he remembered blubbering in class the day Stalin's death was announced and the factory sirens started wailing and the schoolchildren were released to join the crush outside the Hall of Columns where the leader's body was lying in state. One day he and some of the other boys in the class had hidden at the foot of the stairs and peered up, sniggering, as she waddled down, her skirts billowing out. She had caught on to what was happening and sent them all to the headmaster. So much for the inexorable laws of Soviet history!

The professor looked suddenly exhausted, as if he could read Sasha's thoughts but lacked the energy or conviction to take issue with them.

"You can borrow this if you like," he said, holding out the book about Peter the Great. "We'll talk some more, now we are neighbours."

2 Number 14, Sasha's apartment, was on the seventh floor, and was shared with three other families. Your head rang at night with the sound of pans banging and doors slamming shut and voices raised in argument or song in the communal kitchen. Fufkov, the resident bully, a red-faced, sweaty son of the workers who had arrogated a few scarce cubic meters of communal space by installing his own refrigerator in the kitchen (the others with fridges kept them in their own rooms), often got drunk and lectured anyone who couldn't escape on how things were going to the dogs since Stalin died. Down below in the courtyard, you could usually hear the shrill voices of women neighbors engaged in a squabble, or of packs of boys brawling in the playground. This playground was equipped with a plank table for Ping-Pong whose corrugated surface made it so hard to control the movement of the ball that you either became stunningly professional or gave it up.

Everywhere you turned, you were jammed up against other people. There was nowhere to be alone. The authorities claimed that the housing problem had been solved, but Moscow seemed to be bursting at the seams. Still, the block on Peschanaya Street, near the aircraft plants around the old Khodinsk airfield, was a big improvement over the first place Sasha remembered as home. Before the Great Patriotic War, his grandmother, Vera Alexandrovna, had had a whole apartment to herself in a little yellow-stuccoed house in one of the snaky streets behind the Arbat, in the heart of the old Moscow. Sasha's first memories of that apartment dated from the end of the war, when it seemed that the whole of Russia was moving to Moscow. Vera Alexandrovna found that her apartment was being occupied by half a dozen families of evacuees from the front-line zones who showed no inclination to move out. For a time they camped among the rest, and Vera Alexandrovna got used to the sight of her best sheets being laid out to dry over a paraffin stove in the kitchen and the sound of her best crockery being dropped on the floor. Finally, Sasha's grandmother bowed to superior odds and went out ringing doorbells all over the city until she found them the place on Peschanaya Street. That was his grandmother's way. However many times she was knocked down, she would be up on her feet again.

The things about their room in Number 14 that made it personal were Vera Alexandrovna's doing. There was a dark, round table in the middle that displayed her prize possession, a vintage Singer sewing machine, made before the Revolution, that had been passed down to her by her own grandmother and remained in perfect working order. She used it to mend clothes for Sasha and to make dresses for herself, always the same: shapeless, drab, and dark brown, hanging down over her calves like tents. She had a collection of family photographs. There was a grainy photograph of Vera Alexandrovna with her school classmates on the wall, and two pictures of the father Sasha had never known—smiling in an open-necked shirt at a river beach before the war, fierce and proud in the uniform of an army lieutenant on his way to the front.

The room was exactly twenty-four meters square. It had good high ceilings with a center light in a big cloth lampshade that hung low over the table. The wallpaper was pale green, sprinkled with gold flowers. Vera Alexandrovna slept on the big camelback sofa on the left side, next to the heavy sideboard they used to store dishes and cutlers. At night, babushka would put up a folding screen; an old woman was entitled to a little privacy. Nina, Sasha's mother, slept on the other side, next to the wardrobe. Sasha's bed was at the far end, beside the door that opened onto their tiny balcony. If he put his head up against the frame, he could see the sky above the rooftops.

He often lay like that, in the breathing stillness of the night, after his mother turned out the lights. His mother slept on her stomach, face turned into the pillow, like the dead. She was a hard woman to know. Every day she took the trolleybus to the Sokol metro station and boarded a train to the city center, where she had a job in one of the ministries. She was not a bad-looking woman, with a ripe, full figure, dark hair, and big brown eyes, but she minimized her assets. She kept her hair pinned up, dressed in severe, mannish dark jackets and skirts, and rarely used makeup. Her manner seemed to proclaim that she was a *serious* person, with no space in her life for frivolities. She often came home late, and Sasha was given to understand, from an early age, that this had something to do with Party meetings. Their relationship was oddly impersonal. She never kissed or touched him, and usually had little to say to him besides routine inquiries about his progress at school. Sometimes she would read to him when he was little, from Pushkin or Nekrasov or Grimms' fairy tales, but there was never a sense of drama. She worked her way from the beginning to the end of a story as if resigned to a mechanical chore. He preferred it when Vera Alexandrovna read to him. She could mimic all the characters. Best of all, he liked it when she told him about his father and his grandfather and the men of the Preobrazhensky family before them.

"The men of this house," she would say, leafing through the album, "have always been defenders." There were the stiffly posed portraits of his grandfather and his great-uncle with their brides. Both men had died in the civil war, fighting for the Reds against the *Basmachi*, the Muslim bandits in Turkestan.

Or Vera Alexandrovna would pick up a well-used edition of *War and Peace* and start reading to him, yet again, the passage about the battle in the golden fields of Borodino where Napoleon's armies were slowed to a halt at the gates of Moscow. It was from the battle of Borodino that the family derived its name. Sasha's ancestor was a sergeant of artillery, one of those in charge of the batteries on the knoll that became known as Raevski's Redoubt. His men ran out of cannonballs, so he made them fire grapeshot. He stayed with the guns even when the blue-coated French scrambled over the earthworks, flashing sabers and bayonets, and overran the Russian positions. Then he tried to save the colors of the regiment, folding the flag and hiding it under his tunic. When they found the sergeant's body, there were fifteen rents in the flag. As his grandmother read from Tolstoy, Sasha would shut his eyes to visualize the whole scene more clearly: the dark shadows among the woods, the smoke from the cannons like tufts of cotton wool, the teams of frightened horses dragging green ammunition chests. A Russian general, visiting the scene, was impressed by the gallantry of the gunner sergeant, and wrote a report that went all the way to the Tsar. The Little Father rewarded the sergeant's family with a small gift of land and a new surname: Preobrazhensky, the same name Tsar Peter had picked for his Guards.

Sasha's mother didn't like all this harping on family history. Most of all, she hated talk about Sasha's father. It reached the point where Vera Alexandrovna only talked to the boy about his father during the long walks they took together, along the river embankments, or through the Alexander Gardens, in the shadow of the russet walls of the Kremlin.

Sasha's mother never had time for him. When she wasn't at the office, it was always some Party meeting or other. Once, on a Sunday in May, she had arranged to take him to a sports event at the Stadium of the Pioneers, and Sasha was excited, because this kind of thing never happened. But on the way to the metro, they ran into a sharp-faced man in a dark suit whom Sasha had never seen before.

"Good morning, Comrade Krisov," Nina greeted him. Sasha didn't like the way his mother talked to the man. Her manner was almost simpering.

Krisov stood there on the street corner for a good twenty minutes, totally ignoring the boy, lecturing his mother in a high, nasal voice about the work of some committee. Nina smiled and nodded in a way she never did at home.

So they arrived late for the games, and got the worst seats, and all Nina would say by way of explanation was that "Comrade Krisov is the Party Secretary in my department."

From that time on, the idea of the Party and the narrow face of this Comrade Krisov were synonymous for Sasha. He resented the Party for keeping his mother from him, and her for putting it above him. She never tried to explain the point of all this Party work except to say, "I have to support this family." She never explained anything.

"You'll understand when you are older," Vera Alexandrovna would say to him when he complained that it was impossible to talk to his mother. "She's had a hard life, poor thing."

Little by little, from his talks with his grandmother and the things he gleaned for himself, Sasha began to understand something of his mother's hardness. She had met his father in a brief wartime romance. They had just long enough to meet, to court for a week or two, marry, take snapshots, and conceive a child before Sergei was off to the front. Then there was the endless wait, the uncertainty, the rumors of death and disaster, the weary trek along muddy roads, choked with panicky refugees, to food and safety in the provinces. The few letters that Nina received had been written months before; there was no way of knowing whether her husband was dead or alive as she read them. She was little more than a child when she married, swept off her feet by the uniform and the patriotic ardor that infested the air in those days. She tried to behave like a romantic heroine in a movie. Then suddenly she was alone, left to shoulder the burden of bearing a child and caring for it, left to brood over the fact that she hardly knew its father. Oh, Vera Alexandrovna stepped in, solid as a rock, the eternal babushka, feeding the baby, changing its diapers, crooning over it, while Nina went to work in a factory. But Nina made no secret of her resentment; she felt she had been dealt a rotten hand. When the news came that Sergei had been killed, it confirmed her suspicion that the deck had been stacked against her from the start.

She didn't waste time grieving. She abandoned the child to Vera Alexandrovna, attended night school, pursued full Party membership, entered and left the house like an automaton, as if she believed that if only she could purge herself of personal emotions, nobody would bother her or hurt her again.

There was a quarrel going on in the kitchen when Sasha returned home after the hockey game. Fufkov, the neighbor with the refrigerator, had obviously been guzzling vodka all day—or maybe aircraft glue, since he worked at the nearby plant and would sniff or swill anything that had alcohol in it, even paint thinner that he doctored up, when he ran out of money after payday. Vera Alexandrovna was trying to fry up chicken tabaka on the stove. It was one of her specialities. She would chop the bird in half and let it marinate in garlic for an hour before cooking it in a covered saucepan. But Fufkov wouldn't get out of her way, determined to deliver one of his little harangues.

"It's all Nikita's fault that there's no food in Moscow," he was bellowing. You could hear the wretch all the way down the corridor. "Isn't that right, little mother? He takes the food out of our mouths to send to the black-asses in Cuba. And there he sits, grinning like a fat pig. I say fuck our fraternal socialist brothers!"

To stress his point, he brought his fist down so hard on the table next to the stove that the lid came off Vera Alexandrovna's pot, and boiling liquid hissed to the floor. She was going after Fufkov with her stirring spoon when Sasha came in.

Fufkov sidestepped Vera Alexandrovna with an agility surprising in a drunk and pranced over to Sasha. He tugged at his coarse brush of hair, doffing an imaginary cap.

"Good evening, Your Excellency," he greeted Sasha. His face was beet red and sweaty. Fufkov drank the way a man might wake up in the morning and start hitting his head against the wall, and go on banging it until finally he dropped down senseless.

"Go on, try me," Fufkov challenged, squatting down at one of the four tables jammed into the kitchen. He stuck his elbow on top and made a fist. "Let's see if you're a man yet."

"Get away with you." Vera Alexandrovna glowered at him, her spoon raised menacingly.

Fufkov guffawed. "Look at this, fuck your mother. A grown man hiding behind skirts. Why, at your age, I was out getting my bell rung."

Very calmly, Sasha set his boots and his bag down against the wall. But the bag slid down, and Levin's book fell out.

"Well, look at the little professor," Fufkov goaded him. "I know your little secret." He turned to Vera Alexandrovna and said in a stage whisper, "He's been hobnobbing with that Yid who's moved into the building. I told you, everything's going to the dogs since Stalin died." He ran a broad finger up and down his nose. "If you rub it enough," he leered, "you'll get a big nose too."

While Fufkov sat sniggering, Sasha took the chair opposite. His face had reddened; he could feel the heat. He set his elbow on the table, reached out, and laced his fingers through Fufkov's.

With the first lunge, the heavier man almost had him. Sasha's forearm was forced down, till it was only an inch above the table. He could smell Fufkov's stinking breath on his face. He held on, willing all his strength into his right arm, ratcheting up until they were back in the original position. It was over so fast it surprised both of them. A sudden twist, and he had Fufkov's arm pinned to the table. The drunk was so startled that he fell off his seat. When he picked himself up, there was pink murder in his eyes.

Vera Alexandrovna came between them. "Go and see to your wife," she commanded Fufkov. "If she'll have you."

Fufkov stumbled out cursing, and Sasha's grandmother started clacking her tongue at him. "Your father would be ashamed at you."

He didn't argue with her. Neither of them believed it.

Later, when the dishes were cleared away, Sasha turned to the women and said, "I'd like to know how my father died."

His mother's mouth was a straight edge. It might have been drawn with a ruler.

Vera Alexandrovna said, "I'll make some tea." She started to rattle around, getting the kettle ready.

His mother said, "I've told you already." Each word came out like the snip-snip of her scissors. "Your father was killed at the front. That's all we know."

"There must be *something,*" he persisted.

"*All right.*" The words were an accusation. "There's this." She went to the box where she kept her papers. There were several small trays inside. She got to the bottom one, lifted it out, and brought it to the table.

"Here." She thrust the yellowed document at him. "Take it. See for yourself."

Sasha realized that he was looking at a death certificate. It was a standard form, printed on coarse, cheap paper, no better than newsprint. All the authorities had to do was fill in the names and dates. He saw his father's name, written in a spidery scrawl.

He read: "Your husband, Captain of Artillery Sergei Mikhailovich Preobrazhensky, Hero of the Soviet Union, died defending his motherland on April 17, 1945. He was buried in a brothers' grave. Please accept our condolences." The notice was signed with an indecipherable scrawl.

"What is a brothers' grave?" Sasha asked.

"It was a war," Vera Alexandrovna said in a soft, lilting voice, as if she were reciting something in church. "So many bodies could never be found. Or identified."

Sasha's eyes moved from his mother's set face to the remaining papers in the tray.

"Father wrote letters." It was a statement, not a question

"No!" his mother burst out as he reached for the tray. She covered it with her hands. "You have no right." She looked frightened, and it struck him that this was the first time in a long while that she had manifested any sign of spontaneous emotion.

"He has the right," Vera Alexandrovna interposed. "He is old enough."

Nina rummaged through the tray and pulled out a few rumpled letters. The envelopes were soiled and stained. The pages inside were thin and translucent, like ricepaper. Sasha took the letters away to his bed by the balcony and sat up, straining his eyes to make out the minute writing. Vera Alexandrovna started up her sewing machine. Nina went along the corridor to the bathroom. When she came back, she was in her nightclothes. She climbed into her bed and pulled the sheet up over her face without saying good night to either of them. That was one thing Sasha's mother could always count on. Whatever the state of the world, whatever dramas were taking place around her, she could switch herself off like a light.

Sasha did not sleep for a long time after he finished the letters. There were intimate things in them, the longings of a soldier at the front, that embarrassed him because he never thought of his mother as a woman in the sexual sense. But far more troubling was the shift in mood from the early letters, written when the carnage was at its worst and Russia seemed on the brink of utter destruction, and the final one, written when the conquering Red Army was plowing through the suburbs of Berlin. In the first letters, Sergei Preobrazhensky spared his wife heroics and bloody descriptions of the war. He quoted scraps of poetry, asked for news of home, recalled a summer trip to the Crimea. The last letter, from a newly decorated war hero, seemed to be written out of total despair. "I'm sending this with a friend," he began. "I doubt if it would get past our gallant censors."

"When your back is to the wall," he wrote, "the moral sense is numbed. Everything is a matter of survival. To hell with the rest. You step over bodies without seeing them, like so many piles of logs. It's victory that is harder to bear. What the Germans failed to do to our army, we are doing for ourselves. We have become our enemy."

He mentioned the rapes, the pillage, the slaughter of civilians. "Our *zampoliti*—political officers—say that to worry about these things is to fall victim to bourgeois humanism. I wonder whether these years of fighting and suffering have been merely spent deciding whether the concentration camps of tomorrow will be red or brown."

Sasha rolled over on his back. The moonlight, filtering through the curtains, made everything in the room seem ambiguous and insubstantial.

He didn't understand everything in his father's letter. But it was plain why his mother wanted to conceal it. Sasha was angry, and also ashamed. The letter was at odds with everything he had learned about the war—from babushka, from books and museums, from school, where the pupils were enjoined to preserve the "holy memory" of the country's martial heroes. The men of his family had been soldiers, from the battle of Borodino and before. His father's letter seemed to betray them.

The ugly word uncoiled in his mind. Was his father a traitor?

Damn you, he silently cursed the man he had never known. *Why aren't you here to explain?*

He went back to the professor, hoping that he could explain. Levin was friendly, but he found excuses to shift the conversation to safer ground. He gave Sasha more books to read, and he talked about the early history of Russia—the adventures of the Viking marauders who were the original tribe of the *Rus*, the Tatar invasions, Peter's forays into the West—in a way that brought everything to life and made Sasha eager to learn.

"He who controls the past controls the present," the professor remarked to him during one of their sessions.

"Who said that?"

"It's from a book by Orwell. I'm afraid it's banned. You've a natural flair for historical detection, Sasha. You ask the right questions. You ought to pursue this at university."

"I think I'd like to." His talks with Levin had made Sasha appreciate that history had nothing to do with the dull repetition of dates and slogans in his school classroom. History was an adventure, a means of discovering himself as well as the world he had inherited.

At that moment, there was a light tap on the door and a girl walked in. She moved like a cat, with natural, unstudied grace. In an instant, she had slipped across the room and wrapped her arms around Levin's neck. She was wearing a dark, loose woolen sweater a few sizes too big that billowed down to her hips. When she turned to Sasha, her eyebrows arched, slightly mocking, her dark eyes full of fire, he stared down at the toes of his scuffed boots. He had reached the embarrassing age when he thought about girls a lot, but found it uncomfortable to be in the same room with them.

"This is my daughter, Tatyana," Levin said. Sasha was surprised. There was no family resemblance. This beautiful girl, who seemed so sure of herself and her body, seemed to belong to a different world from the professor and his narrow room.

Tanya took charge of the conversation immediately. She started quizzing Sasha as if she had discovered a new game; soon he had forgotten his reserves and was talking as if they had grown up together. She was quick and precocious and laughed easily, and soon she had Sasha laughing too.

"By the way, I forgot to ask," she said. "Which hand do you write with?"

"This one, of course." Sasha held up his right hand, astonished.

"You see?" Tanya said triumphantly to her father. "That's what everybody says. Can either of you explain to me why there are no left-handed people in the Soviet Union?"

Levin sighed indulgently. He had obviously been subjected to this routine before.

"Now *I* happen to be left-handed," Tanya explained to Sasha. "Don't be shocked. It's not my fault. It begins in the brain, like cerebral palsy. But at school, they make me write with my right hand, like you, and then they complain that my writing is sloppy. It's not fair. In a society built on the ideas of the left, everyone should be required to be *left*-handed."

After they had finished tea, Levin said, "Your mother will be expecting you."

Tanya made a face and started complaining about her stepfather. Sasha gathered that he was an important man, a member of the Writers' Union, whose articles appeared in *Literary Gazette.*

Suddenly Tanya sprang up and said, "All right, I'd better go. But I want Sasha to take me home."

"Then don't you think it would be polite to ask him?" the professor said.

Tanya lived with her mother and stepfather in a fancy neighborhood, on Smolenskaya Street between the Arbat and the river, just round the corner from the Foreign Ministry. They took the metro. Sasha was coatless, and Tanya carried her sheepskin coat—it looked American—over her arm. There was a breath of spring in the air, the false spring that sometimes comes to Moscow in February or March, cheating the land so that the buds begin to sprout and the orchards come alive, only to be killed off when the frosts return. Later in the year, after that liar's spring, you would have to range far to find blueberries in the woods.

"When did your parents get divorced?" Sasha asked her when they got off the subway at the Smolenskaya station.

"He didn't tell you?" She gave him an alert, sideways look. "Well, it's no disgrace now that Great Stalin is buried. My father was in the camps. For anti-Soviet agitation. Something he is supposed to have said in one of his lectures. They tried to make out that he was plotting to put a bomb in the University, if you can believe it. They sent him to the camps for seven years. It nearly killed him. After Stalin, he was rehabilitated—one of the first politicals the bitches let out. He even got his job back at the University. But they broke something inside him."

They were on the street. She looked cautiously up and down the row of imposing apartment houses.

"He's a Leninist, you know," she said. "He's a believer."

"I know. We've been talking quite a lot."

"That's our block over there," she said, pointing. "You see, she knows how to look out for herself. When they dragged my father away, they explained to her that an honest citizen has only to ask to get a divorce from someone convicted of anti-Soviet crimes. She got unhitched right away. The next thing, she's in bed with our literary lion Erinshteyn, who makes a fat living by writing whatever they tell him. He used to eat out of Beria's hand. Now he's finishing an article that says that Beria was a British spy."

When they reached the door of her building, she said gravely, "Do you have many friends?"

"Well, not real friends," he admitted. He had never had a conversation like this with anyone at school.

"Let's be friends," she proposed. And without waiting for an answer, she kissed him quickly on the cheek and skipped away into her building. Her lips were swollen, with a faintly violet hue; they looked bruised. There was a memory of sandalwood in the smell of her face and her hair, and nothing of the schoolgirl at all.

3 They grew up quickly, after that liar's spring. They often met in the professor's apartment. But they would also make excuses to rendez-vous in different corners of the city, at galleries and museums, or the zoo, or by the big dipper in Gorky Park. Sometimes, when Tanya's mother and stepfather were out—they attended lots of official functions—they could meet at the apartment on Smolenskaya Street. Tanya, who always seemed to have money and who knew the most surprising people, would play "rock on the ribs" on the phonograph. You could buy these records of American jazz and rock and roll from black market peddlers. They were made from tapes of Voice of America and BBC broadcasts and engraved on old X-ray plates. If you held one of them up to the light, you could see an unknown patient's rib cage. In those days, you could hear Western music wafting out of open windows all over Moscow.

On the living-room sofa in the flat on Smolenskaya Street, in their last summer of school, they became lovers, with musical accompaniment by Dizzy Gillespie. Sasha was nervous. She seemed assured and sophisticated. He was pleased when he discovered it was her first time too. He was awkward, and he heard her suck in her breath in pain, and it was over too fast. But starting over, he began to learn her rhythms and his own, and linger over every part of her long, supple body.

Levin sensed what had happened. Sasha could tell from the way he stared at Tanya the next time they visited him. He said nothing to them, but Sasha went to see him alone and announced that he intended to marry Tanya as soon as they were old enough.

"Don't come to me with that slop," Levin admonished him. "When you've graduated from the university and decided on your future, then we'll see. But listen, Sasha"—and now there was a sort of burr in his voice —"I want you to look out for her. She's not as steady as you. Haven't you noticed how she talks? She comes right out and says what she thinks. She uses words as if there were no taboos. That's very dangerous."

"But things are changing," Sasha objected. It wasn't just a matter of rock on the ribs and boys wearing narrow, tapered pants, he thought. People were speaking up. Especially the poets. Their works circulated in little magazines, typed on ricepaper in editions of ten, twenty, or fifty copies. They called it *samizdat,* "self-publishing," a spoof on the name of the state publishing house, Gosizdat. They gathered in the evening around the newly erected statue of Mayakovsky on the square that bore his name, to read their own verses and those of Mandelstam, Gumilev, Pasternak, and Alexander Galich. And the authorities let it go on. You had to say that for Nikita. He looked like a buffoon, tripped up over his own words, but he had a soft spot for writers. He had even let this Solzhenitsyn publish his novel about life in the camps. It was the talk of Moscow.

"We'll see how much has changed," Levin said skeptically. "Now, keep Tanya away from Mayakovsky Square."

But Tanya wasn't easily ruled. They both entered Moscow University, and attended classes in the old yellow building at 20, Prospekt Marx, that the male students dubbed the Faculty of Brides because it was reputed to attract some of the prettiest girls in Moscow. The location was convenient for both of them. They continued to live with their families, instead of moving into the dormitories around the wedding-cake tower up on Lenin Hills. Tanya registered with the Faculty of Philology; Sasha, with the History Faculty—the professor's influence had told.

Tanya threw herself into everything. They went to the poetry readings in Mayakovsky Square, despite the professor's prohibition, and heard a pale young student called Zhukovsky reading from a ballad that became a sort of password:

> Do not fear ashes, do not fear curses,
> Do not fear brimstone and fire,
> But fear like the plague the man with the rage
> To tell you, "I know what's required!"

Who tells you, "Fall in and follow me
If heaven on earth's your desire."

They heard Zhukovsky read some of his own verses, full of high, windy
words about how poetry was more powerful than the gun. Tanya seemed
fascinated by him then, and later, when a group of them squeezed into a
small apartment to drink coffee and talk excitedly about how they were
going to change the country. Sasha grew impatient with all this talk, and
especially with Zhukovsky, who wagged his finger insistently as he lectured everybody in his high-pitched voice.

There was usually a crowd of hooligans in the square, jeering and threatening. One night, Sasha recognized a Komsomol leader from his own
Faculty among them. They went growling and snapping around the tight
little knot of spectators, trying to scare people into leaving. When the
reading was done and the audience started thinning out, the hecklers
made a grab for the poetry readers. Zhukovsky was thrown to the ground
and Sasha saw the hooligans starting in with their boots. The policemen in
the square turned the other way.

The beating seemed to increase Zhukovsky's fervor. He was unforgiving
toward those who weren't prepared to take part in dissident activities.
"I've heard them all, all the cosy little excuses," he started declaiming one
night, when Tanya had dragged Sasha along to yet another meeting. "You
can't get blood from a stone, isn't that right?" Zhukovsky asked rhetorically. "Anyway, we Russians love to be ordered around. We have no apti-
tude for democracy. What's that you say? Oh, yes, protest will only
stengthen the hard-liners. It will bring the Stalinists down on our heads.
Anyway, it's not the right time. Your exams are coming up, or your mother's sick, or you managed to get your girlfriend in the family way. Yes, I've
heard them all. But you, Preobrazhensky, you're a subtle one. You just
hang around watching us, never arguing, never taking part."

"You can't break an ax with a whip," Sasha said quietly, quoting the
Russian proverb. "The way you're going on, you'll only get a lot of people
arrested."

Zhukovsky flew at him then, and they got into a real slanging-match.
Sasha was angry and embarrassed to see Tanya taking Zhukovsky's side.
He went home before she did, and learned the meaning of jealousy for the
first time. But then the summer came on, and they forgot their disagree-
ments. They bought sleeper tickets on the night train to Leningrad, and
made love in tempo with the gentle rocking of the carriage. They bor-

rowed a car, and traveled the "golden circle" around Moscow to the storied cities of Vladimir and Novgorod.

They were nearing the end of their third year at the university when Professor Levin buttonholed Sasha in the lobby of the building on Prospekt Marx. Above him, on the landing of the stairway, the red cloth under the bust of Lenin had been dragged to one side, and you could see that the plinth below was only plywood.

"I want you to come and see me tonight," the professor said. He seemed to be having trouble breathing.

Sasha began to make excuses. He had arranged to meet Tanya at the cinema.

"Tell her your mother's sick," Levin said. "Whatever you like. But I have to talk to you tonight, and it's best that she knows nothing about it."

Sasha looked into the professor's eyes and stopped arguing. They were open wounds.

Sasha arrived at Levin's apartment at 7:00. The professor locked the door and poured both of them vodka. It was a bad sign, because Sasha had never seen Levin drink.

"You're no fool," the professor said to him. "You can see what's going on. We have been through a time when a lot of young people's hopes were raised. Solzhenitsyn could publish in Moscow. But tell me, where is Solzhenitsyn now? Where is the editor who printed his work in *Novy Mir?* Where is our friend Khrushchev, who was supposed to be responsible for all this liberalism?

"You know as well as I do. The old gang got worried. They thought their feeding trough might be taken away. They said, enough is enough, and booted Nikita out. Now, go anywhere you like and tell me where you can find a book about Stalin's crimes on sale. Listen to the speeches of our leaders and you'll see little phrases creeping back in about our debt to Great Stalin in the war. There's even a move afoot to rehabilitate him at the next Party Congress."

"It's not possible."

"Of course it's possible," Levin snapped back. "But just try to explain any of this to Tanya. She thinks she's leading a charmed life." He took off his glasses and rubbed his eyes.

Then he said, "You know I was in the camps."

"Yes."

"Tanya told you."

Sasha's silence passed for confirmation.

"Well, I'm glad you never asked me about it. But there is something you have to know." He started shaking, so violently that Sasha rose to help him. Levin waved at him to stay in his seat. "I saw someone today," he began again, then checked himself. "No, we must start in the proper place."

4 "Do you know what it is to hate the smell of the pine forest, to hate the smell of woodsmoke even more? I was sent to a logging camp in the Perm region, near a hole called Kuchino. There were a lot of us politicals there in those days. In the winter, the temperature falls to forty-five degrees below. But winter or summer, the workday didn't finish until we had fulfilled our quota. They sent us out into the woods when the snow was chest deep. We had to tread it down, cut down the trees, grope for the branches through the snow and lop them off, and then haul the trunks on our backs to the railroad cars. At night they fed us on slops and locked us up in our barracks, to suffocate in the smoke of wet firewood. Men became so desperate they would do anything to get taken away to the clinic—break a limb, chop off their own fingers, sniff sugar because they thought that would give them tuberculosis. Every time I smell the forest it all comes back.

"The criminals hated us, and the guards egged them on. The trusties—the vipers, we called them—were all picked from this class. A brute called Goga lorded it over our barracks. He bribed the guards to bring him meat, tobacco, even vodka. He used some of the younger ones as his camp wives. Goga really had it in for me. 'I'm a thief, a real man!' That was his theme song. The first time he beat me up, he said it was because that is what kikes deserved. We were enemies of Russia, the whole lot of us. The guards liked to watch.

"For each of us, the politicals, there was some last thing, something private, that you had to cling to, without which you were finished. There was one man who was forever making chess sets out of crumbs of bread, molded with his own spit. I tried to recite poetry in my head, and when I ran out of lines, I tried to make up my own. It didn't come easily. Each word was as heavy as a log. Our veteran, Lieutenant Ivanov, would get hold of a scrap of pencil lead and start designing guns—always the same gun, in fact, a self-propelled monster with all sorts of fantastic embellish-ments. Ivanov, the gunner, was the strongest of us, the only one that even Goga seemed to respect.

"Ivanov kept to himself pretty much, but one day he came to me and said that he had heard that I was helping one of the other zeks to learn English, and that he would like to learn too. After that, we got to talking a bit. He told me he had served with an armored unit in the advance on Berlin. He had been put away under Article 58, like most of us. They told him that his real crime was bourgeois humanism. By his excessive concern for the treatment of enemy civilians, he had defamed the Soviet army.

"One morning, we were roused a couple of hours before dawn, as usual, and ordered to set about cleaning up the barracks. Every clean-up was an excuse for the guards to go ferreting about among the prisoners' private treasures, stealing money and clothes. Our godfather, the NKVD captain, would come sniffing around for hidden books and papers. He would confiscate Ivanov's pencil leads when he found them, but the lieutenant would hide his reserve supply in his mouth, between gum and cheek.

"That morning, we were ordered to smarten ourselves up for an inspection. What a joke! We were shivering scarecrows, in filthy coats patched together from any old rags. Our boots were made with strips torn from worn-out padded jackets and stitched to a bit of rubber. Our families sent clothes, of course. But anything worth having in the packages from home was stolen by the guards or Goga's gang.

"Anyway, we were lined up like conscripts on a parade ground, for the amusement of a bunch of higher-ups—well-fed men from Moscow with round pink faces, warm overcoats, and fur hats. These dignitaries didn't want to waste too much time on us. They were obviously impatient to inspect the contents of the commandant's bar. They nodded at everything.

"Then one of the dignitaries, thicker and more stupid-looking than the rest, clasped his hands behind his back, stuck out his chin, and called out, 'Any complaints?'

"We knew better than *that*. The only sound was from one of the thieves, who let out a fart.

"The dignitaries all started nodding again, as if something significant had been accomplished, and moved on in the direction of their refreshments.

"All except one. I had spotted him earlier, because he seemed to be taking a closer interest in us than his colleagues, and because our NKVD *Oper* was hovering around him like a waiter hoping for a big tip. This one was a chekist—a secret policeman—too, strutting around with a pistol on his hip, turning his squinty gaze on each face as if he wanted to fix it in his memory.

"I admit I was scared when he stopped in front of me. I wondered if someone had ratted on a political argument I had had with one of the other prisoners. I had only gone down to the box once. You sit on a narrow ledge, high up on the wall, looking at nothing, losing count of the hours and the days, till you feel the ledge sawing into your bones. When I was taken there, I found saliva on the walls, saliva streaked with blood. God knows what became of the man before me. The emptiness consumes you, till you start babbling to yourself, until you invite in ghosts. But I don't need to tell you what it was like. I didn't want to go down to the box again.

"So I was trembling in front of the chekist, looking down at his high boots lined with fur, the kind of boots men would kill for twenty times over in the camps. I felt a wonderful sense of relief when I saw him swivel away from me toward my neighbor, the gunner. I even said to myself, *Let it be him.* That doesn't shock you, does it? Brotherhood doesn't survive fear or hunger. Our camp authorities understand that very well.

"The chekist put his thumbs in his belt and said, 'Ivanov?' in a tentative sort of way.

"Ivanov stiffened and mumbled the rest. 'Pavel Mikhailovich, Comrade Major.'

"I hadn't noticed the chekist's rank; it was natural that Ivanov, an army lieutenant, should have done so. But it was also plain that there was something between these two men.

"The chekist ran a gloved finger along the side of his nose, a pulpy sort of nose with large pores. I watched his breath condense in a vapor trail as he opened his mouth to speak. But he thought better of whatever he had intended to say and marched off, with the camp *Oper* trotting eagerly at his heels.

"I saw them pause on the far side of the compound. They looked back at us—or rather, at Ivanov. Our camp godfather was nodding vigorous agreement in response to whatever the NKVD major was saying.

"After that, it was a normal day. We hauled logs until after dark, and sat down to a gruel made of black cabbage, rotten potatoes, and other trash. There were more cockroaches than usual floating in it, but all the same, I was concerned when I saw that Ivanov wasn't eating his share. You had to eat everything you could lay hands on to stay alive. We even scraped lichen off the rocks, when we could find it.

"I whispered to Ivanov, 'You're not eating.'

"He pushed his bowl over to me, and I finished it off. That's the way it is. You wouldn't know if you've never been hungry. Hunger is a nerve that throbs all the time in the camps, like a toothache you can't get at.

"I suppose Ivanov already knew he was going to die. I suppose I knew it too, when he gave up designing his monster cannon and lay on his back on his sleeping shelf, dead to the bawling and brawling in the barracks. Goga had smuggled in vodka, and was selling off his surplus. I remembered then that it was Tanya's birthday, so I spent the last money I had managed to hide on a bottle, although I knew it would be at least three parts water, and gave our gunner a swig. There must have been some humanity left in me.

"Did you ever wonder why my fingers are yellow? I used to dream of shag, when I couldn't get it. I would have given up food rather than *makhorka*, and sometimes I did, to make a trade. Now I've lost the taste for any other kind of tobacco.

"The day after Tanya's birthday, they had us sawing up logs near a river landing, and I squatted down next to Ivanov to have a smoke. He looked terrible. His lower eyelids drooped like a bloodhound's; you could see a watery pink rim inside.

" 'Do you want to talk about it?' I asked. In a place where you can never be alone, you learn not to pry.

" 'I know that chekist,' Ivanov said. 'It's because of him that I'm here.' He took the cigarette from my fingers, inhaled deeply, and added, 'Because I saw what he did.'

"Ivanov looked around. Goga was lolling in the doorway of a leanto, chatting to a guard and enjoying the warmth of his fire. He was out of earshot.

" 'It happened at the end of the war,' Ivanov explained. 'I had a friend, Seryozha, who was in the same unit. He was like an elder brother to me. Once, when the Germans were trying to mount a counterattack, he saved our position single-handed after the other men in his battery had been killed or disabled. He was the best soldier I ever knew, a Russian officer of the old school. But Seryozha had a weakness. He was a bourgeois humanist. Oh, far worse than me.'

"Ivanov's mouth writhed. You couldn't call it a grin.

" 'I confess I didn't always understand him,' Ivanov went on. 'I didn't approve of what our soldiers were doing in Germany, but after what the Nazis did to us, I didn't really care. The Germans had it coming, I thought.

" 'When you've seen enough killing, you're deadened to it. What did I care how many more Germans were slaughtered, how many women were raped? They were no more human to me than that.' Ivanov gestured toward a pile of sawed timber waiting to be loaded onto a barge.

" 'Seryozha was different,' he resumed. 'He was the only one among us who still had the capacity for moral outrage. Like I say, he was from the old school. I remember we were rolling into some nameless village in East Prussia just before nightfall. The first wave had already gone through, and the place was blown to pieces. We came across some old crone lying dead in the middle of the street with a telephone receiver rammed into her twat. Our boys had caught her making a phone call, and decided she must be a spy. Somebody explained that she had greeted the Soviets with tears running down her cheeks, yelling, 'Welcome, *Genosse.*' Seems she was a Party member. And the phones were all dead anyway.

" 'That scene drove Seryozha into a white fury. We were both ready to drop with fatigue, but he kept me tramping up and down the streets of that fucked-up town, ranting that our men were running amok and that this was a judgment on the socialist system. I was trying to quiet him down—you know, the chekists had spies everywhere, skulking in the rear guard, just waiting to send decent officers to the firing squad. He was going on about how the Russian army was being destroyed. He came up with some story about how, when the Austrians wanted to produce a black book on Russian war crimes at the end of the First World War, they could only document two cases of rape.

" 'I was getting pretty nervous, what with the chekists and the possibility that there were still German snipers around. It was a hellish night. The only light came from the fires in some of the buildings. I kept telling him we had to get back to our billets, where there was bound to be plenty of schnapps.

" 'We had just started to retrace our steps when the screaming began. I can still hear that scream. It was high and shrill, but at the same time, it made you feel the girl's throat was coming out with it.

" 'Well, Seryozha might have been struck by lightning. Then he was cursing and racing in the direction of the screams. I chased after him, trying to make him listen to reason. It didn't make sense to get involved, not at the tail end of the war, not with our own men. I got hold of his arm but he shook me off. I slipped on something oily, and came down on my ass. By the time I got round the corner, Seryozha was already ramming himself through the door of a cottage. It must have been a nice place, once. You know, shutters and windowboxes and that gingerbread stuff the krauts like.

" 'I saw the rest through the window.'

"Ivanov had to interrupt himself when the whistle blew and the vipers started herding everyone back to their jobs. I heard the end of it, in whispered snatches, on the way back to camp in the evening, when we were straggling along behind the others and the guard was busy haggling with one of Goga's cronies who wanted to arrange a date with a whore from Kuchino. Such trysts were rare, and expensive, but they could be fixed—if you had the cash.

"When Ivanov got to the window of the cottage, he peered in and saw a couple of bodies lying in a pool of blood.

" 'It was hard to make everything out,' Ivanov told me. 'The only light came from a sputtering oil lamp. I could see a child—no more than a toddler—huddled back in the corner, its face to the wall. There was a table with knobbly legs, and a girl, seven or eight at most. I remember her face. It was oval and smooth like a pebble on the beach. Or should have been. She had been spreadeagled on the table. Now she was bending up from the waist, grabbing at her torn and bloodied dress.

" 'There was a Russian with her. He must have rolled off the table when Seryozha burst in, because he was crouched down against the wall, trying to hitch up his pants with one hand and feeling around for his gun with the other. It looked like he had dropped it somewhere. He wasn't regular army. He was a military chekist, a goon from SMERSH. Seryozha was yelling at him, and he was swaying there, drunk. Seryozha didn't have his gun out, but he had balled his fist, and he was moving in on the chekist.

" 'I thought I'd better get him out of there before it came to shooting, and I went round to the door. Then I saw the other one. He had come in through a door on the far side of the room, behind Seryozha, who couldn't have seen him. He looked drunk too. He had a bottle of schnapps in one hand, and a pistol in the other.

" 'I yelled out to Seryozha, but it was too late. The words were muffled by the crack of the chekist's gun. The bullet got Seryozha right where those bitches always aim, in the back of the neck.'

"The recollection seemed to freeze Ivanov. He fell silent for a time. Finally he said matter-of-factly, 'My shouts accomplished one thing. The chekist turned round. I got a good look at him and he got a good look at me.'

"The chekist Ivanov saw in that gutted cottage, of course, was the man who stopped in front of me during the camp inspection. The chekist had a good memory. Ivanov ran away from the cottage—there was nothing he could do for his friend—but the chekist made it his business to track down the witness to his crime. When he found Ivanov, it wasn't hard for him to fabricate a whole slate of charges against him under Article 58, everything from pissing on Stalin's name to collaboration with the enemy. The chekist was hoping for a death sentence, but the case was prepared in such a slipshod way that Ivanov got off with ten years of forced labor.

"Poor Ivanov. After he had worked off more than half of his sentence, the same chekist was breathing down his neck, still not satisfied, still hungry for blood. The chekist waited just long enough for Ivanov to start to relax before he struck.

"I had got money from Ivanov and bought both of us warm, fresh, crusty rolls from a bakery woman who peddled them, and sometimes herself, around the camps. It was one of those glorious days when the skies are a blue vault and the wind lets up and the light off the snow is dazzling —not that any of us had eyes for those things at the time.

"Goga came up with some men I hadn't seen before. They looked like professional cutthroats. It was odd, because we knew all the people in the camp, and we had heard nothing of a train arriving with a new batch of zeks.

"Goga told Ivanov that he was being reassigned; he'd be working with the new men instead of our regular gang. I had a bad feeling about it, but what could I say? It wasn't the kind of thing you could question. I saw Ivanov stuffing the last of his bread into his mouth as he went off with them.

"Later that day, when we were all out in the forest, I caught sight of Ivanov, quite a long way off. He and one of the newcomers were hacking away at an enormous pine, while another man pushed at the trunk with a long stick. I saw the pine shudder and begin to fall. I couldn't hear anything, because the crash of timber was all around me. But like a fool, I yelled to Ivanov to look out because the tree was falling toward him. He couldn't have heard me, of course, but I saw him start scurrying crabwise out of danger.

"I saw it as clearly as I see you, Sasha. One of the new men stuck out his foot so that Ivanov tripped and went flying. It was quite deliberate. Ivanov was trying to roll away, but the brute shoved him back with his boot, across the path of the falling pine. I don't know if Ivanov screamed. It was over very quickly. The guards came running up and organized a team to dispose of the body.

"The newcomers did not appear in the compound that night. Probably they were packed off straight away, or else they were getting drunk with the guards. I'm sure the whole thing was rigged by our camp *Oper* on the orders of that visiting chekist.

"The man who killed your father got rid of the only witness."

5 Professor Levin slumped into the back of his chair, exhausted. Sasha was breathing in rapid, painful gasps, as if he had been winded running. Long before Levin had reached this point in his story, Sasha had realized that the man who had been shot in the back of the neck trying to save a German child from a rapist was his father.

"You knew the first time we met, didn't you?" Sasha said.

"That Ivanov's friend was your father? Yes, I knew. Ivanov told me the name. I think he wanted to make sure someone would remember."

"Why didn't you tell me before?"

"What would that have accomplished?"

"I had the right to know," Sasha responded bitterly, thinking of the night he had read his father's letters without comprehending.

"Perhaps," Levin conceded. He stretched out his arms, palms forward, like an offering. "But you weren't prepared for the knowledge. It would have eaten at you, like ringworm."

"So why are you telling me now?"

"Because now you *have* to understand. And you have to explain things to Tanya. History has come full circle. It will all be the same as before, the same as it was under Stalin. I was on the trolleybus this morning—" Levin started shaking again.

"Yes?" Sasha prodded him.

"There was a man in the street. The chekist I saw in the camp."

"*You saw him here, in Moscow?*"

"He was as close to me as you are. He even met my eyes. But he didn't know me. He must have seen so many faces in the camps. He was in uniform, with blue tabs."

"KGB?"

"They've made him a colonel. You see now, don't you? You can't fight them."

"Give me his name."

"I don't know. . . . I don't remember."

"I don't believe you." Sasha got up and walked over to Levin's chair. He stood between the professor and the light. In the shadow, Levin looked tiny and frail. He seemed to recoil as if he was expecting a blow.

He said, "You'll never find him."

"So tell me."

A shudder passed through his whole body, and when he said the name, his voice was so thin that Sasha had to make him repeat it. "Topchy."

"Topchy." Sasha echoed the word, letting the clumsy syllables sear into his memory. "He's Ukrainian?"

"I suppose so."

"What else do you know? What section is he in? I want everything."

The professor was trying to roll a cigarette. The trembling seemed to have stopped now he had told it all. "There's nothing more," he said. "Believe me, Sasha, you'll never reach him. Don't even think about revenge. You're just a boy—oh, yes, believe me. What do you imagine you can do to a colonel of the KGB?"

"I can find him and kill him," Sasha said very quietly.

"And be shot in return? Is that what your father would have wanted? Two lives for one?"

"I don't know."

"Besides, how do you propose to find him? Are you going to walk into the Lubyanka and ask to see Colonel Topchy?"

Sasha didn't have a response.

"We've been friends for a long time," the professor said to him. "Trust me when I tell you that emotion is not your ally, and that your enemy is not an individual—not even Topchy—but a whole system. It took me a long time to see all of this clearly. When they first sent me to the camps, I kept thinking that there must be a good reason. I spent hundreds of hours trying to rationalize my arrest in Marxist-Leninist terms. I tried to convince myself that what had been done to me must be in the best interests of socialism, just as I told myself when they denounced the Old Bolsheviks as foreign agents and sent them to the firing squads that it had to be done because the revolution was weak and the people must be taught to revile those who divided us out of honest conviction. I was like a spider whose glands had dried up so it could produce no silk, yet still went on making all the thousands of motions necessary to spin its web."

Sasha went to the window, folding his arms tightly across his chest.

"Do you know what I learned, Sasha?" Levin continued. "I learned that if you want to deal with men like Topchy, you have to meet them on their own terms. You have to learn from them. No, don't be shocked. It's the only way. You won't defeat them by an act of passion, whether it's a single bullet or a poetry reading in Mayakovsky Square. The only way to beat them is to borrow their methods, to lie, to cheat, to make compromises, to be absolutely ruthless in order to get to the top. Do you begin to see?"

The silence, when neither of them spoke, was a leaden weight.

Sasha said, "I'll have to think about it."

"Are you going to tell Tanya?"

"No," he replied without hesitation. Topchy was *his* burden.

"But you will try to stop her getting mixed up with those young fools like Zhukovsky."

That much he could promise. To try.

Sasha reread his father's letters, and understood, for the first time, what he had meant when he said that Russian soldiers had been herded into battle to determine whether the concentration camps of the future would be red or brown. Once the hot passion to seek out Topchy had subsided, he realized that Levin was right about many things. Topchy, wherever he was, wasn't just an isolated individual; he was part of a system, and it was that system that had killed his father and his father's friend. His father had had a vision of Russia. To avenge his death required more than an act of retribution; it meant changing the system. And that couldn't be done the way Tanya's friends imagined, by cranking out leaflets and reading verses beside the statue of a poet who had killed himself. In Russia, revolutions weren't made in the streets. He had often talked with Levin about how all the great reformers in the country's history, for good or for bad, had been autocrats. Even the revolution that was celebrated every autumn in Red Square hadn't come from below; it had been made by no more than a thousand Bolshevik conspirators, skilled in the science of coup d'état.

Thinking about all of this, Sasha decided to follow the professor's advice, to suppress his emotions and learn from the Topchys. He tried to reason with Tanya, but she persisted in playing romantic games with Zhukovsky's group, running around the city, handing out samizdat. His next step was even harder to explain to her.

6 Suchko was not the most popular student in the history faculty. He had a flat, oily face that reminded Sasha of a pancake smeared with butter. He tried to make himself look menacing by narrowing his eyes into slits and pressing his face right up against you. This had its effect, not just

because his breath reeked like an open drain, but because Suchko was the Secretary of the Komsomol bureau for the faculty.

Suchko was no scholar. It was generally believed that he only got through his exams because his professors were instructed to give him passing marks. But he had managed to ingratiate himself with some higher-ups in the Party. His father was some obscure functionary in Dnepropetrovsk. This was a useful connection now that Brezhnev was climbing to the top. Brezhnev had launched his career as First Secretary in Moldavia, and his old gang, the *Banda,* could look forward to plum jobs in Moscow.

All the students belonged to the Komsomol, of course, and were required to turn up for meetings. This was a serious business. If you skipped a couple of meetings without an acceptable excuse, you risked being expelled from the Komsomol and that, in turn, could end your university career. So Suchko was no stranger to Sasha. The Komsomol Secretary was an enthusiastic speaker, working himself up into a lather denouncing foreign influences. Sasha was usually silent on such occasions. But a few weeks after his talk with Professor Levin, he spoke up in support of Suchko's attack on two dissident writers, Sinyavsky and Daniel.

Afterward, Suchko slapped him on the shoulder "You're all right, Alexander Sergeyevich, you know that? You ought to be more active. You've got brains, you could have a big career in front of you. Now look here, I want you to cast your eye over the draft of a speech. It needs a little polishing."

It was a hack job. Sasha set himself on automatic pilot and wrote a whole speech for Suchko in less than an hour. Suchko got a pat on the back from the Party committee, and was suitably grateful to his ghostwriter.

"Come on," he said to Sasha. "I owe you a drink."

Suchko's room smelled of soiled bedsheets and congealed fat. They drank vodka with beer chasers, at a pace that made Sasha feel queasy.

"I know how to look after my friends," Suchko assured him. "You don't need to waste your time burrowing in all those fat books. I've dropped your name to the right people. It's all arranged. We're going to elect you to the Komsomol bureau. You're good with words. We'll put you in charge of ideological discipline. Now what do you say to that?"

It was working according to plan, even faster than Sasha had expected. He affected not to be interested.

"Don't talk garbage!" Suchko interrupted him. "We'll tell you who to look out for. Scum like that snotty-nosed Zhukovsky. I've got his number, all right!" He belched comfortably, and added, "You're one of ours, I can tell. Not like those fucking kikes who are causing all the trouble."

7 He met Tanya in the Alexander Gardens. She seemed distant, and didn't respond to his embrace.

"What's wrong?" he asked her.

"There's a nasty story going around."

"What story?"

"They say that you've joined the bitches."

"*Bitches?*" Sasha flung the foul word back at her. "Who's been telling you that? Wait—I know the answer. It's Zhukovsky, isn't it?"

He thought of the poet with a bleak hatred. Zhukovsky was a fop, in that beret of his, sporting a moustache that he probably imagined made him look like Lermontov. His poems weren't even any good.

Tanya wouldn't face him. "Is it true that you've joined the Komsomol bureau?" she addressed a fat pigeon waddling across the grass.

"And what of it?"

"You know what it means, don't you? They say you've made yourself Suchko's pimp."

"It's not like that at all." He tried not to vent his anger on her, but was shocked by her lack of faith. Zhukovsky had obviously given her a good working over. He'd seen the way the poet looked at her; he was after more than a new convert.

"Did they force you?" she pursued.

"Listen, we won't be students forever. We have to think about the future, start acting like adults."

She sighed and rose from the bench, pale and beautiful.

"Let's go to your place," Sasha proposed. "We can talk about it there." He knew that her mother and stepfather were away. Erinshteyn was spending three months at the Black Sea, courtesy of the Writers' Union, to seek inspiration.

"Not tonight," Tanya said. "I'm going to a meeting."

Zhukovsky again, he thought.

"You're the man to deal with this Zhukovsky business," Suchko told him a few days later, in his most confidential manner. "This time, he's gone too far. Important people have decided to put a stop to it." Zhukovsky's group had handed out leaflets inside the Moskva cinema, denouncing the KGB.

Sasha didn't resist the proposal as hard as he might have, maybe because he resented Zhukovsky's hold over Tanya, maybe because he had already made his choice, and the first betrayal is the hardest.

"The meeting is set for Thursday," Suchko told him. "You will present the bureau report. I've got a few pointers for you."

He gave Sasha a typed sheet summarizing the charges against Zhukovsky. There was no indication of its provenance.

"I know you'll give a virtuoso performance," Suchko said.

Sasha wrote several drafts of his speech against Zhukovsky, and didn't like any of them. The real charge against Zhukovsky was that the man was a vain fool. But they wanted him to make out that Zhukovsky was a tool of Western special services. The only evidence was that some of his samizdat had filtered out to Amnesty International and the foreign press. Suchko was asking Sasha to deliver a catalog of lies. Well, what had he expected? The system was founded on lies. This was the price of admission. Besides —he tried to rationalize—he was just a passive instrument. If he didn't do the dirty work, someone else would. Zhukovsky was finished, and he had only himself to blame.

But he couldn't bring himself to share these thoughts with Tanya. "I'll break it to her tomorrow," he told himself each night. Then the morning of the Komsomol meeting came, and he still hadn't owned up to her.

The lecture hall was crowded, and on the platform were several older men with bulging, self-important faces whom Sasha had never seen before.

When his turn came to speak, he started wading through the prepared text—edited and improved by Suchko and those who gave him his orders —without raising his eyes from the pages. A duplicate of one of the pages had been interleaved by mistake, and the ironclad phrases were so monotonous that Sasha read the first sentence before he recognized his error. Nobody seemed to have noticed.

"Student Zhukovsky's anti-Soviet activities," he wound up, "can benefit only our imperialist enemies. Our bureau proposes that he be expelled from the Komsomol and that the case should be submitted to the Prosecutor-General in order to determine whether Zhukovsky and the members of his underground organization have engaged in anti-state activities as well."

This was received with decorous applause from the platform, weakly echoed by the mass of students in the hall. The roof of Sasha's mouth was dry and sore, as if he had been smoking too heavily. He returned to his seat and avoided looking at Zhukovsky, who was sitting in the front row, legs crossed, head flung back, as if the proceedings had nothing to do with him.

The rest of the session proceeded like a steam locomotive shunting between stops. Other prepared speeches were delivered in tones that ranged from stage fury to the hum of a telephone receiver left off the hook. The resolution to expel Zhukovsky from the Komsomol was passed unanimously.

One of the large, comfortable men from the presidium took Sasha's arm and praised his speech. "You're one of us," he said cheerfully.

Afterward, Sasha hung around inside the lecture hall until the students had dispersed. When he went outside, a few students in Western jeans were gathered around the statue of Lomonosov—the Psychodrom, they liked to call it. There were a couple of ersatz hippies who had taken off their shoes and smeared their faces with bold makeup or poster paint. They paid no attention to Sasha. He crossed the drive, and walked through one of the gateways leading out into Prospekt Marx.

A shadow crossed his path, and he stopped short. It was Tanya. She was very pale, and her skin had an odd, matte texture, as if the life had been drained from it. But her eyes burned into him.

"You—you—" she stammered at him. Unable to complete her thought, she swung the heavy textbook she was carrying at him. He made no effort to stop her. The book thwacked against his rib cage.

She let the book fall and started slapping him. The blows stung, but he stood there unmoving until she had exhausted herself.

"It's over between us," she panted. "I don't care if I never see you again."

She turned to go, and he grabbed at her arm.

She wheeled on him and said, "Ilya was right. You've joined the bitches. I hope they do to you what you've done to him." The tears welled up and flowed over her cheeks. She broke free and started running up the street, veering from side to side to dodge the pedestrians. He watched until she was lost in the crowd.

He turned to find Suchko lolling against the faculty gate, with a faint smirk on his lips. He came up and took Sasha's arm.

"Forget your little Jewess," Suchko counseled. "There are plenty of girls who are willing. You're on the way up."

The Komsomol secretary's oily face gleamed in the sunlight, and Sasha wanted to drive his fist through it. He mumbled something and started hurrying through the crowd in the same direction as Tanya, toward the metro.

He bought a bottle of vodka that cost two roubles and eighty-seven kopeks, the cheapest rotgut in the shop. He found a solitary corner of a playground, tore off the throwaway top, and swilled more of the liquor than he could stomach. By the time he got home, his mind was swinging about like the needle of a broken compass. He ignored Fufkov's drunken bellowing from the kitchen, told his mother he was ill, and threw himself into bed. He stayed there for two days.

When he returned to the Faculty, he appeared totally collected. He had built a wall between himself and Tanya. It mightn't be solid enough to lean on yet, but he kept reminding himself that he had set himself an objective that was more important than his happiness, or Tanya's. One day, he would be able to explain to her. One day, she would understand. Until then, it was better to forget her.

He found release on the hockey rink and in some of his classes in the military *cathedra*. All students were required to do military training. On graduation from Moscow University you were given the rank of reserve lieutenant in the armed forces. But few of the students were interested in a military career. Behind their backs, they called their instructors "High Boots"—*Sapagi*—or *Soldafon*, a made-up word that implied that if you listened to the man's brain working, you'd hear a dial tone. But there was one instructor they all liked, especially the girls, a certain Suvorin. He was young but weathered; he gave the impression of a man with a past. There was a story that Suvorin had been assigned to the university as a punishment, that he'd been involved in secret work in the Middle East, but had got blind drunk and left his briefcase in a Moscow taxi. He was obviously as bored as his students with the theoretical sessions on Marxist-Leninist doctrines of warfare.

Sasha enjoyed the practical sessions, stripping down a kalashnikov or shooting at targets with a makarov pistol. He was the best shot in the class, better even than Suvorin. The instructor began to pay special attention to him.

They put Zhukovsky on trial in a drab stone courthouse in Lyublino, in the southeast suburbs of the city. Tanya and others from the group were kept outside, behind a tall green picket fence and a solid wall of militiamen and civilian toughs who jeered and jostled. Freight trains whistled nearby. In Soviet justice, the purpose of a trial is to make public a judgment that has already been reached. In the case of Ilya Zhukovsky, the only uncertainty was whether he would be sent to a psychiatric institution to be treated for "sluggish schizophrenia"—a wondrous malady, discovered by the celebrated Professor Snezhnevsky, that had no clinical symptoms—or consigned to the labor camps. As it proved, Zhukovsky was more fortunate than some. He got three years in the camps for disseminating fabrications designed to bring the Soviet state and social system into disrepute.

Tanya hurled herself into the work of the defense committee. She tried to organize a demonstration, but hooligans broke it up. She would go to the Hammer and Sickle factory and try to hand out leaflets to the workers at the end of their shift. She had a violent quarrel with her stepfather and took to roaming the city like a nomad, camping out on the floor in other students' rooms—and sometimes in their beds. She accosted foreign correspondents quite openly, pressing them to write stories about the dissident movement.

She was asking to be arrested.

It was Suchko who broke the news. "They're all going to be rounded up," he told Sasha breathlessly. "All the members of Zhukovsky's group." He confided that he had received instructions to arrange the expulsion of several students from the Komsomol. Tanya was at the head of the list. "The Committee's involved," Suchko went on, using the standard euphemism for the KGB. "They've been watching them all along, playing them like fish on a line."

The news blew a hole in Sasha's calculations. He could rationalize what had happened to Zhukovsky, but he couldn't stand passively on the sidelines and let Tanya share Zhukovsky's fate. He had resolved to stop loving her, but he couldn't accept that he had lost her beyond recall.

He rushed home to the room on Peschanaya Street. His mother kept her savings in a shoe box hidden away on top of the wardrobe. Standing on tiptoe, he could just manage to reach it. There was more money than he had expected, tightly wadded in bundles and tied up in rubber bands. He wouldn't need all of it.

He took a taxi to the Yaroslavsky station and stood in line at the ticket office.

"Vladivostok," he said thickly when his turn came. "One way."

They didn't ask for his papers. In those days people were more relaxed at railroad stations than at the airports.

Armed with the ticket and the remaining cash, he went looking for Tanya. He tried the apartment on Smolenskaya Street. Tanya's mother was haughty but scared. "There've been phone calls," she told him. "They wouldn't give their names."

By process of elimination, Sasha tracked her down to a girlfriend's place out in the Lenin Hills, near the main campus. He heard voices inside the apartment raised in argument before he knocked. A nervous, mousy girl with cropped hair came to the door. She told him that she didn't know where Tanya was, but when he threatened to push his way into the apartment, Tanya herself came out onto the landing and closed the door behind her.

"What do you want?" she said, trying to sound casual as she talked around a glowing cigarette. "I thought you'd be busy drinking with your pal Suchko."

"I came to warn you. You're going to be arrested."

"Who's going to press charges—you?"

She turned her back on him and peered out the window, across a desolate expanse of concrete.

"Listen, your only chance is to get away from Moscow, somewhere they won't look for you. I've arranged everything." He produced the railroad ticket, and made her look at it.

She stared at the destination. "Vladivostok?" she said derisively. "So you want to send me to the other end of the earth. Why not Kolyma? It's on the way." Kolyma was famous for its gold mines and the severity of its labor-camp regime.

"Others have got away with it," he explained. "I have a cousin in Vladivostok. I know he'll help you. He's a good man, an engineer. He can get you work. You'll have to change your name. But I promise they won't find you. In the end, they'll forget about you. Everything will blow over."

Her laugh was short and brittle.

"You must understand," he pleaded with her. "They'll send you to the camps. Your father knows what that means. It's beyond imagining."

At that moment, Sasha was ready to throw up everything if he could only persuade her to save herself.

"I'll come and join you as soon as I can," he went on. "We'll be together again."

Perhaps the force of his emotion communicated itself to Tanya, because her sarcasm dried up. But she wouldn't be swayed.

"I'm not going to run out on my friends," she said. "And what about my father? If I run away, they'll come for him. They'll claim he was my accomplice."

"It doesn't have to be like that," Sasha argued. "The families aren't always punished."

"Come on, my father's been in the Gulag already. The men who put him there have long memories. And they're back in their old jobs. Isn't that what you've been telling me?"

"Yes—but—" Abruptly, Sasha changed tack. "At least we can talk to your father," he suggested, hoping the professor would see things his way. "Will you do that?"

She hesitated.

"I'll take you there now," Sasha pressed her.

"All right. But wait for me outside."

She doesn't want the others to see her going with me, Sasha thought, *because they think I'm a stoolie.*

He idled on the corner, in a pool of shadow beyond the sulfurous glow of the street lamp. For a crazy moment, he wondered whether he could somehow force her on to the train.

There she was at the doorway, moving with that sinuous, feline grace. He started to walk toward her, just as two men ahead of him leaped out of a parked car. He saw them wrestle with her, pinioning her arms. A third man flung open the back door of the car—a black Volga—and they hustled her inside. A deep voice commanded, "Put your hands on the back of the seat in front of you."

Nobody paid any attention to Sasha. He walked away, his legs as heavy as pig iron, as the KGB driver started the engine.

Sasha didn't look back.

8 A few days after Tanya's arrest, Suchko asked Sasha to meet him in a room that the Komsomol used for committee meetings. There was a stranger there, a rangy, loose-jointed fellow with alert, cobalt-blue eyes.

"Alexander Sergeyovich, delighted to meet you," the stranger greeted him familiarly, gripping his hand like a metal clamp. "I'm Inspector Lubovin of the Committee for State Security." He flourished his red identity booklet.

"I feel I know you already," Lubovin went on. "I've heard so much about you from our friend here. By the way"—he turned to Suchko—"I mustn't detain you. Comrade Preobrazhensky and I have things to discuss in private."

Trying not to look affronted, Suchko took his cue and left.

"Well, here we are," Lubovin said. "There's a delicate matter I have to raise with you."

"Yes?"

"Just by chance, it came to our notice that Tatyana Levina was at one time your close friend. She's very attractive, in her way."

Sasha sat absolutely still.

"I don't want to cause you any embarrassment. We know everything about you, you can be quite sure of that. Did you get a refund on the railroad ticket?"

The KGB man watched for Sasha's reaction. None was visible.

"We're all human, of course," Lubovin said indulgently. "You're not under suspicion, rest assured."

"What will happen to her?" Sasha said softly.

"To Tatyana? Oh, three years in the camps, if she's sensible. She could do worse, you know. She could be charged with espionage. But you needn't concern yourself. She hasn't said anything against *you.*" The pause allowed Sasha to picture Tanya under interrogation. "I'm confident of your socialist sense of duty," Lubovin added silkily.

"As a matter of interest," he continued, "why didn't you report Tatyana's activities when you first became aware of them?"

"I—I wasn't sure of the correct procedures. And there may have been some personal inhibitions."

"Not now."

Sasha met his gaze. "No, not now."

"Well, I've enjoyed our little chat," Lubovin proceeded briskly. "Now let me ask you. Suppose we need help at some time. Are you ready to assist us?"

"Of course. But I'm not quite sure—"

"*Dorogoy moy.* My dear chap. We're not asking you to become a full-time agent. I just mean, if you notice any unusual behavior, even by members of the Komsomol bureau . . ." He jumped up and slapped Sasha on the shoulder. "I'm sure we understand each other. When you have something, just give me a buzz." He scribbled his phone number on a slip of paper. Like all the numbers at KGB headquarters, it began with the digits 224.

Sasha hadn't called the 224 number, and had heard nothing from Inspector Lubovin, when his turn came to go to military camp. Only male students were taken, in their last year at the university. Some of the others were nervous; the instructors were said to be real bastards. But Sasha was looking forward to clean air and a release from the clammy sense of guilt that he experienced every day in Moscow, where everything held memories of Tanya. Professor Levin had gone to ask about her several times, to the mansion up the road from the Lubyanka that had once belonged to Count Rostopchin. The place was a scene out of Tolstoy: parquet floors, high molded ceilings, glittering chandeliers. Each time, they made Levin wait for an hour or two. Each time, they told him the bare minimum: that she had been sent to a labor center in Kamchatka, that she was allowed a food parcel once a month.

At the camp, they practiced trench warfare, hunkering down while old T-62s churned toward them through the clumps of pines until the treads were grinding above their heads. They were sent across a slippery log bridge over a ditch where a fire had been set with napalm. The colonel who came to watch wasn't satisfied with the size of the blaze. "This isn't a dancing class!" he bellowed. "Pour the shit on!" They did, and the nervous kid running in front of Sasha—the son of a general in the Main Political Administration—lost his balance and fell. He shrieked as the napalm stuck to his hands, his clothes, his face. Sasha helped pull him out of the ditch, ripped off his tunic, and used it as a damper, trying to ignore the sickly-sweet smell of charred flesh. The boy was rushed off to hospital as monstrous black blisters flowered on his exposed skin.

That night, while Sasha was on guard duty across the sandy road—the Commander's Line, they called it—from the cadets' tents, Captain Suvorin came to chat with him.

"Question," Suvorin said in a theatrical hush. "What's a pine tree surrounded by dead wood?"

Sasha shook his head.

"New Year's Eve in the officer's mess." They both laughed, and Suvorin lit up a cigarette. "You're a cool bastard, aren't you?" he said casually. "I was watching you today. You're a natural soldier. You know that?"

He patted Sasha's walkie-talkie. "You don't have to be a *Soldafon*, you know. Me, I've put in for a transfer to the special forces, Spetsnaz. You've got the physique, and the brains. Let me know when you feel like talking about it."

A telegram from his mother came that night. As usual, she had no time for emotion. The message was simply that his grandmother's funeral would take place next Friday. There was no account of how Vera Alexandrovna had died, no expression of loss. Sasha felt surrounded by a hostile emptiness, so immense that it made his ears ring.

He felt the way he had done as a small child, when he wandered away from babushka during an outing to the center of Moscow and was lost in the vastness of gray and ochre walls that climbed toward the sun, so high that it dizzied him to look, and strangers that threatened him like moving palisades. Then she had scooped him up, and the world became near and friendly, as if she had captured the sky in the folds of her dress.

Suvorin was understanding, and arranged for Sasha to leave before the end of the training course.

He returned to Moscow by train. When he reached the building on Peschanaya Street, he found that a crowd had already gathered in the courtyard. There were many faces he didn't recognize. He was surprised that his grandmother, always so private, so self-contained, had so many people who cared for her. The open coffin, draped with a red cloth bordered with a deep black band, stood near the main entrance.

He couldn't take in the whole picture. The voices of the mourners fused in a muted, ominous monotone, like the drone of bees trapped inside a window. His mother was wearing a black scarf over her head and a black dress. She kissed him for the first time he could remember since he had been in the crib, a dry peck that brushed his cheek like crepe paper. There were no tears. He leaned over the coffin, and his grandmother's face was smooth and dumpling-round. The sharp, haughty lines etched from nose to mouth were hardly visible. Vera Alexandrovna looked rather pleased to be where she was.

Men in somber clothes converged on the coffin and hoisted it onto their shoulders. One had a narrow, ratlike face, all squeezed and pointed into a snout from which brows and chin fell away. Sasha recognized Krisov, the Secretary of the Party committee in the Ministry where his mother was employed, the fellow who had organized those endless meetings that had stolen her from him when he was growing up. None too gently, Sasha moved Krisov aside and took his place as a pallbearer. A five-man band struck up the march, and the little procession shuffled off behind them toward the hearse, a squat gray bus with a blue line along the sides. Sasha, his mother, and Krisov were jammed in together on one of the benches inside, next to the coffin.

The cemetery was one of the new ones, out on Dmitrovskoye Chosse.

As Sasha stood by the freshly dug grave, he tried to remember some of the words from the Bible that Vera Alexandrovna, a believer to the end, had tried to teach him. There was no priest among them—his mother would never have stood for *that*—but he felt that his grandmother was owed some Christian memorial.

He was still searching his memory when Secretary Krisov started up. In a high, nasal whine, he recited a string of banalities and half-truths. His voice set Sasha's teeth on edge, like the whirr of a dentist's drill. "Vera Alexandrovna, the wife and mother of socialist heroes, will live forever in our hearts," he wound up. Krisov stood there, all puffed up, apparently waiting for applause.

Sasha was furious. Who had asked this Party hack to say anything? Through all his childhood, this Krisov, and the Party he represented, had stood between Sasha and his mother. Now he had managed to turn Vera Alexandrovna's graveside into a podium. Sasha wanted to smash Krisov's face, to yell at him that none of them—not Krisov, not Suchko, not Topchy—could deprive his grandmother of her vital being, her soul. Laid out in her open coffin, she was still more real than any of *them*.

Someone else came forward, but not to make speeches. A very old, shrunken woman came hobbling through the ranks of mourners until she was standing directly in front of Sasha, stooping over the coffin. She kissed Vera Alexandrovna's forehead and carefully smoothed a long strip of white paper over it. This was the Orthodox passport to the afterlife, the *podorozhnaya*. The words, beseeching the Lord to receive His humble servant, were inscribed in Old Church Slavonic. Her duty performed, the old woman crossed herself with two fingers, in the way of the Old Believers, and shuffled away.

Krisov looked as if his collar was too tight. But some of the other mourners crossed themselves. Every Russian is Orthodox on his deathbed, Sasha thought. It was said that even members of the Central Committee had asked to receive the last rites—insurance against the unknown.

Sasha felt a cold, stinging rain against the back of his neck. He looked down into the waiting grave, where a puddle of rain had already formed. Leaves and twigs and the bodies of dead insects bobbed about inside it. Vera Alexandrovna's face was damp against his lips.

He heard the ringing, implacable sound of the nails being driven through the coffin lid. The undertakers laid ropes under the box and hauled it to the edge of the grave. There was a splash as it dropped to the bottom. Sasha's mother tossed in the first sod of earth, Sasha the next. It thudded against the wood and gave back no echo.

The mysterious words that Vera Alexandrovna had read to him once from First Corinthians came back unsummoned. *"For since by man came death, by man came also the resurrection of the dead."* He understood the words no better now than as a child, but they seemed to steady him, like a railing above a darkened stairwell.

9 With graduation looming up, great things were predicted for Sasha. The Party hadn't failed to appreciate his work for the Komsomol; he was already a candidate member, with the prospect of an influential post as an *apparatchik*. He passed exams with the ease that some athletes jump hurdles, and the head of the faculty assured him, in private, that he would be offered a postgraduate fellowship. Inspector Lubovin had pursued him, lightly reproaching him for never having called the 224 number. Lubovin summoned him to a reception center off Dzerzhinsky Square and told him that a career was open to him in the KGB. He seemed offended when Sasha said he would have to think about it. "Your friend Suchko didn't hesitate," Lubovin told him. "You don't think twice about an offer to join an elite force."

But Sasha said the same thing to all of them: he would think about it.

It was Ilya Zhukovsky's visit that settled it for him.

The poet loomed up like a specter as Sasha was leaving the building on Peschanaya Street. Zhukovsky's appearance was as terrifying as it was unexpected. He had aged ten years in the space of two. His hair, mostly gray, was coming out in tufts. His shoulders slumped forward in front of a concave chest. There was a suppurating scab along one side of his nose. His Adam's apple stuck out like a flint.

"*Suchonok,*" Zhukovsky hissed at Sasha. "You little bitch."

Sasha looked about wildly. None of the neighbors was in sight.

"What are you looking for?" Zhukovsky mocked him. "Are you thinking of turning me in again? You needn't bother. That's what *they* said. I'm not worth bothering about. That's why they let me out early."

His outburst collapsed in a racking cough, and Sasha realized he was dying.

Sasha said, "Why have you come?"

"*Why?*" It was an ugly screech, like a crow's. "Because I want you to know what you did to her. I want you to have to live with that, every fucking day."

He staggered to a nearby bench, and started fumbling for tobacco.

Sasha knew that smell. It was the same rough shag Professor Levin smoked.

"You saw Tanya?" Sasha pressed him.

"I heard all of it," Zhukovsky said, in little more than a whisper. "She was pretty—oh, God, she was always *that*—and some guard took a fancy to her and got her a soft assignment. They keep men and women apart, of course. But every day they would send Tanya over with a few of the lucky ones from her camp to cook for the men who were working on the pipeline. Then it all went sour. Maybe she refused to sleep with her protector, or maybe she stopped screwing him"—he added this with malicious pleasure, as if the words were powdered glass he was blowing into Sasha's face —"or maybe she was trying to organize a political discussion group. You should see our Russian thieves, our real men. They don't take kindly to political discussions."

He broke off in another coughing fit. The rag he pressed to his mouth came away mottled with red.

"So you know what happened?" Zhukovsky resumed. "They made a present of her, first to the vipers, then to the thieves. They threw her to them like a bowl of slops. Do you know what a streetcar means? One climbs on, then the next—"

"Shut your mouth!" Sasha yelled at him.

"Or what? Would you like to beat me up? Go ahead. There's nothing you can teach me about beatings."

Sasha realized he had clenched his fist, and let his hand fall to his side, ashamed.

"Is she—is she—"

"Is she alive?" Zhukovsky taunted him. "Oh, she had spirit, like a wild mare. She wasn't easy to break, not like me. Despite *you.*" His lips curled back in a risorius grin, displaying discolored, almost toothless gums. His face was a death mask as he added, "She never stopped loving you."

"Fuck your mother, tell me!"

"Oh, she kept going for a while. She needed medical attention, of course. The methods are primitive out there, but they got her back on her feet, and packed her off to a prison factory that grinds lenses to sell to the Americans. Who says forced labor is uneconomic? After all—"

"*Tell me!*"

"She found out she was going to have a baby. Not yours, I assume. Our thieves are quite virile."

There was murder in Sasha's eyes, normally so remote.

"She could have got rid of it somehow, I suppose. But at that point, something snapped. I know how that happens." Zhukovsky held up his arms, and for the first time, Sasha saw the ragged white scars across his wrists. "Tanya was more efficient," he went on. "There was some construction work going on at the camp. When nobody was looking, she got hold of a power saw."

He started describing the type, as if he were trying to sell one.

"Oh, God." Sasha's chest heaved, and there was a pounding in his ears. Zhukovsky, the bench, the half-grown trees, and the playground beyond receded into a pink fog. In their place, he saw Tanya in a clearing behind a prison barracks, saw her switch on the saw, set it on the ground, and lower herself, stretched full length, as if she were about to do push-ups. Or make love. He saw the white gleam of her throat as she let herself fall onto the running blade.

Zhukovsky had had his revenge.

Sasha understood that there was only one place for him to go. He went to Captain Suvorin, the military instructor, and said, "Is your offer still open?"

Suvorin raced through the paperwork, eager to get Sasha's signature on the forms. When they had finished, he produced vodka and a couple of mugs.

"We ought to celebrate," Suvorin said. "I'm leaving the university too. I finally worked off my sentence. *Budem zdorovy!*"

"*Budem!*" Sasha chimed in, clinking mugs.

"You're a real sphinx," Suvorin said to him. "I didn't dare ask you this until I'd got you signed up. I know what the others say. They say the army is a swamp. Most of the smart ones, the ones who can take their pick, find something better to do. Now *you*, you had everything open to you. Why the army?"

Because it's in my blood, Sasha thought. *Because I'm sick of betrayals.* Because he wanted to lose himself in the discipline and physical exertion of army life until his sense of guilt and loss had dulled. Because he wanted to get as far away as possible from the Suchkos and the Topchys until he had the means to deal with them. *Because the army is the only institution in the country that has the power—in the right hands—to crush the people who murdered Tanya and my father.*

He raised his mug and said, "Because I like the smell of high boots."

2.

THE AQUARIUM

I do not exhort you to make war without lawful reasons; I only desire you to apply yourself to learn the art of it. For it is impossible to govern well without knowing the rules and disciplines of it.

—PETER THE GREAT, IN A LETTER
TO THE TSAREVICH ALEXIS, WHOM
HE SUBSEQUENTLY PUT TO DEATH

1 The headquarters of the KGB is on public display, with Iron Feliks— a statue of its Polish founder, Dzerzhinsky—out in front. The square on which it stands is named after him, and so is the metro station, and the nearby street where the Moscow District office and the KGB staff club are located. Though KGB officers on their way to work by taxi are inclined to direct the driver to *Detsky Mir*—Children's World—the big toy shop across Dzerzhinsky Square, rather than to Number 2, still familiarly known as the Lubyanka, the Committee for State Security prefers to advertise its presence rather than conceal it. It is officially described as the Sword and Shield of the Party; the people should be reminded that it is vigilant.

The KGB's sister-service, the GRU, is more retiring. Few Russians know that its initials stand for *Glavnoe Razvedyvatelnoe Upravlenie*—the Main Intelligence Directorate of the General Staff. Fewer still are aware that its nerve center is an office complex hidden behind the high walls of the aircraft and rocket factories that cluster around the old Khodinsk airfield. Members of the GRU call it the Aquarium. In all the years he had lived on Peschanaya Street, just a few blocks away, Sasha had never dreamed of its existence.

Except for the few weeks of the year when army units drill on the runways to prepare for the two biggest events on the Soviet calendar— May Day and the anniversary of the Bolshevik Revolution—life at Khodinsk airfield is mostly nocturnal. An Antonov transport plane or a fat-bellied Mi-10 helicopter may land in the middle of the night to unload a Western-made rocket engine or a mainframe computer, which will be rushed away for the defense scientists to analyze and copy. Most of the time, however, the airstrip is the preserve of packs of guard dogs, scores of them, Dobermans and German shepherds that bay in the night like wolves.

The backside of the GRU factory is visible to someone walking along Khoroshevskoye Shosse from the nearest metro station, Polezhayevskaya. It is a gray four-story brick building, caked with filth and soot, with bars in the windows like a jail or a Victorian madhouse. Inside the service, it is known as the Institute of Operational Equipment, and its experts specialize in producing one-of-a-kind gadgets for spies and assassins. Do you need an exploding lipstick or a two-layer film that allows you to conceal the negative of a top-secret blueprint under a harmless family snapshot? Apply here. Some of Russia's most proficient professional criminals have been reprieved and assigned to the GRU factory to advise on safecracking and techniques of surreptitious entry.

The only access route to the Aquarium itself is via a narrow lane flanked by the ten-meter-high blind walls of another classified establishment, the Institute of Cosmic Biology. There are checkpoints manned by soldiers from a special guards battalion, with red tabs on their uniforms, and then a broad open space where some nuggety old men—all of them veterans of the service—can usually be found sunning themselves and playing chess, just keeping a friendly eye on things. In case their attention wanders, the whole area is covered by closed-circuit TV cameras. Off to one side is a big apartment block where some of the staff of the Aquarium live. Directly ahead is a blank yellow structure whose windows all open on to an inner courtyard, a sheath for the main building, which is nine stories tall and mostly glass. To get inside, you have to submit to two more identity checks and a metal detector. Officers of the GRU are not only forbidden to bring any kind of briefcase into the building, but are under strict instructions not to carry anything metallic, not even a cigarette lighter or a belt buckle. Suspenders have a brisk sale among members of Soviet military intelligence.

Captain Suvorin had predicted, before Sasha started his officer training course, that they would pick him for a "special assignment" because of his academic credentials and his flair for languages. Sure enough, after basic training he was plucked out of the stream and sent to a museumlike building on People's Militia Street, screened by dense foliage and an iron latticework fence. In the GRU school, they taught him about the heroes of Soviet military intelligence: about the spy ring, code-named "Dora," that penetrated the German General Staff from a base in Switzerland during World War II; about the network that had stolen the secret of the atomic bomb from Britain and the United States; about successive GRU operatives, from the era of the "Mrachkovsky Undertakings" in the 1920s, who had set up commercial fronts to finance agent operations and induce Western businessmen to export vital technology to Moscow. He was especially intrigued by the stories of Richard Sorge, the celebrated spy who discovered in Tokyo the Nazi plan to attack the Soviet Union, but wasn't believed by Stalin.

He learned tradecraft, and spent a week chasing around Moscow, riding the metro and trying to detect surveillance, looking for good spots to plant dead drops or hold a clandestine meeting. He listened to lectures about the principles of agent recruitment, and about Western counterintelligence techniques. The French and the Israelis, they told him, were killers, ruthless and competent. The Germans were penetrated. Britain was an old lion that had lost most of its teeth, but not its cunning. The Americans were the main enemy as well as the main target. Nobody said in any of the classes, however, that the main competition was the KGB. Sasha had to learn that for himself.

When he had finished his courses, they assigned him to the Second Directorate, which handled agent operations in the Western hemisphere, especially the United States. It was a promising start. With luck, he might progress from shuffling files in the Aquarium to a foreign posting in New York or Washington or San Francisco. But as one of his older colleagues kept advising him, he was going to need some influential friends.

Kolya Vlassov was a hearty fellow who enjoyed playing big brother. "It's easy to see your problem," Kolya would say to him. "It's time you got married."

Vlassov had been talking this way since his own recent marriage to a Ukrainian girl whose father was something in the Party committee in Dnepropetrovsk. He had already served abroad, and liked to laze around with a glass in his hand and reminisce about Scandinavian girls, and saunas, and revels on midsummer's night, when the thousands of boats in the fjords of Oslo were lit up like candles under a midnight sun. But when Kolya started sermonizing about marital bliss, he strongly reminded Sasha of the fox who lost his tail.

"It's Maria's birthday this week," Kolya informed him one afternoon. "We're expecting you."

Sasha didn't need asking twice. He jumped at any chance to get out of the family apartment, which was convenient to the Aquarium but seemed unbearably airless and constricted now that he was alone with his mother. They had nothing to say to each other. She spent even more time than before at Krisov's wretched Party meetings, and Sasha ate at friends' houses or the office canteen.

As a lieutenant without family connections, Sasha didn't have access to the special stores for the higher-ups, so he bought a little bottle of French perfume for Vlassov's wife at the GUM emporium. It was an unheard-of brand, but that didn't stop them from making him pay through the nose. Maria Vlassova received it at the door to their apartment like a ticket collector.

It was plain that Kolya hadn't married her for her looks. Her flat, puffy face with the big nose plopped in the middle vaguely resembled Brezhnev's. The primary appeal, quite obviously, was the father who was something in Dnepropetrovsk.

Maria appraised him as if he were a piece of meat that might have been lying around for too long. At last she nodded her head, as if to say, "It will have to do," and announced, in her surprisingly deep voice, "I want you to meet my closest friend."

Sasha had the situation appraised immediately. Maria fancied herself as a matchmaker.

Her friend was strategically deployed between the window and the table with the drinks and *piroshki*, dominating a group of young men who were vying for her attention. Lydia was conventionally pretty except, perhaps, for the rather solid jawline. Her hair was the color of ripened wheat; her skin was clear and milky white. She was tall—taller than one of the officers who was laughing at her jokes—with a high, full bosom. Her clothes were expensive and flatteringly cut, if perhaps a little too old for her. As she gave her hand to Sasha, he caught a whiff of a scent that certainly wasn't available at the GUM emporium.

Lydia talked about restaurants he hadn't heard of, people he hadn't met, Black Sea resorts he had never visited. She mentioned risqué French and American films she could only have seen at private showings, perhaps in the cinema that Goskino reserved for the Party and government elite. When she cracked a joke, she applauded it with a loud, brittle laugh, and expected others to follow suit. She was rarely amused by other people's sallies. Sasha was mildly aroused by the lazy sexuality he could sense in her, stirring itself like one of the larger predators waking from a nap in the sun. But the brash, brassy exterior annoyed him. Lydia talked as if she had the right to whatever or whoever she wanted.

He slipped away after a while, but Kolya collared him and shunted him off into the kitchen.

"Well? What do you think?" Kolya demanded. He slapped his left palm over his right fist suggestively.

Sasha shrugged.

"Your problem is, you never drink enough to see clearly. Here." He poured both of them a generous slug. *"Davai glaz nalyom!* Here's one in the eye!"

Sasha took a sip. It was Scotch, the real stuff. Kolya poured it down like vodka.

"Good stuff, eh?" Kolya said, wiping his mouth. "Single malt. Lydia brought it. From her father's private stock." He saw Sasha's quizzical look, and burst out, "You stupid bastard! You mean you don't know who she is?"

Sasha said nothing.

"She's the daughter of General of the Army Alexei Ivanovich Zotov, that's all," Kolya announced. He added in a stage whisper, "Now you know what it is to have friends." He refilled the glasses and said, *"Postavish.* You owe me one."

Zotov's name was a household word around the Aquarium. He was a Deputy Commander of the Warsaw Pact and one of the few certified war heroes who had managed to survive both Stalin and Khrushchev. He was one of the commanders who had helped to break the back of the German offensive in the famous Battle of Kursk. He was regarded as a soldier's soldier, not just another political general who knew how to lick asses at the Central Committee. The majors and lieutenant-colonels spoke of him with respect—something that could not be said for more than a few others in the top brass. Sasha had heard someone refer to Zotov as the helicopter general, because of his lightning inspections of military units. He was talked about as a man on his way to the top, a future Marshal of the Soviet Union and a possible Chief of Staff or even Minister of Defense.

"What are you waiting for?" Kolya nudged Sasha. "I'm an expert on body language. I can tell she likes you. You're making a big impression. Remember our illustrious M. V. Frunze." He recited the maxim that every Soviet officer had memorized in class. " 'The victor will be the one who finds within himself the resolution to attack.' "

This show of military science drove Sasha back into the living room, where the party was getting well lubricated and extremely noisy. Someone climbed onto the sofa and attempted a rendition of a Fausto Papette song, before losing his foothold and crashing to the floor, his fall softened by the girl he brought down with him, who started screaming blue murder. Sasha noted that Lydia seemed to be holding her drink pretty well, sticking to Hungarian wine rather than the hard stuff.

Suddenly she was next to him, and he felt her arm fold around his. "I'm bored," she said, close to his ear. "And the racket in here is giving me a headache. Let's go to my place and have a nightcap."

Sasha, who had been mentally preparing his own line of attack, was surprised by the boldness of this proposal. Clearly, the general's daughter wasn't in the habit of waiting for whatever took her fancy.

They flagged down a taxi with a green light in its front window, and the driver seemed happy with Lydia's directions. General Zotov's apartment was in one of the most famous buildings in the city. The Visotny Dom, on the embankment overlooking the river, had been built by Stalin in the same style as the main university building. The massive gray tower was home to scores of Party favorites, to scientists and film stars, academicians and Bolshoi performers, senior officials and others from the *nomenklatura*.

The lobby was huge, with a vaulting ceiling and a marble floor with a star in the middle that radiated in all directions. There was no doorman, only the elderly *liftiorsha*, or elevator lady, perched in the reception area; she knew who belonged and who didn't.

"Good evening, Lydochka," she greeted the general's daughter, with the familiarity permitted a family retainer. She took a good, hard look at the tall young man with the three small stars of a senior lieutenant on his shoulder boards.

The lift was on the same outsize scale as everything else in the Visotny Dom. The car they rode in was the size of one of the smaller rooms in Sasha's communal apartment, with panels of polished wood and lots of gilt around the mirrors.

The Zotovs, father and daughter, lived in a splendid apartment on one of the middle floors of the thirty-five-story tower. Lydia rushed from room to room, flicking on switches, and Sasha's first impression was of light refracted and reflected in a thousand points: from the chandeliers, the mirrors, from rows of crystal glasses in glass-fronted cabinets, from silver coffers and candlesticks. His feet sunk into deep-pile carpets. There were oriental rugs, a baby grand piano—Lydia tinkled a few bars—and a lot of heavy, stolid furniture that presumably reflected the general's conservative tastes. Lydia was showing everything off, as if they were in an auction room. The general's study interested Sasha most. The books were mostly on military history, and they looked well thumbed. The spaces between the bookcases were hung with trophies and plaques from all over the socialist world. There were photos of Zotov with Castro and General Giap and Yasser Arafat. On the desk was a museum piece: an old writing stand with inkwells, surmounted by the double eagle of the Romanovs.

"Where is your father?" Sasha asked.

"Oh, he's away for an exercise in Germany. Then he'll go duck shooting on Lake Varna." The way she described the general's life, he spent most of it away from Moscow. For a month every summer, they both went to Livadia, on the Black Sea.

She took Sasha's hand and dragged him into the kitchen. She pulled open the door of a special refrigerator, and showed him row after row of bottles. There were several kinds of French champagne and, inevitably, she picked the priciest, trailing her possessions in front of his nose. Sasha kept up the facade he had decided to adopt: polished and mildly flirtatious. He was already learning that despite his natural reticence—or more probably, because of it—he could dazzle with a focused charm that he was able to switch on or off at will, like a flashlight.

Lydia brushed against him, as if by accident, as she handed him the bottle of Dom Perignon to open. He wondered how many lovers she had had before, and whether General Zotov had ever found out. Maybe her father checked with the *liftiorsha* each time he got back from giving the satellite armies their marching orders. From the few personal things he had gleaned about Zotov so far that evening, he couldn't imagine that the general was altogether relaxed about his daughter's social life. He might be away a lot of the time, but he sounded as if he was fiercely protective of the only family he had left.

The glasses they drank from were sparkling Bohemian crystal, an offering to the general from the Czechs.

After their second toast, Lydia said, "Now you have to see *my* room."

It was very different from the rest of the apartment. There were posters of Western heartthrobs—Marlon Brando, James Dean—a powerful hi-fi, and a mountainous bed piled high with pillows, some of them lace-trimmed. She motioned for Sasha to sit on the bed while she put on a record. Soon the nudging, teasing music of the Italian pop star who was all the rage in Moscow that year filled the room.

She splashed more champagne into the Bohemian glasses. The wine fizzed, her eyes became misty, and a pink flush spread across her cheeks. He watched the soft quiver in her throat as she swallowed the champagne, the indolent smile that plucked at her lips.

Then she was beside him on the bed. Their lips grazed, then she pulled him against her fiercely, and suddenly they were sprawled full length. He felt the firming pressure of her hand between his legs. She let him explore her body, testing the weight of her breasts, the gentle rise of her belly. But when he began to probe deeper she shivered and recoiled and pressed up against his chest with both hands and pushed him away.

Coolly, as if nothing had happened, she got up and lit a cigarette with an absurdly thin gold lighter.

Sasha felt thwarted and embarrassed. He stood up, turning his back to her to conceal his condition.

She laughed and started rummaging around in her closet. "I'm going to put on something more comfortable," she announced, displaying a frothy white negligée.

But the moment had passed. Sasha felt corralled. Her manner said that she thought she could add him to the inventory of her possessions when the mood took her. The initiative lay solely with her.

At that instant, he thought of Tanya, and wanted to be anywhere other than in that room, with that woman.

He made wooden excuses about night duty at the Aquarium.

She made light of it, but he could see she was surprised and possibly offended. There was a little catch in her laugh, like a zipper that wouldn't close properly.

"I'll call you," he said at the door. They shook hands as if they had barely been introduced.

On the metro, and all the way back to Peschanaya Street, he brooded about Tanya. He told himself he was insane to go on moping over what he had helped to destroy.

At the Aquarium the next day, Kolya Vlassov tipped him a wink and said, "You hooked a live one. Am I right?"

Sasha just grunted, trying to shake him off.

"Come on, it isn't a state secret. Don't tell me you've fallen for her?"

"Later, Kolya. I have to finish a report."

"Listen, you could do a hell of a lot worse," Vlassov persisted. "I wouldn't mind sharing her bed. And the way they live! A dacha in the Silver Forest, stone, mind you, real stone. A palace on the Black Sea, a hunting lodge, whole brigades of orderlies ready to wait on them hand and foot. Just remember, Sasha, we're expecting to be invited if you tie the knot."

Before Kolya would stop, Sasha had to promise to buy him a drink that evening, and they ended up in a restaurant not far from the office. Sasha picked up a few more scraps of information about the Zotov family arrangements. Lydia was an only child. Her mother had been killed in a car crash soon after giving birth, and the general had never remarried. He was married to his profession. Lydia acted as his housekeeper and hostess in Moscow.

Kolya rhapsodized about what an alliance with Lydia would mean: access to the fancy hard-currency stores, dazzling parties, a guaranteed post-

ing abroad, easy promotion. He panted over every detail of the apartment
in the Visotny Dom.

"What are you waiting for?" he pressed Sasha. "You've got to make
your move while the bitch is in heat."

Sasha drank some more, and thought about it, while Kolya embarked on
a complicated explanation of how a four-star general was entitled to an
even higher standard of food than, say, a colonel-general. "Think of it,
Sasha," he was saying, "every apple served on Zotov's table is hand
picked! The tomatoes are four-star quality!"

There was one consuming attraction for Sasha in the situation, and it
had nothing to do with Kolya's vision of creature comfort. The attraction
was power: a shortcut to the top of the military establishment, a means to
fulfill his private agenda. He didn't recoil from the idea of a marriage of
convenience with Lydia. He felt nothing approaching love. But he
doubted that he would ever experience that again, not after Tanya. The
capacity had been burned out of him. On the physical level, there was a
healthy animal attraction. Lydia was no intellectual, but she was smart
enough. He felt that the problem, if he intended to take things further,
was how to win control, how to avoid being smothered by her.

He allowed a couple of days to elapse before calling her.

"I want to thank you for the most beautiful evening of my life," he
began. It was a transparent lie, but she enjoyed it. When he added, "Can
I see you again?" she immediately came back with, "Whenever you like."

That wasn't meant to be taken literally. When they started negotiating
the day, she recited a long list of social engagements. Then she came to
the point. "My father came back earlier than expected. But he has to
leave for Prague on Friday morning. So why don't you come round that
evening? You haven't forgotten where we live?"

The nature of the invitation wasn't lost on Sasha.

He arrived bearing gifts—flowers and chocolates.

She opened the door wearing a very light, summery dress. The way her
nipples were accentuated by the fabric suggested she had nothing on
underneath. As soon as the door was closed, she grabbed him.

The flowers and the chocolates scattered over the floor as she propelled
him backwards along the corridor, toward her bedroom, clawing at the
buttons on his uniform tunic.

They tumbled straight into bed. He began to caress her, but she shud-
dered and drew him deep inside her. She came almost at once, and the

words she gasped jolted him a bit; her father had nothing to teach her about barrack-room language.

They started over again, slower this time, until her body leaped over him like a bird startled from a thicket.

Afterward, she played shy, wrapping herself up in a long, blanketing robe. She picked up the presents abandoned in the hall and arranged the flowers in a vase. When Sasha emerged from the bedroom, buttoning his jacket, she was in the kitchen, laying out platters of caviar and buttered bread.

He kissed her lightly on the cheek. She stood back a couple of feet, inspecting him. Then she stroked one of his shoulder boards.

"The stars are too small for you," she said. "We'll have to do something about that."

They had reached a kind of understanding.

The question of marriage was first raised by Lyda, as he took to calling her, a few weeks later. It was late spring, the time of budding oaks, but cold winds snapped in the streets of Moscow like the whiplash of a winter that refused to die. They had been spending several nights a week together, usually at the Visotny Dom, but once or twice, when the general was in town, at Kolya's. Vlassov and his wife were enjoying the role of go-between.

Sasha and Lydia were in the bath, soaping each other, when he mentioned something he had put out of his mind since the first night in her bed.

He said, "Of course, you're taking precautions."

"Why?" she purred langorously. "We're getting married soon, aren't we?"

There was nothing for Sasha to do except mutter assent. After all, things were going according to plan. But, as usual, she had made the first move, and he had the sensation of mild asphyxiation.

"I told my father about you," Lydia went on. "You're expected for Sunday lunch."

Then she was giggling and groping for him through the soapy water.

2 General Zotov's voice filled the apartment the way a good sergeant-major can command a whole parade ground. He was on the phone in his study, bellowing at some unknown lieutenant. Sasha heard something

about an airlift to Syria as Lydia ushered him into the sitting room and relieved him of the flowers he had brought her from the stall at the Belorussky metro station. He had a gift for the general too, a bottle of Ararat five star, the best brandy he could buy at a normal store. Lydia confiscated it immediately.

"The doctors say he has to think about his liver," she told him. "They said he had a choice. He has so many cases of good cognac ahead of him. He can drink them in one year, or in twenty."

Sasha heard the receiver slammed down, and then a heavy tread along the corridor before Zotov lumbered out into the sitting room. He was in uniform, although it was Sunday, with six rows of ribbons on his chest. Sasha jumped from his chair and stood stiffly at attention. He felt faintly ridiculous, dressed in his one civilian suit.

Zotov stared at him for a moment, measuring him up before he stuck out his hand. He gripped like a wringer. The first thing he said was, "I thought you were an army officer. Why aren't you correctly dressed?"

"I'm sorry, Comrade General. It was a personal visit, on a Sunday, and I thought—"

"When I was your age, we understood that an officer of the Soviet army is on duty twenty four hours a day."

When he scowled, his shaggy eyebrows almost met in the middle. He was a head shorter than Sasha, but everything about him was big. He stood there, his chest thrown forward, his legs planted like tree trunks, then suddenly burst out laughing. "I see you don't scare easily. That's good. Sit down and tell me about yourself. Where do you work?"

"I'm in Department Four Four Three Eight Eight." This was the military cover name for the GRU.

"Don't bother with all that crap," Zotov said. "What are you fishing for at the Aquarium?"

"I'm on the American desk, Comrade General."

"You don't need to call me Comrade General either. You're not on bloody parade. You'll call me Alexei Ivanovich. How do you get on with that woodentop Osorgin?" General Osorgin was the chief of the GRU. Like his predecessors, he was a former KGB professional. In making such appointments, the Party adhered to the principle of divide and rule. There was no love lost between Osorgin and his army subordinates. But his old KGB confrères didn't trust him either, now he was running a rival organization.

"I'm afraid I'm not in a position to pass judgment on General Osorgin," Sasha said.

"I see you've taken up with a diplomat," Zotov said to his daughter. "Bring us a little something, Lydochka. If they learn nothing else in the Aquarium, they learn how to drink like fish."

While Lydia went to see to the drinks, Zotov said, "How did the GRU manage to pick you up?"

"I was at Moscow University—" Sasha began.

"Ah," the general interrupted. "So you're not a strawberry from our field. That's how it is with the GRU. They get a lot of butterflies—*zalyotniki*—who think they're going to be paid to see the world. Well, you needn't take offense. But don't expect a soft life. They'll work your ass off. Now tell me about your family."

Zotov's interest pricked up as Sasha explained that both his father and grandfather were army officers who had been killed in action.

"It sounds like you have quite a tradition in your family. How far does this dynasty go back?"

"To the battle of Borodino."

"And all the men in this line were officers of the Russian army?"

"Yes."

"There aren't many men in our army who can say that. In my case—hah!—they were peasants and privates and bastards, more often than not. I don't know the name of my great-grandfather, and as for the next generation, well, it depends whether my grandmother was lying or not. But your name, now, Preobrazhensky. Yes, that means something." He took a glass of Armenian brandy from Lydia—Akhtamar, his favorite, not Sasha's inferior brand—and added, "Maybe I was wrong to call you a butterfly. You could be from our strawberry patch after all. *Za vashe zdorovye!*"

The lunch was relaxed, and Zotov did most of the talking, recounting wartime experiences. Afterward, he lectured Sasha about the Middle East, which had been absorbing most of his time.

"Fifteen years ago," he said, "the economic warfare experts in your shop—Department Ten—came up with a plan to get the NATO countries by the balls by squeezing off their oil supplies from the Gulf. The key was to build an Arab power that would consistently serve our interests. So we poured weaponry into Egypt, and for a while the plan seemed to be working. Then Sadat turned against us, and those geniuses in the KGB failed to get rid of him in time. But our chance in Egypt may come again, now that the Jews have kicked them all over the map. Things aren't altogether bad. The Arab oil embargo scared the shit out of the Americans. We can use the Syrians and that nutcase Qaddafi as long as we keep an eye on them—I don't trust any of those black-asses. And we've got a big opportunity with our friend who wears the dishrag."

"You mean Arafat?"

Zotov nodded. "The Palestinians are all over the Gulf. With a little direction, they could take over Kuwait or Bahrain like that." He snapped his fingers. "The Arab governments don't give a shit about them, but they all have to pay up for the holy cause. The Americans can't play with them because the Yids run their Middle East policy. They're ours, if we know how to work them." He frowned.

"So what's the problem?" Sasha jogged him.

"The problem is the Americans don't have a monopoly on the Jewish problem. We've got our own little clique, here in Moscow. They want to handle the Zionists with kid gloves." He described a couple of very senior Soviet leaders, including the head of the KGB, as "Yids," and Sasha expressed his surprise. Everyone knew that Brezhnev's wife was Jewish. But the head of the KGB?

"We don't go by the passport," Zotov said. "We go by the face."

The general drained the last of his brandy. "Well, we're not here to complete your education," he said. "I want to know what you think you're doing screwing my daughter."

This was rather more direct than Sasha had expected.

"Lydochka?" Zotov called to his daughter, who had been sent out of the room. "Stop spying at the keyhole and come in here."

She tripped in at once, confirming the general's suspicion, and perched herself on the arm of his chair. Her hand looked like a child's on top of Zotov's clumsy paw.

"Alexei Ivanovich," Sasha said formally. "I would like to ask you for Lydia's hand."

"Just like that, eh?" He turned to his daughter. "So the young fool wants to marry you. What have you got to say about it?"

She threw her arms around his bull neck, then rushed over to Sasha and embraced him too.

"That's enough of the rehearsing," Zotov said.

"Papa?"

"What do you want me to say? It's your life."

They celebrated with champagne. After the first bottle, Zotov said to Sasha, "I suppose you're aware of the conditions. You two want to get married, so be it. But I don't intend to lose my only child. You will both live here with me."

"But we'd be in your way."

"That's the agreement. Now, when are you going to have children? I need a grandson so I can start a dynasty of my own."

The following weekend, on a stroll through the white birches around the general's sprawling dacha, Zotov said, "I want you to tell me, man to man. Do they treat you properly at the Aquarium?"

"I've got no complaints," Sasha replied.

"Well, if you need anything, I expect you to ask. I have some slight influence at Gogol Boulevard."

"Alexei Ivanovich, I'm grateful, but—well, the thing is, this marriage is going to cause talk, and I don't want anyone to think I'm trying to take advantage of my father-in-law."

"*Ne pizdi!*" Zotov interrupted. "Don't talk cunt. Lyda's always been spoiled, and you won't be able to change that now."

That was probably very true, Sasha thought. The reflection didn't raise his spirits as the day of the wedding approached. Kolya Vlassov played best man, and they rode to the Tomb of the Unknown Soldier in a big black Chaika to lay floral tributes afterward. Lydia was already pregnant, although the doctors didn't confirm the fact until after their honeymoon, among the rose gardens of Livadia, in the Crimea.

Back in Moscow, Sasha went to General Zotov to ask for a favor.

"Don't tell me," Zotov said. "Let me guess. You want to go overseas. Lyda's already talked to me about it. We'll work something out when the baby is old enough to travel."

"It's not that. I'd like to get away from headquarters for a while. I'd like some experience of active soldiering."

"What? You mean go to one of the provincial garrisons? You and Lyda both would be bored to death."

"I was thinking of Spetsnaz." Since he had been at the Aquarium, Sasha had met two special forces officers. One of them had returned from an undercover mission in the United States, checking out the ground defenses of strategic air bases in Colorado and Nevada. The other was an instructor at the guerrilla training school the GRU ran near Simferopol, in the Crimea. His special task was to select sabotage agents who could be used to attack command centers and vital communications in Western Europe on orders from Moscow. Both officers seemed to fit Captain Suvorin's description of Spetsnaz: hard, intelligent men, the pick of the crop.

Zotov looked at him closely. "They're tough bitches," he commented. "They'll probably kill you. Why do you want to do it?"

"I want to test myself."

The general approved. "But there'll be the devil to pay when Lydochka hears about it," he observed.

3 On the railroad between Moscow and Gorky is the smoky industrial city of Kavrov. The Klyasma River makes a southerly loop through the town on its way to join the Volga, but Kavrov is not noted for its scenic splendors. It is a place of hulking red brick textile mills, built in the last century, and modern concrete blockhouses, one of which manufactures heavy machine guns for the Soviet armed forces. The city is best known in Russia for its motorbike factory. Life, especially for the younger generation, is drab and provincial. The boys who can't get away to the bright lights of Moscow find release in vodka, brawling, and chasing the girls from the clothing factories. You don't see foreigners in Kavrov. It is a closed city. Its particular secrets are to be found in the pine forests seven or eight miles north of the machine-gun plant.

Hidden among the pines and birches is a huge military complex. It includes a crack airborne division. The most closely guarded facility is the preserve of the Spetsnaz brigade of the Moscow Military District. Its men wear the same uniforms as the airborne, with a tiny difference that only a trained eye would detect. The men of the eight Soviet airborne divisions wear Guards badges, a legacy of World War II; Spetsnaz soldiers don't, because their units are a more recent creation. There are about thirty thousand men in Spetsnaz forces in the Soviet Union and its satellites, divided up into independent companies and brigades, under the supervision of military intelligence. They are kept strictly segregated from other branches of the armed forces. There is no central command, no divisional structure, because the country's masters are nervous that men who are schooled as an elite, and well versed in the arts of political warfare, could develop a pretorian mentality. Only their officers, who are required to be full members of the Party and are subject to extensive loyalty checks, use the generic term Spetsnaz—an abbreviation for "Special Detachments"—and understand the full scope of the enterprise. Units attached in different commands use different names. In Siberia, the Spetsnaz forces are called *Okhotniki*, or Huntsmen. In Eastern Europe, they are *Reydoviki*, or Raiders. What is expected of all of them is unusual, and so are the rewards.

Over Lydia's protests, Zotov had arranged for Sasha to attend the Spetsnaz faculty at the Advanced Parachute Training School in Ryazan. Foreign language study was compulsory, so he chose to perfect his English. The first sentence in the Spetsnaz phrasebooks gave a fair idea of the object of this part of the course: "Be quiet, or I'll kill you." There had been a small compromise with Lydia: Sasha's operational training would take place at Kavrov, within easy reach of Moscow.

The chief instructor at Kavrov was a certain Fyodor Vassilyich Zaytsev, a tough nugget of a man from a family of soldiers and peasants in the Leningrad region. He was a man of average height, but stocky, with short fair hair hacked off in a straight line along the top of his forehead, and a horseradish nose that he was given to rubbing incessantly while talking. He had the pale blue eyes of the North, and wasn't given to saying much unless he was issuing orders. He spoke very slowly; every word seemed to be forged on a blacksmith's anvil. But he interested Sasha, who could glimpse a quick intellect in his eyes, and was impressed by Zaytsev's physical strength.

Captain Zaytsev had risen from the ranks. He came to Spetsnaz the way of many conscripts, virtually by accident. When he was called up for his three years' military service, he was pleased; it was a chance to see the world beyond the village and the *kolkhoz*. He went for his medical inspection to a recruitment office in Leningrad, which his parents, very conservative people, still referred to as Petrograd, in the old way. He was made to strip naked and parade in front of a doctor who seemed to take special pleasure in peering up rectums, while several officers looked on. One of them was from Spetsnaz. He appraised Zaytsev's physique, and announced, "He's for us."

His father had prepared him well for the special forces' grueling physical exercises. Vassily Zaytsev would take him out into the fields to scythe grass—with the warning, which Fyodor never questioned, that if he stopped before the signal, he would cut off his feet. At the end of his three years, he held the rank of sergeant—*makaronik*, his comrades dubbed him, because of the stripes—and his commander called him in with a proposal. "How'd you like to be the first officer in your family? It's better than going back to the village to die of cirrhosis, isn't it?"

So Zaytsev signed on. He was wary of this young cub Preobrazhensky, who came from a different world. What was he doing at Kavrov, this university graduate, this *generalski synok*, this little general's son? He saw Sasha as some kind of joy-rider, a weekend soldier who wanted to impress the Moscow girls. The fact that the brigade commander had told him, straight out, that Sasha was to be looked after because he was General Zotov's son-in-law didn't make Zaytsev feel any better disposed toward him. If Preobrazhensky wanted to play at being in Spetsnaz, fine. He, Zaytsev, would see him sweat.

There was an important exercise coming up, a simulated attack on a mobile NATO command post. Men from the Strategic Rocket Forces—tough bastards, like Spetsnaz—would be playing the defenders, and the chief of Moscow District would be attending in person. The attackers were divided into four-man teams, and Zaytsev picked Sasha for his own group.

They started with a parachute drop into the forest, bailing out at only two hundred meters up. It would have been a sure way to crack your spine except for the containers of carbon dioxide each man carried to puff up his parachute right away. They fell in tight clusters, with their side arms and some heavier equipment—radios, Mon-200 directional mines, Strelas, and antitank rockets. They had a couple of small vehicles, six-wheeled mobile platforms. But when they'd buried their parachutes and scattered liquid chemicals around to baffle the tracker dogs, Zaytsev told his team, "We're not fucking tourists. We're going in on foot. The objective is thirty kilometers away, and we've got two hours to reach it."

As far as Zaytsev was concerned, the weather was perfect. There was a driving rain, punctuated by lightning flashes. As Sasha jogged between the trees, his boots started to squelch; they were soon as heavy as a convict's fetters. When the rain eased off, the forest moaned and creaked and the sky seemed darker than before. They came to a lake, and had to line their ponchos with bracken and grass, cram in their equipment, tie the ends together, and stuff their weapons on top, under the knot, before starting to wade across. The pace was unrelenting, but Zaytsev was breathing smoothly and evenly, through his nose, after nearly two hours. He was surprised to see that Sasha was keeping up better than the others, even though he was lugging a heavy grenade launcher as well as his assault rifle.

They had only approximate map coordinates for their target. Their nominal job was to locate the secret headquarters and call up an air strike by firing the flares Zaytsev had clipped to his belt, along with half a dozen grenades. Zaytsev spotted caterpillar tracks over to the left, and gestured for his team to get down on their bellies. They smelled the cigarette smoke before they saw the sentry, lolling against a tree. He was wearing an American uniform. Before he had even reached for his weapon, Sasha was on him and had his arm around the man's throat.

One of the rules of these games was that prisoners talked, on the entirely rational presumption that, in real life, nobody could hold out for long against the combination of drugs and more primitive methods that Spetsnaz was schooled to employ. Zaytsev brandished a heavy file, just to remind the prisoner about this. Filing away the caps of a man's teeth, in his experience, was a surefire way to loosen tongues. They soon had a detailed description of where to find the hidden command post and how it was defended.

The captured guard was almost as tall as Sasha. Zaytsev glanced from one to the other and said to Sasha, "Put on his uniform."

He sent Sasha in by the front door, along the trail of the caterpillar tracks, while the others fanned out through the forest. Sasha soon found a small army concealed in the forest, with tanks and armored cars, and a strong defensive perimeter. An officer in British uniform called out to him, "Anything?"

"Not yet," he called back.

A sentry in American fatigues, his collar pulled up to shield his neck from the rain, strolled over and started bitching about the weather. "It's all right for the bosses. They're nice and dry while we have to wait around getting pissed on."

Sasha glanced around, but could see no sign of a shelter.

A field officer in a jeep came bumping along, yelling at the men to redeploy for an ambush. They had learned from a radio intercept that the attackers were moving in on the camp.

"The dumb bitches swallowed it," the sentry remarked. "We've got them in the sack. You wouldn't have a smoke, would you?"

Sasha fished around in the pockets of his borrowed jacket and found a pack of cigarettes, soaked through by the rain.

"Keep it," he told the guard, who looked at him curiously.

He started running after the colonel's jeep. There were shouts behind him, but he ignored them. The vehicle was moving slowly, over the ruts, and he took a running jump and swung himself over the back.

The colonel turned round and started swearing.

"Shut your face," Sasha rasped at him, leveling his rifle. "You're prisoners."

The colonel started complaining that he was from the control team, that Sasha was breaking the rules. Sasha ignored this, and made them drive crosscountry until Zaytsev came darting out from behind a tree.

"Get your men out!" Sasha called to him. "It's a trap!"

They pried out of their prisoner the information that their real objective was six or seven kilometers west of the decoy target. One of Zaytsev's men took the wheel, but they kept the colonel to make sure they didn't get lost. A quarter of an hour later, they had breezed through the checkpoints—thanks to the colonel, sitting up front—and piled out behind a mobile command post, consisting of four butterfly trucks parked in a square, their flaps lowered to make a big platform protected from the elements by a canvas roof.

They burst in to find a group of senior officers hunched around a camp table. Zaytsev opened up with his machine gun, firing blanks above their heads. The commander of Moscow District slumped in his seat, his mouth open, his belly hanging out.

"That's it," his chief of intelligence said cheerfully. "We're all dead."

"They bent the rules a bit," the control team ruled afterward, "but you never blame the winners." Zaytsev got a commendation, and he made a gesture that was unusual for him: he invited Preobrazhensky to his quarters.

4   Zaytsev lived in a modest two-room apartment. There were few personal touches, and no concessions to luxury, but you could tell from the freshness and neatness of the place that Zaytsev wasn't a bachelor. His wife was round and pink, with soft cornflower blue eyes. She served them the kind of meal Sasha's grandmother used to prepare: a salad doused in sour cream and seasoned with dill, then borshch, and stewed veal with potatoes. They drank vodka with everything.

At the end of the meal, Zaytsev raised his glass to Sasha and said, "I didn't like you to begin with, I admit it. But I've been watching you. *Nu, ty muzhik!* You're a real man!" It was spoken only the way a peasant could say it. The words sounded rich and loamy. It was the highest compliment Fyodor Zaytsev could pay.

"What made you choose the army?" Sasha asked him.

"You wouldn't ask if you'd grown up on a farm," Zaytsev said. "I went back to my village a year ago, to see my people. Everything had changed. It took me a while to put my finger on it. Then it came to me. The young ones had gone. It was a place of old people waiting to die, and hurrying the process by drinking themselves senseless every day. Agriculture in Russia is dying, and nobody even wants to attend the wake. My father would leave too, but he's an old man, and it's all he knows. To think that once we were able to sell grain to the world!"

It was the first time Sasha had heard Zaytsev string so many words together.

"What went wrong?" he probed further. "Didn't the kids start fleeing the land when Nikita started all those big new projects in Siberia and the Far East?"

"Nikita, fuck your mother! I thought they taught you history at the university. The ruin of our villages started a long time before Nikita. It started in 1917."

He paused, as if he had gone too far.

"Tell me about it," Sasha pursued.

"It's an old story. But you won't read it anywhere. What I know is what my father and my father's father told me. Lenin decreed that the land belonged to the tillers, am I right? Then, the very next year, he imposed a new law, saying the land belonged to the state. They said there was an emergency, so the peasants would have to turn over their crops for free. The peasants obeyed, up to a point, but the authorities weren't satisfied, so they sent out their own bandits—Provision Units they called them—to grab whatever was left. These people weren't Russians, anything but. They were chinks, black-asses, Balts, even Czechs and Hungarians. They didn't give a shit if Russian families starved. They stole the seed corn, shot peasants who tried to save a little bit for their children. Our peasants tried to defend themselves, and the Red Army was sent out to slaughter them."

He paused to refuel, tossing off some vodka from the neck of the bottle.

"There was a breathing space for a couple of years, after the country groaned so loudly that they had to bring in the New Economic Policy. Then the bosses panicked because they saw that independent farmers were beginning to recover and they were no great friends of the Party. So they brought in the collective farms as part of a plan to destroy the successful peasants as a class. Great Stalin called it social prophylaxis. Farmers who knew their jobs were denounced as kulaks. Fifteen million of them were shipped off to plow tundra in Siberia. Most of them died. Stalin deliberately starved millions of peasants in the Ukraine. And who survived and prospered? Loafers and petty functionaries who knew how to crawl to the authorities. That's how it began, Sasha. And you wonder that we can't grow enough to feed ourselves! What is a peasant most attached to? His land! How can you expect farmers to produce when they're reduced to wage slaves? We'd all go hungry if someone hadn't woken up and decided to let the kolkhozniks have a little scrap of land of their own to work in their spare time. Those private plots are maybe three percent of the farmland in Russia, and they produce a third of our meat and milk and two-thirds of our potatoes!"

Sasha was listening very carefully. Those last statistics were unlikely to have come from Zaytsev's father, who was probably semiliterate at best. The man was not only passionate on the subject of what was wrong with Soviet agriculture, he was well briefed, and surprisingly fluent. Like Sasha, Zaytsev must be a full member of the Party, otherwise he couldn't be an officer in Spetsnaz. But he certainly didn't talk like one of the faithful.

"All right," Sasha interjected. "So our agriculture is a swamp. You don't need to tell me. I saw it myself, when I had to go out with the students to help gather potatoes on a kolkhoz. And I've stood in a few food lines too. What do we do about it?"

"It's easy," Zaytsev said. "Easy to dream about. You start by breaking up the collectives, and giving the land back to the farmers. But they'll never do it, of course. They're scared of the peasants, just like Stalin was. They'd start crapping in their pants at the idea that the peasants might get some money and some power and start standing up to the Party." He broke off and looked at Sasha warily. "I've told you all these things," he said, "and you've said nothing about your own ideas."

"There's time for that," Sasha responded. "Tell me one thing more. How many people do you talk to like this?"

"My father. My wife. Now you. Listen, there are no fools in my company."

Sasha resolved at that moment to follow Fedya Zaytsev's career closely. A man who fought like a trained killer and felt like a Russian peasant was a man who could be used. In the weeks that followed, Zaytsev coached him in hand-to-hand fighting, until he had learned all the ways to kill with minimum effort. There were other evenings when, once he had got a good belt of vodka inside him—he favored pepper vodka, one of the tastier brews—Zaytsev shared more of his secret opinions. He startled Sasha one night by announcing, "There never was a Russian revolution. We're still waiting for it. What do you say, learned professor?"

Sasha grunted something noncommittal. He was not ready to reveal himself yet, even to Fedya Zaytsev.

"In the key group of five men that seized Russia," Zaytsev went on, "there were three Jews—Trotsky, Kamenev, and Zinoviev—one cockroach from Georgia, and our famous Lenin, who was half Kalmik and half German Jew."

Sasha assumed that Zaytsev must have acquired this gem from one of the Slavophile leaflets that were circulating around the barracks.

"Do you think there'll ever be a *Russian* revolution?" Sasha goaded him gently.

"There has to be," Zaytsev said passionately. "And I don't mean in another century or so. I intend to be present. Do you think I'm crazy?" Sasha merely raised his glass.

Zaytsev shook his massive head and said, "You don't show yourself, do you, Sasha? Well, that's all right with me. Russia is full of talkers who can expound the most wonderful plan at four in the morning and then, when the sun comes up, they've forgotten all about it and they're too hung over to get out of bed anyway. You listen and remember. I wish I knew what was going on inside that skull of yours."

"I think we understand each other," Sasha volunteered. "You're not one of those who forgets the next day, either."

5 Sasha's Spetsnaz training was cut short because of the imminent birth of his child. He took the train back to Moscow and rushed over to the hospital, where they kept him waiting for hours, through a protracted delivery. When they finally admitted him to the ward, Lydia was propped up against a pile of pillows. Her face was mottled pink and white, but she seemed to him to be suffused with light. She peered up at Sasha, her eyes bright but barely focused. He hardly dared look at the bundle cradled in her arms. She smiled, and he leaned closer. He thought that what he saw was physical perfection. The baby was long and sturdy, with a tuft of white-gold hair on top of an otherwise bald pate. When he pressed his lips to its cheek, it balled its tiny fists and raised a tremendous howl.

"We'll call him Pyotr," he said to Lydia, squatting on the edge of the bed beside her.

"Petrushka," she softened the name. "Petya."

He put his arm around her shoulder. In that moment, in the presence of the mystery of birth, he could forget her airs and her bossiness and the cold reasoning that had led him into the marriage. She was magnificent.

"Thank you," he murmured as he kissed her, and added mentally, *Thank you for making me more than myself.*

One of the rooms in the apartment in the Visotny Dom was turned into a nursery, and General Zotov filled it with soft toys, mostly huge cuddly bears, one of them nearly as big as the baby's grandfather.

Zotov was just as active behind the scenes. Sasha was notified that he would be attending a special course, preparatory to his posting to the Residency in New York. They set him to studying old files, maps, and phone books. He listened to a succession of veterans discourse on the psychology and the weaknesses of the Americans. Even the legendary Colonel Abel was produced for one of these sessions. Abel had once run an Illegals network in New York. Captured by the Americans, he had kept his secrets and was eventually freed in exchange for the downed U-2 pilot, Gary Powers. Abel's voice was thin and reedy, and Sasha had to strain to catch his words, with the snow thudding against the windows, leaving marks like paw-prints.

Word came at last that they would be leaving for New York in the spring. Kolya Vlassov hosted a farewell party. He got Sasha in a corner and said, "I bet they told you all about the FBI, didn't they? How they've got hundreds of radio cars on the prowl, and all the cops and even the firemen report to them?"

"Not quite."

"Well, just you remember, Sasha. The FBI could be on your ass, but it's our brothers in the Committee who are going to stick it to you."

3.

NIKOLSKY'S PROBLEM

Drinking is the joy of the *Rus*.

—THE GRAND DUKE OF KIEV
(ELEVENTH CENTURY)

1 There were cars double-parked on three sides of the block, protected by the black letters DPL on their license plates, defying Manhattan's impatient drivers to gouge a strip off their paint. Large policemen with faces that were maps of Ireland and Calabria stood about in their rumpled blue coats. The precinct house, on the north side of East 67th Street, was a sooty, shadowy place with a flag that sagged from its pole like washing hung out to dry. A few doors away was the firehouse, red brick and businesslike, and next to that, the oriental effusion of the Park East synagogue.

The Soviet Mission occupied a converted cement-block apartment building that would have been at home in the newer suburbs of Moscow. You didn't need to belong to the FBI to guess which floor of the Mission was home for the spies. None of the windows was overclean. But up on the seventh floor, the grime had been allowed to thicken until the glass was opaque. The windows on that floor were never washed, and the blinds were never opened, so the KGB officers who worked on the street side of the building did not have to contemplate the synagogue opposite. The KGB and the GRU shared the seventh floor. As senior partner, the KGB had appropriated the front two-thirds for its Residency. The GRU had to make do with the space that was left at the back.

Everyone in the Mission shared the same bank of elevators, which created a protocol problem. Nobody pushed the button for the seventh floor. Even if everyone knew that you weren't really just a second secretary or a chauffeur or some vague type of attaché, you didn't announce your true functions by getting off on the floor whose windows were never washed.

So the members of the KGB rode up to the eighth floor and walked down the stairs. Their GRU neighbors got off on the sixth floor and walked up.

At the end of Sasha's first week in New York, he shared the elevator with two other people. He had seen the girl before, leaving the Mission at the end of the day. She had quite a pretty face, very fair-skinned with a snub, slightly upturned nose. The rest of her was oceanic, under the kind of dress you associate with advanced pregnancy.

The man was a stranger to Sasha. At first glance, Sasha thought he might have been an American—except, of course, that no American was permitted above the first floor of the Mission. He wore a very well cut suit, a muted pinstripe with a lot of buttons on the cuffs. He was quite good-looking: tall, with wavy hair, graying in just the right places, a strong chin, and a wide, sensual mouth. He was a bit puffy around the eyes, as if he had stayed up too late, and the flush in his cheeks was a little too ruddy. His eyes were the most striking feature. Bluer than Sasha's, vivid, constantly mobile and alert, with a twinkle that suggested both devilment and skepticism. They were eyes that always seemed to be asking the question, *Pizdish?* Are you talking cunt?

He considered Sasha for a moment, then went to work on the girl.

"Well then, Maria," he addressed her, "have you made up your mind when you're going to bed with me?"

Sasha felt sorry for the girl when he saw the way the blush mottled her cheeks. She seemed to be coming out in a rash. She scurried out of the elevator when it stopped on the fourth floor.

The mock suitor mimed despair, then shrugged his shoulders in an odd sort of way, depressing them rather than raising them. As the doors closed, he winked at Sasha. At least, Sasha thought that he winked, but it was as quick as a camera shutter, and he couldn't be sure.

"Good morning, General," the stranger greeted Sasha in a jocular tone. "You're going to the sixth floor, I presume?"

He pushed the button, just to score his point. "Nikolsky, Feliks Nikolayich, at your service." He clicked his heels like a stage soldier.

Sasha shook hands with him.

They were already stopping at the sixth floor. Nikolsky consulted his Swiss watch. "Look here," he announced. "It's already April the tenth, and it's past nine in the morning, and you haven't bought me a drink yet."

Sasha stared at him in the way that he might have examined an exotic fish in a tank. As he got out at the sixth floor, he said, "Eighth, I presume?" and pushed the button for Nikolsky.

It was obvious that this joker was one of the far neighbors, as members of Sasha's Residency referred to their colleagues in the KGB. Nikolsky was far too self-assured to be anything else. But Sasha's chief frowned on fraternization with the neighbors, for the eminently practical reason that they were constantly seeking to recruit agents inside the GRU and to steal its secrets for themselves.

Sasha hurried up the back stairs to the seventh floor, where he shared a cubicle with Churkhin, a case officer who had already had two postings abroad. But Sasha's first port of call was the Referentura, the secret core of the Residency, the place where the records and the code machines were housed. It was built like a vault, and behind its steel shell was a constant hum from the equipment installed to baffle electronic eavesdroppers.

The guardian of this inner sanctum was the head cipher clerk. He was the only man who was allowed to communicate with the Center without the permission of the Resident, General Luzhin. The cipher clerk was indispensable, but his life was not exactly enviable. He and his wife were kept locked up in the Mission like captive animals. The main excitement of their tour had been a bus trip to Niagara Falls, in the company of two dozen other Soviet families. They had left at dawn on a Saturday, arrived in time for dinner, had a quick look at the Falls in the morning light, and been promptly herded back on the bus to New York. The cipher clerk didn't seem to mind. He was a scrawny, bloodless type who reminded Sasha of a plucked chicken.

He grunted at Sasha, unlocked one of his safes, and delivered up the briefcase. Every officer in the Residency had one of these work satchels. Each night it had to be locked away in the Referentura, tied up with string and secured with a gob of wax on which the officer would impress his personal seal with the metal disk he carried on his key ring. The main item inside the satchel was a blue notebook with numbered pages that was used to record every communication to or from the Center, summaries of operations, and agents' code names.

Along with the satchel, the cipher clerk handed Sasha some routine messages from Moscow that had been flagged for his attention. There was unmistakable pleasure in his sallow face as he added, "The boss wants to see you at ten sharp."

General Luzhin, the head of the GRU Residency in New York, was a little man, with a little man's quirks. He liked his visitors to sit on low-slung easy chairs or on a sofa from which it was almost impossible to rise. This didn't quite even up the height differential with a man of Sasha's dimensions, so Luzhin stood behind his desk as he addressed his newest case officer.

"Well?" he boomed in a voice too large for him, his throat trembling and distending like a bullfrog's. "Have you settled in? How do you like your hotel?"

"It's colorful," Sasha replied cautiously.

"I hope you haven't finished unpacking."

"Sir?"

The Resident yanked open the drawer of his desk, pulled something out, and started brandishing it at Sasha.

"You see this?" he roared.

It looked like an airline ticket.

"This is your ticket back to Moscow. There's an Aeroflot flight tomorrow. All I have to do is fill in the name."

"I don't understand," Sasha said evenly. "Is there some emergency?"

"You've been here a whole week," Luzhin bellowed. "And you haven't come up with a single recruitment prospect!"

He's joking, Sasha thought. *Any second now, he'll burst out laughing in my face.*

But the Resident's expression did not relax as he proceeded to deliver a lecture about young men who thought that a foreign tour was a chance to live it up, chase skirts, and go on shopping sprees.

"Now, I'm a reasonable man," Luzhin wound down. "I'm giving you one week more. You can start at the Coliseum. At least you know where that is, don't you? There's an electronics exhibition opening there this weekend. I expect you to come up with something good. Otherwise"—he fanned the Aeroflot ticket—"you know what's in store for you."

Sasha left the general's office still uncertain whether he was supposed to take the man seriously. The service was keen on body counts. In his orientation course the instructors had drilled in, over and over, that agent recruitment was the beginning and the end of foreign intelligence work. The penalty for failing to hook a couple of productive agents was well understood: no more assignments abroad. But Luzhin was jumping on his back when he had barely had a chance to learn the main streets.

When he reached his own office, Churkhin looked at him slyly. Churkhin seemed a cheerful, easygoing sort. Like Sasha, he was listed as a second secretary, but he already held the rank of major in the GRU. Churkhin scribbled a few words on a scrap of paper and pushed it across the desk, like a schoolboy trying to avoid attracting the teacher's attention. That was a habit Sasha had picked up right away. In the GRU Residency, people were given to exchanging certain personal—and operational—messages in writing, less because of the outside chance that the Americans had found a way to listen in than because of the fear that their KGB neighbors had an ear to the keyhole.

"Did he show you the airline ticket?" Churkhin's note read.

Sasha grinned at his colleague. So the general had merely given him the standard welcome.

The Preobrazhenskys and the Churkhins were neighbors in the same residential hotel on the Upper West Side, a short walk away from the river. The Lucerne was a turn-of-the-century triumph in plum-colored stone, with great banded baroque columns on either side of the entrance. It might have been borrowed from the set of an early Hollywood epic. The effect was slightly marred by a tatty blue canopy with white lettering that read, "Permanents—Transients."

One of the permanents, a tiny, elderly Jewish man with a white moustache and bifocals, was taking the air on the porch when Sasha walked up the steps of the Lucerne. He nodded to Sasha, patted the column he was using for support, and spoke around the cigarette that was glued to his lip.

"Like this, they don't make."

There was an echo of Odessa in his voice.

"You got a dent in your car," he went on. They both looked at the white Ford Sasha had left parked at the curb. He had inherited the car, and the dent, from his predecessor. Few people at the Mission were experienced drivers; only a handful had had their own cars in Moscow.

The man on the porch started advising Sasha about a body shop.

"No, Manny went to Florida," he corrected himself. "You should have been here in the old days. This neighborhood used to be something."

It wasn't easy getting in and out of the Lucerne unobserved. The older residents, people who had moved out of nearby brownstones as their spouses died off and the muggings increased, spent a good part of the day in silent communion in the lobby. The desk clerk darted about like a woodpecker and had eyes in the back of his head. The FBI manned an observation post in one of the red brick buildings across the street.

There were a score of Soviet families in the Lucerne. Other Mission families were parked in the Orleans, the Esplanade, the Greystone, up on Broadway, and the Excelsior, across the street from the Museum of Natural History. Hotel managements tended to welcome the Soviets. They were quiet tenants who paid their rent on time.

Sasha liked the Lucerne. There was a sense of freedom, whether or not there was a man with binoculars at a window across the street. He could drive himself to the Mission through Central Park. He wasn't living in a compound, behind closed-circuit cameras and checkpoints, but among foreigners.

Lydia was less impressed. Their small apartment in the Lucerne, with

its efficiency kitchen, was a long step down from the splendor of the
Visotny Dom. The very first night, after Petya had woken them up for the
second time, Lydia announced that they couldn't possibly stay there. She
would write to her father, and he would arrange everything.

"Leave it for a bit," Sasha cautioned her. He didn't want to alienate his
colleagues in the Residency at the very beginning by trading on the influence of his father-in-law, who had just been appointed Marshal and Deputy Commander of the Warsaw Pact. It was better to reserve Zotov's
influence for important things.

For the rest of that week, Lydia had the stores to divert her. The variety
was staggering, even to someone who had been accustomed to the best in
Moscow. She made the grand tour, with Churkhin's wife, Irina, as a
willing guide. They went crosstown to Alexander's and Bloomingdale's,
downtown to Macy's and Gimbel's. Lydia would return each afternoon
with taxi-loads of clothes and cosmetics and electrical goods. By Friday,
when Sasha was called in by General Luzhin for his ritual dressing-down,
she had spent the whole of his monthly salary, paid in cash in advance on
the first day he reported to the Mission.

They dined with the Churkhins that weekend, in a cozy Italian bistro
on Columbus Avenue. Lydia was showing off a new designer outfit, with
matching accessories, and Sasha didn't like the sharp, sidelong glance that
Churkhin threw at him while Irina enthused over it. Even before they got
to the linguine, Lydia started bitching about the hotel, oblivious to the
fact that it had been home for the Churkhins for a year or more.

"Just wait till next year," Irina said. She was large and placid, with an
awesome capacity to put away her food, and she didn't seem to mind
Lydia's airs one bit. "We'll all be moving uptown to the new place."

"What new place?"

"The Sovplex. It's going to be nineteen stories tall, with a school and a
swimming pool and everything."

"They're building it on a hill in Riverdale," Churkhin explained. "That
sounds fancier than saying the Bronx, doesn't it? The theory is that we'll
all be safer from the Zionist crazies up there."

"I see." Sasha did not relish the thought of being shut up in a compound behind fences and checkpoints.

"What really happened," Churkhin confided, "was they held a snap
security inspection after that last defector walked in to the FBI. They
found what you'd expect—one of our top officials was spending his evenings in a topless bar in Queens—and the ruling came down from on high
that it's unhealthy to have Soviet citizens exposed to corrupting influ-

ences. You needn't get depressed. They haven't started construction work yet."

"It will be just like home," Irina gushed.

The woman wasn't overly bright, and she was clearly intimidated by Lydia, but she came up with one useful suggestion that evening. "You'd better get yourselves fixed up for the summer," Irina said. "You can't breathe in this city in July or August. It's like living on a hotplate."

"What do you do?" Lydia asked.

"We have a bungalow," Churkhin's wife responded proprietorially. "Bungalow" was one of the few English words in her vocabulary. "Nothing fancy, of course. But it's at the beach. A lot of Mission families spend the summer there. It's in Far Rockaway."

Lydia stumbled over the alien syllables, trying to repeat the name.

"It's not the Crimea," Churkhin observed. "But still—"

"It's like home," Irina rounded out the sentence. This seemed to be her favorite phrase.

"The reservations have already been made," Churkhin went on. "But with your connections—"

Lydia had evidently been pulling rank on Churkhin's wife. Sasha was glad he hadn't told her about his confrontation with General Luzhin. Who knew what trouble she might try to stir up, through her father?

With or without Lydia's meddling, it was soon plain that something had happened to change the bullfrog's attitude, because the next time Sasha saw General Luzhin, the man was almost ingratiating. He congratulated Sasha on his success at the trade exhibition at the Coliseum, when both of them were well aware that what he had done was perfectly routine; he had picked up a few brochures and had a casual talk with a salesman from a Massachusetts company who would no doubt have drunk with anyone who would pay. Luzhin did not mention the Aeroflot ticket. Instead, he produced a book as bulky as a Manhattan telephone directory.

"Have a look through this and tell me what interests you," Luzhin said.

It was the annual requirements list of the Military-Industrial Commission, the powerful committee in Moscow that supervised the work of all the dozen ministries involved in the defense industry. Each year, the Commission produced a huge catalog of the military and industrial secrets that it sought to steal or borrow from the West, and a copy went out to all of the GRU residencies. The budget available for this kind of espionage was almost limitless, but, more than once, the GRU had been able to get the key to a process that had cost a billion dollars to develop by buying it for a mere few thousand, thanks to the uninformed greed of a secretary or a disillusioned junior executive. Unlike the KGB, which divided its people into specialities and handed out carefully demarcated assignments, the GRU tended to use its operatives abroad like used-car salesmen. They were all in competition with each other to produce the goods at the best premium.

Marshal Zotov's name wasn't mentioned, but Sasha could feel his hulking presence in the room when the Resident asked, "Is there anything I can do for you?"

Sasha seized the chance to bring up the subject of Far Rockaway.

"Nothing easier." Luzhin was only too happy to oblige. "Now next summer," he went on, "I'll see what we can do for you at Glen Cove."

The former Platt family mansion at Glen Cove was the country residence of the Soviet Ambassador, and a favorite retreat for the top brass. Some serious work was done there too: Killenworth was equipped with a sliding roof so the KGB team on the top floor could tune into American microwave transmissions and talk to Moscow via satellite.

"So what do you think?" Churkhin asked as they strolled along the gray, weathered boardwalk beside the beach.

Just like Odessa, Sasha thought. He amended this to Irina Churkhinova's phrase, "Just like home."

It was a warm June Saturday, and forty or fifty Soviet families were camped along the beach with deck chairs and picnic baskets. They formed separate clusters, diplomats with diplomats, KGB with KGB. But it was impossible to keep the children apart. As Sasha watched, Lydia was leading Petya into the water, where older children were engaged in a rough-and-tumble piggyback fight. There was a big splash as a girl went tumbling into the water, and Petya wriggled out of Lydia's grip and ran howling back, his small toes raking the wet sand.

It was a fine, clean, quiet beach: a long strip of shining white sand between the boardwalk and the calm seas inside the breakwater of Atlantic Beach, across the causeway. Behind the boardwalk, and a patch of sawgrass, the houses were all of a kind, small stucco bungalows with a porch out front and a slatted vent up above to let some air in. They were pushed back to back, like railroad cars, with a narrow alleyway between the rows where the women could sit to gossip and watch the kids play ball in the street.

Far Rockaway was a dowdy, mostly Jewish neighborhood on a spit of land between Kennedy airport and the ocean, just inside the borough of

Queens. It was less affluent than the leafier suburbs across the Nassau county line, where they fixed the potholes and people had cleaning ladies and gardeners and the local taxes were twice as high. On the far side of Seagirt Boulevard, beyond what a sign described as a "Voluntary Home for Old Folks," the houses were more elaborate, with a few Victorian survivals, dressed up with chainlink fences and the occasional flowerbed. The Churkhins and the Preobrazhenskys shared a yellow frame house on Caffrey Avenue. Each weekday morning the men would make the one-hour commute through Cedarhurst and up the Van Wyck Expressway to the city, leaving the women and children to their own devices. It was not coincidental that a high proportion of the operational meetings arranged by members of both the GRU and the KGB residencies that summer were held in Queens, conveniently midway between the Mission and the beach.

On weekends, when Sasha and his family made their way down Beach 17th Street to the water, past a children's playground, they usually found a big, ruddy-faced man in a swimsuit with a towel around his neck, working on his Chevy. He was a fixture. On Saturdays, he would have a can of turtle wax in his hand. On Sundays, he would be simonizing the car. He didn't miss a face as the Russians trooped past, checking to see who was walking with whom—an easy way to distinguish intelligence typos from routine diplomats. This FBI presence was obvious and unthreatening, but it had the effect of a sheepdog on a herd. You rarely saw the Russians at the beach wandering off by themselves.

Late that summer, Sasha arrived hot and sticky from wrestling with the Friday night traffic, and went straight down to the beach to cool off. Lydia had bought thick steaks from the supermarket in Cedarhurst, but she overcooked them, as usual. Back at the house, he ate in silence, letting her complaints about Irina and the other wives wash over him in a harmless froth.

His interest pricked up when she suddenly announced, "We're having lunch with the Nikolskys tomorrow."

He remembered the humorist he had met in the elevator at the Mission.

"They're just around the corner," Lydia babbled on. "You know, that nice little white house on Plainview Avenue. Petya plays with their boy."

They heard a car pull up outside, and then Churkhin came rattling into the kitchen with a couple of six-packs, back from the movies.

"Do you know Nikolsky?" Sasha asked casually, fielding the can of Budweiser Churkhin threw in his direction.

"Nikolsky?" Churkhin grinned as if Sasha had made a joke. "Oh, he's a *pyzdobol.* A piss-artist from KGB. He works out of the Novosti office."

Sasha glared at his wife, signaling that they would talk about it later. He didn't want to make an issue of it in front of Churkhin.

Later, in the bedroom, Lydia scoffed at his objections. Why, she saw Olga, Nikolsky's wife, almost every day. She was one of the few women in the Soviet colony at the beach who was worth talking to. They had gone together with the boys to an amusement park.

"What's the matter with you?" Lydia said. "So he's KGB. So what? It's just a family lunch. Anything to relieve the boredom. It's all right for you. You go to the city every day."

It blew up into one of their domestic spats, which erupted as fast—and were as fast forgotten—as a spark from a match that won't strike properly.

When Lydia announced that she wanted to go home for a few weeks, Sasha said nothing to discourage her.

He suspected that Nikolsky had arranged the superficially innocuous contact between their wives in order to bring them together. If the man was working under journalistic cover, it seemed unlikely that he was one of Drinov's people, in counterintelligence. But with the neighbors, you could never be sure. Still, since the lunch invitation had already been accepted, Sasha decided he might as well go along with it and take a look at this *pyzdobol* from the KGB.

2 The man who threw open the door of the house on Plainview Avenue was wearing a black polo shirt and white jeans, and his tanned face was as bright as a mint penny.

"Good morning, General!" Nikolsky boomed. He followed this up with a lopsided salute.

There was a large black poodle in the hallway. Petya darted round the adults to play with it.

"Allow me to present Kipling," said Nikolsky, waving toward his dog.

" 'Take up the white man's burden,' " he recited in English at the top of his lungs as he led them into the living room. " 'Send forth the best ye breed . . .' "

The main feature of the room was a table crammed with bottles.

Nikolsky snapped an index finger against his throat.

"Davai glaz nalyom," he proposed. "Let's put one in the eye."

Lydia asked for a glass of wine. Sasha hesitated over the battery of bottles. But Nikolsky had decided for him already. He sloshed a liter of gin into a tall jug filled with ice, waved a bottle of vermouth above it ritualistically, like a priest swinging a censer, until a couple of drops fell in. Then he served up the drinks in big funnel-shaped glasses with a twist of lemon peel.

"The perfect martini," he announced. *"Nu budem!"*

"Budem," Sasha chorused politely, taking a cautious sip of his cocktail.

He watched Nikolsky toss down his martini in a couple of gulps. He threw his head back in the air and rubbed his chest in small, descending circles. When his hand reached his stomach, he sighed, "Ah, *prizjilas,"* and set about replenishing the glasses. He cocked a skeptical eyebrow as he inspected the level of Sasha's drink, which had barely been touched.

"What's the matter, General? You don't like American cocktails?"

"No, no, it's excellent," Sasha demurred. He knocked off the rest of his drink like vodka and let Nikolsky fill up his glass. But he did not feel comfortable about being hustled into a Moscow-style drinking session by this humorist from the KGB, and resolved to pace himself. Nikolsky had dispatched his second martini by the time Olga emerged from the kitchen.

She was warm and round and made you think of fresh-baked bread, and she obviously adored Nikolsky. She watched him drink with the same helpless adulation with which an indulgent parent might allow a small child to demolish the living room—which is what Petya and his friend, with some help from Kipling, appeared to have set about doing. After a harmless exchange about life at the beach, Olga and Lydia took the children out to the kitchen.

The jug circulated again.

Nikolsky threw himself down on the sofa, sniffed the air, and exclaimed, "That's good! The sea air drives away the smell of high boots. That or the gin."

Sasha chose to ignore this friendly insult.

"I'm told you're a journalist," he said evenly.

"Ah, yes," said Nikolsky. He snatched up a bundle of newspapers at the end of the sofa, ruffled through them, and pulled out a recent edition of a Washington paper.

"You see this?" he asked Sasha, his finger on an article about the CIA. "My latest literary effort."

Sasha glanced at the page. He didn't recognize the American byline. The features syndicate credited at the bottom was equally obscure.

He wondered whether Nikolsky was bluffing. It seemed inconceivable that a professional from a rival service would start boasting to him about a clandestine relationship with an American reporter on their very first meeting. Unless the man was already drunk, or was trying to lead him into similar indiscretions.

Nikolsky threw the newspaper aside and said, "Did you hear about Pelepenko?"

Sasha shook his head. Of course, he knew something about Pelepenko. He was a big man in the Soviet community in New York, a senior Party official who had been rewarded with a top job in the United Nations secretariat.

"There was a big dinner last week," Nikolsky reported. "For one of our delegations. Pelepenko got drunk, as usual, and started drooling down his shirt front. He recovered for a bit and started stuffing himself again as if he had just arrived. Then he started puking, right there at the table, in front of all the bigwigs. Finally they carried him out. Askyerov was there. He's no dummy, even if he is a fucking Azerbaijani. He came away saying that our Pelepenko is living proof of Soviet technological innovation. We have perfected the mobile vomitorium."

Sasha didn't know whether to laugh or not. He had seen Pelepenko at the UN. The man looked exactly like a pig, pink and moist with sharp little eyes. And this was the senior representative of the Central Committee in New York! The Party recognized its natural allies, he thought, mentally assigning this Pelepenko to the same category as Krisov and Suchko.

Nikolsky took to quizzing him about people at the Mission, and Sasha's suspicions intensified. In Moscow, this openness would have been incredible. There was no doubt about it, he thought: Nikolsky was mounting a provocation, trying to suck something out of him that the KGB could use. He was angry at Lydia again for getting him into this situation. He could hear the women's voices from the kitchen, but there was no sign of food, not even a few peanuts, and here was Nikolsky bearing down on him again with the jug. There was a faint throbbing above his eyes. Nikolsky seemed to be feeling no pain.

"This isn't your first foreign posting, is it?" Sasha said, flipping the conversation back to him.

"My first assignment was in London," Nikolsky replied. "Oh, the girls beside the Serpentine on a day like this! Or at a Richmond pub, by the river!" For a moment, he wallowed in nostalgia. "Kosygin came over for a visit while I was there," Nikolsky went on. "He met the government, the opposition, the trade union leaders, the businessmen. But he wasn't happy. 'I want to meet the men who really control Britain,' he insisted. So they introduced him to some lords, hereditary peers who were struggling to keep up the payments on their decaying country seats, and Kosygin was satisfied. Those were the people he expected to be running the country.

"Then they took him up to Liverpool, to look at British industry, and he demanded to go to Blackpool, which is near there. He was under the impression that Blackpool was the only place where the British proletariat is allowed to take holidays. Anyway, it was all arranged. They have these lights along the shoreline for a mile or so at Blackpool, the Illuminations, they call them, you know, fantasy animals and castles and so on. Well, Kosygin loved the show. He insisted on driving back the other way so he could see the Illuminations again. They tried explaining to him that it was a one-way traffic system. He wasn't impressed. For a member of the Presidium, anything can be arranged. Change the direction of the traffic!

"So they went and found someone from the local police and brought him to Kosygin, and the British Foreign Office people tried explaining about the Presidium and the importance of their guest. When they finished, the Blackpool policeman took a good look at Kosygin and said, 'Piss off.' You should have seen the interpreter's face when he tried to translate that! A nice touch, don't you think?"

Sasha was grinning despite his reserve.

Then Nikolsky startled him by saying, "I hope you'll have better luck in New York than your predecessor."

"What do you mean?"

"What, Churkhin didn't tell you about it? He was an earnest sort of a fellow, but no genius. His English was terrible. You don't even hear that accent from Brooklyn taxi drivers." To make his point, Nikolsky switched into English, and Sasha realized that his command of the language was excellent. His speech was clipped and precise. He could have read the BBC news. "Anyway," Nikolsky went on, "this chap was used to service an agent, a manager in one of those companies that make spare parts for the Pentagon. He fixed up a nice little dead drop in Fort Tryon Park, up near the bridge. You know, simple and straightforward: a hole in a tree.

"The arrangement was that the agent would smuggle confidential papers out during his lunch break. Our friend would service the drop, get the documents photocopied, and return them to the same spot an hour or two later. But he was no nature lover. He paid no attention to the time of year. It was nesting season for the squirrels. When our hero went to make his pickup one day, he found hot documents wafting all over the park. You can imagine their condition. Some of the pages had been shredded to line the nest. And there he was, hopping about all over the park, trying to collect every scrap. They had to send everything to Moscow to try and patch it up like new. In the meantime, of course, the missing file was noticed, and your agent was blown. How do you like that?"

Sasha shrugged. He was not amused by the story of the squirrels which suggested, among other things, that Nikolsky knew far more about the activities of Sasha's service than he had any right to know.

"It happens to your people too," he said to Nikolsky.

Nikolsky looked at him mockingly. He took another gulp at his martini, and let the liquid swill around inside his mouth for a moment, so that his cheeks puffed out.

"Oh, yes, we have some prize specimens," he conceded. "Have you met Drinov yet? Well, there you are."

He broke off without explaining.

Everyone at the Mission knew about Drinov, the head of KR Line, the people who spied on the spies. Churkhin had pointed him out to Sasha in the street—a thick, ugly fellow in an ill-fitting suit. By dropping the name, Nikolsky had skated out into the middle of the ice.

He must have realized it, because now he backed off and started talking about New York, the music, the bars and especially the girls. He talked with apparent authority about First Avenue singles bars and quieter German saloons in Yorkville where you could meet amateurs who were looking for a good time.

Lunch was served at last, and they carried the last of the martinis through. Nikolsky seemed inexhaustible. He held forth on everything from the private life of Henry Kissinger to his favorite writer, Mikhail Bulgakov. He claimed to have a first edition of *The Master and Margarita*, a surrealist marvel about Satan's arrival in Moscow that Sasha, too, had read and reread. Carried away by the sound of his own voice, Nikolsky quoted great chunks from memory. He barely touched his main dish, but called for wine and wolfed down the bread on the table, tearing it into strips, scattering crumbs over the cloth.

He addressed little gallantries to Lydia from time to time, praising her summer frock, her hairstyle. Lydia, usually so critical, seemed to be quite taken with him.

"You heard the story of the train, I suppose? No? But you've just come from Moscow. Well, if you insist." Lydia was laughing before he had even begun the joke, which added to Sasha's rising irritation.

"The train is running"—Nikolsky paused to embellish this with his impression of a steam whistle—"and in the best compartment are Stalin,

Khrushchev, and Brezhnev. Suddenly the train stops with such a jolt that they spill their drinks in each other's laps." He mimed this bit by banging his glass down on the table.

"Stalin was furious. He bellowed, 'Why has the train stopped?'

"A railroad official rushed in, pulled off his cap, and started stammering excuses.

"Stalin was decisive. 'Shoot the driver!' he ordered.

"They shot the driver, but the train didn't move.

"Then Nikita piped up and said they were going about it the wrong way. 'Give everybody a wage increase,' he directed.

"The train still didn't move.

"Then our own Leonid Ilyich said, 'Look, Comrades, what does it matter? Let's draw the curtains and pretend that the train is moving.' "

Encouraged by Lydia's rippling laughter—the wine was too much for her in the heat, Sasha thought—Nikolsky improvised on the story.

"While all of this was going on," he continued, "our friend Andropov slipped out of the train, to gather intelligence on the situation for himself. He found a lot of bureaucrats arguing alongside the track. A *muzhik* approached him, drunk, as you'd expect. He said, 'You see, Yuri Vladimirovich, our problem is always the same. All the steam is going up the whistle.'

"Now, isn't that so?" Nikolsky addressed the room. "We Russians are the most impractical, the most philosophical people in the world. All our energy goes up the whistle. Saving your grace, General. *Nu budem!*"

They all drank except Sasha.

Nikolsky leaned toward him and whispered, "*Ty chto mumu yebyosh?* Why are you fucking a cow?"

He produced a liter of French cognac, pulled the cork out, and tossed it aside like the throwaway top of a cheap brand of vodka back in Moscow.

"*Nalivay!*" Nikolsky commanded. He proceeded to pour three fingers of brandy into an outsize snifter for Sasha.

"Listen," Sasha objected. "We can't stay all day. I've got work to do."

"It's not your fault, it's your problem. What's the hurry, General? A job isn't a wolf; it won't run away into the forest. Besides, I want to tell you another story. About Drinov."

As if on cue, Olga rose from the table, taking Lydia with her. Reluctantly, Sasha's hand closed around the brandy glass. He had better hear this out.

Nikolsky made him wait, feeding scraps from his plate to Kipling under the table.

"You can see how it is over here," he finally said to Sasha. "Back home, they can't believe their luck. The President resigns because of—" He spun his finger in a circle around his ear. "They've capitulated in Vietnam. And now the Director of the CIA is running up to Capitol Hill every day to make his confession and receive absolution. It all comes of not reading Kipling in school. Every schoolboy in our country knows Kipling. They probably imagine he's a Soviet author. But the Americans have no talent for imperialism."

"You mentioned Drinov," Sasha reminded him.

"Ah, yes, Dri-nov," Nikolsky echoed, dragging out the syllables. "Well, the Center got so excited by what's going on over here that they sent out a directive, twenty pages, no less. Guidelines for handling walk-in defectors from the CIA. You see, the Center is expecting mass defections from the CIA, what with the newspaper scandals and the sackings and all the rest of it. And who is going to receive all these defectors from the CIA? Our retired soccer star, Drinov!" Nikolsky snorted. "You should just hear him trying to talk English."

He was swaying perceptibly as he got up to fetch the brandy bottle, and he was painfully off-key as he started to recite, " 'Oh, East is East and West is West and never the twain shall meet . . .' "

Leaving Nikolsky's house, Sasha saw a flight of birds winging southward, toward the water. Earlier in the day he had been conscious of the birds flapping about aimlessly. These had formed a perfect V formation, like a fighter squadron at an air show.

"They must know something we don't," he remarked to Lydia. "There's a whole month of summer left."

Not much of it was spent at the beach.

Lydia took Petya home to spend a few weeks with her father, and General Luzhin came up with a special assignment for Sasha.

3 If you are looking for the ideal framework for espionage, you can find it ready-made at the United Nations. You put representatives of countries that are serious about spying in the same committee room as their intended targets, then subject them to a routine of excruciating boredom, from which the only relief is a bar or coffee lounge on the same premises. As if this situation were not already more than promising, in

New York the glass-walled behemoth on the East River is off limits to the police and the FBI.

An hour away from lunch, Sasha's head began to slump forward, and he stiffened his back against his chair, trying to jerk himself awake. The committee was debating the punctuation of paragraph three of a resolution that had something to do with mineral exploration in developing countries. The British delegate was wearing dark glasses. It was possible that he was suffering from eye trouble, but the angle of his head suggested that he was sound asleep.

Sasha returned to studying the man sitting almost directly opposite. He had fine, chiseled features and a thin, military moustache, and was staring absently into mid-space. His attention stirred for a moment, and he met Sasha's eyes, but turned quickly away. Today he was wearing a sober business suit and a white shirt, but the day before he had appeared in flowing tribal robes. A few years younger than Sasha, George Afigbo had already held the rank of lieutenant-general and a seat in the cabinet of his strategically situated West African country. Now, Afigbo was his government's Ambassador-Plenipotentiary to the UN, and the reason Sasha was subjecting himself to the Chinese water-torture of the committee session.

General Luzhin had told him the background of the case. Afigbo had received officer's training from the British, at Aldershot, and from the Soviets, at Simferopol and in the mock-Grecian building on People's Militia Street. Afigbo didn't like the British—he had lodged a formal complaint about racism at Aldershot—but it seemed that he liked the Russians even less.

"Our girls won't go near the black-asses, of course," the Resident explained delicately. "As you recall, we had to ask Castro to send us a load of Cuban girls to keep them happy. But that was after Afigbo's time."

Whatever his feelings about Russians and their women, the West African was ambitious and liked having money to spend. In Moscow the GRU spotted him as a coming man and soon had him on the payroll. Before long, he and a group of young officers had kicked out the London-educated barristers who were trying to run their tropical version of Westminster. Western aid dried up and Soviet advisers flooded in. Then the pendulum swung back, the Russians left, the Americans were suddenly welcome again, and George Afigbo was packed off to study semicolons and attend receptions at the UN.

"It's a sensitive case," General Luzhin told Sasha. "The Center believes that the CIA was behind the last coup. We can't be sure of Afigbo's own loyalties. As you're aware, you can't buy politicians in these places. You can only rent them.

"We've had no contact with the African since he came here. The usual thing would be to fly in his old case officer. We can't do that."

"Why not?"

"Vlassov was declared *persona non grata* after the coup. They put his picture in the newspapers. Every special service in the West knows who he is now. We can't risk compromising the African, not if he can still be used. So it's on your head. I'll fix it so you can attend one of these committees Afigbo is on, as an alternate delegate, so it will be natural enough for your paths to cross. Don't push too hard. If he shies away, let him go for now."

"What was Vlassov's work name?"

"The African knew him as Peter."

In the committee room the representative of Senegal, Sorbonne-trained and a stickler on matters of syntax, was proposing an adjectival adjustment to paragraph three. Sasha caught George Afigbo's eye again and glanced heavenward. He thought he detected a slight wrinkle of amusement around the African's eyes.

Soon afterward, Afigbo got up and left the room. Sasha waited until the door was closed before following. There was no sign of the African in the most obvious place, the bar, where Sasha caught a glimpse of Nikolsky chatting to a Norwegian diplomat who looked ill at ease despite his smooth, urbane features. The Resident hadn't mentioned whether Afigbo was a Moslem.

Sasha caught up with the African in the coffee lounge. At the sight of the Russian, the ambassador made a wide circle, evidently trying to avoid him. Sasha crossed the room and stationed himself in front of a glass case with an elaborate oriental carving inside, a gift from the People's Republic of China. Now the ambassador could not avoid him without ostentatiously reversing direction again.

Afigbo walked briskly forward.

Without turning his face away from the glass, Sasha spoke softly but distinctly in English. "I have a message for you from Peter."

The ambassador's face was a mask. He stopped next to Sasha but swiveled away from him, as if looking for somebody in the lounge.

Sasha did not waste words. He issued precise instructions for a meeting at a small Chinese restaurant on Pearl Street.

As Sasha was leaving the Mission one evening, Feliks Nikolsky hailed him in the street and said, "Both our wives are away. Why don't you let me show you the town tonight?"

The alternative—a frozen TV dinner at the Lucerne—was less than enticing, so Sasha agreed. But his guard was still up. He still suspected an ulterior motive for Nikolsky's relentless sociability.

Feliks didn't talk shop that night. He wanted to let his hair down, and he dragged Sasha from a piano bar on Mulberry Street that seemed to be peopled with *mafiosi* and their girlfriends to an earsplitting discotheque where the genders seemed to be scrambled: Sasha gaped at the spectacle of men dancing with men and girls dancing with girls. "Could we go somewhere more orthodox?" he whispered to Nikolsky.

They ate at an upscale singles place on First Avenue, where Nikolsky netted a couple of secretaries who were visiting town from Hicksville, Long Island. When Sasha begged off, Nikolsky reluctantly returned his own catch to the sea. They progressed to P. J. Clarke's, where a few of the drinkers at the crowded bar greeted Feliks as an old friend.

They traveled uptown by taxi, and Feliks ordered the driver to stop in a tree-lined street.

"Where are we?" Sasha asked, trying to identify his surroundings. He realized, to his astonishment, that they were outside an Orthodox church. Was this some new kind of KGB provocation?

He was reassured, though no less surprised, when Nikolsky made no effort to persuade him to go inside. He cooled his heels on the sidewalk for a few minutes until Feliks reappeared.

"Are you a believer?" Sasha asked Nikolsky.

"Just a seeker," Feliks responded, with uncharacteristic seriousness. "And we Russians have it in our blood," he added, gesturing at the darkened church. "Isn't that so? Besides, it's not so easy to go to church in Moscow."

This was a gross understatement. If Nikolsky's superiors got to hear that he was a churchgoer, he would probably be booted out of his service. This Nikolsky was an odd fish, all right. Sasha began to warm to him.

The next time Feliks slapped him on the shoulder and demanded, *"Ty chto mumu yebyosh?* Let's have a drink," Sasha didn't hesitate.

4 Colonel Drinov might have turned out an excellent fellow, in Nikolsky's opinion, if he had been able to follow his natural vocation as an ichthyologist. Drinov had a small aquarium in his apartment, in which bulbous Japanese fish revolved in what looked like watered ink. Drinov was especially fond of starfish, and made weekend excursions to Long Island and the New Jersey coast. In his office in the Residency, the only clue to this private obsession was a revolting object that he used for a paperweight, a stuffed piranha that Nikolsky had found for him in an East Side store that specialized in amusing gifts. Drinov had accepted the present with solemn appreciation. For the head of KR Line, fish were no laughing matter.

Drinov's other passion was soccer. But he had given up playing years before, and was fast running to fat, the way athletes often seem to do when they abandon sports. Nikolsky had read somewhere that this was bound up with the enlargement of the cardiac vessels. As he sat on the straight-backed chair in front of Drinov's desk, he pictured the colonel's heart as a great hydraulic pump, squirting out waste energy. Drinov's color was high that morning, though no higher than Nikolsky's. Feliks had already made one quick visit to an Irish saloon on Third Avenue, because since he got up, he felt as if a rusty nail were being driven through the back of his head, toward the brain. Then when he got back to the Mission, Kostya, the KGB chauffeur, had waylaid him and suggested a quick inspection of the room where the liquor was stored. Giving Kostya the key to that room was like putting a goat in charge of the cabbage patch.

Drinov fixed Nikolsky with his practiced stare. You wouldn't imagine that a man could look at you for that long without blinking. He must learn it from his fish, Nikolsky thought.

Feliks had no idea of why he had been summoned. Perhaps for a lecture on his personal habits.

Take it easy, you prick, he mentally rehearsed what he would have liked to say to Drinov. *You're no saint either. I know you're fucking the cipher clerk's wife.*

Then Drinov said, "I understand that you know one of our far neighbors, Captain Preobrazhensky."

"Yes, I know him," Nikolsky conceded.

"You haven't reported on this contact," Drinov pointed out.

"Oh, it's just casual," Nikolsky said.

"Nothing that would interest me?"

"Well, he hasn't tried to recruit me for the GRU yet."

This earned a chuckle from Drinov. The KGB poached from the GRU; it had never worked the other way round.

Drinov asked, "How does he seem, this Preobrazhensky?"

"A serious man." Nikolsky shrugged. "Normal family life. No bad habits. Some very important connections in Moscow."

"I see. Well, a report has come to our attention. It appears that your friend Preobrazhensky has been spending rather freely. Expensive jewelry for his wife, furs, that sort of thing. People are asking how they can afford to live this way, whether there is some irregularity concerning operational funds, or perhaps something even more serious."

"What do you mean?"

"Do you know anything about Preobrazhensky's operations in New York?"

"No, of course not."

"We have a report." Drinov glanced at his notebook. "He is involved in running an agent at the UN whose code name is Ibrahim. Do you know who that would be?"

"It's a name from Pushkin," Nikolsky observed. "The Negro at the court of Peter the Great."

"*Pizdish?*" Drinov looked at him in surprise. "Do you imagine that these fellows in high boots read Pushkin?"

"Preobrazhensky might."

"Well, I'm not interested in his reading habits. According to our source, Ibrahim is a double agent who is working for the Americans. Through him, the CIA has managed to establish contact with Preobrazhensky. He's been taking money from the Americans."

"*Ne pizdi,*" Feliks burst out. His gently mocking tone prevented the words from sounding harsh. "I don't know about this Ibrahim business, of course, but I think I know Preobrazhensky. He's not a man who can be bought. So his wife likes to dress up. So what? Her father can give her anything she wants. As for selling out to the Americans, he's the last man in the Mission I'd suspect—saving Your Grace, of course, Vassiliy Ilych."

"It says here," Drinov began, turning back to his notebook, "that Preobrazhensky shows exaggerated admiration for the American way of life."

It struck Nikolsky that the head of KR Line wasn't displaying much confidence in his informant. Drinov was quoting statements of unknown veracity and using Feliks as a kind of litmus test, perhaps to give expression to his own doubts. Drinov's source was obviously a member of Sasha's service. How else could he know about Ibrahim? Perhaps a man Sasha worked with and saw in the Residency every day.

Drinov recounted some statements that Sasha was alleged to have made about America's technological superiority and the greater efficiency of a market economy.

Nikolsky made a noise between his lips like escaping steam. "He might have said that," Feliks commented. "It doesn't make him a traitor, does it? I've also heard him criticize the dangerous and unreasonable level of freedom in this country. He's a soldier, after all. He likes discipline, authority. He despises the Americans because he thinks they've lost the ability to defend themselves."

Drinov busied himself making notes in his private shorthand.

"Is all of this going in Preobrazhensky's file?" Nikolsky asked.

"This is just preliminary checking," Drinov said evasively. "There are certain . . . discrepancies in the original report. This Ibrahim thing will have to be looked into. Listen, your opinions have been very helpful. They tend to confirm my own instincts. Preobrazhensky has an excellent Party record, really excellent. But we can never take chances. Will you do something for me? I'd like you to maintain contact with Preobrazhensky and let me know what you find out. If there are any unusual expenses . . ."

"Don't take this the wrong way," Nikolsky said to Sasha. They were in the corner of a saloon in German Yorkville, the sort of place where you half-expected someone to strut in dressed in lederhosen. There was a large pink-and-white girl by herself at the bar, but for once Nikolsky didn't have eyes for the ladies. He had called Sasha and told him to meet him at the saloon on his way home.

"There's someone in your Residency who has it in for you," Feliks went on. "He's a stoolie for Drinov. And he's jealous enough to go to Drinov with some cock-and-bull story—a story about Ibrahim."

At the mention of the name, Sasha froze. Ibrahim was the code name that had been assigned to his agent at the UN, George Afigbo. Slowly, Sasha set his beer mug down on the table.

"Drinov asked me what I knew about Ibrahim," Nikolsky went on nonchalantly. He left a white moustache on his upper lip as he took a swig of his beer. "I told him Ibrahim is a character from Pushkin."

Who could have told Drinov? Sasha's mind was working fast. So far as he knew, only two others in the GRU Residency knew about his case: General Luzhin and the cipher clerk.

He slapped his hand against his forehead. *Of course.* He shared his office with Churkhin, and Churkhin could easily have picked up the scent. Churkhin knew he was engaged on a special assignment, and the man's attitude had seemed odd in recent months, alternately frosty and overfamiliar. Sasha had put this down to Lydia's showing off, and their move from the comfortable, down-at-heel Lucerne to a grander apartment a few blocks away. Lydia had fixed that when she had seen her father in Moscow.

"Can you guess who it is?" said Nikolsky, as if reading his thoughts.

"I have an idea," Sasha replied.

"It's funny what envy will do," Feliks observed. "It could be worse, you know. We had a case in our own service. They hated each other's guts. One of them sent an anonymous letter to the local security service denouncing his rival. Fantastic, isn't it? But there you are. You can count yourself lucky that your colleague talked to Drinov instead of the FBI. By the way"—he winked at Sasha puckishly—"I don't suppose you really are a CIA agent, are you?"

Sasha swore copiously, and Nikolsky rolled to avoid an imaginary punch.

They ordered kümmel, which seemed the right thing to wash down the German beer, and Sasha said to Nikolsky, "You know I'm grateful. But tell me, why did you warn me?"

Nikolsky winked and held up his empty glass. *"Postavish,"* he said. "You owe me one."

General Luzhin was no intellectual. When Sasha had been invited to the Resident's birthday party, he had confided to Churkhin—the weasel—that he was planning to take a book as a present.

"Don't bother," Churkhin had counseled. "He's got one already."

That had been one piece of honest advice.

On the subject of the far neighbors, the KGB, General Luzhin held opinions that were reinforced by their raw simplicity. The KGB was the enemy, forever trying to steal agents and operational secrets from its sister-service. Sasha remembered what the general had bellowed after a few drinks at the birthday party: "If I catch any one of you farting around with Drinov, I'll cut your balls off."

So Sasha felt confident of his reception as he told the Resident that he had proof that there was a KGB spy in his own office. The general's bulging eyes looked about to pop when Sasha added, "Drinov knows about Ibrahim."

"How do *you* know, fuck your mother?" Luzhin roared.

"I got it from the horse's mouth."

"From Drinov? You've been talking to Drinov?"

"Not him. From someone else."

"Well, spit it out, damn you." At this instant, Luzhin's rage seemed to be focused on Sasha. In the general's eyes, one KGB man was as bad as another.

"He's a social acquaintance," Sasha said. "I'm prepared to give you the man's name on one condition."

"Who do you think you're talking to?" Luzhin exploded. "What condition?"

"If I give you the name," Sasha proceeded patiently, "you must agree not to report it to the Center. This man is in a position to help us. He has done so already, as you can see. But if you mention the name to the Center, well, you know better than I what will happen. The Third Directorate will find out, and he'll be finished."

Luzhin started swearing again, but didn't contradict Sasha. He couldn't deny that the KGB had spies in the headquarters of his service.

"Well," he said, "what are you waiting for? Get on with it."

When Sasha had finished, the Resident stuck his fist under his chin, and brooded in silence for a couple of minutes. He didn't doubt Sasha's word. He had taken a liking to this young captain, who also happened to be the son-in-law of the best military commander—in Luzhin's opinion—that the country had. And he had suspected a leak to Drinov for a long time. There was another agent who had been blown, the one they hadn't reported through the *Kontakt* system, contrary to regulations, to make sure the KGB wouldn't know. The Resident felt in his gut that Sasha was right to point the finger at Churkhin. But where was the proof?

"And so?" he challenged Sasha. "How do you suggest we handle it?"

"I followed him," Sasha said calmly.

"Who? Churkhin? You spied on a brother officer?"

"On a stoolie," Sasha said without visible emotion. "I saw him enter Drinov's apartment, and leave half an hour later. I can give you the exact time and date. Is that enough?"

"I think you'd better help me draft the telegram," said Luzhin.

General Luzhin's message to the Center had a very speedy effect. His superiors in the GRU immediately lodged a complaint with the Administrative Organs Department of the Central Committee, which supervised the activities of both secret services and banged their heads together when required. Neither Sasha nor Luzhin was informed, naturally, of the reprimand issued to Drinov. But within forty-eight hours, orders were issued for Churkhin's recall to Moscow.

And Sasha, who had told himself that he could not afford friends, came to look on Feliks Nikolsky in a new light.

Nikolsky was impossible, of course, a drunkard and a womanizer, totally self-indulgent. Yet he proved his capacity for human loyalty. He was a man you could count on in the trenches. Nor did Sasha doubt that he was a good intelligence professional. He was ready to sabotage Drinov for a friend, yet he would flare up in a white-hot rage when anyone started running down the KGB. He always referred to his organization as *Kontora*, "The Service"—meaning the First Chief Directorate, which was responsible for foreign intelligence—and never as The Committee, the common appellation for the KGB as a whole, as if he wanted to draw as thick a line as possible between his own work and that of the hundreds of thousands of officers and agents involved in crushing disaffection at home.

After the Churkhin episode, Sasha actively sought out Nikolsky's company.

Once, after Sasha had been called to a meeting with some visitors from Moscow, he got back to the Excelsior after midnight, and almost bumped into Nikolsky, who was hurrying out through the lobby.

Feliks raised his hands in mock surrender. "All right, General, I give up! On condition you buy me a drink."

They found a nearby bar, entirely populated, it seemed, by elderly queers.

"I don't like yours," Nikolsky commented, jabbing his chin toward a plump gentleman sporting an ascot.

"I don't like *yours*," Sasha countered.

"So you caught me out," Nikolsky said after a while. He put his fingers to his nose as if he were sniffing a flower. "But she's worth it!

"I got into her bed," he rushed on before Sasha could pose any questions, "the way that Mephistopheles got into the house of Doctor Faust. You remember Goethe's version?"

Sasha hesitated.

"Because of a poodle, a black poodle!" Nikolsky said impatiently. "It was like this. I was walking Kipling in the park, and she appeared from nowhere, like Margarita on a broomstick, with her idiotic little Chinese mutt. Kipling is a sex fiend—he has a problem, a real problem—and he was all over that ball of fluff. It would have been rape in Central Park if I hadn't pried them apart. She was bashful, of course, but one thing led to another. What could be more respectable, more bourgeois, than to meet while walking the dog?"

Sasha refrained from pointing out that this was a favorite cover for whores all over the world. He had no idea who the girl was.

"Oh, I was artful, my dear Sasha. Like Mephistopheles, I tempted her with the pleasures of this world. To be perfectly specific, I got her a job in the Novosti office. She said she was bored, sitting around at home all day. Then I kept her late one afternoon and—there you have it!" He yawned extravagantly. "Lack of oxygen, that's all it is," he said by way of apology. "Her husband was away tonight. For a fucking Turk, he's unusually industrious, I must say. Excuse me," he called to the barman, "could we have the other half?"

Listening to this monologue, Sasha was shaken to realize that there was only one girl Nikolsky could be talking about.

Askyerov's wife, Maya. He had noticed her more than a few times since they had moved into the Excelsior. It was impossible not to notice her. She was all light and shade, a moon-pale face framed by glossy black hair that she plaited and wound up in a chignon. Her eyes flashed like black diamonds. She was tall, long-legged, with a generous, mobile body.

The Askyerovs lived on the top floor of the hotel. Sasha had never seen the inside of their apartment, but it was probably of penthouse dimensions. After all, Maya's husband represented the Party elite. His father was not only the First Secretary of the Communist Party of Azerbaijan, but a man with a lot of influence in Moscow. Young Askyerov held the rank of Counsellor at the Mission, and everyone seemed to treat him with respect, including the Ambassador. But he did not cut an impressive figure—short and swarthy, with a pocked, bulging face. It was hard to imagine that Maya had married the Turk, as Nikolsky called him, for love.

"Do you know the risk you're taking?" Sasha whispered to Nikolsky.

Feliks affected not to hear. "You know the worst thing?" he asked rhetorically. "She wants to go to museums all the time, to look at Great Art. She seems to think that Old Masters improve the soul. Now I can't stand masterpieces. They have a stupid, complacent look about them, like cows chewing cud."

5   The seventh floor of the Soviet Mission was deserted at 4:00 A.M., apart from the security men and the radio operator. In the bowels of the building, Kostya, who was doubling as duty officer, had paused from

his sampling of a fresh consignment of Stolichnaya to present a solitary rendition of an Orthodox chant. The radio operator had dozed off before his machine beeped and began to whir into life. Rubbing the sleep from his eyes, he watched as it spat out the perforated tape. When the transmission was complete, he removed the tape and decoded the first set of digits. Then he got on the phone to Bitov, the cipher clerk.

Bitov, who lived in the Mission building, appeared within a few minutes, wearing a track suit. The man seemed to live for this kind of summons. He whisked the cable away to his strongroom and fed it into his cipher machine. He checked the setting, and then the machine began the automatic translation of the message from the Center.

It was addressed to the KGB Resident and flagged Personal and Extremely Urgent. It conveyed the fact that the Central Committee had approved an active measures operation against a leading American political figure, a man with his eye on the presidency. It contained specific instructions for the use of damaging material that had been prepared by Service A, which specialized in disinformation. The word "immediately" was used repeatedly. "Instruct NORMAN to make contact with VASYA immediately." The message was signed "Alyoshin," the standard code for the head of the First Chief Directorate.

Bitov knew very well that at the Center, where it was nearly lunchtime, they couldn't care less that it was the middle of the night in New York. In any case, it was his duty to pass on a message involving a decision of the Central Committee right away.

The phone rang only three times before the KGB Resident, General Koroviev, answered, his voice thick with sleep.

"Sorry to disturb you," said the cipher clerk. "There's something I have to show you immediately."

"Is it really—"

"Yes, very."

"I'm on my way."

Even at that hour of the morning, Koroviev looked healthy and freshly shaved. Polished and decisive, the KGB Resident was popular throughout the Mission. His own officers called him Ike behind his back because of his strong physical resemblance to Dwight Eisenhower. The professionals respected him as one of their own, a man who, even at his present elevation, was reputed to be acting as case handler for a highly placed mole in the American government.

Koroviev skimmed through the telegram. "Get hold of Nikolsky," he ordered the cipher clerk. "Norman" was Nikolsky's current pseudonym.

Bitov dialed Nikolsky's home number. After a brief exchange, he hung up. "His wife says he's not there," he reported.

"Well, find him," the Resident commanded. "If I can get up in the middle of the night, so can he. Who's on duty?"

"Kostya."

"Tell him to sober up and start making the rounds."

Sasha left his apartment earlier than usual, missing breakfast because of a stupid fight with Lydia that he cut short by walking out the door. He didn't like Petya to see them at each other's throats. Since her return from Moscow she had been worse than ever, trading on her father's name. She had actually got herself embroiled in an idiotic feud with the Askyerovs, all because the Counsellor and his wife had been invited to Glen Cove several times and they hadn't. But he was also aware that the flare-ups between them were symptomatic of another problem he wasn't ready to face head-on. He had married her out of a mixture of sexual attraction and calculation, making an alliance rather than making love. At some levels, the marriage had worked. It certainly hadn't hurt his career, and Lydia was a devoted mother, fiercely ambitious both for him and for Petya. But that didn't always get them through the day. Little things grated, and Lydia seemed shriller than before, probably because there was less between them as man and woman. He took to coming home later, working harder, and certainly drinking more than was necessary, finding excuses not to go to bed until she was already asleep, sometimes sleeping in the other room. She retaliated by buying more clothes and spending hours at the hairdresser or in front of the mirror. It wasn't fair to her, he knew. They had common things to protect, but he shared almost nothing of himself with her. Inevitably, she had started suspecting that there was another woman. Maybe she thought it was their neighbor, Maya Askyerova, Feliks' witch from the park. Maybe that was why she had taken such a savage dislike to the Askyerovs.

Sasha was brooding about this when the elevator creaked to a stop on the ground floor. He was halfway across the lobby when he overheard an unmistakable Russian voice. Even when he was trying to speak in a confidential whisper, Kostya, the KGB driver, sounded like the distant tolling of a bell. He was over to the right of the lobby, his broad back blocking out the door to the coffee shop, explaining something to another Russian who lived in the building.

"He'll be in the shit when he shows his face, poor bastard," Kostya was saying. "I've been looking for him half the night. I'll bet he had one too many and ended up sleeping on the floor somewhere."

Sasha hurried outside, to avoid being noticed. He stopped short on the pavement in front of the Excelsior. A burgundy Volvo, badly in need of a wash and a paint job, was parked illegally in front of him. There was a press sticker on the windshield. There was no mistaking it; it was Nikolsky's car.

Kostya must have seen it too, Sasha reasoned. That meant that Feliks' people knew that he had spent the night at the Excelsior. But they didn't know with whom. Sasha could guess. If the KGB found out that he'd spent the night with Askyerov's wife, Feliks would be on a plane back to Moscow before he had time to pack.

Sasha loitered on the far side of the street, under the sycamores, until he saw Kostya come out of the hotel and drive off. Then he walked west, away from his own car, rounded the corner, and stopped at a phone booth. That was one of the beauties of Manhattan. For a dime, you could make an untraceable call from almost any street corner.

Something stabbed through his sleep, and Nikolsky woke with a raging thirst. His heart seemed to have risen and expanded, pressing painfully against his rib cage like a cork that refused to be pulled. His eyes were gummed up, and when he got them open, liverish blotches were floating about in front of the darkness. His skin was scratchy and dry. He knew exactly how an oyster must feel when it has just been shucked.

He had to shut off that noise.

Nikolsky went groping for the phone, but struck a lampshade instead.

The woman moaned softly and rolled over, burying her face in the pillows, and he remembered that it wasn't his bed, and it wasn't his woman. As he crawled out from under the covers, he saw the silky expanse of her back, the high, firm buttocks, the tangle of blue-black hair.

The phone wouldn't stop ringing.

"Mashka." He shook her gently.

As she picked up the phone, he padded across to the window and pulled back the heavy drapes. It was full daylight outside, but only a thin, wintry light that bleached the sycamores across the street. *Bloody hell.* He had meant to leave before dawn. What had happened to the alarm?

He heard the catch in Maya's voice and turned back to her.

"He's not here," she said sharply into the receiver.

She wasn't very practiced at this, Nikolsky noted. The manner of her denial was already a confession.

He sat down next to her on the bed and squeezed her thigh. She was trembling, but in her black eyes he could see only his own reflection.

Maya put her hand over the receiver and whispered, "He says he's a friend. He says he has to talk with you."

A small dog, all hair and tongue, scampered across the bed and started sniffing and licking at Nikolsky's crotch. He pushed it away and took the phone.

"Who is this?"

"Your people have been looking for you all night," Sasha told him. "There's some kind of trouble. Do you remember my old place?"

There was only a short pause before Feliks said, "Yes."

"Meet me in ten minutes."

They talked in a coffee shop on Amsterdam Avenue, half a block away from the Lucerne. Feliks lacked his usual composure. He all but apologized for ordering a Bloody Mary rather than coffee.

He said, "I had a sort of shiver inside. It's gone now."

"They know you were at my hotel," Sasha summarized. "But nobody asked *me* about it. So it's easy enough. Tell them you were drinking with me. I'll cover for you."

They both understood the stakes. You did *not* get caught screwing the daughter-in-law of a Party boss. But Nikolsky cocked his head and asked, "Why are you doing this?"

Sasha raised his coffee cup in an ironic toast. "Now *I* can say *postavish.*"

6 The journalist described in the cables as Vasya was listed in the KGB files as a *doverynnoe litso*, a "trusted person"—in other words, someone who was considered utterly reliable and could be counted on to perform confidential missions, but was not, in the technical sense, a fully recruited agent. David Frick, otherwise known as Vasya, was not someone with whom Nikolsky, under ordinary circumstances, would have cared to have dinner, even though the man had been to Yale, which Feliks found both surprising and impressive. Frick was lumpish, sloppy around the waist, with lank, unkempt hair that he wore long at the back and sides to compensate for the bald patch on top. He delivered his opinions in a self-important, adenoidal voice, interrupted by asthmatic wheezes. He seemed to have a cigarette for a sixth finger. He smoked even in the middle of the main course, as he was doing now.

Still, Frick had his uses, and he came cheap—a few lunches in one-star restaurants, an occasional plane ticket to Hanoi or Havana, a couple of bottles on his birthday, and, above all, information. On instructions from the Center, and against his own judgment, Nikolsky had pressed Frick to accept a few hundred dollars for a routine chore, collecting State Department handouts. As Nikolsky expected, Frick had turned down the cash. He wasn't a man who could be bought—not in a straightforward way. Now, a research grant from an institute funded by one of the most successful practitioners of trade with Moscow was a different matter. As Nikolsky explained to his superiors, vanity was the key to Vasya, and it had to be turned carefully. Encouraged by judicious flattery to believe that Nikolsky thought he was a magisterial analyst of America's ills, he came out with a flow of enlightening tittle-tattle about people in government and the press corps. Thanks to Frick, Nikolsky had found out about a closet homosexual on a powerful Republican committee.

Frick operated on the fringes of the mainstream press. He had a retainer from a West Coast features syndicate that had been founded in the heyday of the antiwar movement and was still guided by the philosophy that American imperialism was responsible for most of the world's wrongs. Most of what it produced could have been put out, unaltered, by Novosti or *Literary Gazette*, which Nikolsky thought was a serious mistake. For the sake of credibility, he once advised Frick, they had to run more anti-Soviet stories.

Frick was hungry for headlines, and Nikolsky was sometimes able to oblige him, although he was frequently embarrassed by the poor quality of some of the stuff that was prepared by Service A for reproduction abroad. He had counseled against giving Frick a clumsy forgery of a State Department document and, after he was ordered to go ahead, he was not surprised when Frick reported back that he had been unable to get any of the major American dailies to use it. The thing had to be rerouted to New Delhi and Mexico City, where it ran on the front pages of papers everyone knew to be Soviet conduits.

The material the Center had sent in the middle of the night—the stuff that resulted in Kostya coming round to the Excelsior, looking for Nikolsky—was more professional. A source had reported some irregularities in the campaign financing of one of the presidential candidates, a reactionary who was no friend of the Soviet Union. That was the right kind of story for the American press. Frick was able to do his own follow-up, and both he and Nikolsky were rewarded with national coverage.

Nikolsky was a great believer in luck, and faithfully observed his personal superstitions, even though he was forever changing the rules. Some days, black cats meant bad luck; other days, white. Some days, strolling New York's crowded sidewalks, he would veer out into the gutter to avoid treading on a metal grating, as if afraid it would drop open and swallow him up. Other times, he wandered about without caring where he stepped. He was no more consistent than fortune. He knew he'd been lucky after that crazy night with Maya Askyerova. Thanks to Sasha, he got off with a mild reprimand from his boss, General Koroviev. The Resident wasn't going to grind him to pieces for cultivating a friendship with one of the neighbors in the GRU. That was always interesting for the KGB, and after all, Colonel Drinov had requested him to keep an eye on this Preobrazhensky. So Nikolsky just got a slap on the wrist. He was told to make sure the Residency knew where to find him in future, and to get hold of Vasya right away; the Central Committee wanted results.

The episode scared him enough, however, to lead him to break things off with Maya. The girl was a romantic, he discovered, not given to cheating on her husband, but very much given to daydreams about escaping somewhere together. If he could have worked things out the way the French seemed to do so well—a quick embrace *entre cinq et sept heures*—they might have been able to go on seeing each other. But he had already gone in too deep, and with the Askyerov family to worry about, it just wasn't worth the danger. Besides, there was Olga to think about, dear, doting Olga. She was a good sort. It was just that Feliks wasn't made to make do with one woman. So here he was, a few months later, in between girlfriends, watching Frick make a pig of himself, with that blasted cigarette burning at his elbow all the while. Nikolsky briefly speculated on whether Frick had a girlfriend. There was no mention of it in the file, not in all the years the service had followed his precarious career from Saigon to Lusaka to New York. Perhaps he was a pederast. He seemed to know enough of them. Like most Russian men, Nikolsky was a pronounced homophobe. His distaste for Frick increased, but he did not lose sight of the business in hand.

Frick sometimes came up with a scoop unaided. The one that had just come to Nikolsky's attention was a source of possible embarrassment. Fortunately, it had run in a radical bulletin that specialized in digging up dirt on the CIA, and it was unlikely to have reached the Center yet. One of Nikolsky's jobs was to select material from this and similar publications —some of which he supplied—for replay in the Soviet media. From a service viewpoint, Frick's article was first rate: an exposé of underhand CIA operations in Angola, clearly based on an inside source. The difficulty was that Nikolsky hadn't known about it in advance. The Center expected to be forewarned. It would also want to know the source.

"Why didn't you let me know, Dave?" Nikolsky asked Frick as the journalist helped himself to the second bottle of Bardolino.

"I was going to. You didn't show for our last lunch date, remember?"

Nikolsky did. They usually lunched on alternate Fridays, but that day he had had a splitting headache and the thought of Frick's adenoidal monotone was too much, so he had called to cancel.

"You didn't say what you thought of the piece," Frick prodded him.

"I think it's remarkable, really a major breakthrough. It could lead to a new congressional investigation. I must say I hadn't realized that the CIA had been quite so inept in Angola. But of course, you're an expert on Africa."

"Those fuckheads—" Frick began. Sufficiently stroked, he could be relied on to deliver a lecture on any subject at all.

"You obviously had an excellent source," Nikolsky interrupted after a few minutes. "Somebody in the CIA?"

"Ex-Agency," Frick responded, without skipping a beat. "He's terrific. He was stationed in Lusaka. I met him when I was out there, a few years back."

"Oh, yes. Hansen. Seymour Hansen." Nikolsky had done some homework since he received Frick's article.

Frick looked mildly surprised.

"What are his plans now?" Nikolsky pursued.

"Sy's? Well, he's got his pension from the Agency, of course, as long as he doesn't do something they can sue him for. I think he wants to write a book. That's what all of them seem to do."

"Cognac?"

"Sure."

Nikolsky waved for the waiter. "And we'll have some of your fascist cigars, Luigi," he instructed him. Like a number of New York restaurants, this one kept a stock of Havanas, allegedly pre-1959 vintage, for favored patrons. Nikolsky's spirits had lifted considerably since he had confirmed his suspicions about Frick's informant. A CIA man, just retired, who was sufficiently embittered about his former employers to talk to an asshole like Frick. Now, *that* was something worth pursuing.

Fortified by the brandy and the cigar, Nikolsky decided to be reckless.

He leaned across the table and said, "Dave, will you do me a favor? As a journalistic colleague?"

Frick wasn't a complete fool. He waited for the rest.

"I want you to introduce me to Seymour Hansen," Nikolsky said.

Frick wrestled with him for a while, and required pacifying with continued doses of brandy.

When Frick said grudgingly, "You'd better make this worth my while," Feliks knew he had the beginnings of a very interesting report.

7   It was stifling inside the subway car, and Sasha got off sooner than he intended, at 14th Street. He loped up the steps and found himself in Union Square. He paused to buy the late edition from the corner newsstand, then crossed the road and began a leisurely stroll through the park. It was not like the Alexander Gardens, that park. Small knots of drug pushers and derelicts sprawling out on the benches stared speculatively at the big man wearing a light raincoat over his gray suit, then decided to give him a wide berth. Sasha rambled on up to Madison Square, the old potters' field where, under the melancholy memorial to Admiral Farragut, junior executives from nearby insurance companies were buying small pouches of pot from the kind of men they would normally cross the street to avoid. The scene would make a good article for one of the Moscow magazines, Sasha thought; he must suggest it to Nikolsky.

He doubled back to Lexington Avenue and boarded an uptown train at 23rd Street. He was almost certain that he was not being tailed. But he had plenty of time to make sure before he kept his rendezvous with Ibrahim at a restaurant across the river, in Queens. The meet had been fixed for 6:30. He had more than two hours to kill before then.

Sasha routinely spent between three and five hours making sure he was not under surveillance before meeting Ibrahim. Not all his colleagues in the Residency took these dry-cleaning runs so seriously. There was a tendency to get sloppy in a city of endless hiding places, a city so ethnically diverse that you could come from anywhere in the world and still pass yourself off as a native. Besides, the few dozen FBI agents assigned to counterespionage were ludicrously outnumbered by the Soviet community. It was mathematically impossible that more than a handful of the Soviet operatives in New York could be under observation round the clock. Still, Sasha never cut corners. This was partly professional instinct. But he also enjoyed these laundry runs. They gave him a chance to get inside the bloodstream of this diseased but exhilarating city.

He had come to enjoy his meetings with the West African Ambassador. The man had a dry sense of humor, mocking himself as much as others.

He was a valuable source on many things, especially what the Americans were up to in his part of the world. He talked readily enough about his contacts with the CIA, and the questions the Americans were putting to him. Sasha wondered at times whether George Afigbo wasn't playing all of them for suckers. He took the money readily enough, but he never counted it, and Sasha knew that, beneath that shell he couldn't penetrate, the African was more than a mercenary. Ibrahim had his own agenda, and he wasn't sharing it with either the Soviets or the Americans.

Sasha got off the subway at 59th Street, realizing too late that he was uncomfortably close to his point of departure, and wandered east. At a Korean greengrocer's he bought some apples that looked as if they had been polished by hand. Next door was a musty store selling old prints. He went inside and inspected some vintage movie posters. There was one he considered buying for Feliks, Ray Milland starring in *The Lost Weekend.* But perhaps Feliks, penitent after that interlude with Maya, wouldn't appreciate it.

He came out of the store empty-handed and lingered to take a second look at a chunky man near a hot-dog stand who bore a passing resemblance to someone he had seen in Madison Square.

Then he saw her.

It was the hair that caught his eye—thick, dark, lustrous, giving back the afternoon light. But she had done something to it. Instead of hanging loose over her shoulders, it was chopped off in a severe, straight line across the nape of her neck, and parted on the left side.

The clothes were unfamiliar too. She was wearing a soft-knit dress with a curious pattern of white, tawny gold, and browns that might have been an abstract painter's conception of a family of tigers. The dress clung to her body, accentuating the feline grace of her movements.

He had seen her in profile for only a second, but he knew her at once: the long slope of her neck, the bold, arching eyebrows, the slender, undulating body, the miraculous hair, now carved into geometric planes.

He almost called out, *Tanya!* But the word snagged in his throat.

She was already half a block away, walking west on the far side of the street.

He saw her rounding the corner, and was seized with unreasoning panic as she was lost from view. He spotted a gap in the line of traffic and darted out into the street. As the light at the intersection changed from yellow to red, a cabdriver gunned his taxi forward as if Sasha was his target. Sasha dodged the cab, and then a biker who was fast-pedaling the wrong way, no hands, and made it to the other side.

He could not seem to control his breathing; he was panting as if he had been winded. He was vaguely aware that people were giving him odd looks as he plowed through the crowd, searching for the girl. He collided with a fat-bellied man, who spilled his groceries and started to swear and gesticulate. Sasha shouldered his way forward, uncaring. All his tradecraft was forgotten. His whole being seemed to be concentrated in a single purpose.

I'm not going to lose her a second time.

Everything Zhukovsky, the walking dead, had told him about how Tanya had been driven to suicide in the labor camp came flooding in on him. Had Zhukovsky invented the whole story, just to punish him? He had been able to picture the horror of the camp so clearly—even the whirring blade of the power saw under Tanya's throat—as clearly as he had seen her an instant ago, across a Manhattan street. Had he been dreaming then—or now?

He pushed his way through a gaggle of secretaries at a bus stop, and then he could see her mane of dark hair again. She was standing in front of a plate-glass window. He slackened pace until he was only a yard or two away, almost close enough to touch her. Then he stopped and peered through the same window. He half-expected her to turn and greet him.

Instead, she fished around in her bag and brought out a pack of cigarettes—one of those menthol brands, he noticed—and a yellow throwaway lighter. He studied her as she flicked the lighter with her thumb, her right thumb, and suddenly he knew she wasn't Tanya.

Tanya would have used her left hand.

But, even as close as he was standing to the woman, the resemblance was extraordinary, even to the swell of the lower lip, the way the lashes drooped over the dark, liquid eyes. She wasn't Tanya—how could she have been?—but she might have been Tanya's twin sister.

So he was compelled to follow her as she walked toward Lexington Avenue, in the perfect light of autumn in New York, when the excesses of the city's intolerable winters and summers seem almost forgivable.

Now he shadowed her smoothly, fluidly, again the trained stalker. He watched her toss away her cigarette after only a couple of puffs—something that Tanya, seasoned by Moscow's shortages, would never have done—and breeze into a busy department store. It was Bloomingdale's. Sasha had been there with Lydia, but he didn't use it on his laundry runs. It was too close to the Mission.

He hovered round the cosmetics counters for a while, and a pretty girl in a miniskirt and an off-the-shoulder blouse flounced up and invited him to sniff the cologne on her wrist, a new product the store was promoting.

He saw *her* take the escalator, down to the lower level.

When he caught up with her again, she was sifting through the nighties in the lingerie department. She inspected him casually as he crossed the floor, and the mocking tilt of her eyebrows, the way the corners of her mouth turned down as if she were suppressing a smile, were Tanya's too. He felt the giddiness returning, and wheeled away to find himself confronting a dummy in bra and panties that had been arranged in a bizarrely suggestive squatting position, torso flung backwards, legs spread wide. This was not a part of the store where Sasha could easily meld into the background.

He smiled and mumbled, "Just browsing" when a salesgirl came up and asked if he needed help. His accent wasn't flawless like Nikolsky's, but he sounded foreign in a nonspecific way. He could pass for a Dutchman, a Norwegian, a German. Only a trained ear might have detected, from the way he occasionally dropped the definite article, that he was Russian.

He consulted his watch. He still had nearly ninety minutes before his rendezvous in Queens. He stared at the girl and knew one thing for certain: he was not going to leave without speaking to her, without finding out who she was.

He grabbed a couple of negligées from a rack, one black and filmy, the other screaming pink and fluffy, and marched over to her.

He said, "Excuse me," and cleared his throat.

Her look was composed and noncommittal. It seemed to take in all of him, from the scuff on the toe of one shoe to the spot on the side of his chin where he had nicked himself shaving.

"I have no experience in these things," he said to her. "I have to buy a present—it's for my sister, actually—she looks quite a lot like you. Would you tell me which one you like best?"

Her glance shifted from Sasha to the negligées he was clutching in either fist like fish he had just landed. Her nose wrinkled at the spectacle of the pink one.

She frowned slightly, and a tiny line, like an exclamation mark, appeared between her eyebrows. She made a show of inspecting the labels. The corners of her mouth turned down, then up.

"I'd say it all depends on whether your sister is going to wear this before or after her diet," she said.

"Please?" Sasha asked, genuinely baffled.

"Spread them out," she told him. "Go on, spread them out."

When he did so, he saw what she meant. The black negligée was at least four sizes bigger than the pink one.

Her laugh was light and bubbling, like Tanya's. And just as infectious.
Sasha said, "I don't suppose I could buy you a drink?"

She said, "My God, you didn't take that course, did you?"

"What course?"

"Oh, I got a brochure in the mail. It's an option in one of the adult
education programs. 'How to Pick Up Lovers in Bloomie's.' " Seeing the
bewilderment in his face, she took pity on him. "It's okay," she said. "I
think you're a live one. I just suppose we might have that drink."

4.
ELAINE

Passion cannot be beautiful without excess; one either loves too much, or not enough.

—PASCAL, *PENSÉES*

1 Elaine Warner found nothing threatening in the way the stranger approached her in Bloomingdale's. It wasn't the first time something like this had happened. Besides, this one appealed to her. She sensed a raw, primitive strength, yet his manners, and his clothes, were impeccable. He was intense, but in no way pushy. He was more than a head taller than her, although she was no shrimp, and she rather liked the sense of being enveloped. Lisa, her friend at the office, asked her once what she was looking for. "A civilized cave-man," she replied, shocking Lisa, who had mild feminist inclinations. But Elaine hadn't been making much progress. She spent the previous weekend by herself, following the sunlight around her loft like a cat, trying to find the words to finish a short story that was her way of cauterizing the wound left by her last wretched affair. It would probably never get finished; there wasn't much of a story to begin with.

So she was glad to sit with this attractive stranger in the chi-chi eatery around the corner that seemed made for assignations arranged in Bloomie's.

"Elaine," she took the lead in introducing herself.

"Alex." He shook her hand as formally as if she were standing in a reception line.

"White wine spritzer," she said to the waiter. "With my head, that's already serious business," she added for her companion's benefit.

There was an awkward pause.

"At this stage," she said, "I think we're supposed to ask what each other does for a living." The man's eyes hadn't moved from her face. It was such an odd look, as if he knew her already. "Why don't I go first?" Elaine went on. "I'm a librarian, sort of. I work for the X-Tech Corporation. I guess you heard of it? And I'm a writer, would be. As you're aware, the population of Greater New York is entirely composed of writers and actors, most of them waiting for work. But I did get a piece published in *New York* magazine last month. On classic put-downs for use by single girls." This was shaping the truth a little. Her article had been entitled

"On Growing Up Jewish in Great Neck." She wanted to see how he would react. He didn't. He sat there stirring his cocktail, watching her.

"Well," she prompted him. "How about you? Where are you from, anyway? I love your accent."

"Norway," he said, gambling that she hadn't been there.

"Oh, I've heard it's beautiful."

"It's extraordinary," he responded, trying to remember what Kolya Vlassov had said about his two years in Norway. "There are nearly as many boats as people in Oslo, and on Midsummer's Night you can see them all in the fjord, lit up like Christmas trees, under the midnight sun."

"Is it like Sweden, all saunas and free love?"

"Not quite like Sweden." He smiled at her.

"Are you just visiting New York?"

"I work at the United Nations."

"I've often wondered what goes on there."

"It's really very dull," Sasha said. He parodied a recent committee session on the Law of the Sea, which he knew something about since Nikolsky had been the case officer for one of the Norwegian negotiators. He tried to be funny enough to hold the girl's interest, without provoking too many questions.

Then he took the lead, drawing her out on her family, her ambitions to write the Great American Novel, her unsatisfactory relations with men.

"My parents are divorced," she told him. "Twenty-six years of marriage, time to put the kids through college, then they quit. They weren't exactly made for each other. My father grew up on the Lower East Side. The family was so poor they used to get hold of old phone books and tear them up for toilet paper. They came from Russia after one of the pogroms."

Sasha sat absolutely still. It was even possible that this girl and Tanya were related, at the remove of a couple of generations.

"Do you speak any Russian?" he asked, trying to make it sound like idle curiosity.

"No. My father spoke only English in the house. He said we were Americans and had no business thinking about the past. I think he wanted to forget what his own family had been through. He started in business pushing trolleys on Seventh Avenue. He ended up with his own fashion house. But he sweated for every cent."

"And your mother?"

"Oh, she's your archetypal Jap."

"Japanese?"

Elaine burst out laughing. "Jewish American Princess. How long have you been in New York?"

"Nearly two years."

"Jesus. And you haven't heard of a Jap? You must lead a pretty cloistered life at the UN."

"Quite monastic." He smiled at her. The way he said it, and held her eyes until she glanced away, made it a frank invitation.

She felt excited and unsettled, and reached for another cigarette. He struck up a match before she found her lighter. She liked his hands: strong, but with long, sensitive fingers, the nails perfectly groomed.

The conversation turned to easy, commonplace themes. "I play tennis on the weekends," she told him. "And I try to go running two or three times a week."

"I run sometimes," he said. "To be alone. But I prefer less passive sports."

She met his eyes again. They were such a dangerous shade, a gunsmoke gray, and they held such an odd expression, in which she read recognition and puzzlement and boldness. They seemed to reach inside her. The sensation was scary, but not unpleasant. *He knows me.* The thought floated from nowhere to the surface of her consciousness.

He was talking about playing ice hockey in Norway. When he turned the questions back to her, Elaine's responses were a bit delayed, as if she was having a hard time getting across the court to return service.

"Are you still with me?" he said in his deep, vibrant voice. He let his hand rest on hers, and she started as if she had just received a charge of static electricity.

"I'm sorry," she apologized.

"I said I'd like to see you again."

"Of course," she responded automatically.

"Perhaps I might call you?"

"Oh, sure." She took the matchbook from him and scribbled her number inside the cover. "I usually get home around seven," she added, and instantly wondered why she had said that. Yet it seemed so natural.

"I'm afraid I'll have to go," he said, tapping his watch. "I'd rather take you to dinner."

"But the UN never sleeps," she suggested.

"Only the people who have to sit through the sessions."

He put his arm around her back as he shepherded her out into the street, and again she felt that faint electric charge.

She found she had sucked in her breath when he said, "Shall I call you a taxi?"

"It's okay. I'm not scared of the subway."

He walked her to the steps and paused, among the jostling commuters, to squeeze her hand and kiss her lightly on the cheek. She watched him part the rush hour crowd like a curtain as he strode away, and tried to make sense out of her emotions. He hadn't tried to make her right away. That was flattering—or was it? He hadn't given her *his* phone number, which in her experience was a sure sign he was married. He was probably rushing off to meet his wife for dinner. But this was only the surface of things. There was a giddy sensation of plunging from a height. She ought to feel panicked by it, but she didn't. It was like free fall, with the parachute there, primed to open. She had to remind herself that she didn't have a parachute.

When the phone rang, Elaine was glad of the interruption. She had just about decided to tear up the story she was working on. The male character just wasn't believable, even though—or maybe because—everything he said or did was recorded from memory.

She knew the voice at once, with its hard E's, and the odd way of suppressing the definite article. The man she knew as Alex suggested dinner with such solemnity that he might have been inviting her to someone else's wedding. Which was the excuse she had ready-made.

"I thought you'd given up on me," she said. It was more than a week since the meeting in Bloomingdale's.

"But I've been thinking about you. I'm afraid this UN business is very time-consuming."

"You mean, who gets the fishing rights to the North Pole?"

"Exactly."

"Well, I'm afraid I can't make it tonight. I have to go out to Great Neck. My sister's getting married and my mother is going absolutely berserk." This was a half-lie. She wasn't planning to go out until the following afternoon. But she had decided to pace herself. He hadn't bothered to call her for a whole week, during which she had worked on convincing herself that this was proof that their encounter was nothing more than the circumstances might suggest: a casual pick-up in Bloomingdale's. She hadn't quite succeeded. Now she was suddenly breathless, walking up and down, holding the phone to her chest, fighting with the instinct to run out of her apartment and meet him anywhere he suggested.

He mustn't think she was available on demand, she reminded herself.

He sounded disappointed. "May I call you next week?"

"Oh, sure."

Alex still hadn't given her his number. As a married man, he was running true to form. Don't call us . . .

The character in the short story she proceeded to rip up and throw in the garbage can had been married too. Their relationship had lasted longer than the others, almost six months. He was a handsome brute, and knew it, which should have warned her off at the start. But she had let herself get sucked in, until she actually believed that it was love on both sides. Then he had dropped the bomb: his wife had just delivered her baby and family duty called . . .

As she finished shredding her typescript, she resolved not to get burned twice.

So she drove out to Great Neck the next day and watched her mother fluster over last-minute arrangements while Barbara, her sister, coolly chain-smoked and pored over the guest list. Barbara liked designer dresses and Mercedes cars and did everything strictly according to plan. Ira, her intended, was a commodities broker with an affluent paunch who had managed to get her pregnant during the summer. Barbara hadn't hesitated over the abortion. It would never do to disrupt the wedding plans, not to mention the holiday reservations in the Virgin Islands. In Barbara's scheme of things, babies weren't made; they were scheduled. Elaine had gone to the clinic with her sister, expecting a last-minute crisis of guilt. But Barbara went in and out as calmly as if she had gone to the dentist to have a tooth pulled. She might be able to schedule a baby next year.

Looking at other people's lives, Elaine sometimes felt diaphanous, directionless, scarcely formed. From the outside, the lives of others seemed so rounded, so complete. Often she felt envious. But with Barbara, she felt like a claustrophobe trapped in an elevator. Her sister had had her entire life boxed and gift-wrapped.

The sensation of being stuck in an elevator became overwhelming during the marriage service, which took place in a vast reform synagogue with the dimensions of a conference hotel. After the ceremony, video cameras whirred while the hundreds of guests tucked in to a light collation of lamb chops, pastries, and canapés. Elaine's mother, upstaging the bride in a figure-hugging white dress with ruffles, dragged up one prospective suitor after another for her unmarried daughter. All of them might have been Ira's brothers: soft, prematurely old young men with receding hairlines who had clearly lived all their lives in awe of their mothers. One was a doctor, another a corporate lawyer. The only time Elaine managed a spontaneous smile was when the lawyer tripped over a trailing lead from the video equipment.

A couple of hours later, everyone sat down to a five-course dinner, followed by dancing. Elaine saw her father watching her with sad eyes and went over to sit next to him. He had the leathery tan of a year-round resident of Miami Beach, but you could tell that his time was running out.

He kissed his daughter and said, "Look at your mother. She could be the bride." His tone was wistful rather than sarcastic.

Elaine watched her mother kick up her heels on the dance floor. The video cameras ground on relentlessly.

"Ira's a good boy," said her father. "He knows how to work."

"He never had to fight for anything," Elaine observed, staring at her father's awkward, callused hands, and thinking how comical he looked in a tuxedo.

"What about you?" her father was saying. "I worry about you all the time, living by yourself in the city."

She put her head against his neck. "I'm all right, Poppa. Really. I'm finding myself." The wedding party swirled around them, and she thought, *No, not this.*

The following Tuesday, when Alex called to renew his dinner invitation, she said yes, rather quickly.

2 Sasha took the same precautions, meeting Elaine for dinner, that he would have taken before attending a clandestine rendezvous with Ibrahim or another agent. He left the Mission early, and spent more than two hours wandering the city, to ensure that he wasn't under surveillance. The evening ended in Elaine's loft, one enormous room with windows on three sides, littered with her collection of native American art and duck decoys. In bed, he was very conscious that she wasn't Tanya. She was more practiced, more mechanical. She volunteered things that Tanya wouldn't have done, things he would never have asked for. She must have sensed his surprise, because she said, when they were resting, listening to Roberta Flack on her stereo, "Is the missionary posture all that Norwegian girls know?" He took revenge on her for that. The second time, he was sure that her cries weren't faked.

He left in the early hours, trying to reason with himself. This involvement was more stupid than Nikolsky's affair with Maya Askyerova. He couldn't afford it. But the girl was already an obsession—in her resemblance to Tanya, and in the difference from her.

There was a way he could protect himself. Elaine had told him she worked for X-Tech Corporation, which produced advanced data-processing equipment. He could recruit her as an agent. That would provide perfect cover for further meetings, quite apart from the fact that, working in the company library, she undoubtedly had access to all sorts of material that would interest the Center.

No, Sasha told himself, *I'm not going to do it.* The visceral reaction came faster than he could analyze each of the steps involved. But he thought the whole thing through, not wanting to steer by instinct alone.

If he reported Elaine as a recruitment prospect, he would have to concoct some explanation of how he had met her. That wasn't a real problem; he could come up with something. But once he reported her full name— Elaine Frances Warner—her profile would be run through the *Kontakt* system. According to the rules, all foreign contacts had to have their names checked out in a centralized data bank, shared with the KGB. No doubt hundreds of names were entered daily, by Soviet operatives stationed all over the world, reducing the likelihood that any given individual would arouse much interest. There was still the risk that the people in the KGB would know—and maybe even try to take over the case for themselves.

It was only an outside risk, he reasoned. But supposing the GRU approved the recruitment, and then decided someone else should handle the case, because he was involved in running Ibrahim and shouldn't be unnecessarily exposed? Or what if they gave him the case, and he was posted back to Moscow? It had to happen sometime, in two years at the outside. Then Elaine would be passed on to another GRU officer, with consequences that were beyond prediction.

These were all perfectly rational reasons for not telling the Residency about the girl. But the beginning of the relationship, and what was happening now, were not rational at all. He couldn't tell how or when it would end. But he wasn't going to use or betray this girl. Because she was Tanya, and because she wasn't.

In the months that followed, he saw her as often as he dared, never more than once or twice a week, never staying the night. He bought her little things: a scarf, a bracelet, a papier mâché bird from Mexico that went with the brilliant colors of her loft. It was astonishing how little she asked of him, as if she sensed all the taboos that stopped him from giving full vent to his feelings. She hadn't asked if he was married, and he was grateful for that. He felt sure she had guessed. But he would catch her appraising him when she thought he wasn't looking. He tried not to ask himself how long it could go on.

Lydia sensed something, of course, perhaps because he had been more attentive to her than before he met the girl. She released her own frustrations on other members of the Soviet colony, queening it over the wives of his GRU colleagues, and missing no occasion to pursue her idiotic feud with the Askyerovs.

He came home late one night, after visitng Elaine, and found his apartment full of packages from Bergdorf's and Saks. Lydia was sprawled out on the sofa, with a fork in her hand and a plate precariously balanced on the arm. There was a half-empty bottle of wine on the coffee table.

"Who do you think is going to pay for all of this?" Sasha erupted after examining the labels on the boxes and shopping bags.

Lydia had her mouth full of chocolate cake. Her body had thickened since Petya was born. In the past few months she had put on weight at an alarming rate, and had used this as an excuse to buy a whole new wardrobe.

"Did you hear what I said?" Sasha persisted.

"Why should you care?" Lydia sniffed. "You know Papa will arrange everything."

"Don't bring your father into this."

"Well, anyway," she went on, "I can't go back to Moscow without presents for everyone."

"You're going to Moscow?" Sasha echoed. He felt vastly relieved, though this was the first he had heard of Lydia's plans.

"I've already written to Papa. He thinks it would be good for Petya to spend the summer on the Black Sea, among real Russians. It won't make much difference to you. You see little enough of us as it is."

She started attacking the cake again. It was another way of punishing him.

"Lydochka," he said, mildly reproving.

She finished the plate and stretched out on the sofa. Defined by the tight silk of her negligée, her breasts and thighs were like heaped pillows.

She opened her plump, pearly arms to him and he crossed the room obediently.

"I'm not so old," she said, putting on one of her little-girl voices.

"Of course not," he agreed, smoothing her hair.

"I mean I'm not too old to have another baby."

He froze.

"It would bring us together, Sasha. Something's gone wrong between us, and I don't know what it is. Think of what Petya means to us."

He let her tug at the buttons of his shirt, softened by the memory of the first sight of his child in its mother's arms.

"Let me think about it, Lydochka," he said, pulling slightly away.

"Why not now? Tonight?" She was fumbling at the buckle of his belt.

"I'm not ready." He stood up, knowing that the words must sound brutal. She flew at him then, but her bewildered accusations quickly subsided into tears. He held her to him for a long time. Before dawn he made love to her, taking precautions, and watched over her until her breathing was deep and regular. He watched the sky redden as he sipped strong black coffee. *She's not a bad woman*, he thought. He didn't love her, but he owed her better than this. She didn't deserve to be hurt. The trouble was, he couldn't help hurting her. All of them were going to be hurt.

When he saw Lydia off at the airport, Petya was fighting and squealing. The boy wanted to stay with his father, and Sasha had to promise to come to Moscow soon before he would behave.

Lydia said, "This time, I may not come back."

A few days after Lydia had gone, Sasha proposed to Elaine: "Why don't we go away somewhere for the weekend?"

She took everything in hand. She borrowed her mother's car and they drove out to the east end of Long Island, and stood under the Montauk lighthouse staring across the Atlantic toward Europe. They scrambled like children over the dunes and tried to skim pebbles across the choppy water. They drove back through the old whaling port of Sag Harbor and took the ferry across to Shelter Island, where they spent the night in an old clapboard inn in an iron-frame bed that stood three feet off the ground and creaked like a Schönberg symphony.

In the morning, she traced the contours of his face with her fingers, like a blind person, and said, "I only live when I'm with you."

He ached to tell her everything, but he could risk only a partial confession.

"I didn't tell you I was married," he said, watching her. She received the information as calmly as a routine weather report.

"Did you think I didn't know?" she asked. "What's she like?"

"We're separated," Sasha said hoarsely.

"What about children?"

"I have a son, Peter. I love him very much."

"You're not going to get divorced, are you?" She squatted down on the beach and traced the arrowlike print of a sandpiper on the sand with her finger.

"No."

She hugged her arms across her breasts for a moment, as if she were cold. Then she jumped up and cried, "Come on, I'll race you!" and they were sprinting along the beach.

Back in the city, Sasha went out with Nikolsky, pub-crawling up First Avenue.

Feliks needed cheering up. He was worried about his case. Frick, the hack reporter, had done what he was asked: he had arranged a meeting with Hansen, the disillusioned former CIA man. But from the first moment Feliks looked into Hansen's eyes, he sensed there was something wrong. He hadn't gone in like a fool, leaving his backside exposed. Kostya was out there, covering him, making sure that nobody had them under surveillance. Everything seemed to be normal. And this Hansen was outwardly cordial, smiling and joking a lot. But there was no humor in those eyes; they seemed to reach out and grab you like fists.

Nikolsky's suspicions increased after he spun his line about how he worked for an international news syndicate that was extremely interested in exposing the CIA's involvement with South Africa and Israel, and would be willing to pay generously for any first-hand insights that Hansen could offer. The ex-CIA man didn't hesitate. He didn't even ask for Nikolsky's credentials. He just said, "Sure. Tell me what you need to know."

At a subsequent meeting, when Feliks raised the subject of Hansen's book, the American was equally responsive to the idea of inserting a section that would name names of CIA operatives around the world. It was all too easy, Feliks kept thinking. He even wondered if Hansen was wired.

"You're quiet tonight," Sasha jogged him after a few drinks.

"Look who's talking," Feliks responded. "You usually make the sphinx sound talkative. If you really must know, General, I'm worried about my dog. He hasn't been meeting any girls lately. He's horny as hell, and so am I."

Sasha guessed at once that Feliks must have an operational problem. That was the one kind of secret he would never share.

"You remember Mashka? My little witch?"

"Of course," Sasha acknowledged.

"She's still working in the Novosti office. Can you believe it? It's driving me wild."

"Why don't you ask her to go?"

"I did, but she won't leave. You know I can't push."

They drank, and Feliks said, "How's your Lydochka?"

"In Moscow."

"I thought she left weeks and weeks ago. Oh," he interrupted himself, "so it's like that. You haven't been chasing skirts without telling your Uncle Feliks, have you?"

"I think I'll take some leave in Moscow myself," Sasha observed, to deflect Nikolsky. He wasn't going to deliver any hostages, not even to Feliks.

"I suppose Lydia takes after her father," Nikolsky went on. "That's a lot to handle. By the way, I meant to congratulate you. With the Marshal at Gogol Boulevard, there'll be no stopping you."

Sasha said nothing. His father-in-law's promotion had just been made public. Zotov had been appointed First Deputy Chief of Staff and a Marshal of the Soviet Union.

"I don't suppose I told you that Marshal Zotov is one of my heroes," Feliks continued, undeterred.

"Is this another of your jokes?"

"No, no, I'm completely serious. There are stories about Zotov, you know. They say that when Stalin died—no, wait—" He put a finger to his lips like a stage ham. "You'd better ask him yourself."

"Ask him what?"

"Ask him about Beria." After quarter of a century, the name of Stalin's secret police chief still cast a shadow. "Ask him to tell you how Beria died."

3 Sasha returned to Moscow to find the Marshal's apartment in the Visotny Dom deserted. There was a curt note from Lydia to inform him that she had taken Petya to her father's summer retreat in the Crimea, a villa near the Romanov palace at Livadia. "Come if you like," the note ended offhandedly. Sasha smelled new trouble.

He had to use his headquarters connections to get a seat on a scheduled flight from Moscow to Simferopol. There were scalpers at the airport quite openly offering to buy confirmed seats. From the city, it was an hour's ride in a clanking taxi to the coastal resorts. Sasha rolled down his window, loosened his collar, and let the breeze fan his face and neck. Despite the heat, the day was perfect. The air was clean and dry and carried the smell of ripening grapes and magnolias. The contours of mountains and woods were sharply defined. Lombardy poplars marched in lines across the slopes like Tatar warriors in pointed caps.

The palace of white limestone built at Livadia for the last of the Tsars shimmered in the afternoon light. Its columned balconies overlooked the shining waters of the Black Sea and great triangular flowerbeds embellished with ancient Greek marbles. The place where Alexander III had come to die and Nicholas and Alexandra to dance away their fears was now a museum of the people. From the clifftop palace you could take an elevator that descended through tunnels bored in the rock to the beach below.

Few of the villas around Livadia were equally accessible. At nearby Chernomorye was a luxurious establishment used as a hotel by senior officials of the KGB. At Pogranishnik, the KGB Border Guards, a private army charged with preventing anyone leaving or entering the country without permission, had a resort of their own. A short drive away, through the vineyards and rose gardens, was one of the General Secretary's personal retreats. There was a palatial building without a name or identifying sign that was reserved for members of the Central Committee. There were few signs of security around these pleasure-domes, but a curious visitor who strayed too close to any of them would be met by athletic young men in civilian clothes whose duty was to uphold one of the cardinal rules of Soviet democracy: privilege is not for public show.

The marshals and the generals had not been forgotten. Cadets from Simfi and conscripts supplied by the chief of the Military District were engaged in transplanting trees and laying a new path as Sasha drove up to Marshal Zotov's villa. He had to leave the taxi at the gate and subject to two identity checks—the first by one of those polite young men in sports clothes, the other by a uniformed guard—before they let him through. There were running fountains on both sides of the drive, and in front of the large, Italianate mansion, stone sphinxes faced each other enigmatically from opposite ends of a wide terrace. The smell of roses was everywhere.

He found Lydia and the child in the glass-walled loggia facing the sea. In no time at all, Petya had his legs around Sasha's neck and was making his father piggyback him around the garden while he let out Indian warwhoops. Lydia seemed friendly and relaxed, though a little absent. Perhaps the sun and the sea air were helping her to forget the storms in New York.

The Marshal did not appear until dinnertime, and his behavior was ominous.

"Have you left the army?" he growled at his son-in-law, who was wearing civilian clothes. The Marshal was kitted out in full summer dress uniform. Most of his face was an angry red; he had the kind of skin that never really tans.

Sasha mumbled an apology.

"I expect a Soviet officer to look like one at all times," Zotov said. "I told you that when we first met."

After this dampener, they ate in silence for most of the meal. There was sturgeon, of course, the Marshal's favorite dish. Orderlies in white jackets moved back and forth with the regularity of pendulums, adding and removing plates, refilling wine glasses with the excellent local champagne. It was a shame that they hadn't allowed Petya to stay up, Sasha thought. The child's presence always seemed to soften the old man.

As soon as the last plates were cleared, Zotov dismissed both his daughter and the orderlies and demanded point-blank: "Well, what's happened between you and Lyda? Is it another woman?"

"No," Sasha said, looking him directly in the eye. That had been true at the outset, anyway.

"*Pizdish?*" the Marshal responded skeptically in his low, rumbling voice. When Zotov was angry, you could hear the earth move.

"Then what?" the Marshal roared at Sasha. "Lydia came back to Moscow in tears. She went on blubbering until I brought her down here. Is the fat life in America going to your brain? Well? Is it *this?*" Zotov took the bottle of Armenian brandy from the sideboard and waved it around in his great paw.

"We've had some differences," Sasha began, stepping gingerly out onto the minefield. "I think perhaps Lyda expected too much in New York. She wasn't prepared for the problems of life in a large diplomatic colony. I think she presumed too much on your name."

"*Ne pizdi!*" the Marshal snorted.

Sasha did not tell the Marshal about the problem he had had with Churkhin, the man propelled by jealousy to denounce him to the KGB. Instead, he mentioned trivial things, like the fact that Lydia, the week before leaving for Moscow, had prevailed upon the wives of two of his Residency colleagues to serve as cooks for a dinner party. The Marshal nodded; this was something he understood. You didn't walk on the faces of brother officers for no good reason.

"What else?" he demanded.

Sasha told him how Lydia had been promoting a stupid feud with Askyerov and his wife. During a movie screening, at the Mission, she had actually had the gall to go up to them and tell them they were in the wrong seats, that that was where *she* normally sat. Sasha had skipped the screening to meet Elaine, pleading operational duties, but he had heard the story later.

"So what?" Marshal Zotov remarked.

"It's simply not necessary. It creates problems for both of us. This Counsellor is the son of Gussein Askyerov."

Zotov was not impressed by this reference to the First Secretary of the Communist Party of Azerbaijan.

"I don't give a shit about that black-ass," he commented. *Chernozhopi*, "black-ass," was one of his customary terms of endearment for his Caucasian brethren—Azerbaijanis, Armenians, Georgians, the whole patchwork quilt. The Marshal was not a man for fine distinctions.

Quietly, patiently, Sasha attempted to explain that the Azerbaijani Party boss was a man to watch, and that his son commanded a certain amount of respect within the Soviet community in New York because of the family connection.

Zotov was puzzled. After all, Baku was a long way from Moscow. Askyerov had influence, of course, but he wasn't even an alternate member of the Politburo. In defiance of his doctors, the Marshal poured himself a good slug of Akhtamar brandy. That was one thing you couldn't fault the Armenians for—their brandy.

"All right," Zotov said. "So Lyda put young Askyerov in his place. Good. No doubt he had it coming. What I can't fathom is why *you* want to go crawling to that fucking Turk. You're a Russian officer."

This was a slip of the tongue, of course, due to the brandy, perhaps, or the ghosts of Livadia. It wasn't acceptable to talk about "Russian officers." Nationalism was supposed to be extinct.

"I think you may have missed something," Sasha said evenly. "Gussein Askyerov is a man on the way up. In America, even Lessiovsky, even Dobrynin, speak of him with respect. As for the Committee—well, with Andropov and Tsvigun, he's like *that.*" Sasha knitted his fingers together. "And I've heard that Brezhnev decided he's the best administrator in the country since he started sending a special plane loaded up with gifts from Baku to Moscow every week."

This was a daring shaft, and the Marshal pretended it had gone wide. He had his lapses, but nobody, not even Lydia, had heard him criticize the General Secretary—not in Stalin's time, not in Khrushchev's, not in Brezhnev's. The Marshal's restraint did not extend to lesser members of the Party hierarchy. He wasn't frightened of Askyerov. But now he wanted to hear more.

"How do you know these things?" he demanded of Sasha.

"I have a colleague who was in Baku," Sasha lied. His information on the Askyerov family came exclusively from Nikolsky, but he was not going to let on that he had a friend in the KGB. Not yet, anyway.

He told the story of the rise of Gussein Askyerov as he had heard it from Feliks. The Azerbaijani's first claim to office was that he cooked excellent shashlik. At the start of the Patriotic War, Askyerov was a young Komsomol organizer, an Azerbaijani version of Suchko. His experience in keeping card-index files on his comrades made him a natural recruit for the military chekists of SMERSH when they arrived in the region to sniff out spies and traitors in uniform and out of it.

Askyerov made a good impression: eager to please, well groomed, his vivid blue eyes making a striking contrast with his sleek black hair. Tsvigun, the chekist who arrived to take charge of the local SMERSH organization, had a taste for local dishes, especially shashlik. While he roamed the countryside carrying out his patriotic duties on the "invisible front"— such as herding frightened conscripts into battle by putting machine guns at their backs—young Askyerov cooked his dinner and waited to take dictation. "They were as close as two lumps on a skewer," was how Feliks had put it. Askyerov's culinary prowess paid off handsomely. After the war, Tsvigun returned to Azerbaijan as chief of the regional KGB. Within six months, he made Askyerov his number two. And the ascent of the shishkebab man was only beginning.

When Brezhnev came to the top, he called Tsvigun, his in-law and his crony from the old days in the Ukraine, to Moscow to serve as the real power inside the KGB, and Tsvigun, in turn, fixed it for Gussein Askyerov to take over as security boss in Azerbaijan.

"Askyerov didn't waste a single day," Sasha recounted. He started sending lavish consignments of caviar, fresh sturgeon, silks, and crates of exotic fruits to Moscow every week for the enjoyment of his patrons. When they came south, he arranged hunting trips and banquets worthy of an oriental potentate. He supplied women and "business opportunities," of which there was no shortage in Baku, the city of souks, oil derricks, and black market millionaires.

At the same time, he thrust himself forward as the archenemy of official corruption in Azerbaijan. Week by week, along with the caviar, he sent his protector, Tsvigun, dossiers that demonstrated how his nominal boss, the First Secretary of the Azerbaijani Party, was skimming the profits of the black market trade. This First Secretary was too greedy to be smart. He appropriated government money for construction projects that were never even begun, and used the men and materials to put up country dachas for himself and his friends. Anyone could see what was happening. It wasn't hard for Askyerov to make his case. After a while, Tsvigun took the files to Brezhnev, who authorized a follow-up investigation, with the indispensable Askyerov in charge. Of course, everyone knew that Askyerov was involved in the same rackets, but he was a lot smarter than his boss. He was the model of discretion. He collected his pay-offs in person, in hard currency or precious stones. He had a special affection for blocks of pressed diamonds, a popular means of exchange amongst the high rollers of Baku.

"These bloody cockroaches," Marshal Zotov interjected. *Tarakani,* or "cockroaches," was another of his familiar terms for Soviet Caucasians. The etymology of the word had to do with the wearing of a moustache. As a matter of fact, Gussein Askyerov was clean-shaven.

"Get on with it," the Marshal ordered.

"Swamped by the flood of paper from Askyerov's office in Baku," Sasha went on, "Brezhnev decided to get rid of the local First Secretary. This would demonstrate, after all, that our rulers are determined to stamp out corruption. All that remained to decide was who to make the new Party leader. The power of shashlik was proved again. Tsvigun proposed to elevate Askyerov. Why not? He was a good Party man, loyal to the hand that fed him. So Askyerov became First Secretary, and he proved his loyalty at once. He increased the special flights to Moscow, to carry the tokens of his appreciation to Leonid Ilyich and all his new customers."

"Very well, very well," the Marshal cut in. He didn't like these references to the General Secretary. Better to leave *him* out. "I knew some of this already. He's an oily sonofabitch, no doubt of it. What else does your friend have to say about him?"

"There are rumors—"

"What rumors?"

"It's said that he has succeeded in making Andropov his friend too."

"And if it's so?" The Marshal returned to the brandy bottle. Instead of sitting down again, he began to pace the long, marble-floored dining room, hung with nineteenth-century hunting scenes.

"This is the important thing, Alexei Ivanovich," Sasha went on. "Everyone can see that the General Secretary is very sick, a dying man—"

"Are you going to tell him or am I?" Zotov broke in sarcastically.

"Suppose that Andropov takes over," Sasha pursued.

"He won't," the Marshal said firmly. Zotov had long been persuaded that the Chairman of the KGB was Jewish. It was reported that, on his mother's side, Andropov's family name was Erinshteyn which, if true, would have made him a Jew in the rabbinical sense, eligible for Israeli citizenship under the Law of Return. This, however, was not his main objection to the idea of Andropov assuming the General Secretary's mantle. Andropov, like the others in line for the highest office in the country, was a Party man, not a career KGB official. Yet he also represented the authority of the KGB. His appointment to succeed Brezhnev would profoundly disturb the balance between the triumvirate of Party, KGB, and Army.

"If Andropov takes over," Sasha persisted, "Askyerov will come to Moscow. That's why we have to take him seriously. I can't explain it in detail, because there are things I don't know yet, bits that are missing. The man has the gift of making others depend on him. Somehow, he's succeeded with Andropov, just as he succeeded with Tsvigun earlier on. If Andropov takes over," he repeated, "Askyerov is going to be a force to be reckoned with, perhaps KGB Chairman, perhaps something even more important."

The thought of a former KGB Chairman running the country, with a former KGB professional at his right hand, was too much for the Marshal.

"Never again!" he thundered. "Never again!"

This outburst left Sasha somewhat confused. He followed the Marshal, who had flung open the french doors at the end of the room and stormed out into the rose garden. Outside, the moon was bright silver and the sea looked as black as its name.

"Alexei Ivanovich," Sasha addressed him when he had drawn almost level. "What did you mean when you said, Never again?"

"It would be the same as before. The same as with Beria," Zotov said slowly, staring out across the water.

Sasha felt a thrill of anticipation. This was what Feliks had hinted at during their last conversation in New York.

"I heard something about it—about Beria's death," Sasha prompted him.

The Marshal's face clouded. "Oh, you did? I never realized you had such big ears, Sasha. You hear all sorts of things. What exactly did you hear about Beria's death?"

"That perhaps you had something to do with it." Sasha backed away a little, realizing he might have gone too far.

Zotov thrust his empty goblet at him. "Fill that up for me," he said.

4 Out there in the rose garden, alone with his great arms folded across his chest, Zotov could see the whole scene clearly. He was nearly thirty years younger, and could drink a bottle or two of his beloved Akhtamar brandy and still love a woman afterward.

Stalin was dead, people were weeping openly all over Moscow, and Lavrenti Beria, that twisted sadist, lover of underage girls, that *Mengrel* whom Stalin had brought from his native Georgia to command the secret police and direct his last purges, was preparing to install himself as dictator. Beria was parading his pretorian guards, with tanks and machine guns, in the heart of the capital to show who was boss. During his night vigils in the Lubyanka—they were all insomniacs, under Stalin—he was drawing up lists of the next of the Party faithful who would be struck down once his succession was rubber-stamped.

Beria was not an idiot; he was aware that he was not universally loved, and was fully alive to the risk of a counterstrike. His spies were watching the "court divisions"—the 2nd Guards Taman Motorized Infantry Division and the Kantemirov Tank Division—which composed the Moscow garrison. Major-General Zotov, as he then was, was at the headquarters of the Air Defense troops for the Moscow region. It was a good listening post, not least because, in those days, the chekists didn't seem to think that the Air Defense units were worth spying on too closely.

It was Marshal Zhukov who got wind of the fact that Beria had issued a secret order, bypassing the General Staff, to the southern military districts. Units of Caucasian troops—"wild divisions," they were called by the high command—were to be rushed to the capital by rail. With these additional troops, who wouldn't give a shit about firing on Russians and for the most part didn't even understand Russian, Beria's power would be unassailable.

Marshal Zhukov started passing the word around, and once Beria's rivals in the Party leadership found out what was going on, they formed a cabal. Secretly, orders were issued to immobilize Beria's forces and place the secret police chief under arrest. Marshal Zhukov and the Army were only too happy to oblige. The troop trains from the Caucasus were intercepted near Moscow, and Beria's "wild divisions" were disarmed at gunpoint.

Inside the capital, the Air Defense units were the spearhead for the countercoup. Zotov personally supervised the group that seized Beria in his office and dragged him away to the Butyrki prison. Beria seemed to be living in some parallel world. During his first hours in his cell, he hectored and shrieked at his jailers, demanding a hot bath, the best food and wine, even girls—very young ones, the way he liked—as if he were still lording it from his suite in the Lubyanka. When the guards refused, he tried threats. "You can't begin to imagine what will be done to you as soon as I get out of here," he yelled. Then he tried bribes and blandishments. Over and over, he kept calling for the man in charge.

He got Zotov. Major-General Zotov arrived at Butyrki prison with a document in his pocket, drawn up in the proper way, that recorded that Beria had been tried *in absentia* and sentenced to death by firing squad. The sentence was confirmed by the rest of the Politburo, including the men Beria had counted on to raise him to Stalin's place.

When the bull-like Zotov entered his cell, in full uniform with his cap on his head and his pistol at his hip, Beria puffed himself up, the way little men do, and declaimed, "I am a full member of the Politburo. Serious illegalities have been committed, and it is your duty as a general of the Soviet Armed Forces to arrange for my immediate release."

Zotov found this so amusing that he couldn't refrain from laughing in Beria's face.

Beria should have known that the worst was in store, or else why was he having to deal with an army general, instead of one of his own Party brethren, or even a fellow chekist? But his mind seemed to veer off into that parallel world of his.

"Listen to me," Beria said. "If you help me, you'll be rewarded beyond your highest ambitions. I don't know who gave you your orders, but he's finished. You hear me? They're washed up, all of them. Just get me out of here, and I'll remember you. I'll make you a Marshal of the Soviet Union. Just like that. All it will take is my signature."

Zotov stopped laughing. He stood there, impassive, feet planted apart, studying this man whose name had sown terror through the whole country.

"Well then." Beria tried a different tack. He leered as he said, "You ought to consider your family. You can't imagine the things I can have done to them—"

The reason Beria broke off was that no sooner had he threatened to harm Zotov's family—which, to Zotov, meant Lydia, then a cherubic little girl in pigtails—than the general went grabbing for his pistol. Everyone in Russia had a friend or relative who had suffered at the hands of this monster.

"I'll make you a Marshal!" Beria screamed as he looked down the snout of Zotov's gun. The real world was at last beginning to intrude.

"Don't worry yourself about it, Citizen," said Zotov in his low, rough voice, the words dragging like boots over gravel. "I'll be a Marshal without any help from you."

Then he watched the man who had held Russia by the throat rolling around on the stone floor, squealing, squirming, begging for life. The sour smell of urine assailed his nostrils.

Zotov had intended to haul Beria to his feet and hand him over to the guards. But the threat to his family had made him ready to kill. Now the spectacle in front of him filled him with such intense disgust that he resolved to put an end to it.

The former master of the Lubyanka had curled into a fetal position.

Zotov stooped over him, jammed the gun into the nape of his neck, and fired once.

Afterward, nobody criticized him for overzealousness in the execution of his orders. Beria's rivals were relieved, not only that the monster was dead, but that he had been dispatched in absolute secrecy. Before the year was out, Zotov received a promotion and a new decoration. Thirty years on, there weren't many men left in Moscow who knew the truth of how Beria had died. Had it been otherwise, Zotov's further ascent might have been a harder climb. The Party had reason to be wary of a soldier who killed one of its own, even if he had a license.

Marshal Zotov looked around, and found Sasha at his elbow with the brandy.

"Ah, thank you. So people still talk about Beria, do they? Yes, I had something to do with it. But that's all ancient history." He took Sasha's arm. "Now I want to ask you a few things about the Americans. . . ."

5 When Sasha left Moscow, Lydia stayed behind. Their marriage hadn't broken down in any definitive way; they were simply taking their distance from each other. On the Black Sea, they had shared the same bed and he had made love to her dutifully. He felt sure that Lydia understood what had happened. Women always do. He was grateful that she didn't ask any direct questions. But the Marshal, at least, was content. Beneath all the bluster, Sasha suspected, he was a profoundly solitary man, and he was delighted to have repossessed his daughter and his grandson.

"He's the spitting image of his grandfather!" Zotov bellowed, bouncing Petya on his knee. "Blood will tell!" Sasha felt that a new bond had been established between them that first night at Livadia. It was a bond he could build on. Before Sasha left, Zotov said to him, "I want you to keep me informed. I want you to be my eyes and ears, even in New York." And then: "I have great plans for you."

Back in Manhattan, he waited a couple of days before calling Elaine. She sounded tense and withdrawn.

She said, "I'd just about given up on you."

She met him at the door to her loft in a diaphanous wrap, and he was desperate to have her. But she fenced with him, slipping away from his embrace, provoking him but holding him in check. He had never wanted a woman so much, not even Tanya.

"So, how was Oslo?" she asked, and he had to waste time improvising elaborate fictions about a country he had never visited while she poured wine and taunted him from a distance.

Finally, when it became unbearable, he seized her and pressed her close against him, letting her feel his desire, tearing at the fastening of her wrap. He felt her body arch, fitting the contours of his own. Then she broke away.

"Elaine?"

"I have to go to the bathroom," she excused herself. But he could sense that there was something more that was holding her back.

She was gone for what seemed like a long time. For a while, he stretched out on the bed, listening to the rush of water from the shower and the muted noise of a party somewhere nearby, the music reduced to a primal thumping. At least they had time tonight, with Lydia in Moscow. The last few times he had been with Elaine, he had been conscious of her growing more and more tense after they made love, as if she sensed time wearing down to his departure like sand running through an hourglass.

He started to play with the TV set, flicking from channel to channel. The variety of American television, like the variety of American brand names, continued to astonish him. He watched a commercial for a product that was supposed to reduce hemorrhoidal pain. Then the network news came on, and Brezhnev's meaty face loomed up on the screen. Sasha turned up the volume.

"Soviet leader Leonid Brezhnev has reportedly suffered a stroke," the newsman was saying. "Now, for a special report on the men in line to succeed him."

The cameras switched to a studio discussion between a network correspondent and a man with a bow-tie and flesh-colored rims to his glasses who was described as an expert on the Soviet scene. The expert explained to the correspondent that there was a secret war going on in the Politburo between hawks and doves, and that the most crucial thing was that the West should not take any action that might assist the hawks. Then came a good deal of talk about who had stood next to whom on the podium during the last big parade in Red Square.

Sasha, frustrated by Elaine's continued absence, swore under his breath. These so-called Western experts were all alike, he thought. They were forever making the same mistakes, mirror-imaging, using *their* psychology to explain the Soviets, trying to make everything fit in with their preconceptions.

The studio chat continued while photographs of Brezhnev's possible successors appeared on the screen.

And there he was, Yuri Vladimirovich Andropov, with his decorations pinned to his lapel. Why was he only the fourth candidate to be mentioned? What did the expert have to say?

"Andropov can be safely ruled out at the present time," the man in flesh-colored frames said with professorial confidence, "because of the stigma associated with running the secret police."

"Eto polneyshaya yerunda!" Sasha exploded in Russian, just as Elaine came back into the bedroom in her terrycloth bathrobe. "That's rubbish!"

"Is that Norwegian?" she asked, and he thought there was something wrong about the way she said it.

He switched off the television and opened his arms to her. But she slipped away from him again and turned on the overhead light. It gave the big whitewalled loft a mortuary pallor.

She studied him clinically. Then she said, "I don't even know who you are."

In the silence, they could hear the beat of the music from the building across the way, blind and insistent.

"You know all of me," she reproached him with a gesture that embraced her one-eyed teddy bear, her framed snapshots of family and college friends, her decoy ducks on the ledge overlooking a converted warehouse. "And I don't even know what language you speak."

"I thought you said your family didn't speak Russian at home," he said quietly.

There. It was done. He felt that a burden had been lifted from him.

"You knew all along, didn't you?" he said to her.

"No." She shook her head. "Are you telling me you're Russian?"

Her innocence seemed genuine. "Yes, I'm Russian," he responded. "I'm a Soviet diplomat."

"Is that what you were keeping from me?" Her expression surprised him. She looked almost relieved. "Why didn't you tell me before?"

"I was afraid—afraid you might be scared away."

"I don't scare all that easily. In case you hadn't noticed."

He took her hand and said, "I couldn't be sure, not at the beginning. You know, a lot of Americans seem to think that Russians have tails and cloven hooves. You can't blame me for thinking you might have been scared if I'd told you right away."

She stood on tiptoe and kissed him on the lips.

Sasha was amazed by how calmly she was taking it. "You understand that I'm breaking rules," he went on unnecessarily. "We're strictly forbidden to get involved with foreigners."

Her hands moved over his chest. "So you weren't in Oslo," she murmured.

"No, not Oslo."

"And your name isn't Alex."

"Almost. It's Alexander Sergeyovich Preobrazhensky. But you must call me Sasha."

"What else did you lie to me about?" Her fingernails pressed into the flesh above his navel. "You told me you were separated," she reminded him. "Was that a lie too?"

"No. She's in Moscow. There's nothing between us."

"Except your child. Peter."

"Petya," he translated.

"So there'll always be something between you."

She looked into his eyes. They never told you what he felt. Instead, they threatened to draw you into a mystery. She said, "You're not going to leave them, are you?"

He met her gaze. "I don't think so. Not in the way you mean." He hugged her to his chest. "But I'm not going to leave you either."

6 Colonel Drinov was tremendously excited when he called Nikolsky in to see him.

"I've been studying your reports on Hansen," he said. Nikolsky had outlined a plan for using the former CIA man to expose the names of officers and agents of his former organization all over the world.

"As an active measures operation, it's first rate," Drinov said. "Absolutely first rate. But I see two problems."

You don't need to drag the nose to the cunt, Nikolsky cursed inwardly. He had an inkling of what was coming.

"First of all," Drinov continued, "if Hansen writes the book the way you suggest, without getting approval from Langley—which is naturally out of the question—"

"Naturally."

"He would expose himself to legal reprisals. They might even try to put him in jail."

"It's his lookout," Nikolsky observed. He didn't like or trust Hansen. "He can always go and live abroad."

"It's a possibility. But there's another consideration. Hansen hasn't gone public yet. I think we should keep it that way. He wasn't fired from the CIA, he left as an officer in good standing. Isn't that right?"

"That's what he says. We also know he fought with his station chief, and there were those marriage complications."

"That happens in the best-regulated families," Drinov said beatifically. "My point is, we shouldn't regard Hansen as a burnt-out case. Langley is already reeling from all the scandals and exposés. Another CIA man denouncing his service's activities . . . well, it's old hat. There are more useful things we can do with Hansen."

"For example?"

"A job with a security clearance. Come on, what do you think?"

"You mean, ask him to go back to working for the government? I'm not sure the CIA would take him back. Then there's the problem of the polygraph."

"The Americans have an exaggerated reverence for lie detectors. Not everybody's sweat glands work the same. Anyway, it doesn't have to be the CIA. Some other government department, perhaps. Or one of the congressional committees. In any case, you needn't trouble yourself about it."

"I'm not sure I understand."

"Feliks, you've done an excellent job. I'll see that you get your share of the credit, don't worry yourself about that. I'm taking over the case myself. What higher tribute could I pay you than that? Come on, don't take it like that. You know perfectly well this belongs to KR Line. We're talking about a possible penetration of the CIA."

Nikolsky could hardly contain himself. Drinov was a common thief, stealing an agent who didn't belong to him. An agent, furthermore, of unknown reliability. It was just as well that Feliks' blood-sugar count was

low that morning, otherwise he might have erupted more forcibly. Since
he had stumbled out of bed, a couplet from one of Vissotsky's ballads had
been running through his head: "My nerves aren't stretched taut/My
nerves hang down like a washing line."

He stole a cigarette from the pack on Drinov's desk.

"Look, I know I may be sticking my neck out, but I'm sure you're
making a mistake. Hansen hasn't proven himself yet."

"What are you talking about? He's been meeting you, hasn't he? He's
already compromised. And I made sure of it, believe me. Kostya was
covering you on every one of those meetings. We're sure Hansen was
clean."

"How do you know he wasn't wired?"

"Now, listen to me, Feliks Nikolayich." Drinov's tone switched from
coaxing to something approaching a snarl. "That's my business, not yours.
You can complain about it as much as you like, but everything has been
settled with the Center. All you have to do is arrange to introduce me."

"You're going to handle this in person?" Nikolsky burst out, astonished.

"And why not?" said Drinov, becoming friendlier again now that Feliks' protests appeared to have subsided. "These Americans are a piece of
cake. Did you hear what happened in Mexico?" He had evidently concluded that taking Nikolsky into his confidence would serve to mollify
him. "It was a near disaster. Two of our Illegals were picked up."

"Two?" Nikolsky echoed. The loss of an Illegal was about the worst
thing that could happen, after the loss of a cipher clerk. For the service
that captured one, it was like a score in the center of the dart board. "By
the Mexicans?"

"Under American direction, obviously. Well, we put our splendid Ambassador Dobrynin to work. He invited you-know-who to lunch, and explained that this unfortunate episode could pose a serious threat to
detente between our two great countries. It worked like a charm. A call
went out from the Secretary's office to Mexico City, and our Illegals were
put on the next plane to Washington. They were delivered direct from the
airport to our Embassy, fixed up with new travel documents and, whoosh,
straight back to Moscow on an Aeroflot flight. So you see, you needn't fuss
about Hansen. Dealing with the Americans is like—how do they put it?—
like shooting ducks in an incubator?"

"Like shooting fish in a barrel," Nikolsky corrected him, unconvinced.

Drinov planned the meet with Hansen like a military operation. Six members of the Residency, including Kostya, were assigned to mount covering

surveillance. The route that Nikolsky and Drinov himself would follow was plotted out in fantastic detail. It was supposed to end at a safe house in Glen Cove, not far from the Ambassador's residence.

None of this would have counted for much except for the fact that Bitov, the cipher clerk, was taking turns at supervising the battery of scanners that were used to monitor police and FBI radio transmissions. As a radio ham, Bitov was a natural; he took considerable delight in searching for unknown frequencies in between the recognized wave bands. He had the fortune to stumble on a previously unknown FBI wavelength that day, and the signal was unmistakable. But his timing was off. By the time he discovered that the FBI were out in unusual force in Glen Cove, and put out a message to abort the meeting, Drinov was already sitting down to kill a bottle or two with Hansen and Nikolsky.

Drinov was right about one thing. In that era of detente and mutual understanding, there was no question of expulsions. The State Department forwarded a formal protest, which was not made public. However, someone had to take the fall for a bungled operation, and that was certainly not going to be the head of KR Line. Drinov filed a report in which he stated, in lacerating language, that Nikolsky had failed in his duties as a KGB officer, in allowing himself to be duped by a man who had obviously been planted by the American authorities. The Resident, who countersigned Drinov's report, said somewhat apologetically, "It's not the end of the world. Anyway, you've had longer than most. Your tour should have finished already."

" 'If you want to tell the truth,' " Nikolsky quoted, " 'keep your horse at the door and one foot in the stirrup.' " He had just recounted the story of his final encounter with Drinov, which had ended with Feliks spitting on the floor.

"Who said that?" Sasha asked.

"Oh, it's an old Armenian proverb. The Armenians are very smart. You should always look out for them. Look at Askyerov. I'll bet he's part Armenian. He has to be."

"What will you be doing in Moscow?"

"Temporarily unassigned," Nikolsky said cynically. "There's going to be an inquiry. Drinov has seen to that. Oh, well, at least I won't have to live in that white elephant in the Bronx."

Sasha had just received notification that he would be moving uptown to the recently completed Soviet complex in Riverdale. He'd managed to put off the move for months and months. Now the blow had been softened.

They had jammed so much radio equipment into the top floors—up on that hill, they were ideally situated for electronic intercepts—that some of the families were being moved out into nearby residential blocks. Sasha's apartment was in a red brick building with a shoe repair store on the ground level. At least he wouldn't be stuck behind the metal grills and closed-circuit cameras of the Sovplex itself.

"The first thing I'll do," Nikolsky said as he poured himself another drink, "is go to the Theatre Romen." He burst into a rendition of a gypsy song, horribly off-key.

He broke off and said with unusual solemnity, "Sasha, you'll know where to find me. If ever you need anything, anything at all—"

"As a matter of fact," Sasha said carefully, "there *is* something."

"Just tell me her name."

"It's a member of your Committee. His name is Topchy. Did you ever hear of him?"

"I don't think so. Ukrainian, I suppose."

"I know he was in Moscow a few years ago." God, how long *was* it since Professor Levin had told him the story of his father's death? "He's a colonel at least. He could be a general by now." *As my father would have been.*

"Topchy. Well, I'll ask around. Any special reason?"

"It's something personal, Feliks."

"Good enough. Now really, General, why are you fucking a cow? *Nalivay!*"

It was a season of partings. At his next meeting with the agent code-named Ibrahim, the West African Ambassador informed Sasha that he, too, was returning to his own country.

They were jogging around the lake in Central Park. They passed a band of teenage kids with a big box radio that blasted Sasha's eardrums, and a lone fanatic on a bench with a reflector, trying to get a tan under the thin February light.

"What's ahead for you, George?" Sasha asked when they were back on a deserted stretch.

The African was in peak condition. He breathed smoothly and evenly, through his nostrils.

He announced as calmly as if they were reading a script by a Victorian fireside, "I'm going to take over the government."

Afigbo had it all planned. The existing regime had made itself unpopular because of the flagrant corruption of its ministers—one of whom was said to have equipped his residence with a solid gold bathtub—and their highly visible dependence on the United States. Younger officers were restless.

"If I don't do it, we'll get some lieutenant nobody ever heard of," he remarked. "Or maybe a sergeant, like in Sierra Leone."

The African was well versed in the theory of the coup d'état. He had read the masters of the subject: Lenin and Curzio Malaparte. And he had already had some practical experience. "You want a minimum number of people involved," he told Sasha. "The key thing is that the population should remain passive, and that power should be concentrated in a handful of targets. All we have to do is secure the palace, the main barracks, the airport, and the radio station, and the capital will belong to us. That means the country as well. It's not like the Soviet Union."

Afigbo said this with a wry smile, but for an instant, Sasha, who had read Lenin too, found himself wondering: *Isn't it?*

The African had a modest list of things he wanted the Soviets to provide, mostly cash to pay off some of the army commanders. Sasha promised to press his case. He also decided that he would qualify his report. There was no way of telling how long a man like George Afigbo would stay loyal to his benefactors once he had power in his own hands.

7 All of Tom Regan's life was in his face. The skin was loose and crinkled and bunched like a pair of leather gloves that didn't fit right, apart from a raised white scar above his right eye that dated back to his early days in the organized crime division. The web of broken capillaries gave a purplish tinge to his cheeks. His eyes were wary; this was not someone with exaggerated expectations concerning his fellow men. His hair, what was left of it, was cut severely short. "Mr. Regan, he likes a clean neck," his old Italian barber—the only barber he knew in the city who would still cut his hair for a buck fifty—used to say. That was right. Tom Regan liked a clean neck.

He was lightly dressed against the arctic winds that were cutting through the New York streets, in a gabardine coat with a thin wool lining. He was a Chicago man; the cold was in his bones. He grew up in a little box house on a treeless street in a blue-collar neighborhood, and remembered his father, who worked in a rolling mill, as an angry giant who would come home mad drunk and take the strap to whichever of his nine children he could catch. The war was Tom Regan's way out, and after the war, the army helped to pay his way to a law degree, which he needed for only one reason. The kids he grew up with dreamed about being cops or firemen or engine drivers; the only thing he ever wanted to be was an FBI agent. His boyhood hero was Matthew Purvis, the man who got Dillinger.

For six years now, they had had him working in Soviet CI. He would have rather been back chasing Mafia hoods. But he was a brick agent; he did the job he was assigned. And because he was a brick agent, he didn't go much for the briefings on ideology or for intricate theorizing about double and triple agents. What interested him was M.O. and, above all, human failings. These Soviets weren't supermen. They got drunk, they fouled up, and their wives were compulsive shoplifters. They used call girls; Regan had just been looking into a neat little racket that the Cuban service had going at the UN. They flew in hookers from Havana and fixed them up with Cuban press credentials so they could go trawling the delegates' lounges looking for interesting pick-ups. This caused major embarrassment when it was discovered that the Soviets were the biggest customers. No, the Russians weren't ten feet tall. They probably even had kids who didn't understand them. Like he had.

It was a bad neighborhood, the Fifth Precinct, Regan was thinking as he rammed his car into a narrow space. Full of gays and drop-outs and Chinese gangs and kids, like his daughter Sandy, who were going to break their hearts before they ever got what they wanted out of life. He had argued with Sandy not to move out of the family place in Westchester. But no, she was going to be an actress, or a model, or something, and she had to be where the action was. He sensed that she was ashamed of what he did. The kids she mixed with put Che Guevara's hairy face on the wall and thought that Mr. Hoover was some kind of a Nazi. Still, he hadn't completely lost her. It was she who had called him to stop by for a drink. Regan had forgotten it was his birthday. He usually did.

Regan locked the car and stomped heavily across the street. There was a man, a big fellow, coming out of Sandy's building. He didn't look like one of her crowd. He was carrying a newspaper and wearing the kind of comfortable brown double-breasted overcoat that is described in New York as British Warm. The man walked into the cone of light from a streetlamp, and Regan stopped dead at the edge of the street. He knew that face.

He had first seen it in a visa photograph submitted by the Soviet Mission to the State Department and sent on to his office to be checked out two, maybe three years before. He had seen it in a score of pictures since, pictures taken at the Coliseum, at the beach in Far Rockaway, in the restaurant at the UN. Tom Regan was very good at faces. But the name was still eluding him as he started up the stairs to Sandy's apartment. Well, it wouldn't take two minutes to find out. The Soviet was definitely operational, identified as probable GRU. They hadn't managed to nail him for anything yet. Regan had put a surveillance team on him quite a few times, but the Russian knew his stuff. He always gave them the slip, except once, when they were able to tail him out to a Chinese restaurant in Queens. The Soviet must have sensed something, because he turned right around and went back to Manhattan the way he had come. If he had been going to a clandestine meet, he managed to abort it in good time, because they didn't spot his contact although they sat outside the restaurant for a full hour.

Now, what was a Soviet intelligence officer doing in Sandy's grotty building in SoHo?

"You just made my day," Tom Regan announced to his daughter. "Tell me about your neighbors."

Tom Regan was right. It didn't take long to run down the file on Alexander Sergeyovich Preobrazhensky—no wonder that name wasn't on the tip of his tongue!—and to confirm that he was tentatively identified as a major in Soviet military intelligence, known to associate with Luzhin and others in the Residency. It took longer to work out who Preobrazhensky was visiting down in SoHo. Sandy knew only a few of the people in the building. It sounded like there was a pretty high turnover. There were some students from NYU, a couple of gays who ran a boutique on Christopher Street, a photographer. The photographer sounded promising; Abel had used the same cover.

Regan arranged for a stakeout. Within a week, he was examining a nice eight-by-ten blowup. There was the Russian leaving the building and there, framed in the doorway, was a pretty, dark-haired girl waving goodbye.

"I want everything there is on her," Regan instructed the team he had assembled in his new office in the Federal Building. He had preferred the rathole round the corner from the Soviet Mission. "Family. Employers. Personal Habits. Political Affiliations," he rapped out the headings. "Let's get on it."

Two days later, Regan went in to see Murphy, the division chief.

"Elaine Frances Warner," he summarized the facts that his men had assembled. "Twenty-seven years old, currently unattached. Father, Lev Israelyan, son of Naftaly. Born Odessa, nineteen-oh-nine."

"They're Soviets?" Murphy interjected.

"Russian Jews," Regan corrected him. "The family emigrated before the revolution and changed the name. The father made a pile in the garment business."

"So what have we got here? A Line EM operation?" The EM Line people in the KGB Residency handled operations involving the Soviet emigré community. They were always trawling around for people of Russian descent who could be pressured into carrying out espionage assignments.

"Could be," Regan responded. "Except that Preobrazhensky isn't KGB, he's GRU. Also, we've checked out the other members of the family. There's nothing adverse on any of them, except that the IRS ran a couple of audits on the father and the mother collects parking tickets like some people collect postage stamps. The father's retired to Florida. He goes to Israel once a year and stays at the King David Hotel."

"Could be sleepers," Murphy commented. He set about lighting up one of his fat greenish cigars. Regan never could stand their smell. You'd think, now that Murphy was division chief, he could go upmarket a bit.

"Brothers? Sisters?" Murphy pursued.

"One sister, Barbara. She's just had a baby. The husband is a commodities broker."

Murphy grunted. "That could be worth looking into," he said. "A broker told me the Soviets stopped selling gold a few weeks back. Anyone on the inside track could have made a killing."

"I wouldn't know," said Regan. He had six hundred dollars in his savings account, when he last bothered to look.

"What does this Elaine Warner do, anyway?"

"This is the interesting bit. She calls herself a freelance writer, but from nine to five she's working in the library at the X-Tech Corporation."

"Looks like you hooked a big one, Tom," Murphy said. He lolled back comfortably in his chair and put his feet up on the desk. It was well known that X-Tech did classified work for the Pentagon. "We've got a friend over at X-Tech, haven't we? Charlie whatsisname."

"Charlie Macdonough," Regan helped him out. Charlie had worked in CI until leaving for greener pastures.

"Well, go buy Charlie a drink."

"I already did. Charlie knew the girl slightly. He says she's well liked around the office, and nobody's ever criticized her work. He says she doesn't have access to sensitive stuff, but he'll keep his eye on her. He wanted to know if he should tell his boss about the Soviet. That would get

her fired, of course, unless the head of the company is willing to play along
with us. I told Charlie to keep his mouth shut for the time being."

Murphy's grunt suggested approval. "What do you figure this Elaine's
motivation is, if they didn't get her through the father? Is she political?"

"Not unless you count being a registered Democrat." Regan grinned.
"Oh, she made a contribution to the ACLU once. That's about it. She's in
with quite a few media types, but she doesn't write about politics."

"Money, then?"

"She's had a couple of bounced checks, and the credit card company
put a stop on her once. But she pays her rent, and there's always Daddy to
turn to. I doubt if it's money."

"So what's the bottom line?"

"Have a look at this." He pushed a photograph across the desk. It was
one of the pictures taken in the past two days. It showed a strikingly
attractive girl in a leotard doing aerobics in front of a window. It had been
taken with a telephoto lens.

"Holy shit," Murphy said appreciatively. "Is this the one?"

Regan nodded.

"She's quite a looker."

"Exactly."

"What are you trying to tell me, Tom?"

"This is just gut instinct. I could be wrong. But maybe this doesn't have
anything to do with intelligence. My feeling is, this Soviet is hooked on
the girl."

Murphy chewed this over, along with his cigar. "So Preobrazhensky
could be vulnerable," he said at last.

"Maybe."

"But it's worth a shot."

Regan wouldn't go beyond another, "Maybe." He added, "His wife and
kid are back in Moscow." He didn't need to spell out the rest. If they were
looking at Preobrazhensky as a possible defector, this could be bad news.
He might not be willing to sacrifice his family. But if they were looking for
leverage to make him ready to work as an agent-in-place for the FBI, it
might help.

"Have we got the girl's phone tapped?" Murphy asked.

"Sure."

"Okay. Maintain twenty-four-hour surveillance on both of them. Follow
up all your leads. We ought to hit one of them, probably the girl, damn
soon."

New York was a hunting ground for the CIA as well as the FBI. After all, the United Nations was international territory, off-limits to the Bureau—according to the rulebook—but not to the Agency, which had a special division, called Foreign Resources, or FR, to trawl the delegates' lounges. In Manhattan, the two agencies tried to ignore each other's existence, even though their operatives were often rubbing shoulders in the same crowded East Side saloons. When a fight over turf became unavoidable, there was a joint committee in Washington that sorted things out. But it was weighted down with organization men, and when Tom Regan wanted to ask for something from the Agency, he preferred to turn to one of his poker buddies.

He had been flattered when they asked him to join the school. They met once a month, in New York or the Washington suburbs, to play cards with a ten-cent limit and trade shop talk with no limit at all.

Luke Gladden was a charter member of the school, and Tom Regan liked him, despite his Southern accent and a family lineage that reached back to the battle of Shiloh and the sugar plantations. Born and bred in the Mississippi delta, Gladden had the patience and cunning of a riverman.

"Play it long," he advised Regan after he had checked the Agency files. "Preobrazhensky isn't just one of the star operators in the GRU residency. He's the son-in-law of Marshal Zotov."

"Marshal who?"

"Zotov is one of the most powerful military men in the Soviet Union. He has access to everything. You can see what it means. If it's played right, this could be more important than Penkovsky or Popov." These were two moles that the CIA had recruited and run inside Soviet military intelligence more than twenty years before, spies whose product had never been equaled since.

"You know Murphy," Regan said. "He's gung ho. He wants to move in right away. He's got a point. The Soviet's nearly at the end of his tour."

Gladden looked at him thoughtfully. They were both aware that, once Sasha left the United States, the case would be turned over to the CIA. The territorial imperative would not allow Regan's boss to let that happen without making every possible effort to bag a defector for the Bureau.

"Have you got any handle on the girl?" Gladden asked.

"Only her job."

"It may not be enough if it's really a romantic attachment."

They were still talking about it when the others arrived to play poker. Somebody remarked that he had seen the KGB chauffeur from the Mission walking up to the Food Emporium on Third Avenue, tailed by a Chinese.

"Oh, yeah?" Regan said. "He's one of ours."

"No kidding?"

"They assigned him to Soviet CI because they figured that if the Soviets spot him, they'll think the Red Chinese are breathing down their necks. He doesn't speak Chinese anyway. He's from San Francisco."

Loving Sasha made Elaine intensely curious about her own roots. She started reading the Russian classics, and one afternoon of torrential rain she called the New School to ask about language classes.

"The semester has already started," she was told. "But they'll still accept you for the course if you show up for the third session tonight. You'll need to register before five."

At the first hint of rain, every taxi in New York seemed to be either off duty or on radio call. But Elaine managed to hijack one right in front of the X-Tech building, running ahead of a man from the bank next door. Living in Manhattan was a survival course.

The taxi driver was one of the talkative ones, a self-styled expert in palmistry who started displaying sketches he had made of celebrities who had ridden in his cab. Elaine let her mind drift until the driver's voice was just background static. She didn't see the car that pulled smoothly away from the curb behind them and kept a steady distance away from the cab as it made the loop and headed downtown.

"Why don't we do it, lady?" said the man at the wheel. "It would be dynamic."

"Excuse me?"

"Your hands. Let me take a shot of your hands. Then I'll send you the sketch for framing and the full analysis. Your whole life potential. I'll make you a special price."

"Thanks. I think I'd rather not know my life potential."

By the time they reached Twelfth Street, it was as dark as if the sun had set. The gutters were steaming black rivers. The sidewalks were almost deserted. The rain had come like a storm in the desert, sweeping everything loose away.

The New School was a gray modernist structure where the courses ranged from Puff Pastry to The Existence of God. Elaine hurried across a courtyard littered with curious bits of sculpture—a headless torso, another with the head of a ram—to a hall where she was shunted from one computer terminal to a second and on to the cashier and finally handed a printout of her course ticket.

The class began at 5:50 in a chalky seventh-floor room under gaunt strip lighting that turned everybody's face gray. The rain, or the terrors of the course, had washed away all but four of the students. Elaine liked the teacher, a stocky survivor of a Soviet Pedagogical Institute. She wore a voluminous navy print dress and her hair was tied up in a bun. Elaine could imagine her roasting potatoes over a slow fire out on the steppes.

One of the male students complained about the difficulty of mastering certain Russian vowels. "Take the letter *yerih*. We don't have that sound in English."

"Oh yeah?" said the girl next to him. "You oughta come to Brooklyn sometime."

Elaine had trouble figuring out the cyrillic alphabet, but she had a natural ear for pronunciation. Or perhaps it was the months of exposure to Sasha.

"*Ochen khorosho, Yelena,*" the teacher congratulated her after she recited her first sentence. "You can be a good spy."

There was a false note in Elaine's laugh, even though she knew this was only the teacher's routine joke. She had asked Sasha some uncomfortable questions about Russia. Was it true, for example, that dissident writers had been charged with holding the same opinions as their fictional characters, as if Dostoyevsky had been put on trial for the actions of Raskolnikov, the protagonist of *Crime and Punishment?* Was it true that the Soviets were building missiles faster than the Americans? But she had never asked him exactly what he did. If he wanted her to know, he would tell her. If not, well, she preferred not to think about it. But the furtive way that he came and went made her nervous. And lately, she had had the uneasy sensation that she was never completely alone. There was the odd way that Charlie Macdonough, the security man at X-Tech, had dropped by the library when she was working late, tidying her desk. Her ex-boyfriend, the married one, had called her out of the blue to say that someone was asking around about her. And there were those odd clicks on the phone.

The hands of the wall clock swung round to 7:30, and the class said their ritual good-byes in variously accented Russian. There was a jumble of people in the hall. Only one of the elevators was working. Elaine pattered down the stairs, wondering whether Sasha would call tonight. He remained the man on the pay phone. Sometimes he didn't even call for two or three days at a time. Suppose there was an emergency? she had asked.

"I'll try to call you every day," he said. "But if for some reason I can't reach you, and it really is an emergency, you can send a postcard to this box number." He had made her write it down. "Address it to Mister Green. Don't sign your own name. It doesn't matter what you write. 'Wish you were here' will do fine."

"That's original."

"Look, this isn't a game. Promise me you won't write unless it's something really serious."

"How about if I need to make love to you?"

Even then, she hadn't insisted on knowing his real business, although the word "spy" occurred to her. It sounded naughty and glamorous. It made her think of the title of a James Bond movie: *The Spy Who Loved Me.* The trouble was, nothing was ever like the movies.

As she came out of the New School, she was debating whether to go uptown to Lincoln Center and see the Russian film they had been talking about in class. The teacher said it was mystical. The girl from Brooklyn complained that it was so slow you could see the paint drying on the walls. The pelting rain deterred her. She pulled her scarf over her hair, tightened the belt of her raincoat, and began to walk quickly in the direction of the Union Square subway.

A dark blue Oldsmobile pulled up level with her.

"Miss Warner."

She turned to look at the man who was leaning out the window on the passenger side. Under a shapeless hat, he had a face like a road map. She had never seen him before.

"You're getting drowned out there. Why don't we give you a lift?"

She couldn't see the man who was driving. She felt terribly exposed, with the water sloshing against her overshoes and dripping down the back of her neck.

"Who are you?"

"We're FBI agents, Miss Warner. We'd like to talk with you. You'd really be more comfortable in the car."

She started walking on up the street, with the blue Olds nosing along at her heels. But for the storm, the scene must have looked like somebody cruising a hooker.

"Miss Warner?" They pulled abreast of her again. "Would you rather we came to your office?" The man on the street side held out his ID.

Oh, shit. She could just see Lisa's face, and Charlie Macdonough's, and the prim, straight-up-and-down supervisor's when the FBI came tramping through the X-Tech library in their polished wingtips.

She got into the back seat of the car.

"Am I under arrest or something?"

"No, of course not." Tom Regan said. "We just need to ask you some questions about a friend of yours."

"Do the initials GRU mean anything to you, Miss Warner?"

Tom Regan was riding next to her in the back of the car. They were crossing the Brooklyn Bridge, and the whirr of the traffic over the corrugated surface was like the noise of the planes in an old war movie.

"I don't think so," she said.

"But you do know the meaning of the word 'spy.' "

She stared out the window at the lights of lower Manhattan, blurred by the rain.

"We know that Preobrazhensky asked you to obtain confidential company reports from the X-Tech Corporation," Regan said.

"That's not true!" she protested.

"Don't make it hard on yourself, Miss Warner. You know that X-Tech is involved in sensitive Pentagon contracts."

"He never asked me about anything like that," she said fiercely, turning to face the FBI agent. He didn't insist.

"How did you two get together?"

She told him the story of the meeting in Bloomie's.

"And you think that was just coincidence?"

"Yes."

Regan looked at her doubtfully. "Does that kind of thing happen to you a lot?"

"No, it doesn't. And if you're going to ask me any more questions, aren't you supposed to read me my rights, or something?"

"This is just a friendly conversation," Regan said wearily. "Miss Warner, you're an American citizen. Don't you accept that you have certain responsibilities?" In the old days he would have said "patriotic duties."

"You mean I'm not supposed to go out with a man if he happens to be a Russian?" she mocked him.

"Preobrazhensky isn't any Russian. He's a spy."

"What's he supposed to have stolen?"

That's what we'd like to know, Tom Regan thought. But he kept on the offensive. "He didn't tell you his real job, did he? I'll bet there are quite a few things he didn't tell you."

"What are you saying?"

"Did he tell you he's got a wife and kid?"

"They're in Moscow."

"Did he tell you he'll be sent home in a couple of months?"

That shaft found its mark. She looked thrown. She said, "Stop the car."

Regan looked around. They were in a dismal waterside district near the Brooklyn end of the bridge.

"It's not a pretty night to be walking around, Miss Warner."

"Please let me out."

The car slowed to a halt, but Regan squeezed her arm tightly for a moment before releasing her. He said, "Ask him about it. He may not want to go home. He could be looking for an out. If he is, you know where to come."

He gave her his card, with a phone number scrawled on the back. "We'll talk some more," he promised. "I guess your place would be better than your office." The threat was there, beneath the surface of the words. They could get her fired.

But that wasn't what she was thinking about as she scurried up the street like a water-rat toward the shelter of a drugstore. It was the prospect of Sasha leaving her life for good. And the fact that he hadn't even told her.

When she got back to the loft, it was late, and she was soaked to the bone. She took a long, steaming hot bath and wondered whether he had called while she was out. She knew that she ought to warn him. She even considered sending a postcard to "Mister Green" at the post office. But if she told him that she had been grilled by the FBI, she would risk scaring him away and losing everything. She took refuge for the rest of the evening in routine, regular things, in fancy soaps and warm towels, in TV commercials and Cheetos and Diet Pepsi—things that avoided strangeness and threw up walls, however thin, between herself and the terrors of Sasha's world.

Luke Gladden said to Regan, "Let him go."

"But Murphy—"

"Screw Murphy. Consider what we've got. The girl is seriously smitten, right?"

Regan didn't contradict him.

"And she's already fired up by things Russian. Witness her course at the New School."

"What are you telling me, Luke?"

"I'm saying that it doesn't sound to me like the girl is going to give up. She could go after him."

"You mean in Moscow?"

"Well?"

"It's a long shot, Luke. And once the Soviet leaves the States, he's your bird. I guess that wasn't something you'd entirely forgotten."

Luke Gladden busied himself with tamping his pipe. A pipe was a remarkably useful prop when an awkward question came up. By the time you'd finished cleaning or tamping or lighting it, chances were the questioner would have gotten bored with waiting and moved on to something else.

"I'm going to give it another crack," Tom Regan announced. "We could have a defector here."

"I hope you're not going to pitch him direct," Gladden observed. "That might blow the girl's usefulness. There was one Soviet spy who defected for love," he mused. "Agabekov. The very first intelligence defector. But he was a cross-eyed Armenian from Istanbul. I'm afraid it's kind of gone out of style."

8 The final weeks before his return to Moscow whirred past, as if the pages were being ripped from the calendar in whole handfuls. It was hard for him to face what he knew would be the last meeting with Elaine. She had demanded nothing of him, not even false promises. He sensed the depth of her fear of losing him, and it worried him; he stepped warily around it, like a child afraid of a dark, breathing place in the woods.

"I only live when I am with you," she had said, and then slipped away to do indifferent ordinary things so he wouldn't feel obligated to respond. She was often like that, these past months, offering herself with the solemnity with which Petya might offer a seashell or a drawing he had made with crayons, then tiptoeing away, affecting not to notice how the gift was received.

She made me capable of loving again, he told himself. What was that line in the poem by Robert Frost she had quoted, the line she said reminded her of him? "I suffered like a metal being cast." Yes, he had been hardened, tempered—had sought to have the cold, clean edge of a blade —but not beyond understanding what he had sacrificed, in himself and in others, in the process.

He barely slept the night before that last rendezvous, and when he

woke, his sheets were twisted and damp. He boarded the gray metal bus
that shuttled members of the Mission to and from the Sovplex, and as the
doors hissed shut, he felt he was already back in Moscow. He spent the
morning cleaning out his work satchel, getting rid of everything his successor wouldn't need. There, in one of the blue notebooks, were the dates of
Ibrahim's birthday and wedding anniversary. If you wanted to bind a man
to you, he had learned, you should make sure to remember the day he was
born and the day he was married. Agents are often lonely people. Sasha
struck a line across the page and scrawled his name along it, so it could be
consigned, with the others, to the special stove that was kept in the *referentura* for the destruction of classified documents. This mechanical task
helped to calm him.

He took a walk at lunchtime and visited an Irish saloon, a couple of
blocks east of the Mission, that Nikolsky had frequented. A man with a
big, corrugated face positioned himself at the end of the bar and glanced
at Sasha from time to time over the top of his beer. White shirt, close-
cropped hair: the man had FBI written all over him. Sasha looked away, to
a framed poster above the cash register recording the names of Republican
patriots who had survived sentence of death by the British to become
famous men in the New World.

Before Sasha had finished his cocktail, a second appeared, unasked for,
at his elbow.

"What's this?" he said to the bartender.

"Gentleman there says he'd like to buy you a drink," said the barkeep.

"Another time," Sasha said.

As he made his way to the door, Tom Regan said, "Bon voyage," just
loud enough for him to hear.

Sasha didn't pause. That was the FBI's way, he knew. They liked to
trail their coat in front of your face, to make you feel they had your
number—and to make sure you knew where to turn if you ever thought of
defecting.

Defection. It was a sour word in any language, Sasha thought, as he
headed west before turning up Park Avenue, where a sign in front of a
church announced a sermon on the theme of "Adam and Fallen Man."
He stared across the wide expanse of the avenue, at the water towers
above the rooftops, ranging from functional horrors to rococo follies, that
were part of the variety and mystery of Elaine's city. And the thought
flicked at him, like a lizard's tongue, *Can this be my city too?*

Children came skipping across the steps of the National Guard Arsenal,
and he thought of Petya. And then, for an instant, he was engulfed in a

wave of nostalgia. Images of Russia washed over him, images of the limit-less sky over forests and steppes and great rolling rivers. He saw the snow falling from the branches of the firs and rising again in a fine powder dust as the report of his shotgun echoed through the silence of the Silver Forest. He smelled the rose gardens of Livadia, the savor of Crimean vineyards and apricot orchards under the harvest sun.

And he thought of Topchy, his father's murderer, and of the tasks he had set for himself. He was not his own master. He was the servant of a purpose that was dimly shaping itself, something that reached beyond personal revenge. All his life so far had been merely an apprenticeship for that. He had learned things in New York that would help him, not least from George Afigbo, the African exponent of the coup d'état. Better still, he had made a friend in an unexpected quarter, a friend in the KGB. But he had also bent his own rule that no personal attachment should be allowed to interfere with his mission. That had to be set right.

The same evening, he lay cradling Elaine's head in his lap and talked about his childhood, his history professor, and the father he had never known.

"It's a strange thing to live in my country," he told her. "Ninety per-cent of what you are told is a lie, but the lies are more familiar than the truth, so it is the truth that seems unbelievable. There's a permanent contradiction between what you see and what you hear. People get along by rejecting the evidence of their own eyes. But the people are suffocating. It's only the ones on top who can breathe."

"So why are you going back?" she asked softly.

He looked at her sharply. "How did you know?"

She was on the point of telling him about the FBI, but stopped herself. She was afraid that if he knew, he would break off their relationship for good. If he left her now without knowing, there would at least be the hope that she could find him again.

She felt guilty at the deception as she said, "I can sense it from the way you're talking. It sounds like a farewell speech."

He seemed to accept this, because he went on. "I couldn't bring myself to tell you before." Now they were sitting side by side, and he took both her hands in his, enveloping them. "You mean as much to me as my life. But there are things that are more important than my life, things that are waiting for me in Russia."

"Tell me."

"Suppose you were living under an occupation," he said. "Suppose it had claimed the lives of the people closest to you, and you had watched your own generation being turned into cynical drunks. Wouldn't you fight that?"

"I couldn't live with it," she conceded. "But I could go somewhere else."

"I'm a Russian," he said fiercely. "My only future is there. I hope you can understand."

"I'll try," she said, fighting back the tears. "Sasha, there will be another time for us, won't there?"

"I can't promise anything. It's best if you try to forget me."

"Is that what you're going to do—forget me?"

"No," he said simply.

"Then don't ask more of me than you ask of yourself."

When he left, she came down and stood on the steps. He didn't look back.

5.

LIVING
WITH WOLVES

If you live with wolves, howl like them.

—RUSSIAN PROVERB

1 Marshal Zotov discharged one barrel, then the second, at the flight of wild geese winging south, and one of the birds plummeted out of the sky and was lost among the reeds. He let their Bulgarian escorts go fishing for it. One of them, an unpleasant-looking character with a permanent sheen about his face and clothes, waded over and started complimenting the Marshal on his marksmanship.

They were on the shores of Lake Varna, on an estate that belonged to the Bulgarian Ministry of Defense. For the First Deputy Chief of the Soviet General Staff, the entire Warsaw Pact was a private hunting reserve.

After dinner, when they were alone together by a great open fire in the lodge the Bulgarians had provided, the Marshal said to Sasha: "So you want the smell of gunpowder. Is that it?"

Sasha had told his father-in-law that he wanted to return to one of the fighting arms of the Soviet defense forces.

"The reports about you that Luzhin sent back from New York were excellent," Zotov told him. "Luzhin says you have a brilliant career ahead of you in the GRU, or at headquarters. Are you sure you're not just trying to get away from Lyda?"

Of course he was trying to escape from Lydia, and from the memory of Elaine. But he wasn't going to explain that to the Marshal. He made a phony little speech about duty and tradition, and Zotov let it pass.

"If I were your age," Zotov said, "I'd start learning Farsi, or Dari. There's going to be a major blow-up in Afghanistan. We'll be fighting before the end of the year."

"You mean we're going to be directly involved?"

"It's inevitable. We've already received orders to prepare a plan of operations. How much do you know about Afghanistan?"

"Not much," Sasha admitted. In fact, he knew a great deal more than most Soviets, including those who were about to be sent there, because he had been reading western newspapers for the past few years, in addition to picking up occasional rumors from Nikolsky and from people in his own service. "It seems we've been having as much trouble finding a reliable man to run things in Kabul as the Americans had in Vietnam after they got rid of Diem."

"Don't talk cunt! It's got nothing to do with Vietnam."

"I didn't mean—"

"Hold on. I will concede there may be one element of truth in what you said. It's an asshole of a country, Afghanistan. Right on our border, under a fraternal socialist regime, and yet we still can't find a leader to hold things together. Now the Chinese and the Americans are crawling around like lice. If we don't do something fast, those black-asses are going to turn around and kick us out. We had a special meeting of the Defense Council—" A Bulgarian orderly picked that moment to enter the room. The Marshal shooed him away.

"We've always had a problem on our southern flank, God knows," Zotov resumed. "The problem of constructing a scientific frontier. Go back to your history books. Read General Annenkov. Read General Sobelev." These were famous Tsarist commanders who had fought to subdue the martial tribes of what were now the Soviet republics of Uzbekistan and Tajikistan. "None of those fucking Turks have any love for Russia. And the Afghans were always the hardest to deal with. Look at what they did to the British.

"Well, you remember the trouble we had with Daoud."

"Very clearly." Mohammed Daoud had been viewed as a reliable friend of the Soviets until he decided to lock up the leaders of the Afghan Communist Party, early in 1978. The Politburo had often been ready to turn a blind eye to the repression of local Communists in order to maintain good relations with a "progressive" regime, and this was particularly true in its dealings with the Islamic world—witness the cases of Syria under Assad and of Egypt before Sadat threw his Soviet advisers out. In the case of Afghanistan, however, there was alarm that Daoud, lured by the prospect of lavish cash handouts from Iran and the West, was getting ready to break off his close relations with Moscow, and that the arrest of the Communists was only a first step.

The edict was handed down from the Politburo: Get rid of Daoud. From inside their cells, with the complicity of their jailers, the Afghan Communist leaders issued precise instructions for a coup. It was executed with the help of sympathizers in the armed forces, especially the air force, for many years a bastion of Party influence. After President Daoud was toppled and killed, the Afghan Party leaders were borne in triumph in a military convoy, horns blaring, headlights on, from the prisons to the palace.

The Soviets still had to pick a replacement for Daoud. The complication was that the Afghan Communist Party was split into two factions, and the relationship between them was more of a vendetta than a dialogue. There was the Khalq, or "Masses," faction, and then there was the other lot, who took the name Parcham, which means "Flag." The Khalq was the more orthodox organization, ready to follow every shift and eddy in Moscow's line. By contrast, the Parcham faction was suspected of harboring Maoists and Trotskyites—which was why the KGB was allowed to recruit agents inside it.

One of these agents within the Parcham faction, a man regarded by the KGB as one hundred percent reliable, was a politician named Babrak Karmal. This was the man the KGB recommended, after the overthrow of Daoud, as the new President of Afghanistan.

"I have to admit that our friends in the Committee may have been right for once," Marshal Zotov commented after describing this series of events, "But, of course, the Central Committee couldn't accept this Babrak Karmal. Suslov and the ideologues said he belonged to the wrong faction. You couldn't trust the Parcham people, they said. Any one of them could turn out to be a Mao-lover in disguise."

"So they installed Taraki," Sasha observed.

"Exactly. Nur Mohammed Taraki. The little cockroach"—the word *"tarakan"* was also a play on the Afghan President's name—"could spout Marx better even than Suslov. His problem was that he believed every word of it."

At the outset, Taraki did the things expected of him. He invited the Soviets in to supervise the key ministries in Kabul and to run the secret police. He scythed his way through the ranks of the rival faction. Lucky members of the Parcham leadership, like Babrak Karmal, were sent abroad as ambassadors. Many of the others were jailed or shot.

Then Taraki outdid even Suslov's expectations. As a Marxist-Leninist who went strictly by the book, Taraki believed that socialism required the root-and-branch destruction of religion. So he led an assault on the mosques and recruited Party zealots to slaughter the mullahs. Taraki had also learned that socialism requires the abolition of private property. So he grabbed the land from the tillers and announced the creation of collective farms.

"He set out to copy our brilliant Soviet *kolkhoz,*" the Marshal observed. "Suslov, sitting in Moscow, may have thought Taraki was a hero, a model of fidelity. Our advisers down there weren't quite so impressed. The Afghans don't take kindly to anyone fucking around with their land or their religion. I started getting reports warning about a civil war. Moslem bandits were talking about Jihad, a holy war. Taraki was losing control of the countryside. Our people started telling him to slow down. He spouted more Marx and Lenin at them. In other words, he told them to piss off.

"Finally the Politburo had to sit up and pay attention. Enter our new friend, Hafizollah Amin. He reminds me a bit of your pal Askyerov. A real greaser. He appeared from nowhere and was suddenly Taraki's indispensable lieutenant. Taraki brought him to Moscow and he charmed all of them, from Leonid Ilyich down. But we knew even less about Amin than about Babrak Karmal. The KGB had nothing on him. After all, his Party credentials were beyond reproach."

"You mean nobody made anything out of the fact that Amin had been in the United States as a student?" Sasha asked, amazed by this lapse. In New York, Nikolsky had mentioned that the Residency had received a request to check up on Amin's stay in America.

"Nobody thought about him at that time. Amin had the Party's stamp of approval, remember.

"Well, it was becoming plain to everyone, even Suslov, that President Taraki was off his head. He insisted on dealing directly with Leonid Ilyich. He refused to talk to our Ambassador for days at a time. The Politburo finally made up its mind there had been a small mistake. So Taraki was told to move his ass to Moscow in a hurry. They received him with the usual pomp and circumstance, but when he got back to Kabul, he found he was out of a job. Hafizollah Amin had taken over, with our blessing. Taraki just vanished off the face of the earth."

Sasha had seen a report in a western paper that Taraki's body had been hacked into little pieces after Amin had him shot.

"Which leaves us with Amin," Sasha jogged the Marshal along.

"They picked Amin because they thought he'd be flexible. They thought he'd be able to divide the resistance. But Amin turned out to be more flexible than we had reckoned on. He arranged meetings on his own with some of the tribal chiefs, offering deals he didn't tell us about. Now last week—this is the sensitive part, Sasha, I know you can keep your mouth shut—our friends in the Committee came up with a report that caused a near panic."

Zotov summarized the contents of the KGB report, which had been discussed at the meeting of the Defense Council he had recently attended. The KGB Resident in Kabul had sent an urgent message to the

Center stating that President Amin had offered the rebels a power-sharing arrangement. "He is preparing to make an alliance with the most reactionary elements. Then he will turn to the United States and Pakistan for military assistance. There is a high probability that Amin is working in league with the CIA. He has attended secret meetings with identified CIA operatives."

"So there's a possibility that Amin was a CIA agent all along, recruited when he was in the United States," Sasha chipped in.

"That is the KGB's opinion, and the Politburo has accepted it. One way or another, we have to get rid of Amin. You can guess who our candidate to replace him must be."

"Babrak Karmal."

The Marshal nodded. "Third time lucky for Andropov's boys."

"Of course, that won't end the civil war," Sasha said.

"In the opinion of the General Staff—which the Politburo now accepts —there is no way to sustain our position in Afghanistan without using Soviet troops, at least four or five divisions. So you see, you've come back at an interesting time, Sasha. You're looking for a challenge? You've got one. Afghanistan. Go there and be my eyes and ears."

"I don't just want to sit around at headquarters. If we're going into a war, I want to run my share of the risks."

"You *are* hungry for the smell of cordite, aren't you? Well, that's all right. Go back to your friends in Spetsnaz. They'll give you some action."

"How long do you think the Afghan operation will take?"

"Who knows? It depends whether we're allowed to take our gloves off. The Committee assessment is very negative. But I can see a great opportunity here, Sasha. Think about it. Afghanistan is our approach route to the Gulf and the Indian Ocean. It brings us a step closer to controlling the flow of oil from the Middle East. It's a perfect platform for an armored push into Iran. We'll need to go in there some day and sort out those fucking mullahs. We can scare the shit out of the Pakistanis, stop them from sending mercenaries to prop up our enemies in the Arab world. General Annenkov was right. This is our historic line of advance."

He paused before asking, "What do you think the Americans are going to do?"

Sasha said, "I told you before. The democracies have short memories."

"Ah, yes." Marshal Zotov stretched out comfortably and allowed himself a small glass of brandy. "I nearly forgot to tell you the best thing. The Wakhan corridor."

Sasha pictured it on the map: a narrow strip of land jutting out from Afghanistan's northeast corner all the way to China.

"The finest hunting terrain in the world," the Marshal enthused. "I want the horns of a Marco Polo sheep for my dacha. Have you ever seen one of those beasts? Magnificent. Great curled horns. They can stand five feet at the shoulder. I heard that one of the Rothschilds used to go hunting in the Wakhan. Next year, it will be our turn, eh? Now what do you say?"

"*Nalivay!*" said Sasha, filling his own glass to the brim.

Back in Moscow, Lydia packed Sasha's bags for him, and she packed like the soldier's daughter she was: everything with razor-sharp creases, squared away with the fanatical neatness Sasha had had to master to pass inspection during his officer training.

"Both of us married the army," she said accusingly, watching him fasten the shoulder belt over his field uniform. "But my share of army life is waiting."

"It's not so bad, Lydochka. You shouldn't exaggerate. You'll have Moscow, and your friends, and all of this"—he gestured at the splendid apartment—"while I sit in a tent."

"Then why did you volunteer?"

"It's what your father would have done, at my age. Our borders are threatened. It's my duty to serve."

That was the most maddening thing about him, Lydia thought. Whenever she had a legitimate complaint—usually that he had virtually abandoned his family—he came up with an unassailable reason why it would have to wait. *I'm sorry, but officers of the GRU are on duty twenty-four hours a day. Excuse me, but there's a war in Afghanistan.*

"Write to me, Sasha. So Petya will know, when he's older, what it was like."

Sasha thought of his own father's letters from the front, and the terrible line, "We have become our own enemy," and felt suddenly uneasy about the rationale he had constructed for going to Afghanistan.

He said merely, "I'll write."

After two weeks of grueling physical training to work off the residue from the New York restaurants, and another fortnight of briefings that included a crash course in colloquial Dari, Sasha joined the Spetsnaz group that had been assembled in Tashkent. His old friend Fyodor Zaytsev, now a lieutenant-colonel, was there too. Zaytsev was the operational commander;

Sasha had been made chief of staff, a post that was usually reserved for the GRU's designee. He found Tashkent an ugly, sprawling modern city. Most of its oriental splendors had been destroyed in the terrible earthquake of 1966. They paid a visit to the Djuma mosque and the Kukeltash madrassah, but there was only one afternoon available for sightseeing.

At bases just north of the Afghan border, two Soviet divisions, composed of Central Asian soldiers, were waiting for instructions to move. They had been fitted out with Afghan army uniforms. Zaytsev was skeptical about their fighting ability. These conscript divisions were usually employed in construction work and the menial chores of the Soviet army.

"They're *chernozhopi*, same as the Afghans," Zaytsev pointed out.

Sasha, who had followed the Marshal's advice and sought out a copy of General Annenkov's account of the Central Asian campaigns of the last century, remembered the Tsarist commander's injunction not to rely on native soldiers. Britain's reliance on the sepoys, Annenkov warned, was a source of weakness; witness the Indian Mutiny.

Sasha felt largely indifferent to the plight of the Afghans, friend or foe. Like Zaytsev, like the Marshal, he viewed the invasion that was being prepared as a straightforward military operation to defend his country's frontiers: a job of work. He expected that he and his comrades would be judged as soldiers, not on the basis of family or Party connections, and he welcomed that. He was looking forward to proving himself in the first real war that Russian troops had fought since Hitler's defeat. Promotion came faster on the battlefield, and that might assist his secret purpose. But what counted for most was that it was in the field that a man discovered who could be trusted not to cut and run. He needed allies of his own kind. He thought he had found one already in Fyodor Zaytsev. In Afghanistan, he would discover more.

The Spetsnaz group was given a special mission: to support the KGB team that would be flown to Kabul to seize the presidential palace and neutralize Hafizollah Amin. Before Sasha's plane took off, the Central Asian divisions had already received the order to push south, into Afghanistan.

2 The heavy Antonov transport plane bellied down onto the runway of Kabul's international airport, the cargo bays were opened, and Sasha's team drove down the ramp in their jeeps and armored cars. There had been no protest from the control tower at this unscheduled landing. It had

already been secured by Spetsnaz troops in civilian clothes who had flown in on a regular Aeroflot flight.

A fair-haired man in Afghan army uniform came running across the tarmac.

"Preobrazhensky?"

Sasha, in the front seat of his jeep, gave a brief salute. He recognized Colonel Bayerenov, who until a few weeks before had been the director of the KGB's paramilitary training school.

"Deploy half your men to secure the airport perimeter," the KGB colonel ordered. "Follow me with the rest. I'll go in with the first wave. You know your job. Stay back and cover us in case the Afghans counterattack."

"Yes, Comrade Colonel."

It was a strange force that Bayerenov had assembled. Some of them looked over the hill—men in their fifties, or at least their late forties, with sagging guts they hadn't managed to work off in time for this operation. There was a fair sprinkling of dark-skinned Central Asians, who looked a damn sight less conspicuous in their Afghan army gear than the colonel, and who might be presumed to speak Dari, or at any rate Farsi. Well, Bayerenov and his superiors presumably knew what they were doing. The KGB were supposed to be specialists in *mokrie dela,* "wet affairs," weren't they? It's a dirty job, Sasha thought. Let them have it.

Bayerenov had assembled a few tanks and a dozen or more army trucks, no doubt purloined from the equipment that the Soviets had been supplying to Afghanistan in pursuit of their internationalist duty.

The tanks led the way into the city, slowing the pace of the column behind. An Afghan officer at the checkpoint outside the airport stood yelling at them after the tanks crashed through the barrier. A young lieutenant in a following jeep shot him through the forehead, as coolly as if the Afghan were a target on a firing range.

The city was eerily peaceful, the great Shahe Nou bazaar closed and shuttered, the streets deserted until the column neared the palace and soldiers from a loyal Afghan regiment tried to block the road. Bayerenov's men pulled up the flaps on the backs of their trucks and opened fire with their DSK heavy machine guns. Within minutes, the Afghans broke and fled.

These weren't the Afghan fighters Sasha had heard about.

The Soviet force fanned out to cover all three entrances to the palace compound. These were protected by heavy iron gates, and Bayerenov used the tanks to ram them. As the tanks rumbled forward, they came under heavy automatic fire from the palace guards. From where Sasha was waiting the noise was oddly muted, like a series of wooden matches being struck. Now the real resistance would begin, he thought. They had been told that Amin's guards had been specially selected from his own tribe, and they were sworn to defend their leader to the death. But they didn't seem to have anything heavier than a machine gun. With a clash of metal, two of Bayerenov's tanks broke through. The third was stuck in the twisted bars of one of the gates, apparently stalled. The driver was desperately trying to work the ignition, but the engine just groaned and expired.

Bayerenov's squads were racing through the other two gates, ducking and firing. They were all in Afghan uniforms. The only way to tell them apart from Amin's men in the darkness and confusion was that their colonel had told them to put on armbands, which had been hastily fashioned from rags of white cloth. Bayerenov's instructions were precise, and they had been confirmed at the level of the Politburo, which alone had the authority to decide on a high-level assassination. Nobody inside the palace was to be permitted to escape, under any circumstances. The Politburo did not want any witnesses to tell the world how President Amin had died. Bayerenov's men were going in prepared for a slaughterhouse. They were loaded up with spare magazines for their kalashnikovs. Sasha noted that some enthusiasts had taped two magazines together so they could be fed in faster.

"All right, let's move!" Sasha signaled to his men. He led them through the center gate, stepping over bodies that were thrown clumsily about like sacks of grain. Some of Amin's men were still holding out in a sandbagged machine gun post over to the left of the courtyard.

"Cover me!" Sasha yelled to the sergeant who was with him. He was something from a nightmare, that fellow, a hulking Estonian with a face that had been ripped and restitched countless times and was not improved by a black moustache set like a permanent scowl. To top it off, he had his head shaved completely bald. But there was nobody better to have at your back in a brawl. While Sasha zigzagged along the wall toward the Afghans' post, the Estonian dashed out, threw himself down behind a dead man's body and opened up, drawing their fire.

Sasha snapped a magnesium grenade off his belt and hurled it as soon as he got close enough to the bunker. Blinded by the flash, the Afghans screamed and pressed their hands over their eyes. One of them rolled out of the bunker, his uniform ablaze. It was the work of a moment to finish them off.

The shock of the first wave had already rolled over the remaining Afghan defenders outside the palace.

A KGB major was yelling in Farsi at the handful of survivors, telling them to drop their weapons and crawl—"On your bellies!"—toward the Soviet vehicles. Three or four men staggered out from behind their shelters with their hands raised. One of them was bleeding profusely from a head wound that seemed to have claimed his right eye.

The KGB major stepped forward as if to receive the surrendering guards, then hunched himself down, legs wide apart, and opened fire. He was using hollow-nosed bullets that tore the Afghans apart.

He spun round and saw Sasha watching him.

"Orders," he said. Then he added, as if he needed to explain something to himself, "Do you think these black-asses would treat us any better?"

Sasha didn't say anything, but he studied the major's sweaty face and wondered whether his father's killer had looked like this butcher.

A dense cloud of smoke enveloped the main doors of the palace. Inside, the fighting was still fierce. Amin's bodyguards were fighting for every inch of the stairs leading up to the presidential suite. Sasha heard the boom of grenades going off in quick succession.

A man in Afghan uniform came lurching out of the smoke, waving his rifle and screaming something. The words were indistinguishable in the din of battle. The man's face was smudged and blackened beyond recognition, but Sasha knew him from his height and build.

He was conscious of several Russians swinging their submachine guns toward the man who was waving at them. Hot from the killing, their reflexes were so accelerated they didn't allow time for a second look.

Sasha shouted, "Hold your fire! It's the colonel!" But before the first syllable had passed his lips, Colonel Bayerenov's chest was crosshatched with machine-gun bullets coming from both sides of him. It was impossible to identify any single killer. Bayerenov's corpse was thrown back against the palace steps, his head lolling at an impossible angle, his jaws still opened wide in his desperate plea for reinforcements.

Nobody stopped for the colonel. Sasha roared, "Follow me!" and led the second wave into the palace.

By the time he fought his way up to President Amin's suite on the top floor, Bayerenov's picked killers had already located their quarry.

Hafizollah Amin was sitting on a sofa on the far side of a vast reception room hung with silks and finely woven rugs. Behind him was a sight not normally associated with the Moslem conception of paradise: a western-style bar, with a waiter in a white jacket and a gleaming phalanx of bottles.

Conscious of the sensitivities of his people, Amin usually favored fruit juice over spiritous liquors. But tonight, he was drinking scotch out of a chunky crystal glass. He was wearing a flak jacket and a helmet of Soviet design over his evening clothes, but he reached for his drink, not the automatic rifle lying across the coffee table, as the KGB hit-men burst in.

"*Shurawi Zindabad,*" he greeted them ironically. "Long live the Soviets."

His calm resignation was not matched by the bartender, who threw himself down behind his counter, or the beautiful courtesan who was sitting with Amin. He was holding her hand, but she pulled free and ran toward the archway that led to the bedrooms.

Sasha burst into the room in time to see a young KGB officer—the same lieutenant he had noticed at the airport—cut the President of Afghanistan in half with concentrated fire from his kalashnikov. He caught a fleeting glimpse of the ravishing girl who was trying to escape. She reminded him of Maya Askyerova, the one who had fallen for Nikolsky's black poodle. The Estonian took care of her. Instead of wasting bullets, he tore after her, seized hold of her, and wrenched her head round like a wheel until he heard the neck crack.

Now the lieutenant was stalking the bartender, who, realizing he was cornered, was creeping out on all fours. He picked himself up, raised his hands, and started shouting something.

He looked like an Afghan, all right, but suddenly Sasha realized that his shouts were in Russian.

"*Ne strelyaite!*" he yelled. "Don't shoot! I'm Soviet!"

The lieutenant, with his helmet down over his ears, didn't seem to hear, or didn't want to. He seemed to be crazed with killing, like the men who shot Colonel Bayerenov. Sasha grabbed the man's arm so that his shots went wide, shattering lines of bottles behind the bar. The lieutenant rounded on Sasha, and his eyes were like pink glass. He could see Sasha's black Spetsnaz uniform, but he was at a point where he was capable of shooting at anything that breathed. Sasha delivered a quick karate chop; in an instant the lieutenant was on the floor and Sasha had possession of his weapon.

While they were scuffling, the bartender had seen his chance to run out of the room. He must have hurled himself down the circular stairwell because, during the mopping-up later on, Sasha found him cowering in its shadow on the ground level.

"Who are you?" Sasha demanded, dragging the man out by the scruff of his neck.

"Talebov. I'm a lieutenant-colonel of KGB."

Sasha stared at him in disbelief, fingering the trigger of his Skorpion machine pistol.

"I'm sure the commander knows about me," the man stammered. His jacket now looked like a butcher's apron. "I was promised—"

"The commander's dead," Sasha said bluntly.

Bayerenov's deputy, one of the men Sasha had thought looked over the hill, came up.

"You know the orders," he reminded Sasha. "No prisoners."

"This one isn't an Afghan," Sasha said. "He claims he's one of yours."

Lieutenant-Colonel Mikhail Talebov was a lucky man, the only member of Amin's retinue to get out of the palace alive. His story was promptly confirmed by the KGB Residency in Kabul. Talebov was an Illegal, sent to infiltrate Amin's private quarters. He was an Azerbaijani by origin, with a natural flair for oriental languages. He had been given specific orders to assassinate Amin, and had been provided with a special poison that he mixed in the President's drinks. But Amin, with a sixth sense for his own preservation, was forever switching glasses or mixing up unpredictable combinations for himself. Nobody had seen fit to inform Talebov that his job had been reassigned to Bayerenov's hit teams.

Meanwhile, the armored convoys were pushing south from the Soviet bases in Uzbekistan, and the troop planes were rumbling in to Kabul airport. The Soviets did not anticipate much opposition from the Afghan armed forces, once a few key Amin sympathizers had been eliminated. There was a hard core of Communists and Soviet agents in the officer corps who could be counted on to carry out instructions without question. Before the night was over, most of Amin's loyalists would have been removed by KGB-directed squads moving from house to house, barracks to barracks. And the planners had not forgotten the radio.

As soon as the signal went out that Hafizollah Amin was no longer a factor in Afghan politics, Radio Kabul broadcast a remarkable statement by Babrak Karmal, interspersed with patriotic music. Babrak Karmal, describing himself as the legitimate President of the Democratic Republic of Afghanistan, invited his fraternal Soviet allies to come to the defense of his country's revolution, which was threatened by imperialist plots and the secret intervention of the CIA.

This broadcast had been recorded by Karmal at a luxurious rest house in Tashkent. The new leader of the Democratic Republic didn't show his face in Kabul for a week after the KGB had dispatched his predecessor, just to make sure there weren't any unpleasant surprises when he showed himself to his people.

3 Nikolsky woke up before he wanted to, utterly dehydrated, in the middle of a baffling dream. He was attending a grand reception, in a huge marbled hall with endless staircases, balconies, and running fountains. It seemed as big as a whole town. He passed one beautiful woman after another, all in décolleté gowns, until he was at the back of the ballroom, where it suddenly became plain that the whole edifice was incomplete. Not all the foundations had been laid, and at the back the whole structure seemed to be adrift, floating and swaying like a raft. And back there the windows, two stories high at least, had no glass. As Nikolsky tried to steady himself on the heaving floor, a great tide of foul water burst through between the columns, drenching everyone. Or not quite everyone, perhaps, because a cheery round little fellow called Krupchenko came up and made Nikolsky a handsome present: twenty bottles of fizzy red communion wine and a few cases of beer. "Be sure to drink the altar wine first," he cautioned.

As Feliks crawled out of bed and thumped his way to the bathroom, he kept puzzling over the donor. He didn't know anybody called Krupchenko.

He drove himself out to the Village in his Zhiguli. Armed with his dollars and certificate roubles, he'd had no trouble buying the car. He turned off the Ring Road and drove through dense pine forests, past the sign that said "Halt!" and, below that, "Water Conservation District." At the guardpost, where men in khaki uniforms with blue flashes checked his ID card, the bronze plaque amended this to "Scientific Research Center." They let him through to the parking lot, and he walked between neatly cropped lawns to the new headquarters of the First Chief Directorate. They had found some hotshot Finnish architect to design the thing, which was shaped like a three-pointed star, all glass and aluminum. Nikolsky thought it was hideous. But the worst thing about it was that the crowded canteen, where you had to line up for half an hour to get a stale sandwich, didn't even sell beer. This was part of the new drive for efficiency at the workplace. There he was, stranded miles from a drink. It made him quite homesick for the old Lubyanka.

He usually ignored the Soviet press and went straight to the American papers, which were available to his section, although you had to sign each copy out as if it were a state secret. But an item in *Pravda* on the war in Afghanistan caught his interest. It was about the CIA and Chinese operatives who were supposedly crawling all over the place. That's what they told the conscripts in their orientation classes too: they were going down there to fight the Americans and the chinks. Nikolsky wondered whether Sasha had run into any foreigners. The *Pravda* piece cited an article by an American correspondent, D. Frick. Nikolsky swore out loud. So the little shit-eater was still churning it out. He took out his ballpoint and changed the first letter of the transliteration of Frick's name to a P.

One of Nikolsky's colleagues, an Armenian who had spent time in San Francisco, strolled in with a racing form sheet under his arm.

"Well, Agopian," Feliks addressed him, "have you got any good tips for me?"

"I've got a hot one for Sunday. Burilom."

"It had better be an improvement on that last one you touted." Off-track betting, naturally, was illegal. But Agopian was always ready to place a few roubles for a friend.

"Why don't you come and see for yourself?"

Nikolsky considered this proposal. The Moscow Hippodrome wasn't exactly Belmont. The horses were mangy brutes, and everyone knew the races were fixed by the managers. The entrance to the place looked like the Brandenburg Gate—massive columns and heroic statues of rearing stallions and musclebound men trying to restrain them. But the inside was sleazy and faded. There were always plenty of bums and touts hanging around the stairwells under the two-tiered grandstand, which stank like urinals. Still, you could get a serious drink on the terrace from black-market runners who would slip you a bottle wrapped in a newspaper, and the racetrack restaurant, the Bega, was one of the best in the city.

Feliks winked at the Armenian and asked, "Have you got any female company arranged?"

Agopian grinned. "Not this Sunday, Feliks. You'll have to look after yourself. I'm meeting a friend of mine, Colonel Topchy."

Nikolsky tried not to register surprise. Topchy was the man Sasha had asked him to find out about as a matter of great personal importance.

"I don't think I know this Topchy," Nikolsky said nonchalantly.

"He's Third Directorate."

Nikolsky made a face. Everyone in his service looked down on the military chekists of the Third Directorate as riff-raff, low-grade thugs.

"Don't be so snotty-nosed," Agopian reproached him. "Topchy is a great fellow."

"How did you get to know him?" There wasn't much social contact between the two KGB directorates, especially now that Nikolsky's service had been moved out to the Village.

"We served in Baku together. Those were the days!"

Before the Armenian could digress into an account of the delights of Baku, Nikolsky said, "Who was your chief in those days?"

It was Agopian's turn to look startled. "But I thought you knew! Gusscin Askyerov was running our organization in Azerbaijan. Before he became First Secretary."

"Ah, that's right. I'd forgotten," Nikolsky lied. "How were Topchy's relations with him?"

The Armenian made an obscene gesture. "As tight as that."

Nikolsky decided to go to the racetrack that weekend.

Topchy seemed pleasant enough on first being introduced, although his attention was on other things. He had been having a talk with one of the racetrack managers, and was busy scurrying up and down the stairs to deal with the illegal bookies whose turf was the smelly, shadowy corridors under the grandstand.

They all knew Topchy by sight. He would rattle off his bets, hand over the money from a thick wad of roubles, and the bookie would scribble down the details and his assumed patronym, "Vissarionovich," on a scrap of paper and squirrel it away in his pocket. There were no betting slips. This was one place where honor among thieves was scrupulously upheld.

Topchy was sure he had the winner picked for the second race, thanks to his source, and jeered at Nikolsky and the Armenian when they put their money on a horse called Burilom instead.

It was a lackluster lineup at the starting gates. The horses looked undernourished. The jockeys were turned out in a ragbag of garments. One sported a builder's hardhat; another, what looked like an army helmet.

Topchy was pressed up against the railing, yelling his lungs out in between taking a swig or two from the bottle of vodka he had wrapped up in *Izvestia*, when the horse he had picked started into the home stretch. All at once, a black stallion came up fast on the outside. It was Burilom. The lead jockey lashed out viciously with his whip, trying to cut Burilom across the face. This was quite routine at the Moscow Hippodrome. The managers took no action as long as everything had been arranged with them ahead of time.

This time, however, something went awry. Burilom's jockey spurred his horse wide, out of reach of the whip, and streaked ahead to win by more than a length.

Topchy was angry and deflated, complaining loudly that the race had been fixed. He had lost quite a pile. But his spirits revived over the many drinks Nikolsky paid for in the bar of the Bega restaurant, and over the excellent dinner that followed. He thought this Nikolsky was a sympathetic fellow, not like most of those stuck-up people in the First Chief Directorate. Flattered by Nikolsky's interest, he started telling him all about his intimate friend, Gussein Askyerov.

Somehow, Nikolsky managed to drive Topchy home without running foul of the militia, who liked nothing better than to catch a KGB man drunk at the wheel. They parted like old buddies, agreeing that they had to keep in touch.

I'll have something interesting for Sasha, Nikolsky thought. *If the poor sod ever gets back.*

4 Each day that Sasha spent in Afghanistan, he hated the country more. In Kabul, the military headquarters was established in a vast compound near the airport, surrounded by barbed wire and concrete walls and minefields to keep the guerrillas back. The Soviets had their own generators, but most nights, much of the city was blacked out. The capital depended on hydroelectricity from the Kabul gorge, but the rebels knocked out the power lines faster than they could be repaired. The only alternative sources of electricity were a few smelly, broken-down oil generators.

Life in the Shahe Nou bazaar seemed bustling and normal, at least in the mornings. Currency traders still squatted there on their rugs, prepared to change any kind of money, quoting exchange rates that were so exact, so up-to-date, that you wondered if they had a direct line to the exchanges in London and New York. But the Soviets visited the bazaar only in large parties under the escort of armed guards. In the first months, the usual escort was two full truckloads of soldiers. As the random snipings and knifings increased, the guard had to be doubled to four truckloads of troops with kalashnikovs.

You couldn't trust any Afghan, Sasha soon concluded. Every government agency was riddled with spies. The chief of the secret police fled to Pakistan, and his successor narrowly escaped being blown up by a bomb planted in his office by his own lieutenants. Press gangs roamed the streets rounding up young men to serve in Babrak Karmal's army. And they deserted in droves, whole battalions at a time. Rebel prisoners escaped by the hundreds, with the help of their jailers. Even inside the highest circles of the government, the old feud between the Khalq and the Parcham factions was raging fiercer than ever. The Afghan minister of defense, a Parcham supporter, had to be hospitalized after his own deputy, a member of the other faction, beat him up and broke several of his ribs. Whenever government forces were included in a military operation, the rebels received a tip-off in time to get away. When there was no alternative but to turn to the Afghans for something, they were infuriatingly slow, and it was hard to tell whether this was deliberate sabotage. *Nim soat,* "in half an hour," became a maddeningly familiar phrase. It was the standard answer whenever you asked how long it would take to get something done. It could mean anything—a few hours, a few days. It rarely meant what it said.

There was an expression that was even more familiar. You heard it shouted from the back of a crowd, from behind a shuttered window, from children in the street. *Russe murdabad!* "Death to the Russians." They didn't even own the capital. They were just sitting on it, like a sumo wrestler sitting on his opponent.

The hostility of the Afghans was oppressive, but it was less depressing than what the war was doing to the Soviet army. Within a few months, the Central Asian divisions were pulled out and replaced by predominantly Russian units.

"There. What did I tell you?" Zaytsev remarked. The Central Asian troops, related to the Afghans by language, blood, and the Moslem religion, had shunned combat. Some had turned themselves over to the Mujahideen. Sasha didn't doubt that the number who defected would have been many times greater but for the guerrillas' enthusiasm in killing anyone in Soviet uniform before asking questions.

But the country had a corrosive effect on the Russians as well. The rebels, even when they were armed only with First World War rifles, were the best fighters Sasha had ever seen, and they fought with an absolute faith in themselves and their cause. Apart from the border skirmishes with the Chinese, the Soviet army had not seen battle since 1945; the Party leadership preferred, where possible, to pursue its foreign enterprises through subcontractors like the ever-obliging Cubans. In Afghanistan the Russians were soon hunkering down in static defensive positions, using clumsy air strikes to pursue an enemy who was hard to find through mountain fortresses that were harder to scale.

Living in fear, deprived of women—the only ones they saw were hooded from top to toe—and often of vodka as well, the Soviet troops found consolation in hashish. The defensive reflexes of the Politburo and the geopolitical instincts of the General Staff had led them into one of the world's great markets of hashish, a waystation on the hippie trail a decade or so before. Soon Russians from the ranks were trading anything they could steal, including their own weapons, for the fruits of the poppy. Hashish might have fueled the fanaticism of the thirteenth-century Order of Assassins, and of fundamentalist warriors of Jihad since, but Sasha saw no evidence that it was honing the cutting edge of the Soviet army in Afghanistan. On the contrary, soldiers drugged to the eyeballs made easy targets for the rebels.

It wasn't only the conscripts who stole. A colonel was shot for trying to smuggle emeralds out of the country. The gems came from Dasht-i-Riwat, in the heart of a rebel stronghold.

In one of Sasha's first reports to Marshal Zotov, sent through his private channel to the General Staff, he insisted that the war would merely swallow up increasing quantities of Soviet manpower and matériel unless they pursued the offensive in the Spetsnaz style. They had to fight the rebels on their own ground, infiltrate their ranks, use agents to play one movement off against another, and send in elite forces to blow them out of their sanctuaries in the mountains and across the borders, in Iran and Afghanistan. Zotov relayed his enthusiastic endorsement.

There were times Sasha felt utterly nauseated, not by what the war was doing to the Afghans, but by what it was doing to the Russian army. He put none of this in the bland letters he sent home to Lydia, which dwelled excessively on the poor quality of the food. It was the courage and the steadiness of some of his comrades that revived his sense of purpose and encouraged him to believe that, for all of them, the experience could be a decisive watershed.

Sasha went with the Spetsnaz teams on a series of raids into rebel territory, and learned a lot about his fellowmen. From their actions under fire, from the talks they would have at night in the mess or beside a campfire, he found himself grading his fellow officers in terms of whom he could count on, not just for courage in the field, but for the intelligence to understand the type of leadership the army and the country required. As the war dragged on, more and more of the younger officers were outspoken among their own kind about the stupidity of the men in Moscow who had sent them into battle under conditions that they believed made any kind of victory impossible. Sasha listened more than spoke during conversations of this type.

The disaffection extended to some of the more senior officers as well. There was a major-general called Leybutin, charged with an offensive against the rebels in the area around Ghazni, who was particularly scathing about their fraternal socialist ally Babrak Karmal and the people who had picked him for the job.

"It's the old problem," Leybutin insisted. "They won't leave the decisions to the professionals, the men in the field. They can't agree on their objective, and they won't give us the means to achieve it."

"It's called democratic centralism," a young Spetsnaz officer called Orlov observed sarcastically. Sasha had been watching him. He was a more intellectual version of Zaytsev: a man with the reflexes of a professional killer, but the spirit to question the ends for which his talents were being used.

"To fight a war like this, you have to clear out the dead wood," Zaytsev chipped in.

"And the grafters," Orlov added.

They all knew that the worst of the looters weren't conscript soldiers trading for hashish, but people with seats on the Central Committee.

"There's a death penalty for economic crimes, isn't there?" Leybutin said. "They ought to enforce it." He named one individual with an exalted Party rank who had made a fortune by charging the Afghan government a percentage on contracts for Soviet equipment.

"You're dreaming," Sasha goaded him on. "In our society, a man like that is above suspicion."

"Then the time will come when the army will have to clean house," Orlov said quietly.

That silenced the discussion. They all knew Orlov had gone too far. But nobody challenged him, and Sasha lay awake for a few hours afterward, reflecting that the war was molding a new kind of army from the men who served in it: leaner, more exacting, allergic to slogans. It was an army its political masters might have reason to fear.

In a raid against a guerrilla base, or *qarargah*, in the north, Sasha traveled a mountain trail by foot with the Spetsnaz squads. They came to a bridge over a jagged gorge, hundreds of feet above the ice-blue river below. It was a typical Afghan bridge: a couple of narrow tree trunks lashed together,

tapering in the middle to a thickness barely wider than his two boots
pressed together.

A lieutenant in the group, Malenov, whom Sasha had reprimanded for
constantly showing off and exposing himself to unnecessary danger, came
to the middle of the bridge and stopped. He stood there, swaying gently
from side to side, his eyes fixed on the bottom of the gorge.

"Get a move on!" Sasha yelled at him, assuming this was another show
of bravado.

"I—can't," Malenov whimpered.

"What's the matter with you?" Sasha roared. He suddenly realized that
the man was about to fall. He walked back across the bridge to Malenov
and stretched out his hand. "Here. Hold on to me."

He guided the lieutenant, step by step, to the safety of the cliff.

Malenov started stammering his apologies. "It's something I've always
suffered from," he explained. "It's not so much vertigo, more an odd
compulsion to throw myself over a height."

"But you've made hundreds of parachute drops!"

It was the man's way of proving to himself, and to others, that he
wasn't afraid. In the same spirit, when they reached the guerrilla camp,
Malenov was the first into action.

On another operation, in Shindand district, near the border with Iran,
the Estonian sergeant was in Sasha's group. One night, he took off by
himself, dressed all in black, with his black face mask and his chosen tools
of trade: a knife, a pistol, and a stock of magnesium grenades.

Sasha stayed up most of the night with Zaytsev, hammering out the
details for a plan he intended to submit to the Marshal. He was still
waiting for approval to cross the border and take out some of the rebel
sanctuaries inside Iran. But it was clear to both Sasha and Zaytsev that as
long as the guerrillas enjoyed safe haven and a guaranteed supply route
through Iran and Pakistan, where Afghan refugees had poured in by the
million, they couldn't be decisively defeated. Sasha's plan called for Spetsnaz units, guided by agents and informers inside the rebel movements, to
cross the borders and kill or capture the leaders of the resistance.

When he went outside, it was not quite dawn, and the gray light gave
everything the grainy texture of an old daguerrotype. He was surprised to
see the Estonian come striding across the compound, lugging a sack. He
looked more sinister than ever, with a coarse stubble sprouting over his
pate and his cheeks. But he advanced with a bouncing, even jaunty gait.
Sasha was immediately suspicious that the man had been out robbing the
villagers or trading for hashish.

He ordered him to stop and open up his sack.

"Take your pick, Colonel," the Estonian said insolently, dumping the bag on the ground.

Sasha picked it up and shook out the contents. One glance was enough. The Estonian had been out killing, along an irrigation ditch in a fold of the mountains where he knew that some of the Mujahideen hid during the night. He had brought back his trophies: ears, fingers, and other detachable organs that proved the number of his conquests.

Sasha turned away without speaking to the sergeant. The man was a raging beast, more barbarous than those he was fighting. Yet Sasha felt nothing, just the dull pain above his right eye and the sharper pain in his lower back that went with his utter exhaustion. The war was shaping all of them.

Driving himself to the limit helped him not to think about what he had left behind in New York. There were whole days when he managed not to think of Elaine for a single waking minute. But she returned to him in his dreams.

Finally, in the second year of Sasha's war, he got formal approval for a series of cross-border operations that were code-named "Caravan." The Party leadership still wasn't prepared to send Spetsnaz teams against the densely populated refugee camps in Pakistan. They would go on with the same methods as before—the occasional bombing mission slightly off-course, diplomatic arm-twisting, and the myriad forms of political warfare. But Iran was a different affair. The Ayatollah was supplying arms and sanctuaries to the Moslem fundamentalists among the Afghan guerrillas, and had showed he was no friend of the Soviet Union in other ways as well. Not content with humiliating the Americans, he had let a mob invade the Soviet embassy in Teheran. The Ayatollah deserved to be taught a lesson, and he had nobody's shoulder to cry on except Allah's.

5 "It's here." Sasha jabbed his finger at a point on the huge relief map that covered his work table. Zaytsev bent down to look. The place marked was in the desert north of the marshes of the Hamun-e-Helmand.

"It's at least forty miles inside Iran," Zaytsev observed.

"More like fifty."

Zaytsev looked at him. "So you finally got approval. *Ochen khorosho.* It's time we showed those fucking mullahs who to pray to. How reliable is the source?"

"The best. He's one of our own Illegals." Sasha summarized the message he had just received from Moscow, based on the reports received via the Residency in Teheran. Two rival groups of Mujahideen, both supported by the Ayatollah, had agreed to join forces for an all-out assault on Herat. They were now massing in the Iranian desert, at an ancient caravanserai on one of the traditional routes for the smugglers' camel trains. They had picked a place that tested men's endurance: a barren region of treacherous quicksands, with white salt-smears on the lifeless soil. In summer, the land gave back the sun's heat like a metal reflector. From two hundred miles away you could see the mountains with absolute clarity, as if they were within a short ride.

"Our job is to wipe them out before they disperse," Sasha concluded. "It is desirable, but not mandatory"—he quoted the dispatch precisely—"to take Abdol Qari alive." This was the rebel leader who was believed responsible for the assassinations in Herat.

Zaytsev consulted the map again. "That area is totally exposed. There's no possibility of surprise."

"You're right. But it's going to be hard for them to melt back into the mountains if we take them from the air." He drove his right fist into his left palm. "We'll order up an air strike and then take the Caravan team in straight away by helicopter."

"What about the Iranians?"

Sasha shrugged. "Their air force has been rusting away since they kicked out the Shah. They need all the planes and pilots they've got left to fight the Iraqis. They won't do anything except invoke the wrath of Allah. We'll probably be in and out before they even know it."

The Sukhoi fighter-bombers went in at dawn. The drone of the engines carried for miles across the desert, and by the time they reached Abdol Qari's *qarargah*, the guerrillas were already starting to scatter in all directions, on horseback and in trucks and broken-down buses. They even had an old Russian-made tank that must have been captured in fighting across the border. Perhaps it was just for show, because it was abandoned as soon as the jets began their attack, swooping low to strafe the tents and the bearded figures in turbans and floppy woolen hats rolled up at the sides who were tumbling out of the trucks and scrambling to take cover. Some of the Mujahideen were trying to fight back, firing off RPG rockets. But their position was a perfect killing ground for the Soviets. The rebels must have thought themselves secure, so far inside the Iranian border; they would never have let themselves get caught in the open like this in Afghanistan.

Then the big helicopter gunships appeared, buzzing like hornets at the back of the fleeing horsemen. Sasha's group jumped out right in the middle of the *qarargah*, where a few guerrillas were still holding out among the smoking rubble. The Estonian leaped from hut to hut, seemingly indestructible, cutting a swath of death.

There was the crack of a rifle from inside a ruined hut, and the man at Sasha's shoulder gasped and fell headlong.

He heard a shrill cry, *"Allah-o-Akbar!"* and hurled himself into the hut, machine gun blazing.

He found a boy, barely older than Petya, trying to reload an old Lee-Enfield that was taller than he was. He had delicate, almost girlish features, and beautiful almond eyes.

"Harakat!" Sasha shouted at him, gesturing toward the entrance with his gun. "Move out." There was the remains of breakfast on the floor—flat, oily loaves of unleavened bread, a spilled bowl of yoghurt infested with flies.

"Death to Russians!" the boy spat at him. Sasha picked him up bodily and threw him out the door, wondering at the hatred that sustained those people from one generation to the next, and about how many Russians this child had killed.

Zaytsev came riding up on a horse he had stolen from the Afghans. He had several prisoners with him, including Abdol Qari. Sasha was surprised at the man's youth. He appeared to be in his middle twenties. One of the Mujahideen captured with him, a villainous-looking fellow with a hooked beak of a nose like the yellow-chested vultures that were hovering above, could have been Qari's grandfather. There was a terrible fatalism about Qari and the rest of them. They were prepared for death, for any torment of the flesh, if Allah willed it.

They flew back with the prisoners, over mountains whose hollows turned purple as the sun drained from them, to their base camp outside Herat. A Major Mahmoud of the Afghan secret police was already there waiting for them, quivering like a whippet in his eagerness to take charge of the interrogation of Abdol Qari.

"There's a blood feud between their families," the major's KGB adviser whispered to Sasha.

"You're going to let the Afghan run the questioning?" Sasha asked.

"Why not? They know what to expect from each other. The bandits killed about half of Mahmoud's office in Herat. The other half are probably reporting to the Mujahideen," he added cynically. "What a country."

Sasha was aching with hunger and fatigue. He went to find Zaytsev and something to eat. They got hold of some excellent goat's cheese and a couple of bars of chocolate, then ate beside an irrigation ditch on a hill overlooking the valley. The water in the canal tasted as clean and cold as melted snow. Sasha drank greedily. But the stream below them was unnaturally green, almost salad green. The army must have been using chemicals in the area, probably liquid poison to contaminate the wells.

"Don't spit into the well," he quoted the old proverb to Zaytsev. "You may have to drink from it later on."

Zaytsev grunted and went on chewing steadily.

Sasha would have liked to go swimming, but that violent green, and the Afghan abhorrence of any degree of nudity, deterred him. On the far side of the stream, he could see peasants threshing corn the way they had done it from time immemorial, driving yoked oxen around in a tight circle, trampling the stalks with their hooves.

"Do you think it's worth it?" he asked Zaytsev.

"You mean the war? I don't like any of these *chernozhopi,* and I don't like what the war is doing to us. The men don't understand it. They're fed a pack of lies before they're sent out. But you can't live on lies out here. Is it true that they're not sending all the bodies home, to try to disguise the number of casualties?"

"It's true," Sasha agreed.

"We could put up with any number of casualties if the men believed in what they were doing."

"You mean if *we* believed the war could be won this way," Sasha corrected him.

Zaytsev didn't dissent.

"It can only end in one of two ways," Sasha went on. "Either we'll end up swallowing the country whole and spitting out an Afghan Federated Socialist Republic of the USSR, or we'll just declare a victory and go home. The trouble is, our friends on the Central Committee don't see that yet."

"They ought to come down here and watch the black-asses play *buzkashi,* " Zaytsev observed. *Buzkashi* was an Afghan version of polo, in which a headless goat was used for the ball. Hostile tribesmen had been known to use a captured live Soviet soldier in place of the goat. "Is there a way to make them listen, Sasha?" he continued. "Will the Marshal speak for us?"

"He might," Sasha said thoughtfully. "He sees farther than most. He believes in the army more than the Party. I'm in touch with him all the time, even from here."

"That's good. It's time the army found its voice."

Sasha considered this for a moment. Then he clapped Zaytsev on the shoulder and said, "I think I'll go and check on Major Mahmoud."

Zaytsev's eyes narrowed. "I know that bitch. He came along with some of his goons on that raid we made in Shindand district. He deserted under fire, the little prick. I thought for a while that he and his men had gone over to the bandits. When he came crawling back, I wanted to shoot the bitch. Lucky for him one of the commissars showed up."

"Well, let's hope this is something Mahmoud does well."

He had to make an urgent stop on his way to the headquarters compound, squatting behind a tree like an Afghan. However many of those tablets he took, they were never enough to cement the shit together for more than a couple of hours. It was part of Afghanistan's revenge on the *ferenghi*.

Rounding the hill, he caught a whiff of something that he would always associate with the Afghan war, like the stench of carrion: the smell of burning hashish. Down there to his right, partly screened by a boulder, was the Estonian with one of his fellow NCOs. Sasha didn't interfere with them. They had earned their relaxation. But it alarmed him that the Soviet army had learned so quickly to substitute hashish for vodka. You couldn't stop the soldiers trading anything they could lay hands on for the drug—kerosene, diesel oil, looted Afghan property, even guns and ammunition. For the Soviets in Afghanistan, hashish was becoming what marijuana and heroin had been to the Americans in Vietnam. He wondered how that would fit in with Marshal Zotov's scheme of things.

He found Major Mahmoud presiding over a camp table, well protected by a squad of his own men in addition to his KGB adviser.

"Where's Abdol Qari?" Sasha asked.

"He had a weak heart," Mahmoud said straight-faced. "He died under interrogation."

Sasha swore under his breath. The KGB adviser offered him a cigarette. "We got what we needed from one of the others," he said to Sasha in an undertone. "We now know their ringleaders in Herat."

"Next!" Major Mahmoud yelled out.

They brought in the old man, and Mahmoud started hurling questions at him. The old vulture stood there, bound and silent. In response to a further question, he gathered up what little saliva he had in his nearly toothless mouth—he had been denied food and drink—and spat in the major's face. Mahmoud rushed from behind his desk and dealt the Mujahid a terrible blow in the chest with the butt of his pistol.

The old man fell to the dirt floor, his forehead resting on the earth as if he was obeying the call to prayer.

He began to chant. *"Ashahadu anna la ilala illa-llah.* I testify that there is no God but Allah."

"Bala!" Major Mahmoud screamed at him. "Get up!"

Mahmoud had them drag the Mujahid right up to his table. He produced a bayonet and slashed the old man's bonds. Sasha could see the gouge marks where the rope had cut off the blood supply.

Mahmoud grabbed the guerrilla's right hand and slammed it down on top of the camp table.

Holding the sharp edge of the bayonet above the prisoner's knuckles, Mahmoud repeated his question.

The Mujahid started to chant again. *"Ashahadu anna la—"*

Mahmoud raised the bayonet, and brought it down in a rapid chopping motion. When the prisoner was able to pull his hand away, four bloody fingers were left on the table. No sound had escaped from the old man except his patient, monotonous chant.

"Ashahadu anna la Mohammed rasulu-llah," he recited, capping his left hand over the stumps of his fingers, which were spurting blood. It ran down his arms and streaked the sides of his baggy trousers.

Sasha jumped up and started swearing at Mahmoud. Since he was shouting in Russian, the Afghan affected not to understand, even though Sasha was sure he had been to the KGB school in Tashkent. The KGB adviser took Sasha's arm to restrain him.

"We're just their advisers, remember? This is their country. These are their ways. Do you think the bandits treat their captives any better? *S volkamy zjit, po voltchiy vit.* If you live with wolves, howl like them."

"It's not necessary!" Sasha objected.

"Look at that one." The KGB adviser nodded his head at the prisoner. "Do you think he can be reeducated?"

The old man was still at his prayers. He looked like someone who would slit your throat for a couple of roubles, but he burned with the bright flame of a religious martyr.

Mahmoud repeated his question as if there had been no interruption.

He listened thoughtfully as the guerrilla declaimed that Mohammed was the messenger of God, as if this could be the answer he was seeking.

Then he jabbed his bayonet half an inch or more into the old man's flat belly.

This time, the Mujahid groaned aloud, but he went on with his chant. Mahmoud tried him again, with the same results. Finally, Mahmoud wearied of the game, and rammed his bayonet all the way in, up to the hilt.

He wiped the blade clean on the old man's turban, and two of his guards came up to haul the corpse away.

Major Mahmoud smirked, and Sasha realized he would enjoy seeing that man dead. For a treacherous moment he thought, *We've got the wrong Afghans.* He fought to control his reactions, reminding himself that the old man who had been bled in that room like an animal sacrifice had the blood of Russians on his hands.

He had seen enough of Mahmoud's interrogation procedures. But as he was leaving, he saw the next prisoner being dragged in. It was the boy he had captured in that stinking hut in the caravanserai. How old was he? Ten at most.

"Not this one," Sasha said to the KGB adviser in a tone that didn't brook discussion.

The KGB officer entered into a hurried exchange in Dari with Major Mahmoud.

"There's time enough, *inshallah,*" said the Afghan at the end of it.

"Listen to me," Sasha said to the adviser. "I'm going to Herat. When I come back tomorrow morning, I expect to find this one"—he pointed to the boy—"alive."

"Don't worry." The KGB man was too accommodating to be plausible.

Sasha felt a pressing need to go to the latrines, but he waited until he had seen the boy prisoner escorted back to the lock-up. The war, like the country, was merciless. He remembered his reactions when he had first set eyes on the sawtooth peaks of the Hindu Kush. This was not a land that forgave human weakness. And he had accepted that from the beginning. Even the Estonian, a throwback to the eleventh-century Assassins with his hash pipe and his collection of human parts, failed to rouse more than mild distaste. So why did he feel so bitter and angry now? He tried to rationalize his emotions, telling himself that the way the war was being waged would only harden the resolve of the Mujahideen and add to their support among the people. Then he recalled the phrase from one of his father's letters from the front: "We have become our enemy." Yes, that was the danger: what was happening to the army itself. For a start, sadists like Mahmoud had to be put out of business, not for the sake of "bourgeois humanism"—his father's supposed crime—but for the honor and discipline of the army. And because violence was only effective when controlled. He had just planned and mounted a highly successful cross-border operation whose rewards would have been even greater if Abdol Qari were still alive, to be used as an intelligence source, or as a defector who could be displayed on television to demoralize his own followers, or, failing all that, as a hostage.

These were some of the elements Sasha intended to include in his report. He would send it from the command post in Herat that same night, together with his account of the Caravan operation. It would be entertaining to see what kind of protest the Iranians had lodged. And there would be decent food and wine in Herat.

It was dusk as Sasha prepared to leave. The drive to Herat should take forty minutes at the outside, but it was late to be leaving alone. Even during the day the Soviets preferred to move about only in the safety of convoys, sometimes preceded by armored cars and mine detectors. At night the guerrillas owned the countryside. Even in major towns, the bazaars were closing earlier and earlier—in some cases at midday—in expectation of savage fighting as the day wore on.

There was a staff car in the compound, a black Volga. Sasha commandeered it.

Zaytsev came running up. "Where do you think you're going? Dinner's on in the mess."

"I'll eat in Herat," Sasha said.

"Bloody hell. You're not thinking of going by yourself? Hey, you!" Zaytsev called out to a couple of men who were walking toward the barracks. "Get a jeep and a Dashka. You'll accompany Colonel Preobrazhensky to Herat."

Sasha recognized the Estonian and his friend. "You certainly picked a fine escort," he remarked to Zaytsev. "They're having visions of meeting the houris in paradise."

The Estonian did, indeed, look a little disoriented when he reappeared with the jeep.

"They'll go first," Zaytsev said firmly. "I'd rather have those fuckheads run over a mine than you." The guerrillas were cutting up the unexploded bombs that were lying around all over the place and making highly effective mines out of them. They were also getting deliveries of Italian *plastique*, which was no less lethal.

"All right, all right." Sasha patted Zaytsev's arm. "Anything you want in Herat?"

"Well, she'd be about—" Zaytsev defined the measurements with his hands.

"I'll see you in the morning."

Night closed like shutters over the twisting road through the hills. The car bucked under Sasha, and he thought the Estonian must be better off in the jeep. But a sore backside was at least better than falling asleep at the wheel, which he might otherwise have done, passively following the tail-lights ahead of him.

He jerked more fully awake as the jeep ahead veered over to the side of the road. He saw the headlights of a truck approaching them, a big Soviet truck, probably the first of a convoy. He gently depressed the brake pedal, swinging over behind the Estonian.

In the dark of a quarter-moon, he saw only patches of what followed. He heard the driver of the truck honk, as if in greeting, then saw the tarpaulin covering the back of the vehicle yanked up, and a group of men in turbans spurting fire at the jeep. He saw the Estonian, slowed by hash-ish, hurl himself behind the heavy machine gun, but couldn't know that the first bullet from the volley fired by the Mujahideen pierced the left ventricle, the atrium, and the aorta of the Estonian's heart. The jeep lurched off the road, leaving Sasha alone to face the guerrillas in the truck.

He ducked his head into the steering wheel, not fast enough. He felt a scorching pain high up in his chest. His hands fell from the wheel, and the car went spinning off the road. He was coasting close to a cliff, dimly aware of the valley below. The Mujahideen didn't bother to see whether he was dead or alive. The truck followed him off the road, ramming the side of the black Volga, until it teetered over the cliff.

Sasha was hurled around the car like a squash ball as it rolled over and over down the slope to the very edge of an irrigation canal. The pain subsided into a porous darkness. When he came round, the car was lying on its back like a beetle. He was vaguely aware that he ought to be thankful for the poor quality of Soviet gasoline. Otherwise, the car would certainly have burst into flame. Somehow, he managed to wrench the door open. He fell, rather than crawled, outside. Each time he moved, he felt that somebody was beating him down with a red-hot poker.

How much time had passed? There was no way of knowing. He lay on his back, breathing with difficulty, looking up at constellations he couldn't name. *The radio.* He rolled back to the car, but the transceiver was dead.

An instinct stronger than the desire to lie still told him that he couldn't stay there. The guerrillas might return. He started to crawl along the

valley, pausing to wash off some of the blood with the chill water of the
irrigation ditch. There was a fire somewhere ahead. It became his lighthouse. He swam toward it, hand over hand.

He collapsed at the door of a house set in the side of a hillside above the
canal like a beehive. The blackness swirled up and enveloped him again.
Then he was conscious of someone inspecting him, a figure covered in
dark cloth from head to foot like an angel of death, peering through a veil
with eyes that were blacker than the cloth.

The voice that croaked, "Help—a doctor—" in Dari seemed uncon-
nected to him.

The shape disappeared, and he heard voices raised nearby, inside the
house.

Someone—a woman—was screeching, "He's a Soviet! Kill him like a
dog!"

A man's voice, measured and calm, replied, "He has asked for refuge,
and we can't refuse him. Remember *ninawati*. Remember the code."

"But Masoud! His people killed your own son! He's an infidel!"

"He has invoked our law. It is our duty to protect him, even at the
expense of our lives. So it is written."

6 For months after Sasha left New York, Elaine drifted like a rudderless
boat that had slipped its moorings.

The personnel manager at X-Tech called her in and fidgeted, seeking
the right euphemism to tell her she was fired.

"It's all right," she helped him. "I was planning to hand in my notice
anyway."

She had no doubt what had happened. The FBI had told Charlie Macdonough about her relationship with Sasha.

The personnel manager looked less embarrassed. "You're entitled to one
month's salary," he told her. She left him in mid-sentence as he was
explaining about pension rights.

She stayed in her loft for days at a time. When friends called to invite
her out, she gave the same answer. "I'm going away."

She would wake with a start at four in the morning from a terrible,
recurring dream, in which she scaled a great tower, like a broken ziggurat.
Sasha was at the top, but when she touched him, he was cold and hard as
a mortuary slab, and she found that her hand was powdered with a fine

white ash. Then she was falling out of the dream, into the loneliest hollow of the night.

She would sit at her table, with a blanket over her knees, waiting for the throb of the morning traffic to begin, jotting down random notes. *I am a dry husk. I am a field of stubble.*

She felt his absence the way an amputee feels a missing limb and reaches to touch it, despite himself.

She was two months overdue with her rent when her father flew up from Florida to see her.

"I've been worried about you," he reproved her mildly. "You've even stopped answering your phone."

"I'm sorry, Daddy. I've been trying to write."

A practical man, he inspected the refrigerator. He found some yogurt, half a lettuce, and a grapefruit.

"First thing, I'm going to take you to lunch," he announced. "You can't live on coffee and rabbit food."

He guessed far more than she admitted to him. "Forgetting is a survival mechanism," he told her. "You can't drive through life looking into the rearview mirror. Life is all about starting over."

She nodded, and pecked at her swordfish.

"Do you want to tell me about him?" her father asked.

"Not really." It sounded too curt, so she added, "I think you'd like each other."

"So it's not over."

"No." That much he had left her. Hope. *And this hollowness, the aching sensation that I am incomplete.*

Her father had more questions, and she turned them aside as gently as she could.

"There are things that have to be worked out, Daddy. I'm really not ready to talk about it. But thank you."

"I fixed things with your landlord," he said, feeling more secure with tangibles. "But I think you ought to get out of the city for a while. Why don't you come to Israel with me this year?"

So she spent a week with him at the King David Hotel in Jerusalem, and walked the streets of the old city, and met a lively young Sabra called Arnon who squired her around the Armenian quarter and told her he had just completed his annual stint with the commandos. He was alert and attractive, and she knew she was testing herself when she agreed to have dinner with him.

"The Russians are scared of us," Arnon said at one point. "We know them too well. Take me, for example. I have cousins in Kiev."

"Are you in contact with them?"

"They're trying to emigrate. They lost their jobs, of course, when they applied. But sometimes it's possible to talk to them by phone. It drives the KGB crazy, having to listen in to conversations in Hebrew. I'd like to go over there, but it's not easy for an Israeli. And it's forbidden for me because of my military duties. Now you, you're American. No problem. But if they know you're Jewish, you have to watch out. They see Zionists under every rock."

It wasn't this that frightened her. She had thought, many times, of following Sasha to Moscow. It was fear for him, fear of putting him in danger if she tried to see him, that held her back. That, and a greater fear: of going to Moscow and not seeing him, of accepting that the loss was irretrievable.

The wine flowed, and the conversation shifted to lighter topics. But when Arnon took her hand, she shied away so abruptly that she knocked over her glass.

"I'm sorry," she apologized as he mopped wine from his shirt.

"You're not married, are you?" he said, studying her with a slightly mocking smile.

She shook her head.

"But there's someone," he suggested.

"There's someone," she agreed.

"I envy him."

She was grateful for his gracious withdrawal, and they promised to write, the way people do when they want to dress up a flat good-bye.

She never heard from him again. But the holiday in Israel, and the talk with Arnon, helped to form a project in Elaine's mind. It was something that might give her the discipline and the purpose that she needed to cope with Sasha's absence—and to find him again, at least in spirit.

She began roughing out a plan for a novel spanning several generations of a Russian Jewish family. She swallowed her pride and accepted financial help from her father—though she insisted the money was a loan—and rented a tumble-down cottage near the water on the Noyack side of Sag Harbor. She arrived on a raw March day, and tried to stick to an eight-hour working schedule each day. Sasha was a hidden presence on every page she wrote. The writing did not dispel the sense of emptiness that still inhabited her, but for those eight hours it kept it at bay. She made new friends, including an editor who commissioned a couple of articles for a glossy magazine that paid well, and a fisherman who took her out to chase bass. She also discovered, after a few months, what she had known to begin with: she would have to go to Sasha's country.

While the summer people were still flocking east to the Hamptons, she drove back to the city and enrolled for the fall semester of the Russian course at the New School. This time, she managed to show up for the first lesson.

The second Wednesday night, a new student attended the Russian class. He was older than the others, and he wore a worsted suit that gave him a vaguely professorial look, reinforced by his pipe, which he sucked on throughout the class but didn't light.

The teacher introduced him to the others by his first name, Luke. In keeping with the name, he had a leisurely, euphonious Southern accent. It gave a bourbon flavor to the Russian phrases he tried hard to pronounce.

"If they ever develop a taste for Old Grandad in Russia," one of the students said to him as they were waiting for the elevator, "you can do the commercials."

He exchanged some pleasantries with her as they went their separate ways, and she didn't think about Luke until the following week, when he asked her to have a cup of coffee with him after the class.

She inspected him more closely. He was quite distinguished, with his silver hair and his salt-and-pepper moustache. Fifty, probably, but well preserved. She liked his hands; they were fine and narrow, like a painter's.

She said, "This wouldn't be a pick-up, would it? I've sort of given up men."

"That sounds like a New Year's resolution."

She liked the way his chin dimpled when he smiled. There was something reassuring about that.

They went into Beefsteak Charlie's, down the block, and made proper introductions.

"I'm Luke Gladden."

"And you're a Southerner."

"Well, that's a large piece of real estate, ma'am," he said, parodying the style. "I come from Louisiana, and I'm French on my mother's side."

She found herself talking to him readily, maybe because he honed in on things she was ready to share. After prying out of her the fact that she was working on a novel, he didn't pursue the theme—which, for her, was still taboo. Instead, he asked about how she got the words on paper.

"You know what they say," she told him. "Writing is easy. All you have to do is sit down and open a vein."

"I've heard that," he laughed, "and I'm ready to believe it. Tell me something. Do you write fast, or slow?"

"Pretty fast, when I manage to chain myself up and actually do it. That way, it's easier to suspend your own disbelief in what you're doing, easier not to see the blank spaces between the lines."

"That's my experience too. In the riverboat days, on the lower Mississippi, they had some extraordinary races. The captains would rip up the timbers from their own decks to keep the furnace stoked up. Don't you get that feeling sometimes when the creative fires are burning? You consume your own timbers."

"Are you a writer?" Elaine asked, astonished by how close this man from Louisiana had come to her own feelings.

"Just an observer," he replied, and she felt a sudden chill.

To exorcise it, she said, "You didn't ask me why I'm studying Russian."

The silver hair, the courtly Southern manners, the sensitive hands with the discreet signet ring didn't redeem his answer. It was the last thing she wanted him to say.

"I think I know why you're learning Russian."

7 When they threw the stretcher on the ground, Sasha was roused in such pain that he thought they must have broken his back. There were voices all around, harsh and repetitive, like crows'. He was lying in the dust in some open place, with a hot white sun glaring into his eyes. He must have been unconscious for hours. He tried to speak, but his parched tongue wouldn't respond. A veiled woman bent over him, as if to make out what he wanted to say. But instead, she drew aside a corner of the veil long enough to spit full into his face.

He clutched at a word, the word the old man who had come to his defense the night before had used. *Ninawati*, the Afghan code of honor that ordained hospitality for those who sought help. He could only form the syllables with his lips. A white-haired man came near and looked at him with something akin to pity, and he wondered if this was his protector. If so, the man's power had failed, for younger men in turbans and bandoliers came and dragged him from the stretcher into the center of the field. It was almost like a playing field, he thought through a red haze, mostly stamped earth, and there were sticks poking out of the ground, like makeshift goals.

There was the crows' cawing again, and then a new sound, of snorting and stamping, and the profile of a horseman suddenly rose above him, blocking out the sun, as immense as the Hindu Kush from where he lay, helpless and prostrate. The horseman was grinning from ear to ear, and brandishing an unusual weapon. No, more like a hockey stick. The horseman wheeled away, and Sasha felt the hot breath of his mount, and saw that there were others on the field.

There were shouts, and in the thunder of galloping hooves, Sasha recognized a scene he had never hoped to witness firsthand. These Afghans were going to play *buzkashi*, their grisly version of polo, and *he* was the ball.

Not yet, he thought. *Not here. I haven't begun to fight.*

The crows screeched, and he hurled himself onto his side and rolled as far as he could. Something scraped and seared for an instant, and he rolled again to escape a horse's trampling hooves. He was conscious of a rider bringing his mount around, preparing for a second charge.

There was a crackling sound, small and insignificant, like the splutter of a string of Tom Thumb fireworks, and the *buzkashi* players started racing away in all directions, all except one of the riders, who bore down on Sasha swinging his stick in a great arc, like a saber. Sasha writhed, and rolled his body the other way. The movement caused him such exquisite pain that he hardly felt the stab of the horse's hoof as it tore skin and flesh from his lower neck. The rider was thrown from his saddle, but he took the fall well and was up again in an instant, advancing on Sasha with something in his hand that was shorter and more lethal than any hockey stick.

From behind Sasha's head, a man in a black mask came ducking and weaving through the crossfire. Without breaking his run, he pumped a dozen rounds from his kalashnikov into the Afghan's stomach. He crouched low over Sasha, his broad back between the wounded man and the sniper fire from the retreating Afghan tribesman, and felt for his pulse.

Zaytsev pulled off his mask to breathe more freely, and called to his men to bring up a stretcher.

"You'll live, Sasha," he murmured. "You'll tell them in Moscow what kind of games they play here."

A long time afterward—impossible for him to tell whether it was a week or a month—Sasha swam out of his coma like a half-drowned man emerging from the surf. His eyelids seemed to be glued together. When he got them unstuck, his first reaction was to cover them up again with the back of his hand. Light reflected off the white walls and the metal frame of the bed jabbed at him like needles. There were flowers beside the bed, masses of them, yellow and red.

He sensed a woman's shape, bending over him, and tried to shape a name. *Elaine.*

It was Petya who saved him. "Daddy! Daddy!" The boy broke loose from his mother's grip and started kissing Sasha's hand. Sasha couldn't speak, but the tears welled up in his eyes. He was in Moscow.

That evening, Marshal Zotov came to visit. The nurses flustered over the old warrior with his seven rows of ribbons and the big stars on his shoulder straps.

"How are you?" he greeted Sasha.

"Zinda basham," Sasha croaked. "I'm still alive." It was what you said to an Afghan who posed the same question.

"Speak Russian, will you? Or did they turn you into a black-ass down there?"

The Marshal had brought a practical gift, a bottle of his Armenian brandy. The nurses frowned when he set it on the table, but didn't dare to say anything.

"You'd better hurry up and get well," he told Sasha. "Great things are happening, and I need you at my side. I've got plans for you."

"By the way," he added as he was leaving, "you're a full colonel now. And they gave you another gong. The Order of the Red Star."

Sasha could only groan. For a moment, as consciousness receded, he was flat on his back in the dust, with the hooves drumming across the field toward him.

He felt stronger the next day, when the Marshal returned.

"You were damn lucky, you know," Zotov said. "The bullet came that close"—he held up thumb and forefinger, an inch apart—"to your heart." He didn't mention the *buzkashi* match, except to mutter "savages" under his breath.

Seeing that Sasha was more alert, the Marshal launched into his new recipe for Afghanistan, which involved strikes into Pakistan. The Indians were being armed to the hilt; if the Pakistanis refused to seal their border, India could be encouraged to invade. Above all, the Soviets needed to act with maximum force.

"You read Annenkov, I hope?" Zotov had brought his copy along, in case Sasha wanted to refresh his memory. "Yes, here we are." He thumbed the book open and read out approvingly, "Once the enchantment of prestige is broken, once a people accustomed to give way before disciplined troops loses this habit, it becomes indispensable to employ efforts of a very much more powerful character to restore respect." The Marshal slammed the book shut and said, "That hits the mark. We need something like Geok-Tepe." This was the stronghold of the fierce Tekke tribesmen who inflicted a bloody defeat on a Russian column. When the Russians finally captured the fortress in 1879, they slaughtered everyone inside. "Well?" Zotov demanded. "What do you say?"

"I don't know that it will work with men who believe that death is the gate to paradise." Sasha thought of the white-bearded rebel who had gone on chanting the call to prayer after Major Mahmoud chopped off his fingers.

Zotov looked annoyed that his lesson from history hadn't been better received. He said, "No man confronted with death can feel certain about his chances in the afterlife."

"These men aren't like others."

The Marshal shifted his weight on the edge of the bed, and for an instant Sasha felt the earth tremble again under the racing hooves, heard the women's mocking cries, and smelled the rank odor of his own flesh, soiled and damp as if his guts had been laid open. The tang of ammonia that hung about the hospital ward couldn't erase that.

6.
HOUSE OF LIES

I spoke the truth, but no one believed me, so I took to deceit.

—LERMONTOV

1   In his dream, Nikolsky was swimming in a shallow lake, with a slip of
    a girl who seemed to have gills instead of lungs. He pursued her
underwater, but she always eluded him. It was warm in the lake, but the
trees in the park were leafless, and the men who were loitering on the
pathway wore overcoats and fur hats. He realized that they were going
through the clothes he had left jumbled up on the bench. He scrambled
out and ran dripping toward them. A man with a loose, putty-colored face
—it might have been Topchy—inspected him in a leisurely fashion.
"You're wanted right away," he said. They bundled him into his clothes,
but his papers were missing and they wouldn't allow him time to put on
his shoes. A second man, short but very powerfully built, with wiry red
hair and a loud checked suit, was jumping up and down in his impatience.
He looked like a real psychopath, itching for an excuse to give Nikolsky a
good working-over. Then they were hustling him along, but somehow he
managed to persuade them to let him make a phone call. When he dialed,
he heard a plummy English voice saying, "Royal Stationery Office." It
sounded a bit like that girl he had tried to pick up in London.

"Please get off the line," Nikolsky said.

But he was stuck with her, so he began giving her messages to relay for
him. It was terribly important, he kept trying to explain. He wasn't sure
whether she had understood when the connection was broken, and the
men in fur hats were shoving him into a big gray bus, like the one the
Mission used in New York. There were lots of bruisers inside, sprawled out
on the floor, leaving no room to pass; he tripped over their legs as he was
pushed through one compartment into another.

Someone shouted, "Here's the whiphouse!" and he was thrust into a
tiny, filthy lavatory with a heavy metal door that could be forced open
only a few inches before it slammed shut. The ginger-haired psycho was
roaring with laughter.

Then, all at once, they had dragged him into a huge room, packed with
men who had an unpleasant, greenish sheen to their faces and clothes. He
could see Drinov sitting in a place of honor, smirking. A chubby fellow in

the front row bounced up. He had a long, crumpled piece of paper, like a laundry list, in his hand, and Nikolsky realized that it was the list of accusations against him. "My name is Krupchenko," the fat man began.

Nikolsky felt them grab him by the shoulders, and yelled, "Not yet!" He woke to find Olga peering into his face.

"Are you sick, Feliks? It's not like you to talk in your sleep."

"What did I say?" He was suddenly wide awake.

"I couldn't make it out."

"Go back to sleep." He kissed her.

But the baby started wailing in the next room, and she got up to see to it.

He made himself coffee in the kitchen and laced it with a couple of fingers of brandy. When she came in to rinse out the baby's bottle, Olga said, "Is it something at the office?"

"Just a bad dream," Nikolsky smiled at her. What made their marriage perfect, Nikolsky reflected, was that Olga would never insist. He didn't have to tell her that the inquisition into the Hansen fiasco was still going on, and that Drinov was determined to cut off his balls. Still, old Ike, his boss in New York, had stood up for him. There was a chance, just a chance, that they'd post him abroad again soon just to smooth everything over. He knew there was a vacancy coming up in London. If they offered it to him, he would grab it. Maybe he ought to grab it and never come back. Maybe that's what the dream was telling him. The coffee or the thought made him shudder, and he dribbled a bit more brandy into his mug.

Olga didn't pass judgment. She never did. But she said, "Are you going to be late tonight, Feliks?" She was looking as flirtatious as she could manage with her hair still in curlers and a drab flannel nightgown that didn't disguise how much her body had thickened since her last pregnancy.

"Sasha's been promoted," he told her. "We're going to celebrate." He didn't have to tell her not to wait up. But he squeezed her and said, "You're a good kid," before kissing the children and helping himself to another slug to get him through the dry morning out at the Village.

2 If you were going out on the town with Feliks, it was not a good idea to drive, especially in Moscow, where Sasha's special license tags could not be relied upon to have the same magical effect on the militia that his DPL plates had had on the police in New York. Things had happened quickly since Sasha's convalescence. He had been sent to the General Staff academy, and when he came out, it was to find the country with a new leader and his father-in-law, Marshal Zotov, poised to take the final, decisive step toward control of the armed forces. Feliks had been proved right. Using the files of the KGB to mute dissent, Andropov had managed to steal the succession from his many rivals. The last obstacle in his path was cleared when he managed to seal a pact with the Defense Minister. It didn't escape Sasha's attention that the army was already beginning to be acknowledged as a kingmaker.

So the country, having been exposed to the spectacle of old Leonid Ilych dying in front of television cameras and massed crowds over a period of years, was now privileged to hear rumors of Brezhnev's successor wasting away behind closed doors. Such rumors were already circulating—rumors about the arrival of kidney dialysis machines from West Germany, doctors from Sweden. How it would end was a matter for speculation. There was Askyerov, wheedling and conspiring at Andropov's elbow, trying to recruit a loyal cabal of supporters. The KGB, which the two of them represented, had never been so influential. Even the ministry of interior had been handed over to a general of the KGB. But the power of the army had grown too.

"We put Yuri Vladimirovich where he sits," the Marshal had bragged to Sasha after his graduation from the staff college. "And he'd better remember it. He's not our man, of course, not a bit, but he's the smartest of that bunch." Zotov was contemptuous of Brezhnev's cronies; the *Banda*, or "gang," was how Moscow gossip described them. He was particularly scornful of Chernenko, a yes-man and a slogan-maker who had spent his entire life in Brezhnev's shadow, since their early days together in Moldavia, a fistful of real estate on the borders of the Ukraine that Stalin had snatched from Rumania at the end of the war. Chernenko had been Andropov's chief rival until the high command decided to follow the example of the KGB and throw its support behind the former Chairman of State Security. Deals had been made with the Defense Minister and the Chief of Staff, and Zotov, seeing which way the wind was blowing, had gone along with them. But in private, as he said to Sasha, "Andropov is a dying man resting on a house of cards. One puff—" He blew out the air like a bellows.

Lydia had come into her own in the weeks Sasha had spent rebuilding his strength at the dacha in the Silver Forest, fussing over him like an indulgent nanny.

"You see, you need me when you're down," she would say to him, before regaling him with the latest Moscow gossip or a long jeremiad about how Petya was becoming unmanageable, forever scrapping with his schoolmates, or how reliable household help was impossible to find.

She was proud of Sasha's wartime exploits, and showed him off to her friends as if he were an exhibit. Her patriotism was of the raw, old-fashioned kind. It sickened him to hear her recounting a romanticized version of his Afghan campaigns to Petya and her visitors, but he lay silent until he was strong enough to go off on long solitary rambles among the birches.

I've gained more than I lost, he reassured himself. He had found others in the army who were angered by the waste and shame of a war fought by stupid means for stupid reasons. That anger, if harnessed properly, would help to change Russia. He was less alone than before.

He expressed something of this to Zotov after his graduation from the staff academy. He was expecting one of the Marshal's eruptions. Instead, the older man heard him out patiently.

"I hear you," was all the Marshal said by way of comment. "I was at the front myself, don't forget."

The next day, Zotov made his proposal. Characteristically, he delivered it in the form of an order. "You'll come and work for me at the General Staff. As my personal assistant." Sasha had started to point out that this might be less than politic, given their family relationship. Mightn't those who were jealous of Zotov, or nervous of his power, complain that he was practicing nepotism, favoring his own family in just the way that the Brezhnev clique had made notorious?

"You're talking cunt!" Zotov had cut him off. "Let them think I'm vulnerable. Let Askyerov go crawling to Yuri Vladimirovich if he likes. That's fine. It will make all that gang feel more secure. I need a man beside me I can trust completely. I can't tell you everything yet, Sasha. It would be premature. But you've got a good nose. I still remember our little talk at Livadia. You sniffed out Andropov, and Askyerov. You have an instinct for events that have barely begun to shape themselves, trends that others don't see. And since you got your whiff of gunpowder fighting the black-asses in Afghanistan, you've got a sense of the kind of men we need to run things. I know I can count on you."

In his usual style, the Marshal didn't leave space for argument.

He merely added, "Naturally, we'll have to do something about those shoulder straps of yours. It wouldn't do for the First Deputy to the Chief of Staff, a Marshal of the Soviet Union, to have a mere colonel as an assistant."

So Sasha became a major-general, and the numbers on the license plate of his black Volga had the prefix "MO" that was reserved for senior officials of the General Staff. But he wasn't driving tonight.

It was an easy walk from the yellowish mock-Grecian portals of the vast General Staff complex that sprawled along Gogol Boulevard to the beer-bar Zhiguli, where Sasha and Nikolsky had arranged to meet. But Sasha had gone home first to change out of his army uniform, with its intimidating—and possibly compromising—new badges of rank, and re-emerged from the Arbat metro station. Walking along Kalinin Prospekt, with its continuous glass-and-aluminum facade under the stark white tower blocks, Sasha always experienced a vague sense of loss for the priceless architecture that had fallen to the wrecker's ball when he was a boy, being steered around the city in the firm grip of his grandmother.

As always, there was a long line outside the Zhiguli, mostly composed of out-of-towners, stamping their feet to keep warm. Their breath condensed in front of their faces like ectoplasm. They looked at Sasha's foreign-made overcoat resentfully.

A taxi pulled up, and Nikolsky jumped out.

"Good evening, General!" he called out cheerily. "You see, I was calling you the right thing all the time."

Sasha felt real pleasure as Feliks grabbed him in a bear hug. But he was shocked at the way Nikolsky looked. His face was puffier than before, and unnaturally flushed, except for the bags under his eyes, which were a fishbelly color. He was nattily turned out, like he used to be, but his suit had horizontal creases around the middle, as if the buttons needed loosening.

He's in a corkscrew dive, Sasha thought.

Nikolsky squired Sasha up to the glass doors of the bar. Some of the people waiting in line started to grumble and swear as Feliks eased his way through.

"*Izvinite*," he mumbled. "Excuse me. Our friends are inside."

The doorman greeted Nikolsky like an old comrade and ushered them in. Nikolsky shook hands with him, leaving a rouble in his palm. The drunk in charge of the cloakroom barely stirred as they deposited their coats, after carefully stuffing their hats inside the sleeves—an indispensable precaution if you expected to see your hat again.

A thin wooden partition screened the drinking area from the crowd outside. It was dim under the muddy orange lights. The patrons were packed in around square oak tables. But three or four tables were vacant, reserved for special friends of the house—which really meant special friends of the waiters since, in a Soviet hostelry, the waiter is god.

Feliks winked at a tall man in a white jacket who was tramping around the tables with a dozen pint-mugs of beer on a tray. The waiter was florid and big-bellied, but he stomped along like a parade-ground cadet, his spine ramrod straight.

He got rid of his load, and came over to them.

"This is Volodya," Nikolsky introduced him to Sasha. "We all call him Pauk—Spider. Pauk is a man with almost as much influence as the Central Committee. You'd better be careful what you say to him."

Pauk gave them the best table, over by the left wall, equidistant from the bar at the front and the kitchen at the back.

Feliks winked at the waiter and said, "*Po-chut-chut?* A little something?"

Pauk came back with two frothing mugs of beer and a bottle of vodka in a paper bag. Officially the Zhiguli sold only beer, excellent bitter that you could be sure wasn't watered down because they delivered it from the brewery in vats that were hooked up directly to the pumps at the bar. This explained the Zhiguli's popularity: honest beer, at forty-seven kopeks a pint. A favored customer, like Feliks, could naturally arrange to get a bottle of vodka or brandy, but nobody would dream of flaunting this privilege by putting it on the table. This wasn't for fear of the law. In respect of the law, the Zhiguli was well set up. There, sitting by himself across the room from Sasha and Nikolsky, was the beer-bar's mascot, a heavyset MVD man in plainclothes, getting quietly sozzled. No, it was just that you didn't show off in public. Otherwise, you risked getting your face smashed in by somebody who had had a couple of beers and was fed up with queues and empty shelves. So Nikolsky stowed the paper bag away between his feet, tore off the top of the bottle, and poured for himself and Sasha under the table.

"Pauk went to school with me," Nikolsky said, nodding his chin at the waiter. "He was quite a roughneck. The teachers were scared to chew him out. I thought he would turn out a crook or end up wearing high boots like you, General. But you became a real aristocrat, didn't you, Pauk?" he addressed the waiter as he returned with a big plate of appetizers, dry salted fish and *raki*, tasty river crabs. "Now you can turn up your nose at anyone."

"How did he get to be a waiter?" Sasha asked as Pauk hurried off to see to a minor disturbance that had broken out at a table over by the kitchen, where a drunken patron had grabbed his companion by the throat. The militiaman wasn't taking any interest. He went on drinking steadily while Pauk and another waiter frog-marched the drunk out the back. That was the way things were at the Zhiguli. Just try complaining about the bill and the waiters would explain it to you with their boots, out in the men's room.

"Well, Pauk did his military service, of course. Believe it or not, he's a general's son. They made him a guard at one of those test sites they build like stage sets. You know the ones."

Sasha nodded. He had visited one of the nuclear test areas with the Marshal. It was built like a replica of an American town, with live animals in place of people, to check blast and fallout effects.

"After the army," Feliks went on, "Pauk just bummed around for a while. He was a taxi driver for a while, then he landed a job as a telephone repairman at the Centralni Telegraf on Gorky Street."

This detail pricked Sasha's interest. The Centralni Telegraf was Moscow's main telephone exchange. It might be useful to have someone who knew the layout.

"But Pauk wasn't made for regular work. He started hustling, buying blue jeans from the tourists. No doubt he would have ended in a bad way except he fell in with another of our school chums, a real crook, called Arkady, who told him that a waiter in a place like this can take in two or three hundred roubles a night, what with the tips and the way they figure out the bills. Hey, Pauk!" He called his friend back to illustrate his point. "What's this charge for?"

Pauk squinted at the indecipherable scrap of paper.

"Oh, that." He grinned. "That's my collar size."

"Have you got anything planned for tonight?"

The waiter consulted his watch. "I was fixing to leave early and go to Ismailovsky Park. How about you?"

"We're with you." Nikolsky turned to Sasha. "What do you say?"

"Whatever you like." Sasha shrugged. By night, Ismailovsky Park, in the north of the city, was a favorite haunt for dating couples, and the restaurant there had a certain reputation as Moscow's version of a singles bar. "I'd better call Lydia."

They went on drinking and talking about inconsequential things until around ten, when Pauk made his arrangements with the head waiter. It was always possible to get a couple of hours off if you had a spare ten roubles. So far, Sasha and Nikolsky had steered well away from the things they had talked about quite freely in New York—the changes in the leadership, the conditions inside the army and the KGB, the people on their mutual shit-list. They even avoided Afghanistan. Feliks cracked one joke after another, but his humor that night seemed forced.

The taxi ride to Ismailovsky Park took forty minutes. The Restaurant Lesnoi stood alone among the oaks and elms, ringed with private cars, including a big white Mercedes. From the outside, it looked like a modern bistro in Brussels or Cologne, a one-story building with too much glass. Inside, it was a hunting lodge. In the lobby, Nikolsky made a deep bow to a stuffed gray wolf before tossing his fur hat in the direction of its head. The hat missed the ears, slid down the muzzle, and remained suspended from the nose. There was already a pile of coats on the wolf's back, to which Sasha added his own.

Inside, the police were already at work, evicting the patrons from their tables. Officially, the establishment shut down at 10:30.

"Drink up and get out!" a burly militiaman bellowed at one group. As the people rose to leave, he grabbed the glasses that were still part full and finished off the contents himself.

But the militiamen didn't fuss with the drinkers in the booths. Rules were elastic; they stretched or contracted depending on who you were dealing with. They were a colorful crowd, the people in these booths fashioned to look like rustic cabins, walled with raw logs crisscrossed and bound tightly together. There were plenty of Georgians, the kind who are never short of cash. There were some Italian tourists; the band at the Lesnoi was renowned for its version of Italian pop music, and had a singer who did a passable impression of Adrianna Chilintana, who was all the rage in Moscow. These tourists were always well received, because they were bound to have something to trade, if only a pair of decent shoes or a transistor radio. The girls who were squeezed into the booths came from just about anywhere.

"It's not First Avenue," Nikolsky commented, "but it's as close as we come."

One of the militiamen looked at them speculatively, but they were in good hands, thanks to Pauk, who was trading favors with the Lesnoi's head waiter. They were soon jammed into one of the booths, together with some Georgian black marketeers and the girls they had just picked up. The Georgians were friendly-drunk; it was debatable whether they had passed the aggressive stage or hadn't reached it yet.

When the militia finished clearing up the less favored patrons, and their drinks, the fun began. For five roubles the band would play the song you wanted. The Georgians were throwing their money around, and vodka and brandy flowed up and down the table in a continuous stream.

Nikolsky called out to the band, requesting an Adrianna Chilintana number, "If You Don't Work, You Don't Make Love." The girl sitting next to him clapped her hands. She was pretty, with dark curly hair, big eyes, and a slightly upturned nose. Feliks was fishing around for money to give to the band leader. He came up with a wad of rouble certificates. The band leader looked nervous; there were still a couple of militiamen drinking at the bar.

"Don't worry, I'll change it for you," the girl said. "I work in a *beryozka* shop." In a flash, she had pocketed Nikolsky's certificate and given him its face value, ten roubles. It was worth several times as much, since it could be used in the hard-currency stores to buy Western goods.

"Don't you think there's something wrong with the rate of exchange?" Feliks asked indulgently.

"Don't get angry." She nibbled his ear. "We'll settle up later."

"What's your name?"

"Yelena."

"All right, Yelena. Let's see what you've got." Feliks pulled her onto the dance floor, motioning for Sasha to follow with her friend, a pert little blonde who was giggly-drunk. People were swirling or teetering around, swapping partners, and singing along with the band loud enough to bring the roof down. Nikolsky nudged Sasha and said, "*Kogo zgreb, togo yevyob.* You fuck the one you grab. That's the rule here."

Sasha ended up with Yelena. The blonde was all over Feliks. She had got his shirt part unbuttoned and was running her hand up and down over his chest. The Georgians had now drunk enough to get angry. One of them smashed his glass against the table and raised the jagged glass threateningly.

"Leave this to me," Pauk intervened.

In an instant, the two militiamen from the bar were kicking the Georgians out the door. When Sasha and Feliks emerged with the girls, they caught a glimpse of the Georgians speeding off in the white Mercedes. They seemed to be driving straight toward a massive oak, but veered aside at the last moment with a scream of rubber.

There were lots of taxis waiting outside the Lesnoi.

"But where are we going?" Sasha said to Nikolsky as they all piled into one.

"It's all arranged," Feliks reassured him. "Chertanovo," he instructed the driver.

But the man turned around, opened one of the back doors, and said, "You can walk, fuck your mother. I'm not going to Chertanovo."

It was on the other side of the city, one of those districts of faceless concrete apartment blocks that Nikita put up and were sometimes called, in his honor, *Khruschevi*—a play on words between the name of the former Soviet leader and a term that referred to the riff-raff of Soviet society. The taxi driver's reluctance was understandable. Chertanovo was a two-hour drive from Ismailovsky Park. Sasha wasn't amused at the prospect either. "It's late as it is," he began to point out.

Nikolsky wasn't going to be deflected. "I'll pay for the round trip," he said. At the prospect of collecting double fare, the driver's attitude changed dramatically. The blonde dozed off along the way, and only stopped snoring when Feliks started probing aggressively under her dress. Yelena complained about the distance, obviously disappointed that these well-dressed men were taking them out to the sticks. Feliks had to steer the driver block by block through the anonymous maze when they reached Chertanovo. The buildings all looked alike, and were set so far back from the roadway that you couldn't make out the inscriptions on the street signs attached to the walls.

"What do you expect?" Nikolsky said. "This is Bangladesh."

The apartment was cramped but pleasantly furnished. There were African initiation masks in the hallway, fancy wallpaper and drapes that must have been ordered from a duty-free catalog, and a svelte, powerful Scandinavian hi-fi in the living room, which Feliks immediately identified as the Transit Hall. You had to go through the living room to get to the bedroom, which was done up in soft pastels, with a huge, gilt-framed mirror above the bed. Nikolsky sent the girls out to the kitchen to fix drinks and snacks, while he picked up some of the debris. There was a pile of soiled sheets on the floor in the bedroom, which he started stuffing into a closet.

"We have six sets of sheets," he explained to Sasha. "There isn't always time to go to the laundry."

He opened a drawer in the bedroom dresser and showed Sasha pack upon pack of American-made condoms, in every conceivable shape and color.

"Souvenirs of Manhattan," he said.

Moscow's contraceptives factory was notorious for the poor quality of its products. The women said they weren't reliable; the men said they were so thick it was like having sex inside a raincoat.

"Whose apartment is this?" Sasha asked.

"Someone in the Service, a friend of mine. What's the matter? Are you looking for bugs? You needn't worry. To install mikes in the apartment of a member of the Committee, you need the authorization of Chairman Chebrikov, no less. So you see, you're in the safest place in Moscow. Thank you, pussycat." He took a drink from Yelena's friend, the blonde, and slapped her rump. "When my pal was assigned overseas, he wanted to hold on to this place. So I arranged to rent it from him for the princely sum of twenty-five roubles a month. All the same, I'd like someone to share the expenses. Can I count you in?"

Nikolsky tossed off his drink without waiting for a response. "Come on," he said. "I'll give you the grand tour."

There was a poster on the wall in the kitchen, showing a bum in tattered clothes with the inscription "Never Trust a Man Who Doesn't Drink."

Sasha could see the potential: a safe house in Moscow.

"And six sets of sheets," Feliks reminded him. "They're included."

"What about the french letters?"

"Ah, they can't be sent to the laundry. They're optional, as American car dealers say."

Nikolsky was drinking faster than Sasha had ever seen him drink, and his mood shifts were vertigious. One minute, back in the Transit Hall, he had the blonde on his lap; the next, he had packed both girls out to the kitchen again to prepare fresh supplies.

"You'll find everything there, including aprons," he called after them.

"Are you sure you're feeling all right?" Sasha said to him.

"Come on, General, pour the drink and stop fucking around. It doesn't matter. It's all shit. Everything's shit," Nikolsky repeated. "But I have an idea how to get out of it."

He didn't finish, because the girls were back. "I'll do you a favor," he told Sasha. "Tonight, you can have the bedroom. This one's so far gone" —he mauled the blonde demonstratively—"that she'd do it standing up in the hall, if she could stand." Indeed, the little blonde's eyes were unfocused and one of her false eyelashes had come unstuck and was crawling down the side of her cheek like a hairy spider.

When they were alone in the bedroom, Yelena wanted Sasha to put the lights out, and their love-making was urgent and impersonal. He thought of Elaine, and after, he wondered who Yelena had been thinking about.

He woke up a couple of hours later with the feeling that a corpse was walking barefoot down his spine, and found that the girl had appropriated all of the covers. He had to go through the Transit Hall to get to the bathroom—the main disadvantage of Bangladesh. In the half-light he could see the blonde curled up on the sofa, snoring away. He could also see where the draft was coming from. The door to the balcony was open, and Feliks was leaning over the railing, his cigarette aglow, staring out at the lights of Moscow.

Sasha had wrapped one of the sheets from the closet round his waist. He pulled it up over his shoulder like a toga, and went out to join Feliks.

"You remember what the siren Calypso said to Ulysses," Nikolsky said in a low, dreamy voice, as if in the midst of a recital. "She offered him immortality if he would forsake the land of his fathers. He chose to return to the land of his fathers."

He turned to Sasha. "I bet you don't even know what I'm talking about," he said bitterly. "It's all right for you. You're made of titanium. You're indestructible."

"Tell me about it," Sasha said quietly.

Jerkily, Feliks told him about his recall from New York, about how the Hansen affair had caused a scandal, and how Drinov was still after his blood. He explained how frustrated he was with his work at the Village, and with the whole atmosphere in Moscow. He was less than coherent. He strayed off and started talking about the funeral of his hero, the balladeer Vissotsky, who never won the approval of the Union of Writers but had half of Moscow, according to Nikolsky, out in the streets to mourn his death. Feliks had been there too. He described a sea of flowers, and hardened militiamen getting off their horses and joining the crowd.

He started to croon one of Vissotsky's songs: "Why is it the bird, never the bullet, that is stopped in mid-flight?"

While Sasha was still wondering what any of this had to do with Calypso, Nikolsky said, "There's a chance they'll send me back to London. If they do, I'm not planning to play Ulysses."

Sasha was shocked. He and Feliks had been able to talk frankly since they became friends, but now the man was admitting that he was contemplating the worst crime imaginable under the Soviet system: defection to the West.

Nikolsky took a deep breath and clutched his hand to his chest. "Could you get me some water?" he gasped.

He said, "Tachycardia," when Sasha returned with the glass. "Rapid heartbeat. If we were in America, I'd be on Valium, like all those anorexic female executives."

"Have you been to a doctor?"

"What's the point? The problem's up here." Nikolsky cocked a finger against his temple.

"You haven't told Olga about this—this idea about Calypso," Sasha said, slipping into the same euphemism.

"Of course not. You know her. She's old-fashioned."

"I'll tell you what I want you to do," Sasha said. Like many men with natural authority, he tended to lower his voice when he was issuing instructions. "I want you to get some sleep, give your liver some time to work—assuming you've still got one. In the morning, we'll talk."

When Sasha woke up, it was mid-morning on Saturday, and his curly-haired girl had long gone. He found her name and telephone number on a slip of paper on the pillow next to his head. She had vanished like a dream-tiger; he could remember the contours of her body in his fingertips, like a blind man, but not her face.

"They took the bus," Feliks announced when Sasha wandered out into the Transit Hall. "They had to go to work in the *beryozka* store."

Nikolsky seemed at least partly recovered, perhaps because of the bottle at his elbow. *"Opokhmelitsya,"* he proposed. "The hair of the dog."

Sasha shook his head. This didn't deter Feliks. What could?

"I'm sorry about last night," Nikolsky said, once suitably fortified.

"Why be sorry? Yours looked nice."

"I mean what I said. I must have overdone it."

"I really don't remember."

Feliks stared at him before saying, "Thanks." He quickly added, "I was so caught up in my own self-pity I completely forgot to tell you what I've been saving up for months."

"Which is?"

"You remember back in New York, you asked me to find out about somebody, a member of the Committee?"

"Topchy." Sasha inserted the name.

"Well, I've met him. In fact, we've become quite friendly."

What little color was in Sasha's cheeks drained off completely. "Perhaps I'll have that eye-opener after all," he said.

"It started at the racetrack." Nikolsky recounted how he had met Topchy at the Moscow Hippodrome, and arranged several get-togethers since, always ending up at the bar of the Bega restaurant or a nearby hotel.

Topchy had come to regard him as a dedicated race-goer and a source of delightful gossip on the goings-on at the Village.

"Topchy's a big wheel in the Third Directorate now," Nikolsky went on. "A deputy chief, no less. And he's well connected, Sasha. He's got his own line to Askyerov. They were in Baku together, and Topchy knows where all the bodies are buried. He boasts about it, after a few drinks. He says he's a man on his way to the top. But you'll never believe the next bit. Do you know what he said to me, Sasha? He said he'd like a man like me on his staff. He told me that if I ever got fed up with the service, he'd have a job for me back at the Lubyanka, with lots of time to go to the track. How do you like that? He actually asked me to leave the service to go and wallow in that cesspool!"

Sasha didn't say anything for a long time. He experienced a storm of conflicting emotions. There was the hot desire for revenge, now he had located his father's murderer. There was the cooler hunter's instinct that said: Stalk him, wait for a clear line of fire. There was his reaction to his friend's confession in the middle of the night, now shaping itself into a proposal that would dovetail perfectly with the plan he had begun to perfect since he had joined his father-in-law at Gogol Boulevard.

He said to Feliks, "I think Colonel Topchy has done us a favor. Why don't you arrange to work for him?"

"You're not much of a comedian, Sasha."

"But I'm perfectly serious. I just remembered what you were saying last night. Suppose you could have the beautiful Calypso and still live in the land of your fathers?"

3 The great warren of yellow buildings that made up General Staff headquarters sprawled along Gogol Boulevard, facing the writer's monument and an island between the lanes lined with birches and maples where pensioners came to sun themselves and play chess. On the other side, facing the river, was a huge communications tower with a forest of aerials and satellite dishes. A few of the townhouses where Tolstoy's counts had held balls and banquets survived along the boulevard; some had been subdivided into officers' flats. Most of the old Arbat district had fallen to the wrecker's ball in Khrushchev's time. His architects had redesigned the center of Moscow as if no one would own a private car; along the broad, bustling expanse of Kalinin Prospekt, which Sasha could see from his window, there was not a single parking space. One of the clues to

Sasha's new status was that, with his official license tag and his special sticker, he could always command a parking space on the river side of the General Staff building.

Sasha hurried up under the mock-Grecian pediment of the entrance on Frunze Street, and soldiers wearing the red patches of the special Guards Company gave him a brisk salute. He was slightly later than normal, and he paused only briefly in his own office to check for messages and to leaf through the daily intelligence summary from the Aquarium. He was supposed to report to Zotov before he left for a meeting of the Defense Council.

The corridors on the Marshal's floor were as wide as a whole railway compartment, spotlessly clean, lit by fluorescent strips. The massive oak doors of the Marshal's suite were covered in black padded leather, a traditional device to screen out eavesdroppers that had been much favored in Stalin's time, when the building was constructed. But even through the padding, Sasha could hear the boom of his father-in-law's voice. The Marshal was not in a good humor.

"And where were you last night, fuck your mother?" Zotov greeted him. "This is a twenty-four-hour job. I didn't hire you to run around Moscow chasing skirts."

Sasha began to make excuses, but Zotov cut him short. "I don't have time for that now. Are these figures accurate?"

Sasha examined the report from the military command in Kabul. It stated that more than four hundred Soviet soldiers, including a lieutenant-general, had been killed in a single week.

"They're accurate," Sasha confirmed. "The worst of it was that ambush near the Salang tunnel."

Zotov grabbed the document away from him and read out the numbers of trucks, tanks, helicopters, and planes that had also been destroyed. "And another battalion of fucking Afghans turned their weapons over to the bandits," he wound up. "Have you finished that draft?"

Sasha gave it to him. He had been ordered to polish a contingency plan the Marshal had prepared, involving major air strikes against rebel sanctuaries in Pakistan and the doubling of Soviet forces in Afghanistan itself.

"Are you going to present this today?" Sasha asked.

"The boss still has to approve it," Zotov said impatiently. "He's still treading water, like everyone else." He respected the Chief of Staff, but thought he was too much of a politician. Zotov also wanted the job for himself. If they retired the aging Defense Minister and gave the Chief of Staff that job, the way would be clear for Zotov. But, like much else, these decisions had all been left pending while the city discussed the stories about the General Secretary's health.

"There's nobody at the wheel," Zotov said in disgust. "We're getting all the weapons systems we want, no trouble about that, but we're not allowed to use them. Look at the opportunities we're missing. Look at the Middle East. We can put our hand on the oil faucets if we only have the guts to reach out and do it. Look at what we're letting those bloody Pakistanis get away with. Look at these cruise and Pershing missiles the Americans are about to deploy. We were told it was just a political question, we could stop it by psychological warfare alone. Well, we saw all those hippies hold their rock concerts"—the Marshal didn't much care for demonstrators, even when they were anti-American—"and where did it get us? The missiles will start arriving in a matter of weeks. We need to do something to scare the shit out of the Europeans."

The Marshal broke off his tirade and started gathering together his papers. He was voicing a litany of complaints that Sasha had heard often enough in touring the military districts since he had joined Zotov's staff. Everyone seemed to be complaining about a sense of drift, the lack of a helmsman.

"How much longer do you think he's got?" Sasha asked discreetly. There was no doubt about who "he" was. At that moment, the General Secretary was lying strapped to his dialysis machine in the modern clinic that had been erected behind the hunting lodge that had once belonged to Stalin.

"We'll know soon enough," the Marshal said grimly.

"I heard that Askyerov has been making some preparations." It was a chance to see how far the Marshal could be pushed, Sasha thought.

"Oh, yes?"

"He's been mending fences with the old crowd, going around saying that these inquiries into corruption among the Brezhnev family are a disgrace and ought to be stopped immediately. He's picked Andropov's successor, you can be sure about that."

"You mean Chernenko?"

"Askyerov has made his calculations. He thinks it's too soon for any of the younger men to get it. He knows the old crowd will welcome Chernenko because he means business as usual. Askyerov is going to land on his feet, that you can count on. By the way, he's doing quite well out of the war."

"What do you mean?"

"I heard that one of his cronies is collecting pay-offs from the Afghan merchants who are importing boots and uniforms for the army. They pay in afghanis or roubles that Askyerov's people trade for hard currency in the bazaar. Then they triple their profits by smuggling western goods back into Russia."

Zotov looked at him sharply and said, "Can you prove it?"

"Not yet."

The Marshal swore copiously. "That cockroach gets fat while our boys are dying. One day, we'll make an end of these bitches." He stared at Sasha again and added, "I suppose I ought to get nervous when my son-in-law is better informed than I am about what's going on inside the leadership. Where do you get this stuff?"

"I've got a very interesting source, Alexei Ivanich. I must tell you about him sometime. One of these days, he's going to be very useful to us."

Moving the Marshal, he reflected afterward, was like shifting an enormous boulder. You had to begin warily, careful to ensure that it would roll in the right direction. Once in motion, it was very nearly unstoppable.

The second night Sasha spent at Bangladesh, one week later, there were no girls, and Feliks was taking solace in the bottle. His confessions were as remarkable as they had been during the previous conversation. Nikolsky confided that he had taken his baby son to a church to go through the full Orthodox baptism. "As you know, I'm not a believer," Feliks said, and Sasha was reminded of the night in New York when Nikolsky had abandoned the singles bars to light a candle in church. "But it never hurts to take out a little insurance," Feliks added semi-apologetically.

Sasha didn't comment. They both knew what it would mean if Nikolsky were found out. It had been dangerous enough in New York, but here in Moscow, the risk was multiplied a hundredfold.

Feliks was at the bottle again. When Sasha reached over and pulled it away from him, he was too astonished to resist.

"You know what they say," Sasha commented. "First you drink the bottle, then the bottle drinks you. I want to talk to you about Calypso. Do you think you can absorb what I'm going to say?"

Feliks, trying not to appear affronted, lit up a cigarette.

"Has your London posting been confirmed?" Sasha asked.

"It's almost definite."

"I want you to turn it down."

"*You* want me—" Feliks spluttered.

"I was listening to you the other night. I think you meant what you said about not coming back. That's no way out, Feliks. Not for men like you and me. We belong here. If you transplant yourself somewhere else, it would be like trying to live with an artificial heart. Don't think I haven't thought about it myself." For a moment, he saw himself lying on Elaine's bed. She was perched over him, nibbling his lower lip, and her hair grazed the sides of his face like a soft curtain.

"I promise to send my liver home to Moscow for burial," Nikolsky said. "But honestly, Sasha. What do you expect me to do?"

"I told you already. I want you to go and work for Topchy. Listen." He rushed on before Feliks could interrupt. "I can't tell you very much about it, not yet. But there are going to be changes in Moscow."

"What sort of changes?"

"We're going to take back the country."

"*We?*" Feliks echoed him mockingly. "*Kto kogo?* Who-whom?"

"Could you just accept that someone very important *needs* you in the Third Directorate?" Sasha replied, evading the question.

"Aha!" Nikolsky exclaimed theatrically. "Now I'm beginning to see. So the Marshal's still got some life in him, has he? Well, he'd better play his cards close to his chest. *They* haven't forgotten who shot Beria. You and your blessed Marshal want me to be a spy for you, is that it? You're hatching something and you want to make sure you know which of your woodentops at Gogol Boulevard are freelancing for Topchy."

"What do you say?"

"I ought to tell you to go fuck yourself. You know I can't stand the stink of high boots. Anyway, you'll get us all shot."

"I don't think so. I've been thinking about this for some time."

"Even in New York?"

"Even before New York."

"I don't think I know you, Sasha."

So Sasha told him the story of Topchy and his father's death, and then a little of what he had learned from Levin about Russian history. The country could be changed, he argued, but the change must come from above, and it must be sudden, ruthless, and totally unexpected.

Nikolsky fell silent for a while, understanding that Sasha was not accustomed to sharing these things with others. At last he said, "I still know you wouldn't ask me to work for Topchy if you were drunk. You're saner when you're drunk. No, don't say any more. Just let me ask you this, Sasha. Suppose I agree to play your game. Who would ever believe that I would choose to give up a job in London"—he smacked his lips, rhapsodizing the girls by the Serpentine—"to go and work with an asshole like Topchy?"

"You'll think of something."

"I'm not one of your lost soldiers, Sasha. I'm not cut out to be a martyr —although, God knows, I suffer." He stared pointedly at the brandy bottle until Sasha relented.

The next day, Thursday, Nikolsky heard that his London assignment was still under review and that his old nemesis Drinov had been kicked up-stairs. Drinov was to become deputy head of the Second Chief Director-ate, no less. Feliks left the Village early and sat drinking at the Zhiguli until Pauk hauled him out. The following night, he went back. The door-man didn't recognize him at first. With his tie askew, wet patches down his front, and his hat falling down over his ear, he looked like a bum who had been out swilling *samorgon* under a bridge somewhere. The doorman swore when Feliks failed to deposit the usual tip.

Pauk affected not to notice. But after Feliks had gulped down his first pint, he yelled at the waiter, "This beer is half water! I'm not paying for this slop! And I'm not paying for this shit either!" He stabbed a finger at his plate of shrimps.

"Shut your face, Feliks, you're pissed. You'd better settle up and go home."

Without further discussion, Nikolsky threw his plate at Pauk. Food spattered the crowd at the next table. Pauk dumped his tray on the floor, tossed his napkin over his shoulder, and advanced on Feliks with his fits balled. Nikolsky was swinging his vodka bottle like a bat.

When Nikolsky brought the bottle crashing down, narrowly missing Pauk's head, the militiaman on the other side of the room finally bestirred himself.

"You'd better take care of this one," the waiter said to him.

The militiaman swaggered up, the picture of authority, and flashed his identity card.

"Come now, Citizen," he said benevolently, "you've had enough for one night."

"Go fuck yourself," Nikolsky spat at him. "Go fuck your MVD. Do you know who you're talking to, you little bitch? You can't push me around. I'm a lieutenant-colonel in the Committee for State Security."

The excited murmur that spread around the room was like the sound of the crowd when a football team had just been awarded a penalty kick. A KGB man squaring up for a fight with a militiaman. Now, that was some-thing that simply didn't happen, not because the two organizations didn't hate each other's guts, but because the first rule of life for a member of

Nikolsky's service was that you didn't identify yourself except on official business.

Even the MVD man gaped for a moment. This may have been partly because the militia had been slightly less aggressive about penalizing members of the KGB for pecadilloes like drunken driving since Andropov had appointed one of his old KGB cronies to run the Ministry of Interior. You could almost hear the cogs turning inside the squat militiaman's head.

"I know you," Feliks goaded him. "You sit over there on your fat backside, guzzling away like a pig with its snout in the feeding trough. You're paid off by the swine who run this place. They own you."

"If you don't shut up and clear out, I'll have to arrest you," the militiaman warned. He had an audience. He couldn't ignore what this drunk was saying, even if he was a colonel in the KGB.

"Arrest me?" Nikolsky screamed. "Just try it, fuck your mother. I was risking my life abroad to defend our motherland while you were feeding your gut."

The militiaman went for him then. But Nikolsky, remarkably cunning for a drunk, led him a dance round the table, then jumped out when he least expected it and gave him a kick in the groin that left him rolling around on the floor.

Pauk and another waiter got hold of Feliks and twisted his arms up behind his back.

"You asked for this, don't forget," Pauk whispered to Nikolsky while they waited for the MVD paddy wagon to arrive. "I just hope you know what you're doing, Feliks."

They roughed him up inside the van, but not so the marks would show, and just enough to compensate for what he had done to the man in the Zhiguli. They held him at MVD headquarters for a couple of hours, while a full report, backed up by witnesses, was typed up.

"That's it then, Comrade Colonel," the MVD duty officer said to Nikolsky with satisfaction. "Go home, drink plenty of coffee, make love to your wife. You'll be all washed up as soon as this report gets to your superiors."

True to form, the militia improved the report of the incident at the Zhiguli. Not content with describing a physical assault on a member of its personnel, the MVD claimed that Nikolsky had tried to kill the man. Nobody worried about *that* at the Village; revealingly, the MVD had not urged that Nikolsky should be punished for that particular offense. From the point of view of Nikolsky's superiors, the damning charge was that he had disclosed his identity while intoxicated in a public place.

Feliks made no effort to deny this. He didn't even turn up in person in front of the tribunal of inquiry. Instead, he arranged with a girl he knew in a local clinic—his girlfriends were strategically positioned all over the city —to give him a certificate stating that he was prostate with a highly communicable bug. The wheels revolved without him, and word soon came down that he had been suspended from the First Chief Directorate.

Soon after, he met Topchy at the racetrack. The deputy chief of the Third Directorate was in an excellent mood that day, after picking two winners in a row. Even so, he wasn't averse to Nikolsky paying for the drinks.

"I've really got myself in the shit this time," Feliks told him. "They've sent my file to Personnel. They're probably planning to send me to bloody Kazakhstan."

"Those shitholes at the Village don't know a good officer when they see one," Topchy commiserated with him. "Leave everything to me. I've got friends in Personnel."

Topchy was as good as his word. When Nikolsky's former chiefs at the Village were asked to approve his transfer to the Third Directorate, they were only too happy to oblige. "Just what that *alkash* deserves," one of them remarked.

"I came up with something," Feliks reported to Sasha. "If I say so myself, it was an exceptional performance. I trust that the Marshal won't forget what I'm putting myself through. I suppose you know the difference between a photograph and a member of Topchy's section."

Sasha shook his head.

"The photograph is developed."

4 "Do you know the origin of the word 'intelligence'?" Luke Gladden was saying. They were sitting in a wood-paneled sitting room in a Park Avenue club that Elaine had never heard of, and the open fire was hotter than it needed to be. "It's derived from the Latin," Gladden said. He sounded like a patient schoolmaster. "The verb *intelligere* means 'to choose among.' Which is appropriate, don't you think? I find that the only people who are amusing are those who are able to discriminate, if only between the bad and the worse. Are you still with me, my dear?"

"Uh—I'm sorry." She shook herself out of the daze that had come with staring into the flames, the way she had used to do as a child. At school, some romantic scene would come into her head and she would save it up until she got home, and could train herself to see every detail in the fire.

"You have to make your choice, Elaine." It was the closest he had come to hurrying her, in the several meetings they had had since he picked her up at the New School. He had told her that he was from Washington, that he had nothing to do with the FBI, but had certain other connections. She could guess what that meant. She hadn't fled from him the way she had fled from Tom Regan. That was partly because of his gentleness, but more because she was desperate to know something—anything—about Sasha.

"He's in Moscow," Gladden had told her. "He's become an important man, attached to the General Staff."

"Why did you wait so long before coming to me?" she had asked him. As the months had turned into years and she heard nothing from either the FBI or Sasha, she had begun to think that they had all forgotten her.

"I wanted you to be ready," Gladden replied. It was a half-truth. By taking up her Russian language lessons again and planning a visit to Moscow, Elaine had demonstrated that she was vulnerable. But there had been a problem on the Moscow end. They hadn't counted on Sasha getting himself posted to Afghanistan, or that he'd be in the field so long. From what Gladden had observed of the girl, her passion for the Russian hadn't dulled with time. But would that be true of Preobrazhensky too? Well, you played the hand you were dealt. The first thing was to make sure of the girl, this time around.

"I want to put it to you as simply as possible," the CIA man was saying. "You want to see him again. We both know that. But there is no way you can see Sasha—no way that wouldn't spell ruin for him—without our help. We're talking about a meeting inside Russia, not in New York. In Moscow, you have to play by Moscow rules. You'll have to be patient, and you'll have to be disciplined. There are things you'll have to learn."

She seemed to pull away from him, and frightened of losing her, Gladden said, "Don't misunderstand me. I'm not asking you to work for us. You won't be anybody's agent, except your own. We'll help you to meet him, that's all. All I want is for you to tell us what he's thinking. You won't go anywhere near the Embassy, or any of our people over there. I have a friend in Moscow, an old buddy of mine. He's a journalist, a New Zealander who talks like a defrocked bishop. I think you'll like him."

"No." She formed the syllable with her lips before she spoke it.

"What do you mean, no? You *do* want to see him."

Gladden's voice remained soft, but she felt the razor's edge inside the cotton wool. She was resentful, too, that Luke could read her emotions. It was bad enough that, after more than three years, she still hungered for a man who was almost completely inaccessible, without that being known and documented on some floppy disc in the bowels of Langley. She had turned down a marriage proposal and any number of less binding offers. Among her old social set, she fitted in about as well as a nun in full habit. But she couldn't allow Gladden's people to use her need to lay a snare for Sasha.

"I can't do what you ask," she told the CIA man. "You're trying to trap him, and you want me for bait."

"That's not it at all," Gladden protested.

"You just asked me to find out what he's thinking. That's already a betrayal."

"Not if he needs help. Do you imagine that he's happy in Moscow?"

"I don't know. I don't think happiness is what matters most to him, anyway."

"What does?"

"He's driven." She faltered, nervous of telling Gladden more than she intended.

"That's not easy. On the woman, I mean."

"It's not easy for him."

"Look, there are no strings attached. We'll help to put you two together. If you don't feel like talking about it afterward, then fine. What's wrong with that?"

She stared at him, still suspicious. "You could use me to compromise him," she suggested. "Well, that's what you call it, don't you? You could take pictures of us together."

"That's not what we have in mind," he said. "If we wanted to go that route," he added more harshly, "we have all the pictures we need. I shouldn't tell you this," he confided, "but some of your friends in the Bureau wanted to use them on Sasha before he left New York. I managed to stop them."

She shivered involuntarily at the thought that her most secret moments with Sasha had been shared with a spy camera.

"I'm sorry I mentioned it," Gladden went on.

"No need to be sorry. I brought it up." She felt renewed confidence in the man. There was nothing shifty about him. He met her eyes when she asked questions, and he didn't cover his mouth with his hand before responding.

A great pasha of a marmalade cat, the club pet, made its majestic progress toward the fire, then jumped up, uninvited, on Gladden's lap. It purred in measured appreciation as he scratched behind its ears, uncaring about the ginger hairs on his dark suit.

Elaine couldn't be sure afterward whether the cat or the question of the photographs had counted for more. Either way, it was instinct more than reasoning that settled her course for her.

"No strings?" she repeated.

And again he said, "No strings."

"What do you want me to do next?"

"Go back to your Russian class, write your book, put in for your tourist visa. I'm sure there won't be any problem." He patted her hand. It seemed he had the gift of making strays feel safe. "When the time is right, I'll let you know."

5 Andropov's body was on display in the House of Unions for three days, with his decorations laid out on a satin pad at the foot of the bier. On the last day, the corpse was surrounded by an honor guard of the Party elite. All over Moscow and throughout the country red flags of mourning, trimmed in black, drooped at half mast. The official photographs of the General Secretary were also draped in black. Factory whistles, the sirens of the ships on the river, the gun salvoes of the Taman and Kantemirov Guards divisions all marked his passing. But nobody wept in public, as they had after Stalin's death.

On Gogol Boulevard, Sasha was busied with arranging memorial ceremonies in the military districts and even among the "Limited Contingent" of Soviet forces in Afghanistan, as the Moscow papers always described the army of occupation. He and Marshal Zotov both turned out for the funeral in Red Square, standing in places of honor among the army brass. They watched the coffin roll past on its gun carriage, and saw Chernenko, atop the mausoleum, claiming his inheritance, heard him rush through the expected eulogies. "Yuri Vladimirovich lived an eventful, action-filled life . . . remarkable qualities as a Marxist Leninist . . . faithfulness to communist ideals, unbending will, modesty and business ability . . . concern for the working man . . ."

They stood there on the podium, these old men in hats and heavy coats, except for Ustinov in his Marshal's uniform, and they reminded Sasha of a photo he had once seen of Easter Island statues, weathered and eroded, crumbling in front of your eyes. After Chernenko had wheezed his last, they produced Gromyko, another perennial survivor and now a token worker, a press-tool operator from the Likachev auto factory in Moscow, to testify to how Andropov had always had the interest of the proletariat at heart. Then the Defense Minister came to the microphones to report that the men of the Soviet armed forces were gripped by the deepest grief over the death of the General Secretary. Imperceptibly, Sasha shifted from one foot to the other. He could see Zotov's profile, impassive, seemingly hewed from granite. At 12:45 precisely, the guns rang out.

"They had it all sewn up," the Marshal remarked to Sasha after the new General Secretary was named. "Just like you said."

Some months later, Sasha came home to the Visotny Dom to find the Marshal crouched over an elaborate model railroad that he had set up in a back room of the family apartment for Petya, controlling a very realistic O gauge Marklin armored train—a vintage piece that had been presented to him by the East Germans. It struck Sasha that the train Lenin had traveled on from Zurich to mount his coup might have looked something like that.

"Come over here, Sasha," Zotov summoned him. "You can work the points while I pour us a drink. I have a few things to tell you."

Sasha shunted the armored train along a siding.

"All right, that's enough of that," the Marshal interrupted him, holding out a brandy snifter. "We're not schoolboys. Let's toast the new Chief of Staff!"

Sasha stared at him, and the Marshal broke into a broad smile.

"You mean you didn't know?" Zotov guffawed.

"There've been rumors, of course—"

"Well, as of tonight, it's a fact. I take charge at the end of the week."

"Your health, Comrade Marshal!" Sasha exclaimed. He was grinning too. "But how did you manage it?"

"Here's to our esteemed Chairman of the Council of Ministers, Comrade Askyerov," Zotov said by way of response. "We owe it all to him. Fuck him to the nth degree!"

They drank again, and the Marshal explained the game of musical chairs that had made him the master of Gogol Boulevard.

"They put off cutting down the dead wood so long that it started falling under its own weight," he began. "The Prime Minister couldn't work for more than an hour at a stretch—believe me, I've watched the man. Our august Defense Minister never recovered from that last trip to Damascus. Mohammed's revenge. So finally even the boss"—he was still careful to avoid criticizing the General Secretary by name—"was made to see that we need some men who can stand up without being supported on either side. And just look at the prize pair he's appointed. As Prime Minister, Askyerov. As Defense Minister—can you guess, Sasha?"

Through his own channels, Sasha had a fairly good idea. But he waited for the Marshal to answer his own question.

"Serdyuk!" Zotov snorted. "Another chekist! And a fucking Ukrainian to boot! They're going to make him a Marshal of the Soviet Union. And the only shooting he's ever witnessed is the kind they do in a chekist jail!"

"When did you get the news?" Sasha asked quietly.

"Two hours ago," Zotov said, consulting his watch. "We were called to a surprise meeting of the Defense Council. You should have seen the chief's face when they told him. I thought he was going to go for Askyerov with his fists."

The former Chief of Staff had been expecting to get the top Defense job himself. He had made no secret of his view that it was time that a professional soldier took charge.

"They had it all prepared, Sasha. They told the chief they were reluctantly prepared to accept his resignation, on the grounds of his health. But they knew the army wouldn't like it. They're scared of us, Sasha. Why do you think they've agreed to all our weapons projects?"

This was true, Sasha thought. As the civilian leadership faltered, the military establishment had steadily grown in power. Blunders like the shooting-down of a Korean passenger plane and the failure to produce anything approximating a victory in Afghanistan had not altered the trend. The shoddy performance of the Soviet system in every area except military strength had helped to accelerate it. And as traditional slogans and leaders fell into disrespect, the Party was forced to rely more and more on the fear of enemies abroad to rally public support—which again meant building up the army.

"They made you Chief of Staff," Sasha suggested, "because our own people admire you. They think it will make us accept Askyerov and Serdyuk while they build their own power." He paused before adding, "They think they can control you."

"Do you think I'm blind?" the Marshal roared, pouring more brandy. "I know they'll try to keep me on a leash and choke me with it when I'm no longer useful. But I'm on to their game, Sasha. They don't realize what they've done. The whole fighting machine of this country is now under my fist. Think of it. Think what we can become. A country should be like this." He clenched his great paw and raised it aloft. "A country should be like a fist. Instead of *this.*" He let his hand flop open, like a beggar asking for alms.

Sasha watched him as he started pacing the room. The deep-pile rug was not enough to muffle his tread. *It's beginning,* Sasha thought.

"You can change the history of Russia," he addressed his father-in-law's back, mixing flattery with provocation. "The army will stand behind you. And the army is the only institution the people still believe in."

The Marshal swiveled on his heel and stared at him. "You know what they call that kind of talk. They call it bonapartism."

"Not in the barracks," Sasha said softly.

The Marshal pretended to be absorbed in the model railroad. He set the train in motion, then stopped it at a level crossing.

"I think we understand each other," he turned to Sasha. "There are things I don't need to explain to you, nor you to me. You've got your ear to the ground. You've been to fourteen of the districts."

"Fifteen," Sasha corrected him. There were sixteen military districts in the Soviet Union.

"I want you to make me a list. I want the names of the commanders we can count on, men who understand the type of leadership we need. Also of those who will oppose us. Are you with me?"

"Totally," Sasha said with conviction.

"We can't trust anyone to begin with. Not completely," the Marshal went on. "With Serdyuk at the Defense Ministry, the chekists will be crawling all over us."

"We'll be watching them too."

The Marshal looked puzzled. Sasha explained, "I have a source—a friend in the Third Directorate. He'll help us."

"You're insane!" Zotov protested. "He's a provocateur, trying to trap you the way they got whatsisname, that Slavophile in Leningrad." A captain in Leningrad had gathered a circle of ardent Russianist officers and circulated samizdat denouncing "cosmopolitan influences" and appealing for a military regime and a return to the Orthodox church. The circle grew steadily over a period of some months until the KGB, which had helped to set it up, decided it had trapped enough "bonapartists," and arrested the lot.

"I can trust this man," Sasha pursued. He told the Marshal enough about his relations with Nikolsky to see the older man's reaction shift from angry incredulity to admiration.

"I wasn't mistaken about you, Sasha," he commented. He started discussing the personalities of several senior officers in the Moscow Military District, including the commanders of the Kantemirov and Taman Guards, the "court divisions" deployed within easy reach of the capital.

Listening to him, Sasha thought, *It will never work that way. The court divisions are too closely watched, and their commanders are political opportunists. Why are generals always trying to fight the last war?*

"Alexei Ivanich," he said. "You have far more experience than I do, so forgive me if I seem too outspoken. I think your plan could only end in disaster, even with an inside source in the Third Directorate. The Party and the KGB have always looked on the Moscow garrison as the main source of danger. Try anything out of the ordinary, and they'll pounce."

"Have you got a better idea?"

"There are weapons available that they haven't thought about," Sasha said carefully.

"For example?"

"Spetsnaz."

Zotov stared at him with what appeared to be blank incomprehension for a moment, then his big face molded itself into a grin. He remembered that one of Sasha's first requests, after he had joined him at Gogol Boulevard, had been to confirm the appointment of one of his fighting comrades, Fyodor Zaytsev, as commander of the special forces base at Kavrov.

"Very original, Sasha. And how is your friend Zaytsev these days?"

6 Elaine spent the first couple of days in Moscow sightseeing like a normal tourist. They put her up at the Metropol, and the first night she found herself sharing a table with a group of red-faced men who were drinking and eating hugely. "I'm sorry. I don't speak Russian," she said to the one who started trying to pick her up. To her embarrassment, he turned out to be a Scots engineer from Glasgow.

She wandered Red Square, stood in line with the people waiting to view Lenin's embalmed corpse, spent time at galleries and museums. She rode the metro and the trolleybuses, trying to get her bearings. The city looked as drab as she had expected, under a cast-iron sky, and the people had a defeated look, she thought. She couldn't be sure if she was under surveillance, but everywhere she went, she felt that eyes were following.

When she called Guy Harrison, the correspondent Luke Gladden had mentioned in New York, she didn't give her name, feeling sure that his phone must be tapped. He wasn't a bit put out. Harrison had an odd, ecclesiastical turn of phrase. He said, "Bless you, my child," after inviting her to a party at his flat.

"Failed seminarist, you know," he explained that evening, when the other guests had left. "It's the right background for this place. Did you know that Stalin went to a Jesuit seminary? Never underrate a Jesuit."

Harrison's guests were eclectic: an American art dealer, a few diplomats from various European embassies, a dramatically beautiful star of the Theatre Romen who was finally persuaded to sing a few gypsy songs, and a number of sleek Russians who didn't seem at all perturbed about the risks of slipping in and out of the closely monitored apartment block. Harrison himself reminded her of Robert Morley. He had the reassuring rotundity of a man who would rather look at a roast potato than a naked woman, as well as that disconcerting habit of raising his hand to deliver his apostolic blessing. He was accredited to a number of publications in London, Toronto, and Hong Kong. Elaine wondered who else he worked for—the CIA? the British?—and why the Soviets put up with him. These were mysteries that Guy Harrison was certainly not going to elucidate.

"Tomorrow," he told her, "I'll show you the bright lights. Godspeed!"

He picked her up at the hotel, gave her lunch at an Uzbek restaurant, and took her on a spin around the city in his car, a dun-colored Lada that was the only thing about him that blended into the landscape. He showed her the Ministry of Defense, a hulking block of yellow-brown stone with the inevitable neo-Greek portico, on the embankment near the main Aeroflot offices.

"The brass hats are all there for a meeting," he said. "Something to do with Afghanistan and the Paks."

They drove up Komsomolsky Prospekt, across the Garden Ring Road. Harrison had to circle around via a narrow underpass to get onto the Ring Road. He pointed out an old metro station, a one-story building with high wooden doors and a red pointed roof. Park Kultury, Elaine made out the name. It was an old quarter of the city. The houses along the road were three and four stories, off-white and yellow, with narrow slits of windows that opened like shutters at the bottom.

Then they were up on the Ring Road, crossing Krimskiy Most, Moscow's most beautiful bridge. As they drove east, Harrison pointed out the floating restaurant on the river, and the big roller coaster in Gorky Park, on the far side. "The American Hills," Muscovites called it. They recrossed the Moskva River by a second bridge, cutting the loop, and suddenly they were passing Visotny Dom.

"That's where he lives," Harrison said quietly. "He usually drives himself home.

"It's a long shot, I admit," Harrison remarked when he finished explaining his plan. "But I haven't been able to come up with a better idea."

Sasha had been observed following the same route from the Defense Ministry that they had just taken. The road was broad and busy all the way, except for the detour along Novokrynskiy Proyezd, past the old metro station, wide enough only for single-lane traffic, moving at a snail's pace. The old Park Kultury station was quiet, but it was not unusual to see a few people, mostly students from the nearby technical institute, milling around near the doors.

"What am I supposed to do?" she asked doubtfully. "Wave him down like a cab?"

"Don't you think he'll recognize you? It's not as if it's a main road."

"What time will he be coming home?"

"He will leave the Ministry around six."

"Then it's going to be dark," she pointed out.

"You're quite right," Harrison said. "Couldn't you stand under a street-lamp or something?"

"You mean like a hooker?"

"Good heavens, no, it's not like that here at all." Guy sounded quite shocked.

"I'll manage," she said, taking charge. "Providing I can spot him." This was what she was here to do, after all. Dealing with the practical difficulties was a relief from trying to cope with her private doubts. Would he be glad to see her? Had he found happiness with someone else, wife or mistress? Would he suspect that she was being used by Gladden, or someone like him, and cast her out? It was easier to concentrate on what she would wear to the meeting. Something he might remember. Yes, the scarf he had given her in New York, with a vivid paisley design of greens and golds.

"He'll be driving his own car," Harrison went on. "See that one ahead —no, the second car. That's a Volga. Sasha's is like that, only black. He has a special license tag, with the letters MO on the left-hand side. The number is seven-nine-dash-thirteen. But look for the letters MO. They're reserved for senior defense people."

She nodded.

"You must tell me if you're having second thoughts," he pursued. "There could be an easier way. It's just that we haven't come up with one. You can't exactly go knocking on his door in the Visotny Dom."

"I'll do it," she said decisively.

"Splendid. The thing is, his conference ends tomorrow. Can you be ready around three-thirty?"

As she passed the floor attendant in her hotel and opened the door to her room, the only thing she regretted was that they couldn't have attempted the rendezvous today. It would have been better not to have had a lonely evening in which the old fears could spawn new ones.

The sky was oppressive, and the drizzle, light but unremitting, was as cold as melting ice. Elaine felt the snap of the wind against her cheek as she walked out of the Metropol, with a heavy sweater under her black winter coat. Around her throat, lapping over her collar, was the green-and-gold scarf that Sasha had bought for her.

Trying not to seem hurried, she made the usual tourist rounds. She walked down to the GUM emporium, and emerged into Red Square. She lingered at Lenin's mausoleum, and then at St. Basil's Cathedral. She strolled down toward the river and the Rossiya hotel, where she dawdled around the cinema before making a quick exit out the other side to find Guy Harrison waiting for her. They retrieved Harrison's Lada from a nearby parking lot and started their laundry run, along the Embankment, circling around behind the Foreign Ministry and the American Embassy, and finally into the quiet neighborhood around Lenin stadium.

By this stage, Elaine had completely lost her bearings.

"Where are we?"

"Not far from where we came yesterday. It's a good place to check whether anybody's taking an interest in us," Harrison explained as he doubled back, watching the movement of other cars.

Apparently satisfied, he finally headed down to the river and pulled up near a railway bridge, a crude construction of rusty iron girders.

"Andreyevskiy Most," Harrison said. "This is the end of the ride."

She looked doubtful, and he added, "It's all right. There's a footpath. You walk across and you'll find a metro station, Lenin Prospekt, on the other side. You only have to change once. Here, you'll need this." He handed her a five-kopeck piece.

"I'll cover your back," Harrison told her. "If I see anything, I'll meet you at Park Kultury and we'll call it off. They'll know we were up to something, but they'll never work out what it was. Not much of a day for this sort of thing, I'm afraid."

She looked at the sky, which had darkened. There were black scudding clouds out of the west.

"The Lord be with you," he said pontifically. Then he patted her shoulder. "Good luck, love."

She kissed his cheek and pulled her scarf up over her hair.

She crossed the gray embankment and climbed the granite steps that spiraled up to the bridge. On either side of the rails was a narrow pedestrian footpath, a yard or so wide, with a metal railing. She was completely alone on the bridge. There was not even a bird in sight.

The birds have all left Moscow, she thought.

The river was flat and gunmetal gray, and looked as deserted as the bridge. There were no boats, just an old man squatting on the bank with a fishing line.

Far away to her left, she saw the scalloped outline of the Krimskiy bridge, the place of her rendezvous, and understood why Harrison had sent her over the old railroad crossing. If anyone had been tailing them in an automobile, it would take a long time for him to weave his way round to a motor bridge—long enough for Elaine to lose herself on the far side of the river.

The wind cracked like a whiplash, and she steadied herself against the railing. She wondered if Guy was still waiting in his car. His presence, even if slightly absurd, gave her confidence. But when she looked back again, she saw she was no longer alone on the bridge: a stocky man in a parka was plodding along behind her. He did not look to be in a hurry, but his strides were nearly twice as long as Elaine's, and he was gaining on her steadily.

It's nothing, she told herself. *If there's a problem, Guy will handle it. Guy will be waiting.*

But when she looked over her shoulder again, the stranger on the bridge was close enough for her to make out his features. He seemed to be smiling at her, and she didn't like the way he smiled. She moved as fast as she could without breaking into a run, the heels of her boots click-clacking along the path.

She was at the far side now, clattering down the corkscrew steps, and nearly fell where the edge of one of them was badly chipped.

Then she was in lighted streets, among a press of people on their way home from work, passing the inevitable columns of a museum, zigzagging toward the Lenin Prospekt metro station.

She did not see the man from the bridge among the crowd on the platform.

She changed trains once, for the metro Ring. Park Kultury was the first stop on the line.

She was careful to leave by the old entrance, instead of the larger, newer building across the Garden Ring Road.

Elaine was dismayed to find that it was already quite dark outside. Night had descended without dusk. If Sasha came, would he see her? Would she be able to make out his car? The lamps outside the metro station threw a sickly yellow light along the pavement, but everything seemed shapeless, indistinct. A young couple were embracing furtively, in the shadows. A man came out of the doors behind her—not the man she had seen on the bridge, but a handsome, strapping fellow in an expensive leather coat—and looked at her boldly. She consulted her watch ostentatiously. He came up and said something to her in Russian. She shrugged and he pursued in English, "American? French?"

She said, *"Nyet,"* and turned away from him.

He wouldn't leave her alone, and in desperation she hurried back inside the metro station, scrabbling in her purse for a five-kopeck coin to put in the turnstile. She went all the way back down to the platform, making sure that she had gotten rid of the man, before returning to the same exit.

It was already 6:05. There was a fluttering in her chest like a trapped bird.

What if she had missed him, chasing around inside the metro station?

What if she had been tailed, and Guy had been unable to warn her?

She moved just outside the circle of light, trying not to appear as nervous as she felt.

Across the road was a blank wall, and cavernous hollows between the columns supporting the overpass. A black Volga came nosing along the street, and Elaine moved back into the light. The car had special plates, but the letters were wrong. MOC appeared, black on white, on the right-hand side. The car must belong to some Party or government official.

An olive sedan passed by, then a lumbering truck, almost too wide for the space.

There was a gap in the traffic. Then another black car came nosing round the bend, and she knew it was him even before she checked the license number, even though the figure behind the wheel was no more distinct than a silhouette scissored from crepe paper. She saw the outline of his high cap, the long neck, the expanse of chest and shoulders.

She moved without reflecting, without deciding it would have to be done this way, out into the road in front of the car.

Sasha slammed on the brakes and rolled down his window. He leaned out and started cursing at her, then sucked in his breath, drawing back the harsh words.

She blinked up at him, as if startled, playing her role.

He muttered something that might have been "You!"

After that, Sasha did not hesitate. He jumped out of the car, grabbed her arm and pushed her—almost flung her—into the passenger seat. A tiny Zaparozhets squeaked to a halt behind them, but the driver did not honk at the big man in the army uniform who was blocking the road. Sasha waved at him apologetically, climbed back behind the wheel, and eased the car forward and up the approach to Krimskiy bridge.

He glanced at Elaine intently, only once, and drove on in silence, checking the rearview mirror, until they had crossed the river.

"Sasha," she began.

"What are you doing here?" He sounded furious.

"I had to come," she said softly. "I had to see—" She was about to say "you," but amended it to "your city." She could feel the heat of his body. He seemed to be smoldering. "I wanted to contact you," she stumbled on. "But I didn't know how."

This drew no response. He just sat there, clutching the wheel, massive and volcanic.

Then he said, "What were you doing there? At the metro station?"

"I was just wandering around." She knew that she sounded inane and implausible. "I went to the museum—the Tretyakov," she added hastily, as if the name could help to shore up her story. The art museum, re-nowned for its collection of traditional Russian painters, including Levi-tan, was just across the bridge from the rendezvous.

Sasha pulled off the main road and started to meander as if he had lost his way. Then she realized that he was driving like Harrison, checking to see whether they were under surveillance.

"We have to talk," he announced. "Do you have time? Are you meeting somebody?"

"No. I mean, whatever you say."

"All right. I know a place."

He doubled back along the Garden Ring Road, and soon they were heading south.

Sasha parked near a faceless apartment block and told her to wait in the car. He left his cap on the front seat beside her.

When he came back, he said curtly, "It's okay."

They shared the elevator with a pug-nosed woman who stared at Elaine, appraising her clothes.

When Sasha had locked the door to the flat behind them, he said, "Welcome to Bangladesh."

7.

BANGLADESH

The ultimate in disposing one's troops is to be without ascertainable shape. Then the most penetrating spies cannot pry in nor can the wise lay plans against you.

—SUN TZU, *THE ART OF WAR*

1 "This isn't where you live," Elaine said. The living room smelled like an ashtray. There was a lingering trace of a cheap perfume.

"It's a friend's place. We'll be safe enough here."

She stripped off her coat and started picking up plates and glasses.

"Leave all that," Sasha told her. She turned to him and he took her in his arms. The touch of her body made him postpone all the questions he had to ask. *At least we weren't followed,* he had told himself before even opening the door.

He lifted her as if she weighed no more than a down pillow, and carried her into the bedroom.

"I've needed you," he breathed, close to her ear, as he fumbled with the clasps on her dress.

She kissed him and slid away from under him. "Wait," she said. "I never could stand a bed that wasn't tucked in."

He took off his uniform while she made the bed. Then she started undressing on the far side of the room, and they watched each other in the big gilt-framed mirror.

"Do you have such a thing as a bath?" she asked.

"Of course." He laughed. "Where do you think we are?"

"Then let's take a bath together." In the hurried months they had shared in New York, there were so many things they hadn't done. They'd never walked in the park, or gone to a movie, or even taken a bath together.

When the tub was filled the water was too hot, but they jumped in anyway, making a tremendous splash that left a puddle on the floor.

She saw the scar tissue on his chest and traced the lines with her fingertips, as if she were frightened of hurting him.

"Afghanistan?" she asked, and he stopped himself from asking how she knew.

All he said was, "It's not worth talking about."

He wasn't doing much of a job of soaping her. "Well, I guess *some* parts of me will be pretty clean." She smiled at him.

He carried her back to the bedroom before either of them was properly dry, with the only halfway decent towel in the apartment draped loosely over their shoulders. And for an hour or so, their bodies locked together, they were able to forget they were in Moscow, and were breaking its rules. He said her name over and over, tuning her body with his mouth and hands until it sang.

Afterward, he recited something to her in Russian, and she asked for a translation. He picked the words one by one, like pebbles.

> *I have refused to obey.*
> *I have passed beyond the flags.*
> *The thirst for life has been stronger than anything.*
> *Joyous, I have heard the astonished cries*
>   *of the men behind me.*

He broke off and said, "It's about the wolf that escaped the hunters. It's the way I felt, just now."

He spoke with such sadness, using the past tense, that she knew he was slipping away from her. Soon there would be questions. She lay perfectly still, holding her breath, as if the slightest movement would shatter the moment completely. He kissed her, and tasted salt tears. He pressed against her with the whole length of his body, and she clutched at him fiercely. He seemed to radiate heat.

"I never expected you to wait for me," he said.

"I'm no good at waiting. I'm afraid I couldn't seem to do anything else."

"You couldn't know that you'd find me in Moscow," he observed, and she knew it was beginning. She fumbled around beside the bed for her pocketbook, and extracted one of her menthol cigarettes. They watched the smoke coil around an African mask.

"I think you should tell me about it," he went on, still not hurrying her.

"They gave me a tourist visa," she reported. "It was all quite routine. I've been thinking—dreaming—about Russia since you left. I've started work on a novel about a family of Russian immigrants who end up in America. I'm using some of the stories my father told me."

Sasha considered this in silence for a while. Then he said, "Coincidence may work well enough in a novel. I'm not sure that it works here."

"Did you forget Bloomingdale's? We met by chance, didn't we?"

"At the beginning," he agreed. "In New York, yes, it was a miracle. But in Moscow, we're short on miracles. Someone helped you to find me."

His voice was still soft, but his look was so intense that it scared her. "There was nobody."

"It's better that you tell me," he persisted. "That way, I may be able to limit the damage." His eyes never left her face. They reminded her of a gray wolf at the edge of a camp, hungry but wary of the fire, waiting his moment.

She hugged her knees, feeling chill even in the overheated room now that his warmth had been removed from her.

"I'm sorry," she faltered. "Sasha, I had to see you. I would have done anything—"

"*Anything?*" For the first time, he raised his voice.

"No, I didn't mean that," she corrected herself.

"I promise I won't blame you," he said, gentler again. "Not if you tell me all of it. Who led you to me?"

"I love you, Sasha."

"And I've never stopped loving you."

"I never meant to put you in danger." She was sobbing openly now. "It's just that it's been so long, and not one word."

"I know. Don't think I haven't suffered too."

He put his arm around her, drawing her face to his chest, and the smell and the posture were oddly familiar, reassuring. For an instant, she was a little girl again, riding proud in her father's lap on the saddle of a big bay mare at a dude ranch in California.

"Who was it?" he asked again, dragging her back to the present.

She wanted to blurt all of it out, starting from the moment the FBI scooped her up in the rain outside the New School. But then she would have to admit that she had failed to warn him that they were under FBI surveillance in New York because she was frightened of losing him. She was even more afraid of losing him now that she had found him again. So she told him a part of the story, hoping it would be enough to satisfy him.

"There's a journalist in Moscow, a friend of mine."

"Who?"

"His name is Guy Harrison. He's from New Zealand. That's next to Australia," she added, as if this lent weight to the information.

"How did you meet him?"

"I've been writing for a few American publications. One of my editors gave me an introduction."

Sasha allowed this to pass. He let her embroider on these social acquaintances for a while, regaining her confidence, before he suddenly asked, "How did this Guy Harrison know about me?"

"Your name was in the newspapers," she gambled. "When they announced you were a war hero."

"Yes. But how did he know where to look for me?"

"He knew you were working for Marshal Zotov. It's generally known—"

"Not to foreign journalists," Sasha cut her off. "Harrison is much too well informed. Who does he really work for? The CIA? The British?"

She had run out of answers.

"You don't have to say anything more," he told her. "They didn't teach you to lie very well. Did they ask you to try to recruit me?"

"No!" she protested.

"Let me see if I can guess what they said. They said there'd be no strings, didn't they?"

She turned away, ashamed and confused.

"They're playing with us," he said, in a tone that was patient rather than angry. "They're using you for bait. You never feel the hook to begin with."

"Believe me, Sasha. I would never have come if I thought—"

"I know why you came. Whatever happens, I'm glad you did." He kissed her again. "But you must understand that if we're discovered—if your friends are clumsy, let's say, or if they decide to betray us—" She stared at him in bewildered disbelief and he specified, "Oh yes, it can happen. No secret service is a stranger to blackmail, and blackmailers sometimes have to prove they mean business. Let's just say it could be extremely unpleasant. They"—there was no need to spell out who *they* were—"might even shoot me as an American spy."

"What have I done?" Her voice was barely a whisper.

"Nothing, I hope," he tried to comfort her. "Except to give me back my heart for an hour. But you must go and explain to your friends that we can't see each other again, not in Moscow. It would be suicide."

With the slow, disjointed motions of a sleepwalker, she rose from the bed and started to dress. Her body was fuller than before, but her waist was still tiny, and she moved on the small, neatly turned feet of a ballerina. He watched her struggling with her pantyhose, and wanted to hold her again.

"Come to me," he called to her, his arms outstretched. There was no telling how long they would have to wait until the next time.

"If I could think only of myself," he told her, "I would find a way to go back to New York, to be with you. But I told you before, I have a mission that matters more than any individual's happiness. If I betrayed that, you couldn't love me."

"But you won't share that mission. I'm not sure I understand it."

He recited another verse from Vissotsky's ballad of the wolves, without translating:

> *The wolf cannot, must not, act in any other way:*
> *See, my hour has already come*
> *He for whom I am destined*
> *Smiles and shoulders his rifle.*

Elaine could make sense of only a few of the words. Her frown deepened when he said, in English but scarcely less obscurely, "My mission is reflected in whatever you find in me to love."

"And to fear?"

"Perhaps that too."

He drove her from Bangladesh to a Metro station and sped away without looking back, into a tarpaper dark.

"He did the right thing of course," Guy Harrison remarked. "By his lights, that is. I'm sorry, old girl."

"Being sorry isn't enough. I may have put him in danger."

"We took every conceivable precaution," Harrison reminded her. He paused before adding, "He seems a remarkable man. It's the driven men who have always interested me. The ones with a hidden compass. Which way do you suppose his is pointing? You say he's a man with a mission. Is he a man with an ideology?"

"No," she said quickly, hearing him recite Vissotsky's line: *I have passed beyond the flags.* "He's not interested in abstractions. His beliefs are founded in what he has lived. He's not a communist, or a liberal, or a fascist."

Harrison glanced at his watch and said, "It's time for the news." He twiddled with the dial on his radio, and soon the familiar strains of the theme signal for the BBC World Service filled his cluttered living room.

There was a report about a new atrocity by Iranian kamikaze bombers, and when the announcer said, in his clipped voice: "We have just received news of a wave of labor unrest in the Soviet Union, whose leader has not been seen in public for several weeks. An underground trade union that diplomatic observers liken to the Polish Solidarity movement is said to be involved in strike activity in the industrial city of Togliatti."

The rest of the news was routine: a new wrangle within the European Community over subsidies for French farmers, an anti-nuclear demonstration outside an American base in West Germany, a new guerrilla offensive in Central America.

When the broadcast was over, Elaine said, "Guy, do you think the Togliatti business is as serious as they make out?"

"You mean, a Russian Solidarity? Not much chance, I would think. The last time there was a major strike here, the authorities brought out the tanks and heavy machine guns."

"They haven't managed to kill Solidarity in Poland," she pointed out.

"That's completely different. Poland is an occupied country. And the Poles have got the Pope on their side. He's worth a lot of battalions."

An occupied country. The phrase reminded her of something Sasha had said in New York, trying to explain the state of his country, and his own sense of duty toward it.

"The people don't make revolutions in Russia," Harrison went on. "Revolutions are made in their name. And that's a different thing altogether."

"You don't think the strike could be a catalyst for something?"

"What kind of something?"

"Well—" She paused. He had mentioned tanks being used to crush a previous strike. She tried to picture Sasha in command of those tanks, and couldn't. "Suppose they brought in the army."

"Yes?"

"And the army didn't want to obey."

She expected Guy to brush the suggestion aside in his languid way, but instead he responded as a trained intelligence operative, and pounced. "Did Sasha talk to you about it?"

"No, of course not. I don't think I ever heard of Togliatti before now."

"Mmm." He slumped back into his armchair.

She said, "How far is Togliatti from Moscow?"

He raised his eyebrows. "You don't need to know. The place is off-bounds for now, for me, and especially for you. All we need is for you to get yourself arrested. Look, I can see you need a change of scene. Go and enjoy the sights. Take a day trip to Novgorod. Go to the Bolshoi. I've got a little tout who can always get hold of some good seats. I'll send in a report and we'll see what those geniuses in Washington think up next."

She let him ramble on without contradiction, her thoughts focused on Togliatti and its rumored strike. Before leaving New York, she had met an elderly man, a friend of her father's, who was active in the cause of Soviet

Jews, and he had given her a contact she had had no thought of using until now. Why not seek him out? Why not try to get to Togliatti? The venture would give her a chance to test herself as a reporter. It might bring her into the heart of Sasha's country, and its turmoil.

And she sensed, rather than thought, that this might be an act of expiation: for a few days, she would share some of the risks that Sasha had to live with every day of his life.

2 When Misha Repnin read out the speech that had been delivered by his fellow auto worker at the funeral in Red Square, there was groaning and jeering from the men who had gathered in his cramped living room. So Andropov was a true Leninist, a friend of the workers, was he? Well, his much-advertised efficiency drive and his anticorruption campaign hadn't changed the life of the bosses, not so you'd notice, anyway. But Misha and his comrades on the assembly lines at the giant auto plant at Togliatti had felt the effects, right enough. Now there were sneaks hanging around, ready to rat on a man who showed up a few minutes late, or had a bit of a hangover, or "borrowed" a few trifles from the factory store, or did any of the other things that made life bearable. Thanks to this famous efficiency drive, one of the men at the plant had actually signed his name to a letter in the Komsomol paper denouncing "slackness and graft" among his co-workers. Misha had cornered him during the lunch break and told him that if he did anything like that again, he, Repnin, would fix his gearshift for him.

Coming from Repnin, this wasn't a threat to take lightly. He was a stocky young man with plenty of muscle to make up for his beer-belly. He sported a droopy walrus moustache, like his hero Lech Walesa in Poland. The snitches were told to keep an eye on him, but Misha had a pretty good instinct for who he could trust. At night, he would get a few friends together and turn on his powerful Japanese radio. He could get all the foreign broadcasts—German, British, American—and they would listen to what the world was saying about the changes in Moscow and the war in Afghanistan and the East-West struggle. But what most held their interest was the news from Poland. Whatever the authorities were saying in Moscow, it was clear that the revolt of the Polish workers hadn't been broken yet. "If the bloody Poles can do it," Repnin liked to point out to his friends, "if Lech Walesa can set up a free trade union and force the regime to treat him with respect, then why the fuck can't we do it too? Are we Russians or aren't we?"

His fighting words were received with more and more sympathy in the months after the new General Secretary was installed. Nobody had any illusions about what he stood for, this old hack puffing his way through a string of clichés. He stood for more of the same, words in place of reforms, government by the same old gang of geriatrics who had been stealing the workers blind. You only had to look around. The food shortages were worse than ever, while they spent a fortune on crocodile tears for Yuri Vladimirovich. Misha hadn't been able to buy meat or milk at his local shop for months. White bread was almost unobtainable. It was the same all over the country.

"So why can't they feed us?" Repnin would lecture his friends. He was a natural as an orator, and he had been boning up on *samizdat* leaflets that were passing from hand to hand. "Number one, they're too busy spending money—our money—on tanks and rockets. Number two, they won't let the farmers be farmers."

"Why is that, Misha?" somebody asked.

"Because they're shit-scared. Any fool knows that. Just suppose they let the farmers start earning an honest living, so they could put a bit away for their families and might have some incentive to do their job right instead of lying around drunk all the time. What would happen? Why, we might have a new class, a class of independent producers. They'll never allow that. Why do you think Stalin starved the peasants? So there'd be nobody to answer back, nobody who didn't depend on the state for a meal ticket."

"What about Hungary then?" the same speaker asked. There'd been a lot of talk on the BBC about the so-called Hungarian economic model, and incentives for farm production.

Repnin made a raspberry. "They don't give a shit what the Hungarians do. They'll go in with tanks, like in nineteen-fifty-six, if they get out of hand. But with us, it's a different matter. They think if they allow one little crack to develop, it will widen into a huge geological fault, and the whole granite system will be blown to bits."

He was rather proud of this analogy, but it was too high-falutin' for most of his audience.

"What are we going to do then, Misha?" somebody asked almost plaintively.

"Every time we get a new boss in Moscow," Repnin said, "he promises to make things better. This time, we ought to show that we're watching to see if any of the promises are kept. This is the workers' state, isn't it? Let's show them that the workers still have some balls."

After that, anonymous wall posters started sprouting from the walls around the Lada factory, making fun of the bosses both in Togliatti and in Moscow. Askyerov, who as the man in charge of the transportation sector was at least partly to blame for the food shortages, was ideal for caricature. Crude sketches depicted him as a monstrous cockroach feeding off a lavishly spread table while skinny Russian children in rags looked on. Young people started to appear at the factory gates at the end of each shift, handing out leaflets to workers who would accept them. It was a sign of the times that most of the men from the Lada plant weren't afraid to take the *samizdat*. One of the leaflets announced the formation of an independent trade union, the Association of Russian Workers.

When the local Party boss, Muzykin, got wind of this, he flew into a rage. Something had to be done *immediately*, he informed Moscow. Anti-Soviet agitators were taking advantage of the change in leadership to test the determination of the regime. It would be suicidal, he counseled, to tolerate any "controlled experiment" on the Polish model.

The militia didn't waste any time. Everybody knew—or at any rate suspected—that Misha Repnin was a moving spirit in the Association of Russian Workers. It wasn't necessary to wait for proof. Like any good Russian, Misha was fond of his tipple. He was coming home late one night, a little bit merry, and a squad of militiamen, headed by a major, no less, grabbed him right off the street. Nobody could tell for sure afterward whether he had died on his way to the station or after he got there. The militia didn't want to hand the body over to his widow, Aglaya, but there were ugly threats to close down the assembly lines, and after a mob gathered outside the MVD building, the people in charge decided they might as well let his family bury him after all. Misha's neck had been twisted around at a crazy angle. The only explanation forthcoming from the militia was that he had broken his neck in a fall. This version was somewhat undermined by the fact that most of Repnin's teeth were missing, and there was a pattern of blue-black marks, like ink blots, all down his chest and thighs.

Party Secretary Muzykin and the local militia had just provided the Association of Russian Workers with its first certifiable martyr. Even many of the workers who had shunned Misha Repnin's call to organize turned out for his mass funeral. Muzykin panicked and called the Central Committee.

"I need authorization to use regular troops," he told his superiors.

They turned him down flat. What would the world make of the new leadership if it ordered soldiers to put down a peaceful workers' manifestation—a funeral, not a strike—so soon after the death rites of the last General Secretary? Besides, Muzykin's imagination was obviously inflamed. The man must be unstable. There'd been workers' protests in the Ukraine, in the Baltic states, as well as in the satellites. But a workers' revolt in Russia? No, it was unthinkable.

So Secretary Muzykin had to make do with the militia. He had them massed, in their blue-gray uniforms, in front of the Party building, with heavily armed reinforcements of MVD Internal Troops posted in side streets, ready to be brought in if things turned out as he feared.

There was a terrible silence as the crowd advanced through the streets, bearing Repnin's coffin on its shoulders. The widow Aglaya was in the front row, with her three children. But nobody seemed to be leading the marchers. When the crowd swung off the prescribed route, and headed toward Party headquarters, it seemed to be the result of some collective instinct. Their silence, their solidity, seemed to be too much for the first line of militiamen, who fell back and let them through.

When Muzykin, from his window, saw the bier, draped in black and red and strewn with wreaths, sailing up the street, he called down to the militia commander, "Bring up the Internal Troops! And be quick about it!" The men in these units, recruited in other parts of the Union and mostly non-Russians, could be counted on to do what they were told. They didn't care whose heads got broken.

Someone, perhaps a police provocateur, ran out of the crowd yelling, "Murderers! Bandits!" and lobbed a bottle over the heads of the militiamen at the Party building. It smashed against the big oak doors. A second man's aim was better. The rock crashed through the Party Secretary's window. Muzykin was shaking. He was starting to remember the stories he had heard about the food riots in Gdansk, in Poland, when the local Party offices had been set on fire. As if to confirm his fears, someone in the middle of the crowd had unfurled a banner that nobody had seen before. It was white and red, with the word "Solidarity" in Russian.

The Internal Troops marched into the square from two sides, squeezing the crowd like pincers.

"Give them the gas!" an officer yelled.

The tear-gas canisters were fired, filling the square with an acrid cloud. Women and children were screaming. The men were coughing and gasping for breath. As the riot troops pushed in from both sides, the mourners were jammed up against each other, blinded by the gas. When the stampede began, some of the mourners stumbled and fell under the trampling feet. The pallbearers tried to stand their ground, but the human tide carried them away, and Aglaya was left weeping beside her husband's coffin, until a militiaman came at her with the butt of his rifle. When the smoke had cleared, there were six corpses left in the square: two children and two adults who had been trampled to death, a seventy-year-old state pensioner who had suffered a heart attack, and Misha Repnin, the cause of it all.

Party Secretary Muzykin's version of the iron heel was less than successful. The news traveled all over the country. Soon it was being carried over the BBC and the Voice of America. Wall posters started to appear in Kiev and Gorky, in Moscow and Leningrad. Misha's fellow workers at the Lada plant declared an all-out strike. The mysterious Association of Russian Workers appealed, in leaflets and phone messages, for a nationwide show of solidarity. There were walkouts in several cities, even at the Likachev auto works in Moscow, whose spokesman had delivered the eulogy to Andropov, standing shoulder-to-shoulder with the members of the Politburo.

3 Elaine paid a visit to a modest apartment not far from the Lenin Stadium. This was the address she had been given in New York. She traveled by subway and trolleybus, circling around until she was fairly sure she wasn't being followed. She flattered herself that she was beginning to learn "Moscow rules," as Guy Harrison called them. It was a city where habits of conspiracy were easily acquired.

A sad-faced woman came to the door.

"Aaron Semyonich?" she asked.

"I don't know him." The woman was preparing to shut the door in her face, but Elaine quickly added, "Please tell Aaron that Irwin sent me."

"You wait," the woman said. This time, she did close the door.

When it opened again, a man grabbed her arm and pulled her inside so fast that she hardly got a look at him. When she did, she was pleasantly surprised. Aaron was tall and sturdily built, with a high forehead topped by a bright frizz of red hair that made him look as if he had just hit upon some new invention. Indeed, Aaron Semyonich had been a scientist of distinction before he committed the crime of applying for an exit visa.

He asked her a couple of questions to verify that she really had been sent by Irwin in New York, said, "Call me Ari," and got right to the point. "What do you need?"

"The strike in Togliatti," she faltered.

"What about it?"

"I'd like to go. I'd like to write the truth about it."

He peered at her skeptically. "Togliatti is a closed city. No western correspondents have been allowed in."

"I'm not here as a correspondent. I've got a tourist visa."

"Even worse. At best, they'd deport you for violating the terms of your visa. At worst, they'll arrest you as a spy."

"Only if they catch me. Think what it could mean. An eyewitness account by a western writer."

"Do you speak Russian?"

"Only a little."

"Show me."

She told him in Russian about her course at the New School and her family history.

"The accent isn't bad." He nodded. "You might get by if you don't have to say more than a word or two. And you could pass for a Soviet if you dress down a bit. They don't make shoes like that in Russia."

"So you'll help me?"

"I'll think about it. I might know someone." He paused. "But listen, if I get you in there, I can't guarantee to get you out. Like they say in America, we don't sell round trips."

The Politburo met in crisis session with the army chiefs in the Central Committee building on Old Square.

The General Secretary sat silent, weighing the consensus, letting others debate while the stenographers scribbled away at their tables against the wall. Under the light from the chandeliers, the General Secretary's face had the color and texture of frozen poultry. From time to time he would take an atomizer from his pocket and squeeze it into his mouth.

Marshal Zotov was seated opposite Romanov, the former Party boss in Leningrad and one of the contenders for the succession. With his exaggerated tan, this Romanov didn't look much like his namesakes, the former royal family. *He makes himself up like a tart,* Zotov thought.

Gussein Askyerov was doing a lot of the talking. The Azerbaijani managed to fawn and dominate at the same time. "If you'll permit me, Comrade General Secretary," he kept saying, "with your permission—"

He certainly knew how to keep in with the boss, the Marshal thought as he watched Askyerov perform. He had oiled his way into the confidence of Tsvigun, and used him to make his number with Tsvigun's brother-in-law, Brezhnev. Then, with impeccable timing, he had switched his loyalties to Andropov. But as soon as they had Andropov strapped to his dialysis machine, Askyerov had smarmed his way back into the inner councils of the old Brezhnev clique.

"If you'll allow me to say this," Askyerov went on, nodding and smiling at the General Secretary, who had transferred his attention from the atomizer to a bottle of pills—they looked big enough to be horse pills— "we really must show a firm hand. If we demonstrate any sign of weakness, this unpleasantness at Togliatti could infect the entire country. Already, the strike has assumed an overtly anti-Party character."

There were a few grunts of assent. On the second day of the strike, when Secretary Muzykin attempted to deliver a public speech, the roar of the crowd was enough to drown out the loudspeakers. Some of the voices were crying, "Down with the Party!"

"What exactly are you proposing?" Galayev interjected. The youngest man in the room, hoping to survive the rest and inherit their power, he didn't want to be upstaged.

"We must issue a statement at once," Askyerov continued. This was sure to get the approval of the General Secretary, whose main talent was issuing slogans. "We must condemn the saboteurs and explain to the people that the trouble in Togliatti is inspired by foreign elements who are undoubtedly planning to disrupt Soviet production. It is well known that this Misha Repnin was an agent of western imperialism."

Round up the usual suspects, Zotov commented in silence.

There were no objections to this suggestion. But Askyerov was off and running.

"With your permission," he bobbed his almost creaseless face at the General Secretary, "it is now clear to all that the Party and the internal security forces are under siege in Togliatti, which has become a bastion of reaction. The saboteurs will not be defeated without maximum firmness. Am I not right, Comrade Chairman"—this was addressed to the head of the KGB—"that, yesterday alone, there were twenty-seven reported deaths?"

"Just so," General Chetverikov confirmed. Marshal Zotov watched the man closely. He was a lynx, that chekist. Like Askyerov, he had started out spying on the army in Stalin's time. Now he seemed to be playing Askyerov's game.

"We all know what is required." Now Askyerov was addressing the whole room, shifting his eyes—implausibly blue against the olive skin—from one face to another, but carefully avoiding Zotov. "We all know there has to be blood on the floor. But why should we alone be blamed? Why should the Party, the Committee, and the militia have to eat all the shit—if you'll pardon the expression, Comrade General Secretary. Is it not right that the armed forces should share the responsibility for upholding state security?"

The Defense Minister seemed to be taking this in his stride. Perhaps he'd been briefed in advance. But Marshal Zotov, who had not, started to bridle.

"Are you suggesting that regular troops should be used against the strikers at Togliatti?" Zotov demanded clarification. In his first face-to-face confrontation with Askyerov, he was careful to address the Prime Minister by his full honorifics.

"Do you foresee any operational difficulty, Comrade Marshal?" the Azerbaijani responded in his velvety voice.

"I wish to point out," the Marshal went on, "that there is no precedent for this proposed action since the episode at Novocherkassk, more than two decades ago, which had an unfortunate effect on army morale." This was a considerable understatement. The strike at Novocherkassk in 1962 had ended in a massacre. Grisly reports of blood spattered as high as the streetlamps had seeped out to the West and been replayed in Russian over the BBC and the Voice of America.

"I am sure, Comrade Marshal, that you are not suggesting that the Soviet armed forces cannot be counted on to do their duty," Askyerov rejoined, smooth and treacherous.

Zotov stiffened. "I believe we know our duty. I merely wish to observe that it is unnecessary to use the army unless the militia has been overwhelmed." He darted a look at the Interior Minister, who said nothing. "I would add that it is also inadvisable, not to mention *irregular*, to call in the armed forces unless you intend that the troops should use their guns."

"Marshal, you have heard the report from Secretary Muzykin," Askyerov countered. "The situation in Togliatti is extremely volatile. We should not make the error of underestimating our opponents."

"I beg to remind *you* that we are talking about *Russian* workers and their families and that errors may have been committed by the local authorities." Zotov pulled himself up short, conscious that he may have overstepped the line by suggesting that Party officials were at fault.

Askyerov was ready to pounce, but the General Secretary chose this moment to intervene. His words were hard to follow. They came in rapid bursts, punctuated by gulps of air. He sounded like a drowning man who has just been pulled up to the surface.

"Those matters will be subject to inquiry at time fitting."—*gasp*—"The Marshal will issue the appropriate instructions."—*wheeze*—"Who is the District commander?"

"General Leybutin," Zotov replied.

"Can we count on him?" Askyerov asked.

The Marshal stared at the Azerbaijani as if he were something that had crawled out from under a log. "Pavel Leybutin gave his blood in Afghanistan," he said. "He's one of the finest officers in the Soviet army. I trust him as I trust myself."

The Defense Minister glanced at the General Secretary, who nodded assent.

They've worked it all out already, Zotov thought.

"Please instruct General Leybutin to place himself at the disposal of Party Secretary Muzykin," the Defense Minister ordered Zotov.

4 The giant auto plant at Togliatti, named in honor of a famous Italian Communist leader, had, appropriately enough, been constructed under license from an Italian company, Fiat. But the city was closed to the outside world. A visiting team of engineers had been rushed back to Moscow and were being held incommunicado in their hotel. Even the flow of *samizdat* had started to dry up. Most of what appeared in the western press was speculation.

But Aaron Semyonich, it seemed, knew how to squeeze through spaces too narrow for a cat. Elaine was met at the railway station in a nearby town by one of Ari's contacts, a nervous man who was a press-tool operator in the Lada factory. She arrived in Togliatti wearing over her jeans a shapeless coat she had purchased in GUM, on the same day as General Leybutin. She was carrying a purse and a shopping bag with a few necessities in it. Everything else she had left at the hotel, to make herself less conspicuous. She had told nobody where she was going. In retrospect, she thought this was a mistake. Guy Harrison might get worried and start rattling cages. Well, it was too late now.

Her guide, who introduced himself only as Yakov, said that she could stay overnight with his family. But his nervousness was contagious.

"I really don't want to put you out," she said in her fractured Russian. On the way into the city, he started asking her whether she could get someone to write to him, claiming that he was a relative, so that he could apply for an exit visa.

She said uncertainly, "I'll try."

They followed a back road into the town. Elaine heard a noise like squelchy rubber boots over gravel, and when they came to the top of a hill, she saw its origin. Along the highway, over to their left, a column of tanks and army trucks stretched as far back as she could see.

"My God," she breathed. "Do the people know?"

"We have to go back," Yakov said to her. His face was damp.

"No," Elaine insisted. "Whatever's going to happen, the world has to know." She knew that she sounded preposterous, but she was carried along by a giddy sensation, as if she'd been drinking on an empty stomach.

They found a mass demonstration taking place in the center of town. There were scores of banners bearing the symbol of the Association of Russian Workers and the word "Solidarity." Elaine let herself be swept along by the crowd. She didn't stand out in any way. There were almost as many women as men. The human current carried her farther and farther away from Yakov until he was lost from sight.

There was an open space up ahead, and row upon row of soldiers blocking the street. Beyond, the squat facade of an official building. Elaine could not see or hear the exchange that was taking place between Secretary Muzykin and General Leybutin inside the Party headquarters.

"Why do you think you're here, fuck your mother?" Muzykin was screaming. "Give the order to open fire!"

"From what I've seen," Leybutin said doggedly, "this is a peaceful demonstration."

"You didn't see what happened yesterday, or the day before," Muzykin insisted. "Now we have information. They want to burn down Party headquarters. Just listen to them!"

From the streets came the dull roar of a thousand voices calling for Muzykin's head.

"You know your orders!" Muzykin yelled. "They come from the top. Now I'm telling you. Disperse the rioters!"

Heavily, as if his feet were fettered, Leybutin went down the stairs and out into the square.

"Fire over their heads," he ordered.

At the first volley, the crowd wavered, and the people in the front ranks tried to turn and run back. But then the roar deepened, and the crowd surged forward.

Muzykin came hopping out to join Leybutin. "Why are you waiting?"

"They're Russians," Leybutin said quietly. "There are women and children out there."

Muzykin glared at him as if he was thinking of ripping off his shoulder boards.

"I'll do it myself," the Party Secretary announced. "Open fire!" The senior warrant officer, standing next to Leybutin, looked at him questioningly. Reluctantly, Leybutin nodded assent. The warrant officer repeated the order. His voice boomed out over the heads of the troops like a cannon.

Some of the soldiers still hesitated. It was a mixed contingent of conscripts, many of them Russians. Some of the men had been drafted from the Togliatti region and might have had friends or relatives in the crowd. The Uzbeks and Kazakhs in the division, however, didn't have any local loyalities to worry about. Shooting strikers in Togliatti might even have been a more welcome job for them than shooting Afghans. So the Central Asians opened up with their machine guns. The bullets struck their targets with the light plop of pebbles being tossed into mud.

Elaine gasped as a heavyset man tried to elbow her aside. She couldn't move back; the mass of people behind her was solid. The man jabbed his elbow savagely into her stomach, desperate to get away from the shooting.

"Stop, wait," she pleaded, her words lost in the screaming and the rattle of the machine guns.

But he came at her again, blindly, falling on her as if he meant to flatten her on the ground. All his weight came pressing down on her shoulders, and her knees buckled under her. But for the people behind her, she would have fallen. She clawed at the man, trying to pry herself loose. Her hands came away from him wet and sticky, and she screamed when she realized that she was covered in blood. A violent eddy in the crowd dragged her away to the left, and the man's body rolled away from her. He had been shot through the back of the head.

Borne aloft like a cork in the stream, she caught a glimpse of the scene in front of the Party headquarters. Something odd was happening. The soldiers had stopped firing, and broken their lines. They were standing around in a ragged group, leveling their guns at each other. One of them, a swarthy man with a black moustache, was lying in his own blood.

Then she was running with the others, running to save herself from falling under their feet, following the direction they chose. They veered away down a side street, and suddenly a man came darting out of a doorway and grabbed hold of her arm. It was Yakov.

"In here," he said sharply as he pulled her into the building.

There were a dozen people or more crowded into the tiny flat. Elaine looked at the circle of frightened faces. But there was a woman there who looked entirely composed. She was stocky, with a raw look of good health, and she was dressed all in black, with her hair in a tidy bun. She was very definitely in charge. "Make our guests some tea," she issued instructions, as if nothing unusual was going on outside.

"This is Aglaya," Yakov explained to Elaine. "Misha Repnin's wife." They hadn't got used to the hard word "widow."

Elaine couldn't hold the glass steady. Some of the tea sloshed over the rim, scalding her wrist.

"Why did the soldiers stop shooting?"

"Georgi saw it all from the roof," Aglaya said, gesturing toward her teenage son. "When the troops were ordered to open fire, only some of them obeyed. There was a boy there from around here—a Russian," she specified with grim satisfaction. "It was too much for him. He shot one of the Central Asians who was firing into the crowd. It looked as if there was going to be a war between the soldiers, but then their general stepped in. What's his name, Yakov?"

"General Leybutin."

"Well, Leybutin ordered them to cease fire and withdraw."

"I wish I could have seen Muzykin's face," Yakov interjected. "He's the Secretary of our Party Committee," he added for Elaine's benefit. "He ran away to hide when the soldiers left."

"I saw him!" Georgi said excitedly. "He had to climb out a back window! There were flames coming out of the building."

"You mean they stormed Party headquarters?" Elaine asked.

"They took the place apart," Yakov confirmed. "They ransacked the files. I never thought I'd live to see anything like it. Party documents are blowing around the square. They say several militiamen were killed too," he added grimly. "There'll be the devil to pay."

"By tonight," Aglaya said, "the news will be all over the country. Yakov says you're a journalist." She turned to Elaine. "I hope you will write our story so the world will know that they couldn't kill Misha Repnin."

Yakov shook Elaine awake before dawn.

"What time is it?" she asked blearily. As she uncoiled herself on the sofa, she became conscious of the other people in the room, busily engaged in gathering their belongings.

"We can't stay here any longer," Yakov said urgently. "This is one of the first places they will search."

"What's happening?" Now Elaine was fully awake, and could read the fear in the others' faces. Even Aglaya, so proud, so contained the day before, seemed pale and edgy.

"We received a message while you were asleep," Aglaya said. "Muzykin didn't waste any time. He went to Moscow himself and arranged everything. General Leybutin has been placed under arrest. A new district commander is arriving today. They are bringing in special troops—Chukchis."

The word seemed to create a chill among the Russians in the room.

"The Chukchis are born killers," Yakov explained to Elaine. "They're an Arctic people. The men are bred to be hard and merciless. They provide a lot of the guards for the uranium mines—and shock troops for the MVD."

"I think I should stay," Elaine said.

"You must go." It was Aglaya who spoke. "Go and tell the world what they're doing to the workers of Togliatti."

The streets were bleak and unnaturally quiet as Yakov led her away from the center of the city. They pressed themselves into a doorway as a military convoy roared past, led by a jeep with a heavy machine gun mounted on the back.

"They're going to the auto plant," Yakov whispered. The workers had seized the factory and were holding it against all comers. In the distance, Elaine could hear the crackle of small-arms fire and the deeper crump-crump of mortars or rockets.

"But the workers aren't armed," she said.

Yakov shrugged. "There are rumors that some of the Russian soldiers joined them. I don't know if that's true. They've already begun the court-martials. Some of the soldiers who refused to obey orders have been shot. They say a whole regiment is going to be disbanded. The men will be sent to the labor camps."

They walked for what seemed like hours, creeping along, ready to take cover at the sight of a uniform. Beside a rough track leading across the fields, Yakov said, "I can't come any farther." He pointed ahead. "You'll be able to get on a train at the next village. It's not far."

Waiting in line at the railroad station to buy her ticket for Moscow, Elaine started fishing around for money in her pocketbook. She must have injured her left hand during the jostling in the street, she thought. The fingers felt stiff and arthritic. She felt a sudden, searing pain in the joints and her bag fell to the ground, spilling most of its contents.

An unpleasant little man who had been lolling over by the platform, undressing her with his eyes, came hurrying over to help.

"It's quite all right, thank you," she said.

But he insisted.

She saw the blue corner of her American passport jutting out from under a wad of tissues, and scooped it up before he could, hoping he hadn't noticed.

He didn't bother her for long after that, just long enough to hear her destination when she got to the head of the line. As she moved out onto the platform, she saw him strutting off in the direction of the stationmaster's office. But there was no sign of him when the train pulled in, and once she had found a seat, she stopped worrying about him and began to compose her first article on the strike at Togliatti.

"He claws with his dying hand," Marshal Zotov told Sasha in disgust. He had been describing the meeting at which the General Secretary had issued his instructions for the mopping-up at Togliatti. They were in the Marshal's office on Gogol Boulevard, which he preferred to his suite in the Defense Ministry, because he felt farther away from his Party overseers.

"They all went along with him, of course. He pants, and they tremble. The Chukchis were Askyerov's idea, naturally. One of these days I'm going to crush that cockroach under my heel."

"What about Pavel Leybutin?" Sasha asked. He had admired the general since he had seen him in action in Afghanistan.

"Some of them wanted to shoot him," Zotov reported. "I did my best. I told them they couldn't afford to make a martyr out of one of our war heroes. Now they're going to send him to the Serbsky Institute for psychiatric examination."

He started drumming his fist on his desk.

"Here's what I want you to do," he instructed his son-in-law. "Go to Togliatti for me. Make me a full report. Those bitches are going to be held accountable for this. I also want complete reports on the state of army morale."

Sasha made a few notes, then sat there, expressionless, meeting Zotov's gaze.

"Always the sphinx, aren't you, Sasha? I know what you're waiting for. You think it's time to move, don't you?"

"I don't need to conduct an opinion poll to tell you what the younger men are saying."

"And they could be right. I don't need a report from the Kremlin clinic to tell you that our Party leader won't be with us very long."

"And then?"

"They're all poised to stab each other in the back. But Askyerov is going to be the kingmaker, that's staring us in the face. He's no fool, I'll give him that. He won't try to take the laurels for himself. He'll put in a man he thinks he can control as General Secretary, while *he* runs the machine. He can count on Chetverikov, Serdyuk too. And we can be sure of one thing, Sasha. If Askyerov gets his hand on the wheel, it won't be long before they're trying to pack *me* off to the bloody Serbsky Institute." He paused. He had his office swept by a trusted man, an army technician, every day, but even so . . .

"You remember those Spetsnaz exercises we discussed?" he said to Sasha. "I don't think we should wait any longer."

5 Sasha picked up Zaytsev at the station in his own Volga and drove him to Bangladesh. The Spetsnaz general was wearing civilian clothes under protest, stiff and uncomfortable in his old suit and worn overcoat with a couple of buttons missing. On the way, Sasha recounted what he had seen during his visit to Togliatti. The Chukchis had done a thorough job, favoring the bayonet over the bullet, exacting revenge for the sacking of the Party headquarters. "When I saw what they did at the auto plant, where some of the workers tried to make a stand, I thought I was back in Herat," Sasha reported.

"What about Leybutin?"

"He belongs to the KGB now. I saw a preliminary report from the Serbsky Institute. They've decided Pavel had a drinking problem, and was seeing white mice instead of imperialist saboteurs. Maybe Feliks can tell us something."

Zaytsev wasn't trying to disguise the fact that he was less than enthusiastic about going to his first meeting with Sasha's friend in the KGB. When Sasha said, "We depend on Feliks," Zaytsev shook his head as if his collar were chafing him. His first impressions of Nikolsky left him looking positively depressed.

Feliks came bounding out of the kitchen sporting a new apron with a picture of a kangaroo and the inscription "I Love Australia," and a tray loaded up with brandy and snacks which he deposited, with the poise of a professional waiter, on the coffee table in the Transit Hall. The door to the bedroom was open, and Sasha winced internally as he observed the familiar bundle of soiled sheets on the floor. Zaytsev's glance roamed across the sheets, the unmade bed, the dirty glasses standing around on every flat surface in the living room.

"How long are we going to spend on business?" Nikolsky inquired cheerfully as he poured out the Akhtamar brandy. "Shall I call one of my chickens and ask her to book a couple of her friends for later?"

Zaytsev stared at him balefully. But Feliks wasn't in the least put out. "My apologies," he said ironically, waving a hand over the plates of appetizers. "This is not from the great Maxim's in Paris. But in view of the food situation in our great agricultural nation, it's the best I could do. Now really, General"—this to Zaytsev, who hadn't touched his drink—"ty chto mumu yebyosh?"

Feliks proposed a couple of toasts, while Zaytsev sat silent and angry, waiting for Sasha to call him to order.

"Don't sit there like a boiled potato," Feliks goaded him. "Give us a toast!"

"Very well." Solemnly, as if he were standing for a hymn in church, Zaytsev got to his feet. He raised his glass and said in his deep, gravelly voice, "Let the earth be a soft bed for the dead of Togliatti."

This sobered even Nikolsky. They all drained their glasses and sat in silence for a long moment.

"The bitches," Zaytsev said. "They used the army for their dirty work in Togliatti. Thank God we still have men like Pavel Leybutin."

They drank again, to the cashiered general who had refused to go on killing Russians.

"It won't end well with Leybutin," Sasha remarked to Nikolsky. "We received a report from your respected organization that claims he was suffering from white disease."

"I never had it myself," Nikolsky said, unable to resist a joke even under the least humorous circumstances, "but a friend of mine had it. I went round to his place, and there were white mice running around all over the floor." Nobody laughed, and he went on, somewhat apologetically, "They're putting Leybutin under intensive care."

"What exactly does that mean?" Sasha asked.

Nikolsky took out a piece of paper. "I made a list. These are the drugs they've prescribed for him."

Sasha glanced through the list. The first drug prescribed was aminazin. He was familiar with its effects. After being treated with aminazin, university professors were unable even to read.

He handed the paper to Zaytsev, who looked at it and swore, "*Svolochy.* Scum. They want to turn his brain into mashed potato." He returned the list to Nikolsky and said, "How did you get this?"

"I work for Colonel Topchy."

"In the Third Directorate?" Zaytsev looked sideways at Sasha as if to say, *I warned you.*

"Just so."

Zaytsev withdrew into himself again.

Sasha took charge of the conversation. "Take off that fucking apron and sit down," he told Feliks. "I've brought you together for a serious reason. We represent three powers in this country: Spetsnaz, who are the best fighters we've got; our honorable chekists"—Nikolsky took a bow—"and the General Staff, including Zotov. I can tell you within these four walls that Marshal Zotov feels just as strongly as we do about Togliatti. I am sure you understand that, in his position, he can't express his views as strongly as he would like. Even so, he opposed the use of the army in Togliatti in front of the whole Politburo."

"They won't forget that," Zaytsev remarked.

"No, they won't. I've known each of you for a long time," Sasha went on. "I know I can trust you completely. There is only one institution left in Russia that retains any real integrity and popular support." Nobody dissented. "We can't allow this gang to destroy the reputation of the army the way it has destroyed the reputation of the Party."

"What exactly are you suggesting?" Nikolsky asked.

"The Marshal can't move without support. We are going to provide that support."

"For what? For a military coup? Now really, General"—Nikolsky poured himself another drink—"this isn't West Africa. We're not jungle bunnies, or comic-opera Latin colonels. We're allergic to coups."

"I think I've learned something about coups," Sasha continued. "You don't need to involve many people, and you don't need popular support. All you need is a clearly defined center of power, and a passive population that is used to following orders from the top. The daughter of Peter the Great did it with only four hundred men."

"You're not drinking enough, Sasha," Feliks said. "You've got no business talking like this when you're sober. Come along, General," he prompted Zaytsev, "*you* tell him he's insane."

"Bloody hell!" Zaytsev erupted. "With just my own boys, just one Spetsnaz brigade, I could do it myself."

Nikolsky covered his eyes with his hand and groaned.

"Tell us about it, Fedya," Sasha said.

"The Politburo meets every Thursday at four in the afternoon, am I right? Well, all you have to do is smuggle in a few special teams, surround the Central Committee building, and grab the bitches when they're all sitting together in the same room. I would be master of Moscow, and the rest of the country would do my bidding. Moscow rules, doesn't it?"

"Excuse me," Feliks objected, "but do you really imagine that everyone would jump to attention for an unknown paratroop general?"

"Maybe not," Zaytsev agreed, darting a glance at Sasha. "But if the orders were signed by the Chief of Staff, the army would obey. That's all that counts."

"Haven't you forgotten a few details?" Sasha chipped in. "It wouldn't be enough to capture the Central Committee building. You'd need to worry about the militia, the airports, the broadcasting and communications centers, not to mention our friends at the Lubyanka."

"Fifteen hundred men," Zaytsev said. "And a back-up force, in case the Dzerzhinsky Division was mobilized. That's all it would take. The planning would have to be perfect, of course. We would need floor plans of all the targets. We'd need secure assembly points. We'd need to rehearse every move."

"That can all be arranged," Sasha said.

"I know a waiter who worked in the telephone exchange," Nikolsky interjected.

Zaytsev glared at him, apparently thinking that this was another joke in doubtful taste, and said, "Our biggest problem is security. If the Marshal is with us, only a handful of people would have to be fully indoctrinated. The rest will simply do what they're told. We need to be extremely careful who we include in the inner circle. There are chekists everywhere." From the way he went on staring at Feliks, it was plain that Nikolsky hadn't yet passed muster as far as Zaytsev was concerned.

"Fedya," Sasha began, "perhaps I should have explained." He started to recount how Nikolsky had gone to work for the Third Directorate at his request, but Feliks cut him off. He was angry and aggressive now, wounded by Zaytsev's refusal to trust him.

"Our *muzhik* general is absolutely correct," Nikolsky said. "You can't be sure of anyone, not even in your famous Spetsnaz. Not even among the group you've picked for your very special exercises. Oh, I see you're both surprised I knew about that. Well, let me show you how I found out."

He produced a document from his pocket, an official KGB report. Sasha glanced at the name of the sender.

"Major Suchko," he read out.

"That scum!" Zaytsev exclaimed. "He's the head chekist at my base."

"Big round face, very oily, breath like an outhouse?" Sasha asked.

"That's the one."

"I know this Suchko," Sasha said, remembering the Komsomol organizer at university who had helped to destroy Tanya. "You'd better take a
look at this."

He passed the document to Zaytsev. Suchko's report discussed "anti-
Soviet" tendencies among the Spetsnaz and airborne forces stationed at
Kavrov. It included some poisonous remarks about General Zaytsev himself. But what most startled Zaytsev was that it identified several KGB
informers at the base. One of them, Captain Vassily Artamonov, was a
man Zaytsev had trusted completely, and had included in the group he
had selected for the special exercises.

"God, I can't believe it."

"You needn't worry too much, General," Nikolsky said. "This report
was never received."

"What do you mean?"

"I mean that I intercepted it. It never reached Topchy's desk. Lucky for
you, wasn't it? No action will be taken. But I do agree with you that you
ought to be very careful about who you trust. I'm not in a position to read
all of Topchy's mail."

"I'll take care of this right away," Zaytsev said to Sasha. He got up and
put out his hand to Nikolsky. "Are we friends?"

"Aargh, I never could stomach the smell of high boots." Nikolsky
pumped his hand. "Now, if you two are finished with your plotting, it's
not too late to call a girl I know. . . ."

6 "You must be out of your bloody mind," Guy Harrison told Elaine
when she gave him the typescript of her article on the massacres in
Togliatti. Guy was wearing a smoking jacket whose original color might
have been wine red. He shuffled over to the sideboard and turned up the
volume on his radio. The music sounded as if it had been composed by a
committee.

"It's a bloody scoop, I'll grant you that," Harrison said with grudging
admiration. "And the writing isn't half bad, if you take out some of this
tabloid stuff." He quoted a line about the smell of fear.

"Will you send it off for me?"

"In the beginning was the word," Harrison intoned. "Once a hack, always a hack. How could I say no? It would be like denying an alcoholic a drink, or a dying man the last rites of Mother Church. I'll talk to a chum of mine at the Embassy. This ought to go out in the diplomatic bag." He paused and scratched his stubbly chin. "I really ought to warn you," he went on. "Certain people aren't going to be overjoyed by this little foray of yours. Now don't get your knickers in a twist. I'm just here to minister to the needy."

He stood next to the window and peered out from behind the drapes.

"Are you sure they didn't spot you in Togliatti?"

"I—I don't think so. I couldn't swear to it."

"Hmm. Well, it could just be my friendly shadow."

"If the KGB saw me in Togliatti, wouldn't they have arrested me?"

"They're not all simpletons, my love. They might have preferred to follow you and see where you led them. After all, the official line is that the strike is the work of foreign agitators. By the way, I hope you weren't planning to put your byline on your piece. Not if you were thinking of staying on here for more than twenty-four hours."

She looked offended for only an instant. Then she murmured, "Oh. Yes. Stupid of me."

"If I were you, I'd hop on the first plane out of here. Then you can write what you like and put your bloody photograph on the cover of the rag, for all it would matter. That's what I'm going to say to our American friends, too. Frankly, I don't know whether they'll want to listen. You see, I tried to ring you up after you went missing. It seems there's some kind of a panic on in Washington."

"What kind of panic?"

"Listen, my love. I'm just a boy from the bush. I carry messages back and forth and that's all, remember? Somebody's flying in from Washington this week to explain it all."

"Luke? Is Luke coming?"

"They didn't see fit to tell me. No names, all right?"

She frowned and said, "I don't want to see him."

"You mean Luke Gladden? I thought he was something of a father figure."

"He's using me. Or trying to."

"He kept his promise, didn't he? He gave you Sasha." Harrison saw her tense, and hastily added, "If I were you I'd forget about your Russian prince and the bloody CIA and get on that plane back home. I'll deliver your regrets to our visitor from Washington. You can take your copy with you. I'll even give you an introduction to my editor, the old vulture."

"Thanks, Guy," she said curtly. "I'm staying. Now how about my piece?"

"They pay by the column inch, and the rates were determined at the beginnings of the Gutenberg era. But do you think 'From a Special Correspondent' would do you for now?"

"I suppose fame can wait," she said, trying to adopt the same bantering tone.

"Good girl. Now what about an early lunch? You'd better brief me about what's going on in this bloody country. I wouldn't want my editor to think I was losing my touch. Did I tell you what he asked me for a few weeks back? He wanted a seven-hundred-word feature on the General Secretary's talent with the banjo. The same old wheeze we got with Andropov. FILE SOONEST ON ANDROPOV'S REPORTED PENCHANT FOR JAZZ, SCOTCH, POP AMERICAN FICTION."

"So what did you do?"

"I filed, of course. They ran my piece under the title 'He Came from Alma Ata with a Banjo on His Knee.' "

7 In time of war, Soviet Spetsnaz forces have the following functions: to neutralize enemy command centers and hunt down and eliminate the enemy's political and military leaders; to identify and help to destroy nuclear bases and other key defense installations; to disrupt power and communications systems. The training exercises that Zaytsev's brigade, reinforced by several independent companies, began in the forest north of Kavrov, seemed to conform completely with the combat role of the special forces, except for one unusual detail. The commandos were rehearsing the seizure of command centers in Moscow.

Vassily Artamonov came sidling up to General Zaytsev to ask about this.

"It's a new scenario," Zaytsev told him. "The enemy is presumed to have seized the capital. Our mission is to spearhead a counterattack to retake Moscow."

"There must be some real optimists in the General Staff," Artamonov remarked.

Zaytsev watched the young captain closely as he strolled away. It was still hard to accept that the man was a traitor. Spetsnaz officers were required to be Party members, of course, and were given the most thorough security screening. It was possible that Artamonov imagined that he was fulfilling his duty to the Party by ratting on his comrades to the KGB. But it was more likely that he did it for money, or through naked ambition.

He called over his chief of operations, Lieutenant-Colonel Orlov. He had briefed Orlov on Nikolsky's revelation as soon as he returned to the base.

"It's all arranged," Orlov said. "Artamonov is going on the next parachute drop."

Orlov went with the team himself. They were dressed in standard Airborne uniforms, minus the Guards badges. The men were carrying D-5 parachutes with their rifles lashed to the sides.

As they were boarding the plane, Captain Artamonov fell back.

"What's the matter with you?" Orlov demanded.

"I've got cramps. Must be something I ate."

"Get on the plane." Orlov gave him a rough push. "You're an essential part of this exercise. Nobody's going to give a shit about your belly when the real shooting starts."

They dropped from five thousand meters. As the men bailed out, the first stage of their parachutes, the stabilization canopies, opened.

Orlov held Artamonov back until everyone else had jumped.

"Now you," he said softly.

As Artamonov jumped, Orlov hurled himself after him. The colonel's boots slammed into Artamonov's back, but the force of the blow was softened by the equipment he was carrying. Then they were locked together, spinning round and round in midair, the stabilization canopies snagged and useless. Artamonov was flailing out with his arms, trying to get beyond Orlov's reach. Then the colonel was on him again. He got one arm under Artamonov's chin, and seized hold of a leg with the other. He looked as if he was trying to break the man in two. They were spinning faster and faster, and the ground seemed to be flying up to meet them; the tips of the pine trees loomed up like stakes in a bear pit.

Orlov knew he was falling too fast, 120 miles per hour, maybe faster. He summoned all his strength, and jerked Artamonov's head upward and back until he heard the bones crack. Then he spread his arms like a swimmer doing the butterfly stroke, trying to move clear of the body.

He had removed the automatic opening device from his main chute. Now he pulled out the pin. The parachute failed to open. The lines must have got snarled during his struggle with Artamonov.

With the ground rushing toward him, he clawed at the pin on the reserve chute strapped across his stomach. It fluttered open.

He braced himself for the shock. It came almost at once, all along the left side of his body. But he went on falling until there was a sudden wrench and he was left dangling like a hanged man, twenty feet above the ground. His reserve parachute had snagged in the branches of a giant fir.

Some of the men came running toward him. "Are you all right, Colonel?" one of them shouted up.

Orlov swore at them to cut him down.

He felt a shooting pain as he hit the ground, but nothing seemed to be broken. He looked around for Artamonov. The dead man's chute had opened automatically. His body lay where it had fallen, limbs spread out in a ragged cross.

When Orlov made his formal report to Zaytsev, he said, "Captain Artamonov was unfit for Spetsnaz assignments. He failed to maintain his physical condition, and broke his neck in the fall."

8 "You'll have to tell her yourself," Harrison said to Luke Gladden. "I'd still bet London to a brick she'll never do it."

And she'd be right, the CIA man thought.

"It's time we stopped pussyfooting around," the head of Soviet Division had told him at Langley. Gladden's boss, Joel Carson, favored the coinages of Teddy Roosevelt. Carson had been studying the files, and had reached the conclusion that the Agency was missing the best opportunity it had had to penetrate the Soviet General Staff since the days of Penkovsky. Carson wasn't a fisherman, like Luke Gladden. He liked shooting clay pigeons, an affluent sport that required hair-trigger reflexes rather than a patient affinity with the elements. "We've got him by the balls, haven't we?" Carson had asked rhetorically, referring to Preobrazhensky. "If he won't cooperate, we can break him."

Luke Gladden had never believed much in blackmail, not when it came to recruiting good agents. The best were the ones who came to you because of their private agenda, men with a mission. He might have argued more vigorously with his boss had he not been fully aware of the pressure that Carson was under. The White House had asked for an assessment of what was going to happen in Moscow when the new General Secretary gasped his last, and some bright spark on the NSC had come up with the idea that Marshal Zotov was the man to watch. The President himself had

asked for a full personality profile, and had been deeply alarmed by what
he got. Zotov was viewed in Washington as a super-hawk, a man who
wouldn't hesitate to use the military might of his nation where its interests
were threatened, in the Middle East, in Africa, or in Western Europe.
Zotov was said to be the moving force behind the Soviet arms build-up in
India, and behind a Soviet plan to invade Iran and choke off the oil supply
routes to the West. The Pentagon experts regarded him with respect, as
one of the most able men in the Soviet military establishment. So the
CIA's Soviet Division had been tasked, as a matter of urgent priority, to
gather every available scrap of information on the Marshal and the poli-
cies he was likely to promote if his power increased.

Gladden had arrived with a diplomatic passport in an assumed name,
supposedly attached to a delegation that had been sent to discuss the
renewal of cultural exchanges between the Soviets and the Americans. He
had decided that he wasn't going to risk a clandestine meeting in Moscow,
where his every movement would be watched. He couldn't rule out the
possibility that Elaine was now under KGB observation too, given her mad
expedition to Togliatti. So he arranged for Harrison to bring Elaine along
to the Embassy for a reception.

Guy didn't warn her. As they circulated among the guests, she with her
white wine, he with a large whisky, he just took her arm and whispered,
"Awfully stuffy in here. Why don't I show you the pictures next door?"

Luke Gladden was waiting for them in the library, next to an open fire.

Elaine stopped short in the doorway when she saw him. Gladden looked
plausible and elegant, as always, in his muted pinstripe. The setting reminded her powerfully of the evening they had spent at his New York
club, when he had talked her into letting the CIA arrange her meeting
with Sasha. *You never feel the hook at first,* Sasha had warned.

Gladden took his pipe out of his mouth as he advanced toward her,
evidently bent on planting a kiss on her cheek. She moved crabwise into
the room, avoiding him, and stationed herself behind a wing chair.

"What do you want?" she demanded.

Gladden glanced at Harrison, who merely folded his hands over his
expansive belly, disclaiming responsibility.

"I think you'd better sit down and tell me what happened," Gladden
said to her mildly.

"I told Guy already."

"I'd like to hear it for myself."

"I don't think I have anything more to say to you."

"That's not going to help him, you know." Gladden paused, hoping that she'd ask for an explanation. She didn't. *Mustn't push,* he reminded himself. *We could lose both of them.* Harrison had shuffled off into a far corner of the library, where he was ostentatiously inspecting a copy of the Federalist Papers.

"I brought you a copy of your article," he said, and held out a clipping from the London paper that Guy described as "the rag." She came out from behind her chair to take it from him. The piece was signed "By Our Special Correspondent." She noticed that the cuts had been minimal, although the London editors had added a photo that certainly hadn't been shot in Togliatti.

"You were very brave," Gladden told her. "But you could have got yourself into a lot of trouble running off like that."

"I wanted to do something that could make a difference."

"To *his* people?"

She nodded. "In a way, they're my people too."

"You really feel that strongly about them?"

"I do now."

"Will Togliatti make a difference?" he pursued. "Does writing about it help?"

"I don't know," she said uncertainly. "It helped me. I have the sense that everything is picking up speed. I guess I want to be a part of what's happening here."

"You're very much a part of it, Elaine. That's why I've come. For Pete's sake, sit down and have a drink."

He waited until she was seated with a glass in her hand before he added, "We think that Sasha could make a difference."

"How can you know that?" She left her drink untouched, as if anything from this man's hands might be tainted.

"You know him, Elaine. Is he the kind of man who could accept what the army was ordered to do at Togliatti?"

"No."

"That may be why he's in danger."

This time, she gave him his opening. "What do you mean?"

"We received information from a highly—uh—sensitive source. Another purge is being prepared. Sasha's name is pretty high on the list. Certain people have got hold of some extremely compromising dossiers."

Luke Gladden didn't particularly enjoy having to lie, but he usually managed it with panache. He told himself that this was the playwright manqué coming to the fore.

"Sasha has to be warned," he pursued. "I want you to see him again."

"He'll never agree," she protested.

"He needs our help," Gladden continued. "Just tell him what I said.
Tell him that we need to meet him as soon as possible. He can choose the
time and place. That's all there is to it."

She turned her face away to the fire, and the light gave her face the
flush of ripened apricots.

She said, "Sasha thinks it's suicide for us to meet in Moscow."

"It's suicide if you don't warn him."

She faced him. Everything about him was so damn plausible, so reassuring. Even the mild aroma of his Virginia pipe tobacco. She said, "How
can I trust you?"

He played it as a soft lob. "Have I ever lied to you?"

"I don't know."

9   In his time at Kavrov, Suchko—whom Sasha correctly remembered
     as the Komsomol bully at Moscow University—had realized his full
potential. He had degenerated into a swaggering, drunken lout, incoherent after lunch, and sometimes before, sloppy and running to fat. Recruited by the KGB upon graduation, in acknowledgment of his gifts as an
informer, he had first been assigned to the Fifth Directorate to spy on
dissidents and Jews. He set about his work with gusto, but he was too
crude even for his superiors. After he beat senseless a professor of biology
—a man who had received several international awards and been nominated for a Nobel Prize—Suchko was shunted sideways, into the Third
Directorate. He felt at home with the Topchys, and they with him.

But Suchko was bored with life at Kavrov, where those stuck-up bitches
in Spetsnaz wouldn't give him the time of day. The officers clammed up
whenever he entered the room, and Suchko guessed that it was their
commander who was giving the lead. He loathed Zaytsev, that caricature
of a man's man, with a passion. Often he had tried to catch him out, by
suggesting, for example, that the Togliatti business was a disgrace. But
Zaytsev always eluded him, volunteering nothing of his own thoughts.

It was the *stukach*, Artamonov, who gave him the first clue that something wasn't quite right at the base. The way Artamonov told it, Zaytsev
and some of his officers had formed what amounted to a political society.
They sat around at night discussing Afghanistan, the East-West conflict,
the Togliatti strike, even the country's economic problems and the leadership itself. All outside Party auspices. Suchko wondered why he'd received

nothing from headquarters except a routine acknowledgment since he'd sent in that report. Now Artamonov had got his neck broken in a bloody parachute jump. There was something wrong about that too, but Suchko couldn't get anything solid to go on.

He was diverting himself in his flat with a stupid little shopgirl from the town who had the hots for the Airborne and thought he was an army officer. When the phone rang, he had just succeeded in unhooking her bra.

"Yes?" he snarled. The girl seized the chance to move away from him and rearrange her clothes.

"This is Malenov," said a guarded voice at the end of the line. "I've got something interesting for you. We ought to talk it over straight away."

"Come round and have a drink." Suchko's voice was thick and slurred, but his mind was suddenly alert. He had marked down this Captain Malenov as someone he might be able to use. He understood Malenov's type well enough. The man was a coward-bully, someone who had tried, all his life, to hide his basic weaknesses behind a mask of arrogance and physical toughness.

"I'm duty officer tonight," Malenov explained. Through his mental fog, Suchko could see the picture clear enough. There was Malenov sitting all alone, feeling sorry for himself, stewing with envy of comrades who'd been promoted faster than him. Comrades like Zaytsev. After all, they were both veterans of Afghanistan.

"I'm coming over," Suchko announced. "I'll bring a bottle with me."

He let the shopgirl escape, fastened his zipper, and headed out toward the duty room. He greeted the sentry at the checkpoint with a floppy salute.

It was nearly midnight, but Fyodor Zaytsev found it impossible to sleep. Sasha had called during the day to say, in circuitous language, that they might have to move faster than anticipated. He wondered if the rumors that the new General Secretary had been rushed off to the clinic for an emergency operation were true.

Zaytsev got out of bed and dressed, padding around the room with his shoes in his hand so as not to wake his wife. He glanced at the phone in the living room, the direct line to Gogol Boulevard that Sasha had had installed by military technicians to bypass the KGB monitors. If that phone rang, it would be to tell him to start the engine of the coup.

He threw his overcoat over his shoulders and went outside. There was the tang of pine resin in the air. He wandered along the sandy road, past the tall antennas of the communications building and a long line of single-story barracks, toward the airstrip. Nearing the checkpoint, he saw the light in the duty room, and decided to drop in and have a smoke with Malenov.

He remembered Sasha's story about Malenov's behavior in Afghanistan, the way he had taken fright crossing a log bridge over a mountain gorge. You had to admire a man like that, who faced up to his fear, Zaytsev thought. Malenov might be scared of heights, but despite that—or because of it—he had the best record in the brigade as a parachutist.

He was nearly up to the window when he realized that Malenov wasn't alone.

Who was that with him? Orlov? The blocky silhouette came between the light and the window.

In the instant that Zaytsev recognized Suchko, the KGB man bent down to pick up the phone on the duty officer's desk. This single motion convinced Zaytsev that Malenov had betrayed them. Why else would Suchko be using his phone in the middle of the night?

The general didn't hesitate. He burst into the duty room, tugging at his pistol. Malenov glanced up, and his jaw dropped open.

Suchko was breathing noisily, through his nostrils, but otherwise seemed perfectly at ease. He gave Zaytsev a cursory look and went on dialing. Without looking up again, he said, "Don't try anything adolescent, General. The game is over for you."

Malenov, who knew Zaytsev better, was more realistic. He sprang from his chair and hurled himself at the Spetsnaz commander. But Zaytsev's reflexes were as quick as ever. He stepped aside nimbly, dodging the blow, and delivered a karate kick to Malenov's chest. The younger man was dead before he hit the floor.

Suchko was fumbling for his own weapon, but his holster was empty. Fuzzily, he blamed this on the shopgirl who had teased him and wrestled with him. Maybe he had dropped the gun when he rolled off the sofa. Then he remembered. He had let her play with it. He saw her caressing the barrel with her fingers while he groped under her skirt; that seemed to excite the little whore. It was fortunate for Suchko that he had lost his pistol, because Zaytsev was already on top of him, ramming his head back against the wall. He slid off his chair and was left lying on the floor like a beached whale.

Zaytsev put his foot on Suchko's belly while he picked up the phone, broke the connection, and then dialed Orlov's private number.

When Orlov arrived, he didn't ask any questions. They hauled Malenov's body into the bathroom. The colonel arranged to replace both the duty officer and the guard at the checkpoint who had seen Suchko arrive.

All this time, Suchko lay on the floor, shaking a little.

Zaytsev grabbed him by the collar and pulled him up to his full height. "We'll take you home," he said.

"I'll forget everything, I swear it," Suchko stammered.

"Of course you will."

Something about Zaytsev's tone made Suchko tremble more violently. When they got back to his quarters, he looked longingly at the liquor cabinet.

"Go ahead," Zaytsev said obligingly. "Here, I'll pour."

Suchko gulped it down gratefully, and Zaytsev refilled his glass.

"What about you, General?" he asked, beginning to regain some confidence now he was back on his own turf.

"Well, just a small one," Zaytsev responded.

Suchko had never seen the man smile before. The liquor created a warm glow in his stomach. He accepted a third glass, and began to feel positively euphoric. "You were quite right, of course, General," he said. "Malenov was a fool. Not a patch on a man like you. You did the right thing. It will look fine in the report, just fine. I'll say he was drunk and fell under a truck."

"That's an excellent idea."

Zaytsev took the tumbler away and shoved the bottle into Suchko's hand.

"*Iz gorla budesh,*" the Spetsnaz commander said. "Go on, take a swig."

Suchko took a small swallow, and started to feel queasy. Colonel Orlov came over and jammed the neck of the bottle into his mouth. Some of the vodka dribbled down over his chin.

"No, really, I've had enough," Suchko began to protest. But Orlov came at him again, forcing his jaw open. Quarter of a bottle must have gone down. Suchko was coughing and spluttering. Then he started throwing up over the rug, a yellowish-green bile like a cat that has been eating grass.

Orlov was waiting with a second bottle.

"What are you trying to do?" Suchko exclaimed, but his tongue seemed to have swollen and the words came out in an incomprehensible gurgle.

"Drink!"

Suchko felt something jabbed hard into the base of his stomach and opened his mouth again. The liquid went down like molten fire. He was drowning in it.

He was barely conscious when they carried him out to his own car. Then they were driving somewhere. He could see the lights of the base, whizzing like fireflies. Then they were pushing him onto a metal ladder; the rungs clanged under his feet. He tried to get off, but there was one of them pulling and the other shoving from below. They manhandled him up the ladder like a sack of potatoes until he couldn't see the ground anymore. When they reached the top, they left him winded, swaying about on top of a tiny platform without a railing. It might have been the top of the world.

"Where—"

"You take such an interest in our activities, Major Suchko," Zaytsev said patiently. "It's really time you tried one of our parachute jumps."

Then Suchko understood where they were. They were on top of the tower the Spetsnaz people used for practice jumps, two hundred feet up, maybe more. More recruits had broken bones trying to jump from the tower than dropping out of planes.

"Holy Peter," Suchko croaked.

"He can't even swear like a man," Orlov spat.

They threw him down head first, just to make sure. Drunks sometimes had the luck of alley cats, their nerves and muscles loosened by alcohol. Suchko didn't.

"Do you think there'll be an inquiry?" Orlov asked.

"Everybody knew he was a bottle-jockey," Zaytsev said. The danger, he thought, was that Malenov might have talked to Suchko before he had caught them together. Nikolsky would be able to find out about that. In the end, there was bound to be some sort of inquiry. But maybe, before it got underway, everything would have changed. . . .

In the meantime, they had to dispose of Malenov's body. Zaytsev decided to follow Suchko's suggestion. They put the informer's body on the road and ran him over with a truck.

10 Sasha followed a zigzag course on his way home from Gogol Boulevard. He circled around behind the Metropol, and he couldn't have analyzed why. He didn't seriously expect to catch a glimpse of Elaine. The last thing he wanted was another of their "chance" meetings on the street. Anyway, for all he knew she had left Moscow already. Yet he was drawn to her presence.

But he counted the minutes, as he usually did, and arrived at the metro station where he had arranged to meet Nikolsky a couple of minutes before Feliks did. Zaytsev had given him a delphic description of what had happened at Kavrov on the telephone; now it was urgent to establish how much of the truth was known in the Third Directorate of the KGB.

They talked in the car. The heater needed fixing, and it was chilly inside, but at least Sasha was sure there were no bugs.

"Topchy's completely in the dark," Feliks reassured him. "But there's bound to be some kind of investigation. Who ever heard of a chekist falling off a parachute tower? It would have been smarter to have Suchko fall out of bed. I just hope there weren't any witnesses."

"How long before they start asking questions in Kavrov?"

"Well, Topchy will have to pick a new man to replace Suchko, and then he'll have to inform your august colleagues. It could take a few days. Topchy has been rather preoccupied of late."

"Good. As long as we have a little time. Have you heard anything from Kuntsevo?"

Feliks shrugged. "The old man can hardly sign his name. Askyerov is already in charge."

"I know. I had a talk with the Marshal this morning. We found out that Askycrov has given orders to form two completely new army divisions, made up of troops from the Caucasus. His own people, of course, men he can trust to pull the trigger when he tells them."

"If they're not busy running away," Nikolsky said scornfully. "How did this get past the Marshal?"

"They didn't tell him. Askyerov and the Defense Minister arranged the whole thing by themselves. They used Togliatti as a pretext They claimed that they need a bigger reserve of reliable troops in case of further labor unrest. Of course, they're setting up a pretorian guard. Doesn't it remind you of something?"

Feliks hesitated for only a moment. "Beria!" he exclaimed. "The wild divisions! What did the Marshal say?"

"He remembers," Sasha said. "He's running out of patience. He'll be ready to move when the time comes. But there's something that's very important, Feliks."

"Yes?"

"We all have our own ideas of what ought to be done for the country. We need to pull them together, to make a synthesis. Otherwise, we'll be navigating without maps."

"Have you talked to Zaytsev about this?"

"Oh, yes, Fedya has some very pronounced ideas about agriculture. I think the Marshal will approve of them. I talked to Kolya Vlassov, too."

"Vlassov?"

"At the Aquarium. He's a budding diplomatist. I want you to think about what we're going to do with your honorable chekists, Feliks." He consulted his watch. "Now I'm going to drop you at the metro. I promised to be home before Petya goes to bed."

He had started to slow the car when he turned abruptly to Nikolsky and said, "I think you once mentioned you had a friend in the Tourist Department."

"Mitik? Oh, he's a good sort. But I don't think he's serious enough for you, Sasha."

Sasha was on the point of asking Feliks to try to find out, discreetly, whether Elaine was still in Moscow. He suppressed the words that had already formed. He was sure of Feliks, but it would be inviting discovery to go making inquiries in the Tourist Department of the KGB.

"Oh. I see," he said lamely. Feliks gave him a curious look as he left the car.

Lydia came to the door of the family apartment as he turned his key in the lock.

She was wearing a bathrobe and the kind of face pack that made her look like a plaster cast. She no longer bothered about how she looked when she was alone with Sasha in the house, but would spend hours preparing for a social event. Sasha had noticed how the younger officers paid court to her, and realized that he was supposed to feel challenged. He didn't. There was no rancor between them, but not much pretense either. Each of them recognized the marriage as what it had become: a convenience, a well-appointed terminal for travelers who were planning to leave for separate destinations. When they made love, which was rarely, it was comfortable and undemanding. They had not slept together since Sasha had taken Elaine to Bangladesh.

"I want you to tell me what happened today," Lydia said to him, folding her arms the way she always did when she wanted to take a stand. "Papa came home in a flaming temper and has locked himself up to get drunk."

"Let him," Sasha said. "He's got reason. Askyerov is behaving as if the General Staff was a mausoleum."

"Askyerov? Always the same cockroaches!" In the privacy of the Visotny Dom, Lydia was given to using her father's abusive slang. "I had tea with Katenka today. She was telling me that Askyerov gave his wife an emerald necklace. The stones were as big as *that.*" She made a circle, her forefinger grazing the joint of her thumb.

Sasha's attention flickered. He regarded Katenka as one of the more featherheaded of his wife's friends. But he started when Lydia added, "Katenka says the emeralds were smuggled out of Afghanistan. Is it true there's an emerald mine in Afghanistan?"

"Yes, there is." *And our men are dying to put baubles around Madame Askyerova's neck,* he told himself. *It has to end. One way or another.*

"We've already eaten," Lydia said. "But I can warm up something."

"Where's Petya?"

"Watching TV. I told him he could wait up."

Petya had the door shut—he liked to create his private world—and he had whole companies of toy soldiers lined up on the floor. He came running to embrace his father, and Sasha let him swing from his neck while he swiveled on his heels.

"There was a film about Pavlik Morozov," Petya reported excitedly when he had slid down.

This wasn't one of Sasha's favorite subjects. Pavlik Morozov, the legendary hero of the Pioneers, was a central figure in Soviet iconography. He earned his fame as an informer. When young Morozov found out, in the dark days of the Twenties, that his father was selling false papers to wealthy peasants who had been exiled for hoarding grain, he informed on him to the authorities and bore witness against him at his trial. His father's friends took their revenge by dragging the boy off to the woods and stabbing him to death.

"Well, what did you think about Pavlik Morozov?" Sasha asked his son.

He watched the small face crease in a parody of his own frown. "I'm not sure," Petya said solemnly.

"You must have some opinion."

"I mean . . . I don't think what Pavlik did was right. I would never do that to you."

Sasha laughed. But even muted by the sound of the announcer's voice on the television, it seemed to him that his laughter was unnaturally loud.

He said, "I hope you'll never have cause."

Petya came over to him, not looking at him directly, the way he always approached when he wanted to ask for something.

"Dedushka gave me a tank today," the boy began. "It's a T-seventy-two, I think. It works by remote control. He says he's going to let me ride in a real one."

"Your room looks like a battlefield already," Sasha complained gently. The Marshal was always bringing the boy toys, usually with a military bent: plastic tanks and howitzers and fighter planes, machine guns and grenades, whole battalions of model soldiers. Sasha didn't resent the presents. But, as he ruffled his son's hair, he resented the fact that the Marshal spent more time with his son than he did, and was perfectly ready to make him conscious of it. "I believe he's more my son than yours," the Marshal had said only a week or two before, not entirely in jest. "He looks like me. It's the blood winning out."

"Are you going to be with me tomorrow?" his son was asking, looking at the floor.

The next day was Sunday. There had been little difference between one day of the week and another in Sasha's life for a long time past.

That's all that he's asking, Sasha thought. *My time.*

"Yes, I'm going to be with you," Sasha said. "If you like, we'll go somewhere by ourselves. Without any women around," he added, as if to include his son in a grown-up male conspiracy.

"Let's go to the American Hills!" the boy shouted joyfully.

"Not the Devil's Ring?"

"Oh, yes! That too!"

Sasha laughed, and thought the sound was better. It might be the last Sunday they would have together.

At the entrance to Gorky Park was an immense triumphal stone arch leading through a high metal fence. The park was crowded, and Sasha had to stand in line for fifteen minutes to get tickets for the rides. Then they had to wait in line again to get on the roller coaster. To ease the wait, Sasha bought ice cream, thick, frozen cream glazed with a rich coating of chocolate. His son's eyes were shining with excitement as they finally reached the head of the line. When a car creaked to a halt in front of them and discharged its passengers, he jumped into the front seat; Sasha got into the seat behind him. A teenage girl with her young sister came and squeezed in next to them.

Then they were climbing in a laborious upward spiral. Sasha looked across the amusement park. There was a blare of loud music from another of the rides, the volume was turned up to mask the screams as the flying saucers whirled, rising higher and higher into the air. He could see people hanging upside down from the cockpits of whizzing propeller planes. He craned his neck as they reached the top of their ascent, to look over to the Moskva River. The sun caught the cables of the Krimskiy bridge, giving it a silvery sheen. He thought of Elaine, and how her face had crumpled when he had told her they couldn't meet again. Would she go on waiting for him, when he had given her so little cause for hope? Would he be able to find her, if he had the freedom to choose only for himself? Would Petya like her, or resent her? The questions became too painful, and he tried to push them away. He reminded himself that he could not afford distractions now; since Kavrov, his course was set on iron rails.

Their car hung there for a long moment above the steep descent. The tracks seemed to fall straight down. Then they were falling too, hurtling along at ever-increasing speed, and the teenage girl next to Sasha was screaming and clutching at his arm, and he heard Petya screaming too, and saw the child beside him wriggling and bawling, trying to get out of the car. Sasha himself felt a sudden fear, the fear of powerlessness in that vertical descent, the knowledge that, however much he wanted, he could neither get off the roller coaster nor change its course until the end of the ride. The little girl next to Petya was rocking from side to side. He put his hand on the child's shoulder, gently restraining her. Then they had reached the bottom, and were slowly trundling up the next of the "American Hills." When the ride was over, they all laughed at each other in relief. But Sasha had the sensation that, in his own life, he had only completed the ascent of the first slope, and was swaying above the gulf that had opened ahead of him.

"That's the trouble," he said to the girl who had been so frightened. "Once you get on, you can't get off."

8.

TOPCHY'S
SOLUTION

If you had a bite, played your fish, and the line
broke, don't waste your time asking questions.

—GOGOL, *DEAD SOULS*

1 Yurovsky, of the Second Chief Directorate of the KGB, was a patient
fisher of men. He liked to trawl for as long as possible before he
pulled in the net. His special responsibility was American tourists, and he
had a large apparatus, including the staff of Intourist, at his disposal to
make sure that no one of interest slipped through the mesh. Almost everyone was of interest. There was that case, only a month ago, of a real estate
salesman from Bethesda, Maryland, who had been married for sixteen
years but preferred boys. As it turned out, he had some very interesting
Washington clients on his Rolodex.

Yurovsky was intrigued by the report on this American girl Elaine
Warner, who had been observed boarding a train for Moscow at a station
just outside Togliatti. Informers in the strike-bound city had already reported the presence of foreigners, including a girl matching Warner's
description who had visited the family of Misha Repnin. Yurovsky had a
copy of the girl's visa application in front of him, together with some
notes from the consular official who had processed it. She was a Jew, of
course. Her father had come from Odessa, and had known Zionist affiliations. It was therefore possible that she was engaged in Zionist agitation,
like that stupid bunch of students from Columbia University who had just
been intercepted at Leningrad airport trying to smuggle in propaganda
leaflets.

But it was equally possible that Elaine Warner was a CIA agent, sent to
Togliatti to establish contact with the leaders of the underground labor
movement. That was worth exploring. So instead of booting her out of the
country, Yurovsky had her watched, and he did the job properly. Twenty
men were detailed to follow her in shifts. There was no shortage of manpower in Yurovsky's section. Even if she was a professional, it was highly
unlikely that she would realize she was under observation.

The operation had already produced results. She had been observed
attending a reception at the American Embassy in the company of Guy
Harrison, a suspected agent of Western special services. The following
night she had gone with Harrison to a performance at the Theatre

Romen. It was only a matter of time, Yurovsky calculated, before they would assemble the proofs that would totally discredit the Russian imitators of Solidarity.

He decided that he would like to take a look at the girl for himself. Even in the drab visa photograph, she was quite striking. So that morning he joined one of the surveillance cars that tailed her as she left her hotel. It was suspiciously early; the subways had been running for less than an hour. They watched her walk along Marx Prospekt and vanish into the Sverdlova metro station. One of Yurovsky's men, loitering across the street, crossed over quickly and followed her down. She took the green line, but got off at the next station, switched platforms, and doubled back the way she had come. She made two more changes, and took a brief taxi ride, before Yurovsky received a radio signal that she was entering a car park near the river, not far from the Visotny Dom.

It was a clandestine meet, he concluded. *It had to be.*

He ordered his driver to head for the Visotny Dom. They were halfway there when another radio message crackled through: "She's approaching someone. . . . He's in army uniform. . . . I think he's a general."

"A general?" Yurovsky echoed, incredulous.

"One star. . . . Now they're talking. It looks like he knows her. Do you want us to move in?"

"No. Are you getting anything from the directional mikes?"

"We're trying, sir. There's a lot of static. It seems they're arguing. She's saying he has to meet somebody. He says something about Delhi."

"Delhi?"

"I think that's New Delhi, India, sir."

"I know where it is!"

"He's breaking away from her. He's getting into his car."

"Get the license tag!"

"She's leaving the other way. She looks really upset. Shall we follow her?"

"Follow both of them!"

Yurovsky reached the car park too late to see the general for himself. It was hardly believable—a Soviet general meeting a Jewish-American girl who had been involved with the saboteurs in Togliatti. Well, it wouldn't be hard to find the man. There couldn't be many Soviet major-generals who lived in the neighborhood of the Visotny Dom.

The group that assembled at Bangladesh that night was larger than before. In addition to Sasha, Nikolsky, and Zaytsev, there was Kolya Vlassov, now one of the senior men at the Aquarium, a young general from one of the Airborne divisions, and a colonel from the Strategic Rocket Forces.

"You know what they used to say," Feliks murmured to Sasha. "For a secret meeting in Moscow, three is already too many." That had always been true. Confine a meeting to two people, and if you were betrayed, you knew for sure who was the informer.

Then and afterward, Sasha seemed more than usually guarded, and Feliks sensed that it wasn't just because of the size of the gathering. Nikolsky tried to liven things up with a few jokes, one of them at the expense of the General Secretary's notoriously promiscuous daughter.

"Do you know what she puts behind her ears to attract men? Her knees," Feliks answered his own question.

Only Vlassov and the Airborne general laughed.

"There's not much time," Sasha brought the meeting to order. "The General Secretary has been taken to the clinic at Kuntsevo. The Marshal is very concerned that Askyerov won't wait for the death certificate before he makes final arrangements for the succession. You've all heard the news from the Caucasus."

It was, indeed, the talk of the messes up and down the country. Many of the Russian officers were openly furious that the Defense Minister had rubber-stamped the order to form two Caucasian divisions without consulting Marshal Zotov. Nobody doubted that the initiative came from Askyerov, or that the Prime Minister was seeking to create, in these "wild divisions," an armed force totally loyal to himself.

"There's more," Sasha continued. "The Marshal has received information that the wild divisions are going to be brought to Moscow."

"To Moscow?" Zaytsev exploded. "Those black-asses? It's not possible."

But every man in the room realized that it was, and their discussions gained further urgency.

When the others had left, Nikolsky said, "I thought I might go to hear the gypsies sing tonight. Why don't you come? God knows when we'll be able to do it again."

Sasha shook his head.

"There's something wrong, isn't there?" Feliks pressed him.

For a moment Sasha was tempted to share his burden. But he shook off the mood quickly. How could he tell anyone that all their efforts had been placed in jeopardy because Elaine had waylaid him in a parking lot and relayed a message from the CIA—a threat that, unless he agreed to deal with them, they would use their dossiers to destroy him? He couldn't believe that Elaine understood the full meaning of the words she repeated, but the meaning was there nonetheless. He had played for time, telling her to inform her controllers that it was impossible to arrange a meeting in Moscow, but that he would agree to a rendezvous during his next visit abroad. As it happened, he was supposed to accompany the Marshal on a trip to New Delhi in three weeks' time. Maybe the CIA would leave him alone until then. At the pace that things were moving, it would be time enough.

"Go to your gypsies, Feliks." He patted Nikolsky's shoulder. "But keep your head clear." The news about the General Secretary had come from him. Thanks to Nikolsky's relationship with Topchy, they had excellent inside information on Askyerov's activities. They depended on Feliks to tell them when it was time to move.

Nikolsky arrived at the Lubyanka rather late the next day. He had stayed at the gypsy club into the early hours, giving himself over completely to the wild intoxication, followed by exquisite melancholy, that the music inspired. It was the most dangerous music in the world, more dangerous than alcohol or hashish. It broke down all of a man's reserves, it opened cravings as limitless as the steppes. Feliks' club, an hour's drive from the center of Moscow, wasn't for tourists. It was for those who *knew*. They still drank *charochki* there in the old way. Several times, the singer—the great Tamara Fedorovskaya—placed the huge beaker of champagne on its plate in front of Feliks. Then she would burst into song, and the whole troupe would take up the chorus. When they were done, Nikolsky would stand—less steadily as the night wore on—bow low, and drain off the whole drink at once, turning the glass upside down to show that not a drop was left. He never failed in his duty.

By the time he got home it was too late in the day to bother with sleep. He had breakfast with his children and indulged in a long, steaming-hot bath. On his way to the office, he felt perfectly composed, suffused with a pleasurable sadness, bittersweet as a slice of lemon fished out of a glass of gin.

Topchy was no stickler for office hours. On the other hand, if he wanted you, you had better be available. He wanted Nikolsky that morning. He was visibly excited, more elated than angry.

"Alexander Sergeyovich Preobrazhensky," he greeted Nikolsky. "You knew him in New York, didn't you?"

"We had a few drinks," Feliks conceded. "He's not very amusing. You know how these woodentops are."

"I've been going through the file," Topchy went on. "There's something that was never cleared up. One of our contacts, a fellow named Churkhin, made the allegation that Preobrazhensky was in contact with the CIA. Do you know anything about that?"

"I never believed it," Nikolsky said cautiously. "I think Churkhin was trying to get a bonus. It happens all the time. As I remember, Churkhin went home with his ass in a sling." He was desperately trying to work out why Topchy should suddenly have decided to investigate Sasha. Had there been a leak from Kavrov?

"I want you to track down this Churkhin and see what he has to say. Get on it right away. There's no time to waste."

As Feliks returned to his own office, his delightful gypsy hangover supplanted by near panic, he was trying to work out how to get a message to Sasha. Better to wait, he decided, until he had managed to sniff out how much Topchy knew. He called records and told them to put a trace on Churkhin. If they were lucky, the bitch had got himself shot in Afghanistan. But somehow, people like that managed to survive.

Gussein Askyerov received Topchy around noon, in a splendid suite at the Rossiya that was reserved by his Armenian associate for confidential meetings of this kind. The Prime Minister's eyes glistened as he listened to Topchy's account of the meeting between an American girl, a suspected CIA agent, and the son-in-law of Marshal Zotov.

"How did you find out?" Askyerov interjected.

"Yurovsky's men were trailing the girl. They asked my section to identify the general."

"Yurovsky is a thorough investigator," Askyerov said in a neutral tone. Topchy understood the undertow. *We don't own him.*

"I want to take charge of the case myself," Topchy said. "This is Third Directorate business." He mentioned other peculiarities in the case, including Churkhin's report. He suggested that Churkhin's testimony had been suppressed by Zotov to protect a member of his own family.

"Let me see if I have the whole picture," said Askyerov, steepling his fingers. "The girl is no ordinary tourist, and we have circumstantial evidence that she is in contact with Western services. We know that she has attended one—probably more than one—clandestine meeting with Preobrazhensky. We know that Preobrazhensky is not only Zotov's son-in-law, he's the man's brain as well."

"And he has access to everything that crosses the Marshal's desk," Topchy added.

"Which means," Askyerov pursued, "that Zotov is either an accessory to espionage or too incompetent to be in his job."

"That's how it looks," Topchy encouraged him.

"But can we make it stand up?"

"Just give me a few days."

"We don't have that much time." Askyerov uncoiled himself from his armchair like a lizard and moved, with no sense of haste, to the liquor table, where he poured himself a glass of some sweet fizzy drink. "I am going to Kuntsevo this afternoon."

Topchy didn't say anything. Kuntsevo meant the Kremlin clinic, where the General Secretary had been in intensive care for more than a week.

"What I am about to say doesn't leave this room," Askyerov said, fixing Topchy with his stare. "An emergency meeting of the Politburo will be convened tomorrow morning. We need a hand at the wheel. This time, we're not going to wait until the body is cold. The General Secretary will sign whatever I put in front of him. There's only one man who would dare to oppose us openly. I want to break him tomorrow morning. Then we can put reliable men in the high command. Do you understand what I'm saying? When Marshal Zotov leaves the Central Committee tomorrow, he will no longer be Chief of Staff."

Askyerov sucked at his drink. Topchy thought it looked like liquid shit. He eyed the cut-glass decanters of whisky and vodka thirstily, but wasn't offered anything. Maybe since his last trip to Damascus Askyerov was starting to remember that his family were once Moslems.

"What you have told me has great possibilities," Askyerov resumed. "Our friend the Marshal is popular in the officers' messes. It's too dangerous just to tear off his shoulder boards, especially after Togliatti. We might create another martyr in uniform, like Leybutin. We have to crush not only Zotov but the very idea of Zotov, the way Stalin dealt with Tukhachevsky. You may have supplied the means. But I can give you only twenty hours. Can you do it?"

"We need a confession," Topchy volunteered.

"Whose confession? Preobrazhensky's?"

Topchy played with his earlobe. In his experience, in time, and under proper care, any man would confess. One of the great achievements of their form of society was that the victims always felt guilty. Topchy said, "I would need full powers."

Askyerov snapped his fingers, and the Armenian left the telephone. He had been engaged in sorting out a number of housekeeping problems, ranging from the dispatch of a special consignment of cement for the

Prime Minister's villa in the Crimea to the private screening that night of a new soft-core film from Sweden.

"Get hold of Chetverikov," Askyerov instructed him. "Tell him that Colonel Topchy is in charge of the case of the American girl because it involves military security. Arrange for Colonel Topchy to be delivered the necessary arrest warrants." He turned back to Topchy. "How many?"

"That depends on the results of the interrogation."

"Six warrants," Askyerov told the Armenian. "Leave the names blank. Anything else?"

Topchy looked longingly at the liquor table.

"Help yourself," Askyerov said. "We know each other well enough," he went on while Topchy sloshed scotch into a heavy-bottomed glass. "You know that I don't forget a service. I was already planning to make you head of the Third Directorate. That's worth a couple of stars."

Topchy's smile came and went like a facial tic.

"What do you want? Chetverikov's job?" Askyerov studied him. "Don't be too impatient, my friend. There's a time for every purpose."

In the afternoon, Nikolsky went to Topchy to report that Churkhin was currently stationed in Alma-Ata. He was half-expecting to be ordered to fly out there to interview the wretch. But Topchy seemed to have lost interest in Churkhin and his allegations.

"Shut the door, Feliks," he said. The scotch had made him more jovial than normal, but Nikolsky backed away from the fumes. The effects of his sleepless night, and the *charochki*, were beginning to tell.

"I told you you'd do well if you stuck with me," Topchy reminded him. "Well, after tomorrow, you'll see I'm a man of my word."

"What's happening?"

Topchy put a finger to his lips. "Not a word, mind, not a word! I have it on the highest authority. The Politburo is meeting at eight o'clock. There'll be great changes, Feliks, you'll see."

Then he was correct and official again. "Get me the papers on that new man we're sending to Kavrov. I think I'll take them over to Gogol Boulevard myself. I want to see what those bitches are up to."

On his way out, Nikolsky passed Skvortsov, on his way in, and noticed that the man was armed. Skvortsov was a typical product of the Third Directorate: a swaggering, foul-mouthed lout. Topchy used him for his dirty work.

As soon as he had forwarded the transfer forms that Topchy had requested, Feliks left the Lubyanka to find a safe phone. They had less than seventeen hours.

Elaine had stumbled out of the parking lot near the Visotny Dom through a cold sleet and wandered the embankment, bareheaded, until her hair was wet and matted. The river was the gray of tarnished pewter. The sky was pressing down on the city like a vast metal lid.

The moment Sasha had recognized her, his face told her how wrong it had been for her to come. He had the look of a cornered animal. His eyes darted all around, seeking a way of escape, as she nervously repeated Gladden's message.

"Do you understand it?" he asked her. They were standing side by side, not looking at each other, as if they were strangers waiting for different partners. "I warned you it might come to this."

Then she understood, and hated herself for her stupidity. Gladden had duped her. It was Gladden's people who had the compromising dossiers. They were trying to blackmail Sasha, as he had predicted. And they were using her to deliver the threat.

She began stammering excuses.

"Don't," he silenced her. "There's no time. You wouldn't have come if you'd been thinking clearly. I know what drove you. I feel it too." The words touched her like a brief caress. But his final statement was clipped and impersonal: "You will go to your friends and say I agree to their terms. But I cannot meet them here. Tell them it will be Delhi, in three weeks' time."

Then he had turned on his heel and marched off to his car.

Elaine watched him drive away. The embankment seemed strangely deserted, except for a man reading a newspaper on a bench, and she felt terribly exposed. She saw a taxi with its green light on, and ran out into the street to wave it down. She drove straight to Guy Harrison's apartment block. It was mostly occupied by foreign correspondents, and one of the inevitable KGB goons was squatting in the middle of the steps. He made no effort to shift his bulk to let her pass, and she had to climb around him. He shouted a coarse joke after her as she went inside.

"Fuck you!" she called back, and he showed a row of broken teeth, yellowed like one of the meerschaums Guy kept on his desk. She was angry with the whole world.

"Fuck you too!" she yelled at Harrison when he finally answered the doorbell. The rims of his eyes were red, flecked with white. He looked like an aging basset hound.

"Steady on," he said. "It's too early in the day for that sort of thing."

While Harrison brewed tea, she sat on his disheveled sofa and described her meeting with Sasha.

"So it's New Delhi, is it?" he said thoughtfully when she had finished. "I think I saw something about a trip the Marshal is going to make. Well, the Reverend Gladden ought to be able to live with that."

"You can tell Luke that I think he's a bastard." She couldn't find a word that seemed strong enough.

"He may have been called that before," Harrison observed.

She watched him take a pinch of snuff; the man was a walking museum of Anglophile eccentricities. He started sneezing copiously and dabbed at his bulbous nose with a spotted handkerchief that had obviously been used for this purpose before.

"I've never seen Sasha frightened until now," she went on. "He looked like a man on Death Row. I can't believe Gladden used me like this."

"He was carrying out orders."

"That's been said before too."

"I'd better hop round to the Embassy," Harrison said. "Why don't you make yourself at home? You look like you could do with a hot bath."

"I'm going back to New York, Guy. There's nothing left for me here. I want to leave today. Can you arrange that?"

"I'll try."

He went away and made phone calls. The first flight he could manage to get her on, using all his connections—including a girl at Aeroflot who liked to be kept supplied with the latest pulp paperbacks from the West—left the following day.

When he came back to report the news, she was peering down into the street from behind a curtain.

He followed the direction of her gaze. There was a man propped up by a streetlamp reading *Pravda*, and another beside the main entrance.

"Just the usual hoods," Harrison said. "You don't think you were followed, do you?"

"I don't know."

"Gladden's men had the meeting covered. I'm sure they would have intervened if they saw anything. But look here. I really think you should stay here until tomorrow. You'll only be miserable at the Metropol."

"What about my clothes?"

"I'll have your things brought round. There's plenty of room, and you'll feel a lot safer. You needn't worry about your virtue. I'm not the marrying kind. Oh, dear, I didn't shock you, did I?"

She managed a wan smile, and Guy left the room as lightly as a man of his girth could manage. For a couple of hours she fiddled with his short-wave radio and wondered whether there was any world where she and Sasha would be free to love, until she fell into an uneasy sleep. She dreamed that she was riding on horseback through a snow-covered forest, with a pack of baying hounds at her heels. Something started from cover, and the hounds overtook her and charged after it. Luke Gladden rode up beside her and shouldered a rifle. She saw he was aiming at Sasha, who was backed up against a fir, inside a circle of snarling dogs. She was struggling with Gladden, trying to stop him, but she felt the gun kick and saw the snow falling from the branches, and looked at her own hands, and found they were spattered with blood.

Harrison insisted on driving her to the airport himself. She would pick up the New York connection in Geneva, and fly on home by Swissair. She had been quite emphatic that she did not intend to sit on a Soviet plane all the way to New York.

Elaine watched the windshield wipers scrape back and forth. Small pellets of hail pounded the roof of the car like buckshot.

"I told Gladden what you said," Harrison reported. "He said to tell you there was no other way. And that he meant what he said about Sasha needing help."

Elaine said nothing.

Almost halfway to Sheremetyevo, she realized that Harrison was looking into the rearview mirror more and more frequently.

"Are we being followed?" she asked, turning to look at the car behind them. It was a black Volga, like the one Sasha was driving the night she stopped him beside the bridge. But there were four men in the car, all wearing hats.

"Farewell party," Harrison commented. "If it's us they're interested in, they're not making any secret of it."

Suddenly the Volga pulled out into the middle of the road, forcing a car traveling in the opposite direction to veer aside.

Harrison swore as the driver of the Volga swerved across their path without warning, so that he had to ram his foot down on the brake pedal. Harrison's car went into a skid, and before he had mastered it, they were bumping along the shoulder of the road.

Three men emerged from the Volga and took up positions around them.

"Who are they?" Elaine whispered. "KGB?"

"Leave it to Uncle Guy." Harrison sounded his usual unflappable self, but he was having trouble controlling his sweat glands. He was mopping his brow with the back of his hand as he got out of the car.

Elaine heard him engage in a brief exchange with the Russians. He sounded more adenoidal and antipodean, trying to communicate in a foreign language, and he didn't seem to be making himself understood. He was saying something in a loud voice about the rights of the western press, invoking the name of his London paper, when an enormous bruiser in a dark overcoat that came down to his ankles slammed his fist into Harrison's midriff. Guy staggered backward, gasping for breath, and toppled over.

Elaine immediately leaped for her door and started running blindly along the side of the road, against the direction of the traffic. A couple of motorists started hooting at her. She felt a tug at her coat, but broke loose and stumbled on. Then her head was wrenched back, as if someone was trying to tear her hair out by the roots. She lost her footing and would have fallen on her back, but the man who had hit Guy threw a massive arm around her waist and lugged her back to the others. She screamed and kicked, and he gave her hair another savage twist before tossing her into the back seat of the Volga, climbing in beside her.

Doors slammed, the engine revved, and suddenly a figure loomed up in front of the car. Through the misted-up windshield, Guy Harrison, his arms upstretched, looked bloated and undefined, like a drowned man floating up from the ocean depths. The Russian driver accelerated, and she saw Guy hurl himself to one side. The men squeezed in on either side of her wouldn't let her turn round to see if Guy was dead or alive.

2 "Who are you? Where are you taking me?"
The first time she tried to ask a question, the big man pulled her hair again. The next time, the smaller man on her left, who was sniggering and stripping her with a rapist's eyes, stuck his hand between her legs. She spat at him, but the saliva wouldn't come. They rode out the rest of the journey in silence.

They found out about Togliatti, she told herself, trying to find some reasonable explanation. *They traced the article to me. They're trying to scare me into admitting something.* But she couldn't shut out the terror that they knew about Luke—and Sasha. She saw him again in the dream, with those hunted eyes, flattened against a tree. *Whatever happens, I won't betray you,* she promised. She had to concentrate, focus her mind on anything but him, on the slaughter in Togliatti, on her sister's wedding, on horseback riding with her father, anything but Sasha.

They sped into the center of Moscow and dragged her into a house on a street she didn't know. She said to a man in uniform, "I'm an American citizen and I demand to speak to the American consul." Everyone seemed to think this was highly amusing. They shot her full of something that was probably supposed to make her talk but instead left her retching all over the well-worn rug. Then a man was booming questions at her in Russian, questions about Sasha that confirmed her worst fears. It helped that she couldn't understand him very well. She bent her mind to reciting all the poems of Robert Frost she could remember. She had worked her way through the repertoire and was starting over when they brought in another interrogator, who put questions to her in English, but his accent was so thick and his vocabulary so sparse that she didn't have to feign incomprehension. But she couldn't miss one phrase. It reverberated through all the questioning.

"We know you're CIA."

But they hadn't mentioned Luke Gladden. That must mean they didn't have all of it. Not yet.

After dark, they moved her to another place in a closed van. Nobody told her where she was going, but when they set her to wait in a sparsely furnished office under the rapist's eyes and she heard voices raised in argument from a neighboring room, something told her it was the Lubyanka. *Funny,* she thought. She had read that they stopped bringing prisoners to the Lubyanka after Beria's death. She felt wonderfully detached from the situation, even from her own body.

They moved her to yet another room, and she kept repeating to herself, over and over, *I won't betray you, Sasha. I never met you.*

Everything was slightly out of focus. She looked at the man behind the desk. His features were loose and slightly disarranged. He was a plasticine head a child had thrown on the floor in a temper.

He rapped out some more questions, about when she had met Sasha, when he had started working for the CIA. His Russian was hard to understand, and her attention was drifting, her head was swirling . . .

Topchy brought her out of it with a slap that burst her upper lip.

"Give her another shot," he ordered Skvortsov, who was holding the syringe with the scolopomin. "And get Feliks in here to translate. Maybe he can charm the bitch."

This time, the drug had something closer to the desired effect. When she came round, she couldn't stop talking. She was running from the mouth, the victim of some kind of verbal diarrhea. She tried to talk about anything except Sasha and Moscow. She gabbled on about Great Neck, her family, her problems with New York publishers.

Feliks was in his own office, leafing through an internal directory, mentally erasing the names of the men who would be removed if Sasha's plan succeeded. There would still be a security service, of course. He smiled to himself, remembering a London production of a French play he had seen years before, in which a revolution takes place while most of the capital's leading dignitaries are sheltering in a bordello. When the revolutionaries take over, the only man who keeps his old job is the chief of the secret police. Yes, but there would be no place for the Topchys in the new Russia.

Skvortsov came barging in. "The boss wants you to help out with an interrogation."

"An interrogation? Here?"

Nikolsky was even more startled by the scene he found in Topchy's office. He grasped its essentials at once, however, from the questions Topchy was shouting. The girl was somehow involved with Sasha, and Topchy was bent on using this to destroy him. Feliks had no idea what, if anything, she might have to confess. He had to find out before she started telling them.

Topchy provided the opportunity, by announcing that he was going to take a leak.

Feliks followed him out, and found him standing in front of the urinal with his hands on his hips, as if inviting the world to acknowledge how big a man he was.

"She's not bad," Feliks remarked casually, stationing himself at the next stall. "Do you think Preobrazhensky was screwing her?"

"I don't give a shit," Topchy said. "She'll confess she was the bitch's CIA contact. We've got pictures of them together."

"Here in Moscow?" Feliks asked, incredulous. He couldn't believe that Sasha, always so careful, so hidden, could have committed this folly.

"Where the fuck did you think?" Topchy said impatiently, zipping up his fly. "Now let's go and milk the bitch."

Feliks could not afford the luxury of analyzing what might or might not have happened between Sasha and the American girl. They were using scolopomin, and he had seen its effects before. With the dosage they had given her, she would soon be telling whatever she knew. At all costs, he had to prevent that from happening.

A man was leaning over Elaine. His eyes were kind, and his English was so perfect, so soothing, that for a moment she thought it was Guy Harrison. "Why did you discuss New Delhi?" he was asking, and then she realized he was just the interpreter, translating for that poison dwarf behind the desk. But he took her hand as he spoke, and somehow his touch, his whole presence, seemed reassuring. The man in charge started jotting down notes, and in the next instant, the interpreter was bending down, so close she could feel his breath as a warm breeze in the shell of her ear.

"Don't answer," he whispered, and she gaped at him.

"Isn't it true that you arranged for General Preobrazhensky to attend a clandestine meeting with the CIA in New Delhi?" the interpreter went on in a louder voice.

She felt an overwhelming desire to answer. He put his arm around her, as if to comfort her, but the pressure around her throat became more and more intense. She felt she couldn't breathe. Her senses were muddled. She heard a Russian voice raised in anger, but that came from miles away. The room around her, bleached by the harsh surgical light, turned purple and then black.

"Are you trying to strangle her, fuck your mother?" Topchy yelled as Elaine blacked out. "Get away from her!"

He rushed over and dragged at Nikolsky's shoulder.

"I'm sorry," Feliks said. "I must have gotten overexcited."

"This isn't the place for your sexual fantasies," Topchy roared at him. "Try to bring her around," he instructed Skvortsov.

"She's out cold," Skvortsov reported. He gave Nikolsky an odd, sidelong look, and said, "What was that you were whispering to the bitch before you knocked her out?"

Feliks tried to make light of it. He slapped his hand over his fist suggestively and said, "I just wanted to show her my appreciation."

But Topchy's suspicion had been aroused.

"We talked about Preobrazhensky before," he reflected aloud. "You spoke up for him, as I recall. Why are you trying to protect him?"

"That's absurd," Feliks protested.

"But you're friends, aren't you?"

"We served together. That's all."

"When did you last see Preobrazhensky?"

"Oh, years ago," Feliks said airily. He realized he had made a mistake when he saw the look of pleasure on Skvortsov's face.

"Skvortsov told me he saw you with Preobrazhensky in the street," Topchy said slowly. "I was meaning to ask you about it."

"Oh, that," Feliks rejoined, wondering if Skvortsov had tailed him to the Bangladesh or the rendezvous outside the Sverdlova metro. "That was just a chance encounter. We hardly said two words."

"You're not as smart as you think, my dear Feliks," said Topchy. "Skvortsov gave me no report. I think you have quite a lot of explaining to do."

"Maybe he's the one we ought to interrogate," said Skvortsov happily.

When Elaine came round, she could focus, but things had changed in a way that was inexplicable. The interpreter, the man with the round, self-indulgent face who had whispered to her to hang on, was suddenly the victim. He was stripped to his shorts, and they were working him over, concentrating on the soles of the feet and on jabs to the kidneys. Like a counterpoint to his grunts of pain, she heard the ticking of the clock on the wall, and looked up to it. It had to be wrong, she told herself, another element in their efforts to dislocate the senses, because according to the clock, it was more than twelve hours since Guy had started out for the airport.

"I don't want to prolong this, Feliks," she heard the man in charge say to the one they were roughing up. "And frankly, I don't have time to. You tried to sabotage this interrogation, and the reason is perfectly clear. You're involved in an anti-state intrigue with Preobrazhensky. Both of you, and the little tart over there, are working for the CIA. We'll stop this nonsense as soon as you confirm what we already know."

The prisoner's only response was his labored breathing.

The rapist said, "Want me to give him a shot?"

"No, there's a faster way. Get rid of his jockstrap."

The scene that was played out in front of her eyes was too graphic for any horror film, though she kept thinking she was in one. The colonel—she must have heard someone mention his rank—went back to his desk and yanked open the drawer. They dragged Feliks forward and spreadeagled him over the desk, so that his testicles were dangling over the open drawer.

"I'll ask you once more," the colonel said. "Will you confess that you and Preobrazhensky were recruited by the Central Intelligence Agency?"

Feliks yelled something that might have been "Yes" as Topchy grabbed the handle of the drawer and made as if to ram it shut. Topchy let him feel the pressure, then relented.

"I see that you're ready to talk now," Topchy said to Nikolsky. "Your wife will be relieved—if you ever get to see her again." He paused to check that his tape recorder was still running.

"Well, you can sit down over there," Topchy told him, releasing him from the drawer. There was no move to return his clothes, and Feliks was still on the edge of panic. He couldn't resist the urge to touch himself, to make sure he was still intact.

His whole body was shaking, and he felt a shooting pain from his kidneys. But his mind was working again. He would agree to anything, he resolved, as long as it didn't threaten the plan itself. Nothing Topchy had said suggested that he knew anything about that. The man was pursuing a vendetta for Askyerov, and didn't yet realize what he had stumbled across. The girl had actually helped to keep him in the dark. Nikolsky confessed to everything Topchy thought to ask: *yes*, he was an American spy, *yes*, he and Sasha were paid every month in Swiss accounts, yes, yes, yes. His compliance stopped them from using the drugs, which would have cost him any measure of self-control. And he could deny it all later. So long as the plan remained secret, there was a fighting chance.

3 "Find out where Preobrazhensky is," Topchy instructed Skvortsov when all the questions had been answered to his satisfaction.

The general, it transpired, was not at home. He had spent the whole night at Gogol Boulevard, which pricked Topchy's curiosity. What was Preobrazhensky doing at General Staff headquarters a few hours before the members of the Politburo were due to assemble? Tidying up? Burning files that could be compromising to himself and his father-in-law if there was an inquiry?

Preobrazhensky was no fool, Topchy reasoned. No doubt the man had guessed what the Politburo meeting was going to bring, and was trying to prepare for the consequences. If even half of what Nikolsky had admitted was true, the young general had plenty of cleaning up to do. Topchy's attitude toward the confessions he extracted was that of a commercial artist toward his designs: he didn't necessarily believe in the integrity of the product he was presenting. Nikolsky's confession was a little too eager, and consequently somewhat lurid. It would serve the purpose in hand admirably, but left Topchy wondering whether there was something he had overlooked.

He saw now that the whole affair went deeper than he had originally suspected. There was a nest of them, including a man planted in his own office, spying on the Third Directorate! He remembered now that it had been Nikolsky who had reported on the curious events at Kavrov. Feliks had been even more off-handed than normal, trying to divert him with a hot tip for the third race on Wednesday evening. "Don't trouble yourself about Kavrov," Nikolsky had told him. "It's all in hand." There were no signs of any irregularities, Nikolsky had insisted. Everyone knew that Suchko was a drunk. There were several witnesses, including a shopgirl he'd been trying to screw, who said he'd been reeking of booze the night he fell to his death. "Couldn't tie a rope, the poor bastard," Nikolsky summed up.

Topchy thought it smelled funny at the time, but he'd gotten into the habit of relying on Feliks, and he pushed the business out of his mind. Now he experienced an unpleasant, crawling sensation down the back of his neck as he remembered how Preobrazhensky had just stood there, with that vacant look in his eyes, when he had raised this business of Kavrov in the Marshal's suite at Gogol Boulevard.

A KGB man with his neck broken in a Spetsnaz base. . . . An army spy inside the KGB itself. . . . An American agent. . . . Where did it all lead?

Preobrazhensky was the common link. There was something very unsettling, yet also familiar, about that man. Topchy couldn't quite put his finger on it.

Skvortsov rolled in, waggled his eyebrows suggestively, and snapped a finger against the side of his neck.

"Why not?" Topchy agreed. "We've earned it." He was tired, and his sciatica was starting to play up again. He kept a couple of bottles in his safe for just such occasions. Fuck the regulations. They weren't made for deputy chiefs.

He ripped the top off a bottle of vodka, sloshed some of the contents down his gullet, and passed it to Skvortsov, who took a big gulp without bothering to wipe the neck, then belched contentedly.

Topchy rubbed his eyes and consulted his watch. It was only 3:12 A.M. He felt he'd been up a lot longer than that. But wait, his watch had stopped. He swore copiously. The watch, which was gold-plated with quartz action, had the name of one of the most prestigious Swiss manufacturers on the dial. It was a gift from the Armenian, Askyerov's crony. It was supposed to run for a year before being recharged, and he'd had it only six weeks. The thing was a dud, or a counterfeit. Come to think of it, was that casing really fourteen-carat gold? It looked a bit tarnished. Well, he'd see to it that they paid through the nose before he was through, Askyerov and the Armenian both.

He wrenched the bottle away from Skvortsov.

"What the fuck is the time?"

It was past five. In just a few hours, the members of the Politburo would all be converging on Old Square in their fat limousines. Topchy felt a spasm of pain in his left leg, and then in his lower back, and dosed himself with another swig from the bottle.

He stared at the phones on his desk, irresolute. Should he call Askyerov with the good news that they had more than enough to hang Zotov's son-in-law, and therefore the Marshal himself? Why bother? He answered his own question with another. If Askyerov was awake, he could sweat it out for a bit longer. That way, he might be all the more grateful when he got what he wanted. Topchy visualized the scene now, as he arrived at Askyerov's residence, just as the Prime Minister was preparing to leave for Old Square. That would be the perfect moment to put the squeeze on. Why settle for promotion to chief of directorate? Hell, Askyerov could make him Chairman of the KGB.

This reflection cheered him up considerably. He handed the bottle back to Skvortsov, who fell on it like a man who was dying of thirst.

Topchy pulled a paper out of his pocket. It was all the authorization he needed to deal with Preobrazhensky. It was an arrest warrant, nicely official. All he needed to do was fill in the name. A private line to the Chairman of the Council of Ministers certainly helped to cut down the paperwork.

"What do you say, Vanvanich?" he consulted Skvortsov. "Shall we go round to Gogol Boulevard and stick a needle up that bitch's ass?"

"Why not?" Skvortsov grinned stupidly. He emitted a sound like old plumbing.

Then Topchy frowned. There was something he couldn't afford to forget. What was it? Fatigue and vodka were clouding his brain. Oh, yes, Kavrov. There was something very wrong about that. He ought to check.

"Get on the phone to Kavrov," he instructed Skvortsov. "I want to talk to what's-his-face." His speech was slightly slurred.

"Who?"

"Our man with the Spetsnaz brigade. The one who replaced Suchko. What the hell is his name?"

Skvortsov couldn't remember either. It seemed to take him an awfully long time, as well as further lubrication, to place the call. Then he had trouble communicating with the man on the other end of the line.

Topchy grabbed the receiver away from him and yelled into it, "Who is this?"

The man on the other end was almost inaudible. Topchy assumed he was drunk or half-asleep.

"Pull yourself together and do what I say," Topchy roared into the phone. "I want a full report on Suchko's death—a *new* report. Have you got that? I want it on my desk by noon today. It will state that we are investigating new leads that suggest that his death was not accidental. Yes, that's what I said! Are you deaf? What's that?"

Topchy could only make out a succession of grunts. They sounded accommodating.

"Listen," he went on. "Is there anything unusual happening down there? Anything that doesn't seem right? What's that? Well, get your ass outside and check! You're a military chekist, fuck your mother! If you see anything out of the ordinary, call me at once. Do you understand?"

When he slammed down the phone, he found that Skvortsov had managed to finish off the vodka. The idiot was holding the bottle upside down, a lopsided grin on his face. Topchy looked at him in disgust. Then he opened the safe and took out a second bottle.

"Go and wake up the others," he instructed Skvortsov. "Make sure that everyone is armed." He slammed the metal door to the safe shut and started fumbling for his personal seal. When he had his papers, and the last of his precious liquor reserve, sealed up tight, he took a quick look at Nikolsky in the adjoining office. He was still laid out on the table. He looked bloated and bled-white. The girl was pretending to be out to the world too, but he could see her pupils stirring under the lashes. He made a little bow to her. Major Furtsev, who was standing watch over both of them, with his pistol on the table at his elbow, looked almost as pale as Feliks. He was too squeamish for this line of work, Topchy thought. He must remember to transfer Furtsev to something more appropriate, like supervising the flowerbeds at the dacha he would soon be able to enjoy. He made a motion as if to toss the bottle to Furtsev, but thought better of it, and brought his arm back abruptly.

"I won't be long," Topchy said.

Furtsev was already on his feet, and his upper lip was trembling, it was hard to say whether with fear or anger.

"You have to let me call in a doctor," Furtsev said. "Nikolsky needs immediate medical attention."

"You're a babysitter, not a fucking wetnurse."

"He's been unconscious for more than an hour," Furtsev went on.

"He's going to be out for a lot longer than that." Topchy waved the bottle at Furtsev to dramatize his point. "We're dealing with a case of treason, Comrade Major. Perhaps you have heard of the crime? Some very big people—oh, yes, some real brass hats—are going to get themselves chopped off at the knees as a result of this. So what you do is, you sit at your desk there and you play with yourself and if anybody except me comes in demanding access to your prisoners, you shoot to kill."

Furtsev's mouth dropped open.

"Anything can happen tonight," Topchy said with satisfaction. "Anything at all. Now I have to go and sniff high boots. Cheer up, *dorogoy moy.*" He patted Furtsev's plump, almost hairless cheek patronizingly. "We're all going up in the world."

Topchy strutted out into the corridor, and a wild kind of exhilaration came over him, like a blast of hot air from a furnace. The sensation was compounded with nostalgia, a harking back to a place and a time where none of the normal rules applied. He saw himself, young and strong, in his chekist's leather coat, roaming the blasted landscape of East Prussia like a power of nature. There were Skvortsov and the others, cracking jokes, and that, too, evoked scenes from the past, from his early days in the Lubyanka—before anybody thought of trying to clean the place up—when drunken chekists roamed from cell to cell in the middle of the night, beating up prisoners or blowing their brains out.

There would be explaining to do later, of course. But by then, the case would be sewn up tight, Preobrazhensky and his father-in-law would be broken like wooden toys, and Moscow would be under new ownership. He imagined himself presiding over that vast, opulent office one floor above, with its fine mahogany paneling and luxurious oriental rugs, the one reserved for Dzerzhinsky's heirs.

Then he felt a painful, burning sensation, as if hot coals were falling through his bowels, and rushed out to the bathroom.

4　The cars were waiting in the Well, the courtyard inside the old seven-story building, the original Lubyanka. The massive iron gates leading out into the alley behind KGB headquarters were dragged back. Topchy let the bottle circulate and Skvortsov, sitting in the front seat of their Volga, kept turning around and proposing toasts.

From time to time, Topchy would growl at him, "Shut up, you piss-artist," but there was no force of reprimand in the words. Topchy was in excellent spirits. Since he had emptied his bowels, he felt invincible. As their little convoy sped through the deserted streets, other scenes from the past returned to him. He saw the faces of men he had killed and enjoyed killing. He saw the haughty features of a Russian army officer, the one who had been bleating over the fate of a German whore in some nameless village in Prussia at the end of the war, as if one life more or less—especially a *German* life—mattered a damn in the midst of all that car-nage. Topchy relived the almost sexual thrill as the big gun kicked back in his hand and he watched the dark stain spread between the officer's shoul-der blades. The fool had it coming, he reflected. He was a real *byvchy,* a throwback to the Tsarist officer caste. Just like that arrogant bitch Pre-obrazhensky.

In the frosty stillness, the mass of the General Staff complex, its enor-mous communications tower and its forest of antennas and satellite dishes rising above the roofline, seemed more daunting than usual. But Topchy had his driver pull up right in front of the main entrance and then strut-ted in as if he had just bought the deed to the property.

A soldier with the red tabs of a special guards company insisted on inspecting all of their KGB identity booklets. He asked Topchy to sign the admissions book while he got on the intercom to his duty officer.

"I see. . . . I'll have to check," the duty officer's voice crackled back when it was explained to him that the KGB men were on their way to visit Major-General Preobrazhensky. The guard set down the receiver.

"What is the reason for this delay?" Topchy glowered at the guard, moving as if to go past him toward the elevators.

"We have to locate the general, sir," the guard said stiffly. "It should only take a minute."

One of the elevators descended, the doors opened, and the duty officer appeared, all smiles and servility.

"Allow me to escort you myself, Comrade Colonel," said the major.

"I know my way."

"But really, sir. It's no trouble."

Topchy looked at the major curiously and shrugged. The man was obvi-ously just following regulations. How these woodentops in the army loved their standing orders! No Soviet army major was going to interfere with a KGB colonel in the execution of his duty.

Topchy, Skvortsov, and two assistants—one man had been left outside, with the cars—rode the elevator with the duty officer to the seventh floor, then followed him along a white-walled corridor and through an outer room to the leather-padded "Beria door" that screened Sasha's private office. Another army major was sitting at the desk in the outer office. He stood to attention when Topchy came in. Then he rapped on the frame of Sasha's door.

"Come in!" Sasha's voice boomed from within.

The door swung open, and as he stepped into the frame, Topchy saw his victim lolling back in his chair, a mug of steaming coffee in front of him on the desk. There was a radio playing in the office. Topchy realized, to his surprise and delight, that Sasha was listening to the BBC World Service. One more item for the dossier.

"Well, Colonel," Sasha greeted him. "It's good to see that our friends in the Committee get up early."

"You seem to get up early yourself."

"You've heard the news, I suppose." Sasha cocked his head toward the radio. There had still been no announcement in Moscow on the state of the General Secretary's health. But there were reports in the West that the man had suffered a terminal stroke and that the knives were out among the leaders disputing the succession. One London tabloid, which had distinguished itself in the past by claiming to have found Martin Bormann hiding in Brazil, had garnished the Moscow story with rumors that the General Secretary had been shot by the son of a disgraced Party official. "I wonder if anybody has told the General Secretary he's dead yet?" Sasha summarized. "What do you think?"

"There will be changes, I suppose. If it's true." Topchy hovered there in the doorway, not wanting to rush this moment of pleasure. "By the way, do you get all of your news from the BBC?"

"Oh, no. Sometimes I listen to the Voice of America. But I prefer the accent of the British announcers. But please"—Sasha played host—"won't you sit down? Would you like some coffee?" He raised his own mug. "I'm afraid it's the strongest stuff we serve here."

Topchy threw himself down on a chair, completely confident of his ground, with Skvortsov and the others blocking the doorway behind him.

"Oh, this is charming, General," he said to Sasha. "There you are, drinking your coffee. Take your time. I want you to savor every sip. That's the last coffee you're going to get."

"I'm not sure that I understand you." Sasha remained perfectly relaxed.

He let his arms swing down along the back of his chair, where his uniform jacket was draped.

"I'm taking you to Lefortovo so we can have a nice long talk," Topchy said.

"You mean I'm under arrest? May I know the charge?"

"Article Sixty-Four. Betrayal of the motherland. The penalty—"

"I know the penalty," Sasha said with seeming indifference.

Topchy felt acutely disappointed. Why didn't the man react?

"You'll be shot," Topchy informed him. "But not until you've answered all our questions. You'll wish that I'd shot you tonight." He toyed ostentatiously with the butt of his Makarov.

"On whose authority are you making this arrest?" Sasha asked lazily.

Visibly annoyed, Topchy pulled out the warrant and threw it on the desk. Dammit, how could Preobrazhensky just sit there?

With his left hand, Sasha picked up the warrant, and scanned it. He said very slowly, "I'm afraid you have made a mistake, Colonel Topchy. This document has no meaning in this building."

This was too much for Topchy, who sprang from his chair yelling, "Stop the bullshit! We've got the goods on you, fuck your mother! And now you're coming with us. Vanvanich!"

Topchy had his gun out. When nobody came to his aid, he looked around, over his shoulder. Skvortsov was still blocking the doorway, but he was goggle-eyed, his tongue was protruding between his teeth, and his broad face was flushed angry red, verging on purple. At the same moment, the soldier who had been silently and expertly garrotting him with a length of nylon fishing line released his grip, and Skvortsov fell in a heap. Topchy turned to Sasha, and saw a second soldier emerge through the door to the back room, cradling an automatic rifle.

Topchy was reduced to making an incoherent gargling sound.

"Take his gun," Sasha ordered his bodyguards. "And dispose of the others. I'll deal with this one myself." He had brought his right hand out of his jacket pocket and was leveling a P-6 at Topchy's chest.

"You can't do this," Topchy tried again when they were alone.

"That statement is anachronistic."

"What's going on, fuck your mother?"

"It would take too long to explain." Sasha released the safety catch on his pistol. His tone hadn't altered. He sounded completely detached. It was that, more than what he had seen done to Skvortsov, that told Topchy he was a dead man.

The blood drained from his face, and he turned away from Sasha, his shoulders hunched. He looked old and blanched, scuttling sideways like a hermit crab.

"Turn around," Sasha said evenly. "I am not going to shoot you in the back the way you murdered my father."

Topchy turned around, his fear mingling with intense curiosity.

"Your father? What are you talking about?"

"I'm sure you remember. It happened in East Prussia. Years later, you had a man killed in the labor camps because he had seen you do it."

"It's not possible." Topchy gaped at him.

"The man you had murdered in the camp was Lieutenant of Artillery Ivanov. The man you shot in cold blood in East Prussia was Captain Sergei Mikhailovich Preobrazhensky. He was a Hero of the Soviet Union."

"Your father." Topchy rubbed his face with his hands. "I thought there was a look about you. How long have you known?"

"All my life. All of it that matters."

"They couldn't have told you the whole story." Topchy saw a chink, and tried to wriggle through it. "Your father was a fine officer. It was a terrible mistake, but those things happen in a war. People's nerves are stretched beyond endurance. You can't imagine what it was like at the front."

"This is the first time in your life that you've seen the front." The words were as precise, as implacable as nails being driven into the lid of a coffin.

Without haste, Sasha extended his right arm so that his pistol was pointing into Topchy's face, his left arm folded behind him as if he were engaged in a dueling contest. Topchy jerked sideways at the last instant, so the bullet drove through the socket of his right eye. His head seemed to explode as he fell, spattering blood and brains across the wall on the far side of the room, over the space where the portrait of the General Secretary had hung.

Sasha stepped over the body. He felt as if a yoke had been lifted. He threw open the door and told his adjutant, "I'll move into the Marshal's office until this war is over."

9.
THE COUP

The moment you decide an event is impossible and therefore stop directing your attention to it is the moment when it will take place.

—GENERAL PETRO GRIGORENKO

1 The lines of the Moscow metro converged on the center of the capital like the spokes of a bashed-in wheel. At 5:30 A.M., when the trains started running, Zaytsev's advance squads began to arrive in twos and threes at Vodnny Stadium, north of the airport, and at Sokol'niki. The weather was on their side. With the bite of winter in the air, it was natural to go about in overcoats or parkas, which made it easy for the Spetsnaz teams to conceal the tools of their trade: Malish mini machine guns, P-6 pistols, knives, and magnesium grenades.

Orlov arrived at Dzerzhinsky station a few minutes before six, and emerged from the pedestrian subway on the far side of Kirova Street. There, in the middle of the traffic circle, was the statue of Iron Feliks, his back confidently turned to the gray stone building that had once housed the All-Russian Insurance Company. The streets were almost empty. It wasn't hard to identify the KGB guards in civilian clothes loitering around the entrances to the Lubyanka. They were obvious bruisers, stocky, hard-faced types from the Ninth Directorate. Orlov spotted two at the front of the building, and a third on the near side. There would be more around the back, and around the new headquarters block that had been built for the Second Chief Directorate.

Orlov ambled along the pavement, checking that his own squads were in place. Two of his men were inspecting the windows of Detsky Mir, the children's department store. Another came strolling along Prospekt Marx, the first of the group that had arrived at the Sverdlova metro station, a few blocks away. Orlov glanced at the battered steel watch on his thick wrist and continued his walk, branching off along Dzerzhinsky Street. The line had not yet begun to form in front of the KGB's neighborhood *Gastronom*, which was celebrated for the quality of its food. The shelves were usually cleaned out half an hour after the doors were opened at 8:00 A.M. Orlov glanced, with no apparent interest, at two Spetsnaz troopers who were lolling outside.

The KGB guards in the square looked relaxed. As Orlov doubled back toward the Lubyanka, he observed one of them exchanging pleasantries with a statuesque cleaning woman as she passed. The guards' main function was to shield the Lubyanka from terrorist attack, but nobody—not the Ukrainian nationalists, or the Crimean Tatars, or the Jewish refuseniks —had ever tried to get inside the building. The closest thing to a terrorist assault that anyone could remember was when a drunken Armenian had tossed a bottle of champagne through one of the windows in 1976. The bottle landed intact on the desk of a surprised, and presumably gratified, duty officer.

Then Orlov saw what he was waiting for. A big green army ambulance, with a red cross inside a white circle on its side, came lumbering up Kirova Street. The colonel raised his wristwatch to his ear, as if to see whether it had stopped, and the men who had been watching for this signal started moving into position.

Orlov walked round the side of the Lubyanka to Entrance Six, one of the two reserved for the First Chief Directorate and the Border Guards. He stopped just short of one of the KGB watchmen, who stared at him but did not speak. The guards had instructions not to shoo tourists away; the Committee had its image to protect.

"Smoke?" Orlov inquired pleasantly.

At the same instant that the guard growled his refusal, Orlov felled him with a single slicing blow along the side of the jaw, aiming for the brain stem.

A second guard turned to see what had happened, but before he could utter a sound, one of Orlov's men sank a knife into his throat. It was an ingenious weapon, the Spetsnaz knife. You pulled the switch and it fired its blade like an arrow, accurate over a distance of several yards. For reasons Orlov had never bothered to question, they called it a French knife. Whatever its origin, it had been fully naturalized.

The ambulance, borrowed from the Khodinsk airfield, where Vlassov had been in charge for several hours, was already drawing up to the curb, and the first body was loaded into the back. As it continued on a slow circle of the Lubyanka, coming out through the alley that made a dogleg around the back, the other KGB guards were piled in like logs. His task complete, the driver headed back to Khodinsk; nobody was likely to challenge a military vehicle along the way.

No one had raised the alarm. There was only the rumble of the early-morning traffic, the sounds of the city stretching and groaning as it came fully awake.

Followed closely by two of his men, Orlov marched through the high double doors at the front of the Lubyanka as if it belonged to him. At the same time, other squads tackled the remaining entrances, all except Entrance Two, which was kept permanently shut. They found some of the doors locked, but had come prepared for that with skeleton keys.

There was a mousetrap inside the main entrance: a space in front of a second set of doors with small glass panels through which the uniformed security men inside could squint out at anyone attempting to enter the building.

Orlov nodded at the man behind the glass, pushed open the door, and gave a hearty "Good morning!" He reached under his coat, as if to fish out his identity card. Instead, he brought out his P-6 and fired point-blank through the screw-in silencer into the KGB guard's face. The man slumped heavily across his table. There was an ugly, ragged star at the back of his head where the bullet had escaped.

It took scarcely longer to deal with the guards who were napping in their room off the hall. One of the Spetsnaz troops set about stripping the KGB uniform from one of the corpses. The jacket was tight under the arms, but at least it did not show bloodstains. He took the place of the dead man at the table near the main doors. The pattern was repeated, without a hitch, at the other entrances.

Orlov sent a small detachment to break through to the basement, where the KGB switchboard and communications center was located. There were only two operators on duty at that hour of the morning, and neither was allowed time to give the alarm. An army technician took charge.

Another team worked its way through to the inner doors that opened onto the courtyard inside the old part of the Lubyanka. The men who worked at KGB headquarters called it the Well. For countless victims of Yezhov, Yagoda, and Beria, it had been the lobby of Hell. The lone sentry at the massive iron gates leading out into the alley was swiftly dispatched.

The honor of occupying the office of the Chairman of the Committee of State Security on the fourth floor fell to a young lieutenant, Mikhailov. The Chairman's vast office, embellished with oriental rugs and mahogany paneling, straddled the old and new sections of the building. Mikhailov ripped the portraits of Dzerzhinsky and the General Secretary from the wall, and set about breaking open the Chairman's personal safe.

Two-man squads roamed the corridors of the Lubyanka, all of which were confusingly alike. The walls were painted to resemble oak, the parquet floors were sheathed in worn-out linoleum, dirty brown with traces of a yellow pattern. Light filtered down through big white globes suspended on metal rods. Most of the offices, too, were uniform, painted a harsh, surgical white above a pale blue dado, generally empty except for the standard-issue items: a writing table, a big metal safe closed up at night with a wax seal, a second long table for meetings in the rooms of the department chiefs.

Orlov knew exactly where he was going; he had been over the floor plan with Zaytsev a dozen times. He turned left, past an elevator with a thick metal door, solid except for a tiny peephole—it had once been used for Beria's cells—and hurried up a broad staircase, taking the steps two at a time. Zaytsev had charged him with a special mission: to secure the records of the Third Directorate, especially the lists of KGB spies inside the armed forces. He had been warned that he might encounter a chekist called Feliks Nikolsky. Under no circumstances was Nikolsky to be harmed.

The Third Directorate, on the second floor, seemed to be awake earlier than the rest of KGB headquarters. Orlov's party were challenged by a duty officer. They shot him on the spot. But a second KGB officer darted from a doorway at the end of the corridor and squeezed off several rounds from his pistol. Orlov threw himself back against the wall. The man behind him sucked in his breath sharply as a bullet nicked his shoulder.

Orlov swore softly. They had been told that nobody in the building, apart from the security detail, would be armed. Before 1979 officers at KGB headquarters had been permitted to keep personal sidearms in their safes. Then a KGB officer took his gun home with him and shot his wife and his wife's lover. New regulations went out. But it seemed they hadn't reached the Third Directorate.

Orlov turned to the wounded man at his elbow.

"Give me that," he hissed, reaching for the Malish. He gestured to the third man in the squad. "Around the other way," he whispered. "We'll take them from both sides."

Gripping the mini machine gun like a pistol, Orlov started to zigzag along the corridor, keeping his body low. He saw a shadow at the end of the corridor, and fired a short burst. He heard a door slam shut. Then something else took place that he had no reason to expect. A woman started to scream, a sudden, piercing cry that was instantly stifled. It came from the big corner office, which Orlov knew must belong to one of the top men in the Third Directorate, perhaps the chief himself.

He waited till the third man in the squad came loping toward him from the other end of the corridor.

They both hovered for a moment, their backs against the wall on either side of Topchy's door.

Then Orlov signaled, "Go!"

The Spetsnaz commando—a tough captain who had risen from the ranks and was credited with more than twenty kills in Afghanistan—leaped forward and crashed the door open with his boot. Then he was down on his belly, firing into the office a few inches above body height so as to numb resistance without killing anyone till they had taken the measure of what was going on in the room.

Orlov lunged forward after him.

There were four people in the office, one of them a naked man lashed to a chair. There was a second prisoner, a woman.

The KGB man who had fired at them in the corridor didn't seem to have the stomach for a fight. He dropped his gun and nervously raised his hands.

Orlov's eyes shifted to the far end of the room. At first, he could see only the top of Major Furtsev's bulging skull, the receding hairline that came forward into a widow's peak, as he surfaced from behind the writing table. Furtsev had a telephone receiver in one hand. Orlov could not see the other hand.

"Get up!" Orlov yelled at him. "Hands behind your neck!"

Major Furtsev moved slowly as if to comply, sliding around the side of the table.

The naked prisoner shouted a warning, and made as if to drag himself and the heavy chair across the room.

Orlov fired as soon as he saw the pistol, but not before Furtsev got off a single shot, aiming not at the Spetsnaz soldiers but at the male prisoner. The burst from Orlov's Malish stitched a ragged diagonal pattern across the major's chest, as if he had been flung against barbed wire. He died with a sound of water being sucked down a drain.

Orlov rushed to the prisoner, who had toppled sideways still bound to the chair. A mulberry-dark stain was spreading across the floor from an open wound the size of a fist. Orlov had seen stomach wounds like that before, and he knew that you didn't get over them.

"Who are you?" he asked, pressing his lips close to the dying man's ear. He seemed to be beyond speech. Orlov took out his knife and gingerly cut the bonds so he could lay the prisoner flat on his back.

"Who are you?" he repeated his question to the girl, who gave a foreign name in heavily accented Russian.

"American?" Orlov asked.

She nodded, waiting for him to release her too.

"What about him?" Orlov jabbed his shoulder toward the man on the floor.

"I heard them call him Feliks. His clothes must be in the next room."
One of Orlov's men went out and came back with Nikolsky's KGB
identity pass.

"He was trying to help me," Elaine said in a murmur.

"I don't understand."

She groaned and said, "Could you *please* do something about this?"
twisting her ankles and wrists inside the ropes.

When Orlov had cut her loose she tried to stand, but her legs buckled.
She felt stabbing pains as the circulation returned. Orlov took her arm to
support her. For a moment, she thought it was Nikolsky. Faces blurred
into a continuum.

Orlov let the girl stagger over to the table. She bent over the dying
man, stroking his hair. Colonel Orlov had no instructions about an American girl. But she was somehow connected to Nikolsky, and he had precise
orders to protect Nikolsky. He would have to hold the girl until Zaytsev
arrived. The general would decide.

There was a shuddering sound from the man on the floor, like the
banging of a clapped-out old refrigerator against a wall.

"Can you get a doctor?" the girl asked.

"It's too late," Orlov said. He was thinking, *It would be kinder to shoot
the poor bastard.*

"You could *try,*" the girl said accusingly. "You can't begin to imagine
what he has been through." A tear rolled down from her cheek over
Nikolsky's forehead. "I just pray that he's beyond feeling anything."

Nikolsky did not hear this exchange. He had been drifting for a long time.
At one point, he felt an exquisite, searing pain, but then it seemed to him
that he was floating on his back down a broad river—the Dnieper, perhaps
—toward a sunlit sea. The banks of the river resembled the walls of
Topchy's office, but they stretched outward and backward into the far
distance as the stream widened. Then it was no longer the current that
carried him but waves of music and the distant riverbanks were the walls
of a magnificent concert hall, in which the Moscow Symphony Orchestra
was tuning its instruments, preparing to play.

Nikolsky watched the conductor raise his baton. Then the conductor
paused and turned to look at Nikolsky, who was sitting there in the very
first row, and for some reason the conductor was no longer a man with
white hair and a black tie but a ravishing gypsy singer. He felt that he
knew her. Of course. She wasn't a gypsy at all. She was Maya, Maya
Askyerova. She leaned over him, smiling, and her raven hair flowed down,

brushing his face, enclosing him like a tent. The orchestra struck up a wild gypsy melody, and the girl was singing her heart out. Her voice soared and swooped like a hawk, carrying him with it. Then the girl was bowing and backing away from the stage, and he wanted to rise and go with her. But there was somebody behind him who kept tapping on his shoulder, tapping and tapping, until, not wanting to, he was compelled to turn around in his seat and look into the mild, china-blue eyes of his grandmother.

He knew that she had no place being there in the concert hall, because surely she had died years before.

Nikolsky's grandmother was kind but insistent. "Feliks," she said, "they're all waiting for us. Hurry. We can't stay here any longer."

"But babushka," he was protesting, "I have to talk to that girl."

"It's too late, my child. We must go now. Look, here's nice Mister Krupchenko." And there, sure enough, was Krupchenko's little beaming round face. Where on earth had *he* come from?

"There are some irregularities," Krupchenko said rather apologetically.

And his grandmother was plucking at his sleeve and drawing him along after her in a strong, fluid movement, like an irresistible undertow. The walls of the concert hall were lost in an infinite distance. The music was sucked away. The figure of the gypsy singer became tinier and tinier until she and the orchestra and the whole concert hall were compressed into a single, failing point of light.

Colonel Orlov put his hands on Elaine's shoulders and gently drew her away from the table.

"He's gone," Orlov said.

"Who are you?" Elaine whispered.

"Orlov," he said, slightly inclining his head.

"You're not KGB?"

"I am a colonel of the Russian army," Orlov said with pride.

"I don't understand what's happening."

"I can't tell you anything. Don't worry, it will be clear soon enough."

She wanted to ask him about Sasha, but she did not know how far she could trust this grim, taciturn soldier in civilian clothes who had invaded KGB headquarters with a gun in his hand, for reasons she could not begin to comprehend.

The phone rang, not the ordinary line via the KGB switchboard, but a special circuit.

Orlov stared at the instrument with its flashing light as if it were an unidentified animal.

Elaine said, "Topchy."

Orlov turned the same stare on her.

"Colonel Topchy," she specified. "It's his goddam office." Then she was sobbing again, reliving the horrors of the night, seeing Topchy's face as he shoved at his desk drawer. Her sensation was like vertigo. She felt she was toppling over a precipice.

She was pulled back by the stinging sensation where Orlov had slapped her cheek.

"Will you be quiet?" the colonel said.

She nodded.

The phone was still ringing. Orlov picked up the receiver. "Duty officer," he said.

"Let me speak to Colonel Topchy." The voice on the other end of the line was rounded, almost fruity, and familiar. Orlov was reminded of a speech that had been telecast only a few days before.

He cleared his throat and reported, "Colonel Topchy is away from the office on an operational matter. May I take a message?"

"No message," said the caller, and hung up.

Orlov looked at the American girl and wondered why Prime Minister Askyerov would be calling a KGB colonel on his direct line at 6:30 A.M.

2 From Kavrov to the center of Moscow was a drive of four hours, more or less, under good conditions. Just after 1:00 A.M., Zaytsev had left the base with half of the Spetsnaz brigade—five hundred men—squeezed into a dozen Ural personnel carriers. The moon, when it showed through the clouds, was almost full, mantling the sandy patches among the pines with a powdery white, as if the first snows were falling. Zaytsev rode in a jeep at the head of the convoy with his radio operator and the lieutenant who had helped to dispose of Suchko's body. They drove right through the town, past the Victorian bulk of the motorbike plant and the machine gun factory; night maneuvers by army units were nothing unusual in the closed city of Kavrov.

Three and a half hours later, they crossed the Moscow Ring Road on Volokolamskiy Chosse, avoiding the outposts of the traffic police. Zaytsev, no Muscovite, had to check his street map before they found the right turning off Leningrad Prospekt. But as they neared the Khodinsk airfield, he recognized familiar landmarks.

The entrance to GRU headquarters and the airport was heavily defended and, for the first time, Zaytsev's convoy was forced to stop. The officer at the checkpoint was not satisfied with Zaytsev's written orders, issued above the signature of the Chief of Staff, and they were made to wait while he went to telephone. One of the guards strolled around the back of the jeep, peering curiously at the radio transmitter and the heavy machine gun that was inadequately concealed under its waterproof cover. Zaytsev could sense that his men were jumpy. He saw the lieutenant reach down instinctively and grip the barrel of his kalashnikov. Zaytsev patted his forearm.

"Easy," he murmured.

When the duty officer came back, he was more respectful.

"General Vlassov is expecting you, sir." He motioned for the guards to stand aside, and climbed up onto the side of the jeep to escort them in person to a parking area around the side of the GRU buildings, at the edge of the runway.

Alone at Marshal Zotov's desk, Sasha wondered how many people were awake in Moscow at that hour of the morning. Since he had pulled the trigger and killed Topchy, he had felt a tremendous sense of release, bordering on elation. There was no longer room for doubts. Wherever it might lead him, his course was set. He could no more turn back to his previous existence than the bullet he had fired could reenter the barrel of the gun.

Still, there were questions that troubled him. Why had Topchy come for him in the middle of the night, suicidally sure of his ground? Surely Topchy would never have acted alone. Who had authorized his arrest? Why had Nikolsky, Topchy's confidant, failed to warn him? Had he been betrayed?

A snatch from one of Vissotsky's songs, Nikolsky's favorite, ran through his head and wouldn't leave him, like an itch that he couldn't reach. *"Why is it the bird, never the bullet, that is stopped in full flight?"*

And he had guessed the answer to the first question. He saw the sly look on Topchy's face, and then he saw himself with Elaine in the parking lot near the Visotny Dom when, crazy and tearful, she had taken both of their lives into her hands. Topchy had found out about the girl.

He stared at the phones on the Marshal's desk. Should he call her hotel? But the call almost certainly would be monitored. And what if she wasn't there? What could he accomplish? If he knew Topchy, the KGB would be holding her somewhere, as witness—and perhaps as hostage—in Lefortovo, or Butyrki, maybe in the bowels of the Lubyanka itself. If the girl was in danger, she was beyond his help—for now. In a few hours, they would rise or fall together.

In the meantime, there were practical things to attend to.

It was Kolya Vlassov who had explained things to General Luzhin. Until the previous day, Luzhin had been the deputy chief of the GRU, the top career army man in the service. As of today, he was acting head of the service, with Kolya as his chief of operations.

Like Sasha, Kolya had advanced to the rank of major-general. Unlike Sasha, he had stayed in military intelligence for nearly his entire career, although tanks had been his early and enduring love and he had managed a short stint with an armored division. After getting kicked out of West Africa, Kolya had spent most of his time at headquarters, which had done no harm to his career at all. He had served his term in Afghanistan, like the others in Sasha's inner circle, apart from Feliks, and it had shaped him, as it had shaped them all. Sasha took to meeting him for the occasional drink or dinner *en famille;* after all, he had Kolya to thank for his marriage, and therefore his relationship with the Marshal. More from what was left unspoken than from what was said, he realized that Kolya was one of them, and that Kolya, as a senior and well-connected officer at the Aquarium, could be extraordinarily useful. Kolya was invited to Bangladesh for the first time only a few days before the coup. Not only did he pledge instant support, he helped to refine all their plans. For one thing, he pointed out that Luzhin, Sasha's old boss in New York, remained a fervent admirer of the Marshal and was at daggers drawn with the chief of his service, who had been imported from the KGB in keeping with the Soviet tradition of divide and rule. For another, he stressed the fact that the Aquarium had remarkable potential as an operations center in Moscow. The Khodinsk airfield was the best guarded and most secret in the whole region. There was even a metro line that ran straight from the front door of the Aquarium under the Kremlin.

"Leave it to me," Kolya said when Zaytsev asked how many men he would need to seize control of the Aquarium. "General Luzhin will make everything possible for us. All I need is an order signed by the Marshal. Luzhin will enjoy carrying it out, I can assure you of that."

Kolya had another bright idea. The elderly commandant of the Tank Academy was another admirer of the Marshal's. He had served with Zotov in the Battle of Kursk. A "personal" message from the Marshal could work wonders in that quarter too.

Nobody was wasted. Pauk, the waiter from the beer-bar Zhiguli—

Nikolsky's friend—had joined the Spetsnaz team assigned to take charge of the Central Telephone Exchange on Gorky Street, near the sand-colored mass of the Ministry of Interior. Pauk was looking forward enormously to lording it over those bitches who had given him hell when he was a junior engineer. It promised to be even more fun than fixing the bills at the Zhiguli.

Other squads were assigned to the state broadcasting center and the major airports, and were already converging on their targets, ready to swing into action at the prearranged time. There weren't enough of them to control everything. But if the first stages of the operation went according to plan, they wouldn't need to.

3 Nobody walked in the park opposite the Central Committee building; it was a place where everyone kept off the grass. The ground rose quite steeply between Serova Passage, at the foot of the hill, and Old Square, at the top. The solitary drunk who was attempting the climb was reduced, more than once, to scrambling on hands and knees. As he reached the top, his feet, dragging through the dry leaves, made the sound of stiff brown paper being shredded. He took a pull on a bottle of some unidentifiable stuff, *samorgon* perhaps—cheaper than vodka and more lethal—and marched unsteadily toward the square, where there seemed to be more police about than usual, diverting traffic, milling around the entrances to the Central Committee building. The drunk collared a militiaman who was patrolling the sidewalk, where there was reserved parking for some of the higher-ups. Many of the spaces had already been claimed by black Chaikas.

"Iz gorla budesh," the drunk proposed to the militiaman. "Take a swig." The militiaman grinned and wagged a finger at him.

"Tell me, chief," said the drunk. "Why are the bosses here so early? Is it true that they're going to lock up all the Jews?"

The militiaman laughed and shooed him away. It was nearly 8:00 A.M., and the last of the long line of Zils snaked through the General Secretary's gate into the L-shaped courtyard inside the Central Committee building. This was the most exclusive parking lot in the city. The sentries at the gate—tough Kremlin Guards in militia uniform—only admitted Zils, the Rolls-Royces of official Moscow.

Gussein Askyerov's limousine was the last to arrive. The Prime Minister's normally bland, shiny face was as gray as that of the drunk in the park, who had now subsided into an ugly, liquid cough that made it sound as if his whole insides were stirring. Askyerov rubbed the loose flesh under his chin as if his collar were choking him. His restless eyes darted everywhere, noting the tight squad of Kremlin Guards deployed near the General Secretary's private entrance, the personal security men in somber civilian suits hovering around the official cars. He was alarmed that Topchy had still not reported back. Almost an hour before he had ordered one of his closest aides to track Topchy down. There had been no word since then; it was as if Moscow had swallowed both of them up. Askyerov had called the Lubyanka a second time, only to be told that Topchy had not come back and his aide had not arrived. Askyerov still lacked the proofs he had been promised, the material that would bury Marshal Zotov as a pawn of the CIA. It had occurred to him that Topchy could be playing a double game, that he might even have warned the Marshal.

But what could Zotov do? the Prime Minister asked himself as he got out of his Zil. He felt calmer now, enclosed by the sturdy walls of the Central Committee.

He quickened his stride to overtake a stocky man with cropped hair the color and texture of lint who was approaching the General Secretary's entrance. He called out, and Serdyuk paused to let him catch up.

"Any news?" Askyerov asked the Defense Minister in an urgent whisper. "Any unauthorized military movements?"

"Relax." Serdyuk took his arm. "Everything is as it should be. I checked with Moscow Military District myself."

"What about the Guards? What about the Kantemirov division?"

Askyerov had a particular suspicion of this celebrated tank division, part of the Moscow garrison.

"Confined to barracks, on full alert," the Defense Minister reassured him.

"And the Caucasian divisions?"

"The advance units"—Serdyuk consulted his watch, a gold-plated Rolex—"should be landing about now. The rest will be here by midafternoon. Don't worry. Nobody's going to fight. Moscow belongs to us."

On the second floor, instead of entering the meeting room through the antechamber, like the other officials, Askyerov and Serdyuk passed through an outer office into the private sanctum of the General Secretary. They lingered there for a moment while Askyerov tried for a third time to reach Topchy. This time, there was no answer on the direct line. Sitting there in the General Secretary's chair, behind the big desk topped with green felt, Askyerov felt uncomfortable. He picked up the cream-colored phone, the Kremlevka line. He wanted to call the Armenian, the link between himself and Topchy. Maybe the Armenian would know what had happened. Askyerov dialed all four digits before he realized that the Kremlevka line was dead.

"What is it?" Serdyuk asked, seeing the Prime Minister's mouth tighten.

"Here. Try it yourself." Askyerov passed him the receiver.

It was inexplicable. The Kremlevka line was operated round the clock by KGB technicians for the benefit of the top circle of the *nomenklatura,* those who rated four-digit telephone numbers as well as Zils.

The two men in the General Secretary's office looked at each other.

"Get Chetverikov in here," Askyerov ordered the Defense Minister. "Don't mention this to anyone."

"What's happening?" the KGB chief demanded when he came in with Serdyuk. "Everyone's waiting in there."

"Including Marshal Zotov?"

"Including Zotov. Though he looks more asleep than awake."

Askyerov grunted. Zotov's presence was a good sign. For a moment, when he discoverd that the Kremlevka line wasn't working, the Prime Minister had experienced the strangest, most unsettling premonition that the Marshal had found out his plan and had already launched a preemptive strike. It was absurd, of course. In the Soviet Union, the military were bound hand and foot. Zotov couldn't possibly have forgotten what had happened to some of his predecessors who had developed bonapartist tendencies—to the illustrious, self-important Zhukov, given the boot while he was out of town on a junket in Yugoslavia, to Biryuzov, blown sky-high in his plane a few years later. Anyway, the Prime Minister reasoned, if Marshal Zotov was hatching a plot of his own, he couldn't possibly be fool enough to deliver himself up as a hostage by attending the Politburo meeting that particular morning.

"Find out what's happened," the Prime Minister ordered Chetverikov, who called his deputy at home on a white phone reserved for family and personal calls. Within five minutes, the KGB general called back with some story about a technical malfunction. He promised it would be corrected within the hour.

"Well?" the Defense Minister prodded Askyerov. "What are we waiting for? Let's get it over with."

Askyerov's enemies had complained, more than a few times, that the man could smell danger. Intuition, nothing else, had stopped him from attending a meeting in Baku where cutthroats hired by one of the black market operators he had been milking were lying in wait for him. Now, though he reasoned that there was no cause for fear—not with Zotov sitting there in the Central Committee room, surrounded by Party officials who would vote as Askyerov instructed, and armed men who would fire on his orders—wordless, unreasoning instinct held him back, like a cobweb across his face.

Since he could not explain this to Serdyuk and Chetverikov, he said, "I'm not sure that we're ready. That evidence that I mentioned to you, on Zotov. I don't have it yet."

"Evidence, fuck your mother," Chetverikov snorted. "Make your move, then we'll see about evidence later on. For now"—he jutted his shoulder out toward the door leading to the meeting room—"you own the people in there. But if you delay—well, I won't vouch for later. Zotov is definitely up to something, but he thinks he has a whole week to play with. You can't risk giving him time, not even a single day. Break him *now*."

Serdyuk was nodding vigorously.

Askyerov sighed and went into the General Secretary's private bathroom. When he came out, he said, "I'm ready."

Twenty-six men were already seated around the long, polished wooden table in the center of the meeting room. There was a portrait of Lenin over the General Secretary's door, through which Askyerov and his companions made their entrance. Over to the left was a table for assistants, with a battery of phones in various colors, and a second table for a pair of girl stenographers. Behind were tall windows overlooking Kuybishev Street, with heavy brown-and-gold drapes. Up to the level of Askyerov's eyebrows, the walls of the Committee room were paneled with pale wood; the paint higher up matched almost perfectly. Chairs had been placed around the walls to accommodate some of the less senior officials, men who belonged to neither the Politburo nor the Secretariat nor the top level of the cabinet or the high command. Askyerov meant to show that the decisions taken here commanded broad support.

He took his place, to the right of the empty chair that belonged to the General Secretary, and opened the rust-colored leather folder in front of him.

The glare from the ceiling, where four big white glass lampshades were suspended like inverted mushrooms, was not flattering to the men around the main table. Askyerov scanned their faces: faces like cracked ice, faces like pillows squashed and pummeled out of shape through many sleepless nights, faces of weary, cynical survivors. Even Galayev, a stripling by comparison with most of them, looked older than his years. Romanov's color was a startling orange that morning; he had been overdoing his fake tan. Few of the men in that room liked Askyerov, but many had reason to fear him. Some had been caught in his sticky web of favors, accepting opulent gifts that had never been reciprocated. Others were scared by what General Chetverikov's dossiers might contain. The minority who had kept their noses clean might well have been daunted by the combination of power represented by the two men seated close to Askyerov: the Defense Minister and the Chairman of the KGB.

The Prime Minister's eyes flickered across to Marshal Zotov, who was sitting almost directly opposite, his eyelids shut, his hands folded over his expansive belly as if he had nodded off. He looked as harmless as an old sheepdog dozing in the sun. But Askyerov wasn't deceived. Zotov was the one man in the room who could break the spell.

"I have just come from the General Secretary," Askyerov began. "I regret to have to report that his condition is terminal. It's only a matter of days. In his wisdom, out of his great love for our country, the General Secretary has dictated his political testament, which I propose to read to you now. He has asked me to convey to you that its contents are merely suggestions for our consideration. His concern is for continuity in these dangerous times we are going through. With your permission."

He paused, to see whether anyone would dare to object. No one did. There was a slight rumble from the Marshal, and his eyelids opened a fraction. Then he hauled himself upright and consulted his watch.

Don't worry, Askyerov addressed him mentally. *It will be over for you soon enough.* It had been necessary, of course, to interpret the General Secretary's wishes somewhat freely in the document he was about to read. The man had deteriorated sadly in recent weeks. He couldn't even control his bladder. But the signature at the bottom was real, all right.

The first brigade of Askyerov's "wild divisions" was flown in from the Caucasus on board Antonov transport planes. To the pilots' surprise, Moscow air control diverted them to the Khodinsk airfield. The ramps were lowered, and the men began to disembark. Most of them were still milling around while their officers tried to get them sorted out into platoons and companies, when half a dozen tanks emerged from the cover of the buildings around the airfield. They were an odd assortment, of different vintages. They were demonstration models, borrowed from the one army institution that was permitted to keep tanks permanently stationed within the perimeters of the capital: the Moscow Tank Academy.

But the effect, as they flanked the thin line of troops advancing on the Caucasian brigade from front and back, was sufficiently dramatic.

Kolya Vlassov came riding up in an armored car and called for the brigade commander to come forward.

"You are relieved of your duties on the orders of the Chief of Staff," he announced curtly. "You will instruct your men to lay down their weapons."

As he spoke, the tanks lowered their guns to head height.

The Caucasian troops, whose orders to advance on Moscow had been a mystery to them from the start, had no fight in them. They piled their rifles in stacks and sat around talking and swapping cigarettes, until they were herded away into nearby warehouses.

The main force from the Caucasus was intercepted at a railhead forty miles south of Moscow by men of the 105th Airborne, who also had precise instructions signed by the Chief of Staff. They, too, were disarmed. They were informed that their divisions had been disbanded, and were allowed to go home on the same trains that had carried them north —except for the officers, who were placed under arrest.

A second Airborne division was deployed on the road between the capital and a base twenty miles to the southwest that was occupied by the Dzerzhinsky Division, the KGB's private army. Fully motorized, and equipped with tanks and armored cars, the Dzerzhinsky Division posed the most imminent threat to the coup.

The same planes that had brought the Caucasians to Khodinsk were used to ferry more troops to the capital from Kavrov. The commanders of the "court divisions"—the Kantemirov and Taman Guards—had received orders from the Chief of Staff to maintain their forces on maximum defensive alert.

Meanwhile, Zaytsev used the Well, inside the Lubyanka, as a rallying point, massing several hundred men in a variety of uniforms and disguises for the most critical phase of the operation.

Askyerov was halfway through his reading of the document he had described to the Politburo as the General Secretary's political testament. He paused to pour himself a glass of mineral water, and waded on.

"Militarism is antithetical to the Marxist-Leninist tradition," Askyerov read out. "Our armed forces have always been dedicated to the cause of world peace and the cause of proletarian internationalism. No conflict is possible between the high command and the Party, which is its guide and mentor."

He glanced over the edge of his folder at Marshal Zotov. The Marshal's attention seemed to be focused on his watch, as if he was counting the minutes until the conclave was over.

He read on. "Bonapartism, however, has been encouraged by foreign special services in their unremitting efforts to divide and weaken the Soviet people."

Zotov gave no sign of having absorbed this. The man actually yawned—copiously, insolently—and Askyerov again wished that he had the dossier Topchy had promised. Never mind. He could break the Marshal without it.

He sped through the rest of the edited text. He relished the surprise and the delight in the face of the youngest man in the room, Galayev, as it dawned on him that he would inherit the title of General Secretary. The title, not the functions. Askyerov was no fool. He wasn't a Russian, or even a Ukrainian, and he knew that the Marshal wasn't the only one who called him black-ass or cockroach behind his back. Let someone else bask in the limelight. He would content himself with the real power.

He had reached the peroration. Predictable, but then you could never fault the General Secretary for being excessively original. In the silence around the table, people cleared their throats, vied for the bottles of mineral water, doodled on their pads. Galayev's face was pink and bright, like a happy pig. Only the Marshal remained totally impassive.

I've got you now, Askyerov thought. Before Galayev could begin the improvised speech he was obviously itching to deliver, Askyerov took some notes out of his pocket and recalled the meeting to order.

"The General Secretary's concern about bonapartist tendencies in the armed forces," he resumed, "is well placed. With your indulgence, I would like to draw your attention to a number of unfortunate recent occurrences following the sabotage attempt in Togliatti. I am sure that our distinguished Chief of Staff will share our concern."

Like a picador, he had placed another shaft, but the bull still refused to be goaded into action.

He resolved to be more daring. "Comrade Marshal, it has been said that you yourself encouraged anti-Soviet elements in the officer corps by your negativism in respect to Party policy over Togliatti and Afghanistan and other critical issues." His voice was as sweet as halvah.

That lance had found its mark. Zotov shifted in his seat. He said in a hoarse voice, barely more than a whisper, "Whoever says that is talking through his asshole."

Askyerov's flow was interrupted by the rattle of small-arms fire close at hand. The Prime Minister and several of the others jumped to their feet. The KGB chief, Chetverikov, had his hand on the butt of his pistol. Marshal Zotov looked as bewildered as the others.

A bulky man, his cap askew, stuck his head through the door. It was General Rostov, the head of the Kremlin Guards, a miner's son, and an old classmate of the Marshal's.

"What the hell is going on?" Askyerov screamed at him, losing all his composure.

Rostov seemed as confused as the men around the table. He mumbled something about unidentified "traitors" and "mutineers" who were trying to storm the building. "We'll soon have them sorted out," Rostov promised.

Romanov, with his folder under his arm, started sliding along the wall toward the General Secretary's inner sanctum.

"Where do you think you're going?" Askyerov shrieked at him, glad to have someone to bully. "Get back to your place!"

The artificial tan no longer concealed Romanov's pallor, especially around the eyes, where his skin looked like crumbling parchment.

Rostov reappeared at the door.

"Yes, General," Askyerov greeted him. The shooting seemed louder, and nearer.

"I don't know who they are," Rostov fumbled. "But they're professionals, and they've got automatic weapons. I've been trying to call up reinforcements."

"Well?"

"I can't get through to MVD headquarters, or the Dzerzhinsky Division. The lines are dead."

Askyerov remembered the break in the Kremlevka line. It hadn't been a false alarm after all. He fiddled with the knot of his tie, already tight against his throat.

"Call Moscow District," he ordered.

"I tried that too," General Rostov reported. "They won't send troops without a confirmatory directive from the Chief of Staff."

Both men stared at Marshal Zotov. "Is this *your* doing?" Askyerov yelled at him.

Zotov remained impassive, arms folded across his chest.

"I have to get back to my men," the commander of the Kremlin Guards excused himself. As he opened the double doors, the acrid smell of burning fabric filtered through. There was a fire somewhere in the building. There was a muffled explosion, and the dreadful sound of a man spitting his lungs out.

Askyerov ordered Serdyuk, the Defense Minister, to get on the phone to the commander of Moscow Military District.

"You know what's going to happen to you," he threatened Zotov, toying with the small pistol in his pocket. "I know this is your doing."

The Marshal paid no attention. He had taken to doodling on his pad, a very realistic impression of a gallows.

Serdyuk was still bellowing at an unresponsive telephone operator when the tall bay windows exploded into a thousand knives.

"Oh, God, I'm shot!" the Defense Minister exclaimed, inaccurately, as a splinter of glass stabbed his temple, gushing blood into his eyes. He dropped the phone and tried to staunch the bleeding with a handkerchief.

Then they were all coughing and choking as a stinging yellow gas billowed into the room. Tears streaming down his cheeks, bent double by a racking cough, Askyerov saw several dim figures swing feet first through the broken windows, suspended from ropes. They were a nightmarish apparition, dressed all in black, with black ski masks over their heads that revealed only their eyes and mouths. They jumped lightly to the floor with the rolling ease of parachutists and began to fan out around the room, their automatic rifles at the ready.

"Spetsnaz," someone muttered.

Conscious of his status, Askyerov puffed himself up and stammered, "What is the meaning of this?"

"Shut your face!" This came from a compact, muscular man who had begun to circle the table with a slightly bowlegged gait. "All of you: hands up!"

Only Chetverikov failed to obey. He pulled out his pistol. But before he could use it, the Spetsnaz leader dropped him with a single shot.

Somebody was hammering on the door to the conference room. At a nod from their leader, two of the men in black positioned themselves on either side, their machine guns at the ready.

The Spetsnaz commander continued to circle the table, peering into each man's face. He stared at Askyerov for a long time, and it seemed to the Prime Minister that his eyes were unnaturally bright against the black mask, the pupils elongated like a jungle cat's.

Finally, the man in the mask came to Zotov. The Marshal had his hands raised, like everyone else. Across the table, he could see Chetverikov's corpse, thrown back against the wall, where his chair had fallen. Zotov was breathing deeply and evenly, showing no emotion.

Two paces away from him, the Spetsnaz leader snapped smartly to attention, saluted, then grabbed the bottom of the ski mask and wrenched it up over his chin and his nose.

"General Zaytsev." He announced himself as stiffly as if he were on a parade-ground. "Commanding officer of the Spetsnaz brigade. I am awaiting your orders, Comrade Marshal."

"*Zotov!* It's you!"

This outburst came from Askyerov. Purple-faced, the Prime Minister was wagging his finger at the Marshal.

Zotov did nothing without deliberation. Slowly he got to his feet, acknowledged Zaytsev's salute, and plodded around the table to Askyerov's place.

The Prime Minister wriggled in fear and indignation as the Marshal clamped his huge paw on his shoulder, dragged him from his seat, and propelled him toward the door, beyond which the clatter of automatic fire and the cottony thud of distant explosions could be heard.

Using Askyerov as a human screen, Zotov advanced toward the main doors.

"Open them," he commanded the Spetsnaz troopers who were standing guard.

The doors opened outward. As they were flung back, a KGB sentry was thrown off balance and was catapulted over the shoulders of one of his comrades who was squatting at his feet, returning the fire of the attackers who were advancing room by room, corridor by corridor, toward the Politburo's retreat. There were a dozen or more KGB men outside. They didn't know how to respond to the spectacle of the Chief of Staff clutching the Prime Minister like a rag doll so that his toes barely scraped the floor.

Zotov roared over their heads, in his sergeant-major's voice, "*Rostov!*"

His uniform in rags, his face blackened as if he had been crawling down a mineshaft, the commander of the Kremlin Guards came staggering toward the door.

"General Rostov," the Marshal said formally to his old classmate, "everything is under control. Order your men to cease fire immediately."

Rostov was an army man, after all, even if he was in charge of a KGB unit. He hesitated for only a moment.

When the shooting had subsided, the Marshal said, "As Chief of Staff, I relieve you of your responsibility to protect these people." He shook Askyerov as if to demonstrate who "these people" were. "Order your men to lay down their arms. No harm will come to any one of them. You have my personal guarantee."

Rostov confirmed the order.

"Zaytsev?" The Marshal looked over his shoulder, and the Spetsnaz general came hurrying up. "You will place yourself under General Zaytsev's orders," he instructed Rostov.

The Prime Minister, whose chin was now supported by the Marshal's massive forearm, was in no position to object.

"Whatever you say, Alexei Ivanich," Rostov said. He sounded slightly dazed. "But are you sure you know what you're doing?"

The Marshal responded by dropping Askyerov like a sack of flour.

4 They had not forgotten the man on his deathbed in the clinic among the birch woods. At the same moment that Zaytsev's men were surrounding the Central Committee building, two five-man teams commanded by a young major called Metkov were speeding south through the Moscow suburbs toward Stalin's former dacha at Kuntsevo. They had borrowed their cars and their uniforms from the Lubyanka. They crossed the bridge over the Serun River and followed a twisting road through forests that swallowed up the light. The lead car came to a halt in front of a pair of high metal gates, electronically controlled. A discreet plaque announced the Cardiac Hospital of the Fourth Medical Directorate of the Ministry of Health.

The duty officer wasn't sufficiently impressed with the cars and the uniforms to open the gates right off. After all, the guests of the clinic included the General Secretary of the Soviet Communist Party. He came swaggering out and yelled through the metal bars, "Show me your written authorization."

Major Metkov jumped out of his car, obviously delighted to oblige. He came right up to the gates, but was speaking so softly that the duty officer had to lean forward to catch what he was saying. In that instant, Metkov got hold of the man's right ear and jabbed his knife up into his belly, just far enough for him to feel the sharpness of the point.

"Open the gates," Metkov said between his teeth. "Tell them."

As the gates swung back, the duty officer broke free and began running up the drive. Metkov flicked the switch on his knife, next to the guard, and the blade flew straight as a bullet and sank deep into the duty officer's back.

Two of Metkov's men took charge of the guardhouse. The rest proceeded in the cars past a two-story hunting lodge, fashioned from Karelian
birch, toward the modern glass-and-metal hospital wing hidden in the
woods behind it. Metkov saw a very old man in a wheelchair being taken
on his morning outing by a male nurse. He looked crumpled and disjointed, like a bird that had struck a windshield in midflight.

Metkov strode decisively across the lobby of the hospital wing toward
the elevators, while four of his men headed for the stairs.

A flustered receptionist came rushing over, but didn't dare question
Metkov's curt explanation: "Orders of the Central Committee."

There were more guards on the floor reserved for the General Secretary,
but they were men of the Ninth Directorate, and they didn't interfere
with a man wearing the uniform of a KGB colonel.

Metkov burst into the General Secretary's suite. There was a group of
haggard men in white coats, a woman sobbing.

"What the hell—" a startled doctor began.

"I have a message for the General Secretary, on a vital matter of state
security."

"You're too late, Colonel," the Kremlin doctor said wearily. "The General Secretary is no longer at this address."

Metkov looked past him. The General Secretary's loose, familiar features were eggshell white. The sheet had been pulled down to his chin.

10.

NALIVAY!

I have to harvest grain, but I have no mill; and there is not enough water close by to build a water mill; but there is water at a distance; only I shall have no time to make a canal for the length of my life is uncertain. And therefore I am building the mill first and have only given orders for the canal to be begun, which will the better force my successors to bring water to the completed mill.

—PETER THE GREAT

1 There were times when Marshal Zotov reminded Sasha of the general in Gogol's *Dead Souls*, a man "who, though he could be led by the nose (without his knowledge, of course), if he got an idea in his head, it stuck there like an iron nail: there was no pulling it out again."

It was impossible for the Marshal to conceive of a clean break with the past. He was the reverse of a revolutionary; he could only understand the present in terms of what had happened before. With a little help from his son-in-law, he had identified Askyerov as an enemy who had to be crushed, because he saw him as a second Beria. Now that supreme power had suddenly been handed to him—by a Spetsnaz general in a black ski mask—he could only imagine what to do with it by establishing precedents, even though it was doubtful whether there were any that could provide a solid handhold in the maelstrom that had started to shake Russia.

But the Marshal made a brisk beginning. Back in his own office on Gogol Boulevard, he received generals and admirals and issued a stream of orders that Sasha had drafted for him. The very first decree that he signed declared that because of "extraordinary threats to state security," full powers had been assumed, on a temporary basis, by the Chief of Staff. Any instruction emanating from Moscow would be valid only if it bore the Marshal's personal seal. The members of the Politburo were being held in protective custody pending a thorough investigation of a plot against the Party and the state.

Another directive ordered the release of General Leybutin from the Serbsky Institute. Sasha sent a special team to collect him and bring him direct to headquarters.

Leybutin looked better than he had feared—paler than normal, perhaps, with his uniform hanging a bit loose, but his eyes were steady and alert.

"How far did they go?" Sasha came straight to the point.

"Not far. They gave me the usual things, to loosen the tongue. The serious treatment was supposed to begin a few days ago. For some reason, the bitches postponed it."

"Are you up to handling something really important?"

"Of course."

"Pavlik, I watched you in Afghanistan, then at Togliatti. You were never afraid to take a stand. We need you with us."

"Would you mind telling me what the hell is going on? I've been in the loony bin, don't forget."

"We're making a revolution," Sasha said quietly. "It's only taken us nearly seventy years since the last one."

"You mean you're going to finish with the Party?" Leybutin said with a mixture of excitement and incredulity.

"It may come to that. There's still a lot to be decided. For now, we've got our work cut out just ensuring that our orders are obeyed in Moscow. Are you with me, Pavlik?"

"You know I am."

"All right. I don't trust Gukhov. He had too many friends in the Central Committee and he likes the fat life too much. I want you to assume command of the Moscow Military District straight away. It's all arranged. You will report to me personally. You'll need these." He handed Leybutin a document, stamped with the Marshal's seal, confirming his promotion, and copies of several directives that were being sent to all the army district commanders.

Leybutin's narrow face cracked into a grin as he scanned a decree instructing the district commanders to place all KGB offices throughout the Soviet republics under military control, and to arrest all Third Directorate personnel.

"The men won't have to be asked a second time," he commented. "But what about Party officials?"

"What about them?" Sasha shrugged. "They have been told to remain at their posts, to carry on as usual, that special instructions will follow."

"And when they do?"

"That's something we still have to agree on among ourselves. And it's one more reason I want you with me in Moscow. Now, there are some details we need to discuss." Sasha spread out a large-scale map of the Moscow region on his desk and began explaining his ideas on the redeployment of the Kantemirov and Taman divisions, to relieve the airborne forces that had seized the airports and railheads, and to tighten security around the perimeters of the capital.

General Gukhov, the commander of the Moscow Military District, didn't take his abrupt dismissal lying down. He arrived at Gogol Boulevard in the company of a formidable delegation, including Marshal Vorontsov, the commander of Strategic Rocket Forces, and an old rival of Zotov. They insisted on seeing the Chief of Staff at once. They got no further than Sasha's outer office. He had them relieved of their duties and placed under close arrest. Then he went up to the Marshal with a list of other senior officers whose loyalties were questionable.

Zotov glanced through it, and nodded his weary approval. "Make the changes," he said. "Let's hope that there's an end of it. If the country sees that we're not united—"

"The army is solid," Sasha interjected. "The men are with us. We only have to worry about a few politicians in generals' uniforms. The others will obey without question. That's the way they've always lived."

"All right, all right, but we have to justify ourselves to the people, and we have to do it in a way everybody can understand."

"We've already issued several statements," Sasha pointed out. "I have a group that is preparing a basic policy document that should be ready for your approval in a matter of hours. Even though the people have been told little, I believe that they're with us."

"I've come to a decision, Sasha." Marshal Zotov got up and lumbered around his office, shoulders forward, his hands behind his back, like a bull circling the ring, gathering speed. "I'm going to summon the entire membership of the Central Committee to Moscow. You remember 'Fifty-seven, don't you?"

Sasha nodded, while thinking that the precedent didn't apply. In 1957, when a cabal on the Politburo was getting ready to dump Khrushchev, Marshal Zhukov had come to the rescue by using the army's transportation networks to rush all the members of the Central Committee to Moscow, where they voted obediently to keep Nikita in his job. Now Zotov wanted to assemble the Central Committee in the same building that had just seen a shoot-out between Zaytsev's men and the KGB guards, counting on the bulletholes in the walls, no doubt, to keep the Party delegates in line.

"Just what do you think you're going to accomplish?" Sasha asked. "Do you imagine they're going to proclaim you a national savior?"

"They might elect me General Secretary."

"They might," Sasha conceded, "if they thought they could keep their jobs. Is that what you want?"

"All we have at the moment is a holding operation. We need a stronger basis, something that can pull everyone together." He bunched his fingers into a fist. "We've been ruled by the Party for more than two-thirds of a century. We need some kind of Party endorsement, the way the Tsars needed the blessing of the Church. We can't change everything overnight."

Sasha said, "We just have."

The Marshal studied him. "Don't be too hasty, Sasha. You put on a first-rate technical operation, and you'll be given full credit. But remember who's in charge. I want to be kept fully informed. I want copies of every directive that goes out from this headquarters. Am I making myself understood?"

"Perfectly."

As Sasha walked back to his own office, brooding over what the Marshal had said, one of his aides intercepted him.

"Your wife's waiting for you," he reported.

"I thought it was understood no civilians were to be admitted to this building."

"Yes, but under the circumstances—"

"Tell her I'll see her at home tonight."

"She's got someone else with her. Olga Nikolskaya."

Feliks' widow. He had already received a report from Orlov. The details were confused, but Sasha had understood them well enough. He had given instructions for Elaine to be kept in protective custody until the situation had stabilized. One of them, at least, had been spared. What on earth could he say to comfort Olga, when only the pressure of events prevented him from experiencing the void that Feliks' death had opened in his own world?

But he said to the aide, "Bring them into my office."

Lydia was subdued. She looked at him with a kind of pride. But he also sensed uncertainty and fear. Neither he nor the Marshal had said anything to prepare her for what had taken place.

Olga's face was red with weeping. He opened his arms to her, and she fell upon his chest.

"All of us loved him," Sasha said quietly. "And all of us will remember that but for him, this day would never have come."

"He left something," Olga said, pulling out an envelope. "He gave it to me just yesterday. He said I was to open it if anything happened to him. But I think he meant it for you as well."

Sasha glanced through the letter, scrawled in Feliks' minute hand. Feliks described the dream of a Russia "in which God and the people will be rehabilitated like the survivors of Stalin's terror." He expressed his fear that the "old gang" would cling to their privileges under the protection of "the generals they bought long ago," and that a militarized dictatorship could still prove that "imperialism is the highest form of communism"—a dictum that would have Lenin rolling in his grave.

Sasha lingered over the closing lines, a couplet from Vissotsky:

> *I want to believe that our dirty work*
> *Will permit you to see the sun tomorrow, without bars.*

He folded the letter and handed it back to Olga.

"You have to do something for him," Lydia said. "He ought to be buried in the Kremlin Wall."

He looked at her and wondered whether she, or her father, would ever be able to comprehend Feliks' letter.

Olga was shaking her head. "Feliks would never have wanted anything like that."

Sasha saw a place in his mind that Feliks had described, the place where Vissotsky was buried, and knew what to do.

"Is Father going to be the new General Secretary?" Lydia asked, shaking him out of his reverie.

"No," he said firmly, and ushered them out.

2 The borders of the Soviet Union were sealed, international telephone services were cut, and a total embargo was imposed on foreign news reports. Harassed Foreign Ministry officials knew about as much as, and often less than, the ambassadors and attachés who called them, demanding information. Guy Harrison prowled the streets like an alley cat, counting tanks. He managed to sneak a photograph of the bullet-riddled Central Committee building, but the sentries caught him and smashed his camera, after offering to smash his face.

While Russia turned its back on the world, the wildest rumors were accepted as fact, and, indeed, were hardly more sensational than the reality itself. The London *Times* ran an editorial entitled "The End of Soviet Communism," but a sober hand added a final question mark. The Communist press, both in Eastern Europe and in the West, began by putting a brave face on affairs with articles about the need for "resolute measures" against "imperialist intrigues" and "industrial sabotage," but soon lapsed into an embarrassed silence. From Peking, the Hsinhua news agency commented that the "fascist coup" in Russia had demonstrated the quintessence of Soviet revisionism. In Paris, the Soviet Ambassador paid a courtesy call at the Elysée, advised the Socialist President of France that his home country had passed under the sway of "Slavophile fascists," and asked for political asylum.

In Washington, the alarm bells were ringing. Since the first announcements had been carried by Moscow radio and TV, a crisis team had been assembled in the War Room in the White House basement.

"There are large-scale troop movements going on all over the Soviet Union," a senior Defense official reported. "Satellite reconnaissance has also detected several previously unknown ICBM silos in the Soviet Far East, targeting our military bases. Furthermore, two-thirds of the Soviet nuclear submarine force is reported at sea, a much higher proportion than normal."

"What are you saying?" the National Security Adviser asked. "That this whole thing could be a blind? A cover for a preemptive strike?"

"We know that Zotov, like his predecessor as Chief of Staff, is well versed in strategic deception. By closing down all normal channels of communication and leading us to think that they're in the throes of a bloody leadership struggle, the Soviets could conceivably be hoping to catch us off guard. We can't rule it out at this point. They've left us literally in the dark, sir."

"Are you suggesting that Marshal Zotov isn't actually the one minding the store over there now?"

"I don't have sufficient facts to pass judgment on that, sir. But if he is in control, I'd say we're in a lot of trouble."

"Joel." The National Security Advisor cocked an eyebrow at Carson, the head of the CIA's Soviet Division. "What's your people's appraisal of Zotov?"

"He's fairly primeval, even for a Russian," Carson responded. "I'd say that Zotov's idea of a Soviet security zone is a chain of Finlands or Bulgarias stretching all the way to the English Channel. According to sources with access, he has a plan to invade Iran, which would destabilize the whole Gulf area and panic the Saudis. He's contemptuous of the United States. He doesn't think we've got the stomach for a fight. He's violently anti-Semitic, and wants to avenge Israel's humiliation of Moscow's Arab clients on the battlefield. A few years back he authored an article in a

Soviet military journal that some of our people read as a thinly veiled justification for a nuclear first strike."

"Not somebody it will be easy to do business with."

"Not at all. Our reading is that one of the factors that precipitated the coup—if that, indeed, is what it is—was a rift between Zotov and the political honchos over the use of military force. He wanted to raise the stakes in Afghanistan, send combat troops to Angola, and so on. Our reading is that he will be more prepared than the men he has ousted to risk general hostilities. I think we have to prepare for the worst-case scenario: that we could be dealing with a bunch of mad bombers in the Kremlin who are actually prepared to start a nuclear war."

"Does anybody disagree?" The National Security Adviser glanced around the room. There was much tamping of pipes and clearing of throats. "All right, I'll get this to the President right away. He'll want to start battening down the hatches. We'll reconvene at three."

Before the crisis team reassembled, the President had issued the order to place all American forces on full alert and had requested his country's NATO allies to follow suit.

A time of revolution is a good season for insomniacs. The lights burned all night on the Marshal's floor at Gogol Boulevard, and both he and Sasha became round-the-clock residents of the building. Since the normal channels of command had been superseded, every kind of inquiry was brought to them. Was *Pravda* to continue publication? If so, who would act as censor? The Party offices in Togliatti had been sacked. Were any reprisals to be taken? The First Secretary of the Party in Moldavia had been caught trying to cross the Rumanian border under a false passport. What was to be done with him? Younger officers had organized revolutionary military committees in a number of districts, in solidarity with the men who had seized the Politburo. Were they to be given official recognition?

Few people had any firm idea what direction the country's new masters intended to steer; it was enough that they represented a break with the past. Despite the ban on public meetings, students and workers organized demonstrations to show their support. The day after the coup, ten thousand people assembled in Red Square, and no one interfered with them. The next day, there were two hundred thousand. Some of the demonstrators displayed the banners of the Association of Russian Workers, the underground union organization. Others, ultranationalists, swaggered around in their leather jackets, promising a purge of "cosmopolitan elements." There were people wearing crosses and carrying icons, and a madman who clambered on top of Lenin's Mausoleum and claimed to be the grandson of the Tsar until the guards pulled him down.

There was no organized resistance, not yet. Headless, the vast body of the Party seemed to be paralyzed, if not lifeless. There had been a few minor incidents, dogfights between army units and KGB or MVD personnel who refused to obey the directives from the Chief of Staff. In Eastern Europe, there were ominous rumblings that could presage an avalanche. Polish workers had taken to the streets in their millions, apparently convinced that the hour of liberation was finally at hand. Rumania's dictator had made a speech that suggested he was about to defect from the Warsaw Pact. There was rioting in East Berlin, and the East Germans had sent a special mission to Bonn. But in Moscow, and in Russia as a whole, the coup seemed to be uncontested. Askyerov and the other members of the Politburo were being held under armed guard at the Aquarium, pending the Marshal's decision on their fate—a decision that he was still resolved to share with the Central Committee, whose members were now arriving by plane and limousine, under army escort, for the special meeting scheduled to begin at 4:00 P.M.

Sasha arrived at the Marshal's office with Zaytsev in tow. According to the clock, it was nearly lunchtime. The Marshal's eyes were bloodshot, and the raised vein along the side of his temple was throbbing. He had the drapes pulled against the wintry light outside.

"You ought to take a nap for an hour before the meeting," Sasha suggested.

"There's no time," Zotov said impatiently. "I'm still working on my speech. Here, take a look at this."

Sasha took the paper from him. It listed the names of a dozen members of the Central Committee, half of them with high military rank.

"What's this?"

"These are the men who are going to nominate me as the next General Secretary," Zotov explained.

Sasha dropped the paper on the Marshal's desk and threw himself down on the sofa. Zaytsev remained standing.

Sasha said, "I think you ought to reconsider, Alexei Ivanovich. Fedya, show him the cables."

Zaytsev marched up to the desk and deposited a stack of telegrams from military headquarters all over the country.

"Everywhere, our orders are being obeyed," Sasha summarized. "Everywhere, people are rejoicing. They're celebrating the overthrow of a regime, not just a government. You don't need to go through with this charade of the Central Committee. If you do, you'll risk losing some of the support we already enjoy. You've said yourself that the Party is dying. Now is the moment to finish it off. You've created the perfect opportunity."

"What are you talking about?"

"Lock up the Central Committee the way we locked up the Politburo. All of them in one room—think of it! We won't have a chance like this again."

"And then what, Sasha? Answer me that. A military junta? The return of the Romanovs? Civil war? The people may be with us today, but don't be so sure about tomorrow. We need continuity."

"We need *this*," Sasha said calmly, placing a document in a slim red folder in front of the Marshal.

"And what's this, fuck your mother?" the Marshal glared at the title page, which announced "The Draft Program of the Military Revolutionary Committee." He barely glanced at the first page before erupting, "Either you think you're a poet or a stand-up comic." But he went on reading.

The opening paragraph read as follows:

The ideology of Marxism-Leninism, which has brought the people only misfortune and suffering, has been lifted from our society. The Communist Party of the Soviet Union, the exponent of this ideology, is dissolved. Ordinary members of the Party are released from all their obligations toward it. They are no longer required to pay Party dues. Members of the Politburo and the Secretariat are being held under detention. They will be brought to trial by people's courts to answer for their crimes. Other Party functionaries are required to register with the nearest military headquarters. They have no reason to fear. They will be offered the opportunity to return to the occupations they practiced before they became political careerists. Those who had no professional experience prior to their employment as Party officials will be offered vocational training. The All-Union Council of Trade Unions, which never in its entire existence represented the interests of the workers, is also dissolved.

Zotov snorted, but read on. Paragraph Three stated that

The operations of the Committee for State Security, at home and abroad, are suspended. Individual officers who have not been involved in crimes against the people will be considered for assignment to a new department. The Chief Intelligence Directorate of the General Staff will assume primary responsibility for national security. The militia have been placed under the authority of the Ministry of Defense.

Sasha watched the older man's face closely. It seemed to relax slightly as he scanned one of the sections that Feliks had proposed, on freedom of religion and the reopening of the churches that had been closed in the course of the long war against the country's believers. The Marshal actually appeared to nod his agreement.

Better if he can accept, Sasha told himself. Without the Marshal as their shield, they could never have made their elaborate preparations for the coup. When it came, the Marshal, like the others in the Central Committee, had been taken by surprise. But within hours, he had come to believe that it was *his* coup. It wasn't the first time he had borrowed an idea and made it his own. Perhaps he could do so again. Sasha hoped so, not only because, without Zotov, rifts within the armed forces might begin to open, but because he genuinely liked and respected the old warrior. And after all, he was the man who had shot Beria. That should make him a hero of any truly Russian government.

Zotov voiced no objections as he read:

Because of the lack of experience of democratic development in our country, and as a safeguard against chaos and anarchy, all political activities are strictly forbidden until civil order has been guaranteed. Providing they respect this regulation, political emigrés who left the country under the former regime are welcome to return at their own expense. They will no longer be considered enemies of the people under a Soviet legal code that has been abolished.

There was a lengthy section on economic reforms. Sasha thought of this as the "Zaytsev Plan," since it was in Fedya's house, after the grueling Spetsnaz exercise that had pitted them against each other, that the necessity for placing individuals in charge of their own fortunes had come home to him. The collective farms were to be abolished, and land redistributed to individual farmers, "so that Russia can feed herself again." The profit motive was to be recognized in industry, and light manufacturing was to be opened up to the private sector.

"Utopian," the Marshal muttered.

His frown returned as he came to the section on foreign policy, which

was terse. The basic drift was that it was sufficient for Russia to be *inde-structible;* the country did not need foreign adventures that wasted the resources required for reconstruction at home. Sasha's document stated

> The Military Revolutionary Committee harbors no aggressive designs. In order to prevent civil disturbances, we will maintain a military presence in Eastern Europe. But the citizens of the member-countries of the Warsaw Pact, no less than our own people, will be afforded the chance to develop their own course of political evolution.

The Marshal choked on the Afghan section, which was unambiguous:

> A schedule will be announced for the phased withdrawal of the occupation forces, whose original deployment was a major blunder by the former Soviet regime. The Military Revolutionary Committee will convene a conference at which all the principal factions involved in the Afghan conflict will be urged to participate in a power-sharing arrangement. The Committee is ready to sign a nonaggression pact with a coalition government representing all the popular forces in Afghanistan.

The Marshal slammed the red folder shut and threw it in Sasha's direction.

"You know what you can do with this!" he bellowed at Sasha. "I'll never accept it. I'm surprised at both of you." His glance shifted to Zaytsev. "You've fought those black-asses in the field in Afghanistan."

"Exactly," Sasha interjected. "We've seen what the war is doing to the army, and we don't believe it's worth the cost."

"Your whole approach is wrong," Zotov went on. "It's not just Afghanistan. You seem to want to back off from all our internationalist responsibilities, forfeit the influence we've acquired. You seem to imagine that the Americans and the rest of our enemies are going to love us just because we're wearing shoulder straps. You're making a big mistake. You've seen these?"

He held up some satellite reconnaissance reports.

"The Americans are mobilizing in a big way. I bet they're shitting in their pants. This isn't the moment for us to start swallowing the isolationist slop they gulp down like Coca-Cola. It's the moment for us to stand up and show that we're strong. That will help us bind the country together.

That's what I intend to tell the Central Committee, and they'll vote my way. You can count on it."

He rose, as if to dismiss his visitors.

"We have a different perspective," Sasha said. "We think that our most pressing priorities are on the home front. We've got nothing to fear from the Americans. I've seen them. Their politicians and their media prefer to deny they have any enemies, so they don't have to pay the price of standing up to them. If we make a gesture to them now, they'll shower us with gifts."

He bent down to pick up the red folder, which had landed on the floor.

"You didn't just suck that out of your thumb overnight, did you?" The Marshal returned to the attack. "Why didn't you tell me about this earlier on?"

"I didn't know whether you were ready to accept it."

"Ready?" Zotov mocked him. "Well, you were damn right. You have one or two ideas we can use, I'll admit that. But you can tear up this foreign policy shit. We'll do things the proper way."

"You mean you're going to preserve the Party."

"It will be our show, Sasha. You know that. There'll be changes, of course. But not all at once. We have to bring people around, build support."

"And disappoint all the hopes we've raised? Don't you see the people are with us? How long do you think they'll be on our side if they see that the system is going to stay the same?"

"I've made my decision," the Marshal said. "You are both dismissed."

"Not quite," Sasha responded. He held up the red folder. "We would like you to broadcast this to the people tonight, as Chairman of the Military Revolutionary Committee."

"Perhaps I haven't made myself clear," Zotov erupted. "You can stick that academic twaddle up your ass. We have to live in the real world."

"I'm sorry, Alexei Ivanovich. But with or without you, this is the way it's going to be. We didn't risk everything to end up with some kind of Soviet Jaruzelski. We would like you to lead us—"

"That's very gracious of you," the Marshal interrupted.

"But only if you are willing to accept the changes that Russia needs. I beg you to reconsider."

"Zaytsev!" Zotov roared at the general. "Don't just stand there like a dummy! Remind your friend that we still have discipline in the Russian army."

"I would have obeyed any order from you until now, even at the risk of

my life," Zaytsev replied. "But Sasha is right. You must do as he suggests."

Marshal Zotov's eyes seemed about to burst from their sockets. "Are you both insane?" he roared. "Do you dare to threaten me in my own office? I'm not fucking Askyerov. I'll place both of you under arrest. Believe me, Sasha. I'll do it."

"Then go ahead."

Zotov rang his secretary. "Who's on guard duty?"

"Major Petrov, sir."

"Send him to me at once."

He banged down the phone and said, "I'm prepared to forget this, Sasha. Your apology will be sufficient. Come on, spit it out. There's time."

"I can say I'm sorry, Alexei Ivanovich, and I mean it from the bottom of my heart. I'm sorry that a line has been drawn between us. I'm sorry you couldn't cross to our side. I'm sorry you insist on remaining in the past."

"Have it your own way, then!" the Marshal roared at him. "Don't think I'm going to make it easy for you because you're married to my daughter! You forgot to do your duty on that front too! I can see you make it a habit to let down your family."

Sasha folded his arms and stared at the ceiling.

Major Petrov marched in, armed to the teeth. The Marshal didn't recognize him. He was in Airborne uniform. He clicked his heels and saluted.

"Major," Zotov instructed him, "you will place these two officers under arrest for gross breaches of discipline and confiscate their sidearms."

Instead of obeying, Petrov turned and looked quizzically at his commanding officer, General Zaytsev. "It's all right, Petrov," General Zaytsev said. "The Marshal is overtired. He's been up all night. I want you to arrange an escort and take him home. He is to remain there for the next week for recuperation. Got that?"

"Yes, sir!" Petrov responded cheerfully.

"You bitches!" Zotov yelled at all of them. "This is fucking mutiny!"

"There's time for you to think again, Alexei Ivanovich," Sasha said to him as Petrov led him toward the door. "We're doing what the people want. You ought to be with us, not against us."

Zotov replied with a stream of profanities. Then he shoved his big face up against Sasha's and muttered, "How could you do this to me?"

Sasha slowly recited, "If you live with wolves, howl like them."

3 With the arrest of the Central Committee and the confinement of Marshal Zotov, Sasha held absolute power in Moscow. For most of the day the radio stations had been broadcasting military music and Tchaikovsky; Moscow television was off the air. At 7:00 P.M., the "1812 Overture" was interrupted.

"Attention! Attention!" said an unfamiliar announcer. "Stand by for an important communiqué." There was a pause. Then a tape recording of Sasha's voice came over the air waves.

"Fellow citizens," it began. "The dictatorship of the Communist Party has been ended. According to the decision of the high command of the armed forces, full powers have been transferred to the Military Revolutionary Committee, which is resolved to put an end to the corruption and tyranny of the former regime and restore the spirit of true democracy. Martial law is in force. We expect all citizens to remain calm, to avoid demonstrations, and to observe curfew regulations. All citizens are required to remain in their homes between the hours of 10:00 P.M. and 6:00 A.M."

Sasha summarized some of the key points in the program. He concluded: "The name of our country, which has been tarnished in the eyes of the world and our own people by the actions of the former regime, has been changed to the Union of People's Republics. The rights of all nationalities and religious communities within the Union will be upheld."

Vassily Fedotov, a taxi driver from the Eleventh Garage, had just dropped a passenger at the Rossiya when he heard the news. He set his headlights on high beam and started driving around the center of Moscow. Soon a procession had formed, and the blare of car horns chorused the church bells.

On Lenin Hills, university students broke into the building that housed the relay radio transmitter and took over the special network reserved for civil defense announcements. When Sasha's broadcast was repeated an hour later, the amplifiers carried it all across the campus.

An elderly couple paused by the swimming pool that Stalin had built over the rubble of the Cathedral of Christ the Savior. Dabbing at her eyes, the woman said to her husband, "Listen, Petrushka, listen to the bells."

"It's like the old days," he said. "It's like the birth of a Tsarevich."

At Gogol Boulevard, Sasha worked deep into the night. The office he had taken over was like a revolving door. Men in uniform rushed in and out, bearing messages, needing instant decisions. Leybutin came in with mud on his boots and dumped an object that looked like a piggybank on Sasha's desk. It was solid gold.

"What's this?" Sasha asked.

"We dug it out of Askyerov's backyard. There were six more like it. You wouldn't believe it, Sasha! His dacha was fitted out like a bloody emporium. He had a dozen big American freezers packed with prime meats, like a fucking supermarket! Whole arcades stuffed with fancy perfumes, video recorders, cameras, you name it! He had a Rolls-Royce and three Mercedes, and a whole library of pornographic smut. Oh, yes; show him, Vanya."

Leybutin's aide produced a sack full of Askyerov's favorite staple from his old freewheeling days in Baku: blocks of pressed diamonds.

Leybutin wanted to form a flying squad to deal with graft. In his no-frills, soldierly way he proposed to call it the Anti-Corruption Command.

"You don't need my authorization," Sasha said. "You're in charge of Moscow District. You ought to get some of those investigators who were on the tail of Galina Brezhneva. As I recall, there was an honest man in the Prosecutor's office, perhaps not the only one."

"It won't be hard," Leybutin said. "There are plenty of people who are ready to spill their guts, if only to save their skins. And the gang haven't had time to hide their loot."

Sasha turned the gold pig over in his hands. "Don't forget Askyerov's Armenian," he said softly. "He was holding parties in the Rossiya three or four nights a week, spreading gifts and starlets."

"None of those bitches was clean!" Leybutin exclaimed. "They were all in it up to their necks! If the people could only see—"

"That's an excellent idea," Sasha chimed in. He turned to Petrov, who was fighting a losing battle with the phones. "See if we can track down Kozlov," he ordered.

"Yevgeny Kozlov?"

It was a household name, like Vissotsky. This Kozlov was a popular journalist and balladeer who had got himself booted out of the Writers' Union after somebody ratted on an amateur satirical review he had taken to holding in his apartment on Friday nights. His usual butt was the lifestyle of the Party elite.

"Find him and tell him we're making him head of state broadcasting," Sasha went on. "Tell him to clean out the TV studios, hire anyone he wants, and start telecasts tomorrow evening. His first project"—he turned back to Leybutin—"will be to work with you, Pavlik. Get your boys to show him Moscow. Let's get all of it on videotape—the cars, the lovenests, the caches of black-market goods. We'll show all of it on TV, day after day, night after night. The Secret Lives of the Party Bosses. Well, Kozlov will think of the right title. That's his job. We'll show their fat mugs, and we'll run little excerpts from those speeches they made about Leninist principles and socialist morality. Then we'll show how they lived up to all those fine words."

Kolya Vlassov was waiting at the door. Sasha had entrusted him with provisional responsibility for foreign affairs. Kolya had a huge grin on his face.

"What's so funny?"

"We just received our first congratulatory telegram. At least one foreign government has decided to recognize us."

"Who is it from?"

"It's from West Africa. From someone both of us know."

Sasha took the cable. It read: "Heartfelt congratulations to my most gifted pupils. We welcome you to the ranks of the national liberation movements." It was signed: "General George Afigbo, Chairman of the Provisional Military Council."

"Our first ally." Sasha chuckled.

"I think the British could be next," Vlassov reported. "Her Majesty's Ambassador is urgently requesting a meeting. I think they've decided to recognize us."

"The lion may have lost its teeth, but not its cunning," Sasha said reflectively. "What about the rest of the Europeans?"

"I think they're holding their breath, waiting to see whether we stand or fall. The French have an internal problem, as you're aware." The French Communist Party, still allied with the Socialists, had denounced the officers' coup as a conspiracy against the Soviet workers, funded by the CIA. "The krauts don't know which way to jump. Our people report that the East Germans have gone rushing to Bonn with proposals for immediate reunification. They're scared shitless that their own people are going to string them up from the lampposts."

"Perhaps they will. But we can't tolerate any move toward German unification. Get onto our people at Karlshorst. Inform the leaders of the German Democratic Republic that they will break off the negotiations with Bonn or suffer the consequences. NATO won't oppose us. This is in their interest as well as ours. What about the Americans?"

"They're scared. You've seen the report." He gestured to the GRU intelligence summary in its gray folder on Sasha's desk. Since the declaration that an anonymous officers' group had seized power in Moscow, the Washington Administration had ordered a full-scale mobilization. On Wall Street, the Dow-Jones industrial average had dropped nearly 100 points in a single day, and the price of gold on the commodities markets had soared $113. "I think they were happier with the devil they knew," Vlassov commented. "They suffer from the illusion that anyone in uniform is bound to be trigger-happy. Their Ambassador is requesting a meeting too. I think it's just a fishing expedition. They don't know how to deal with us. They're scared we're going to bomb them into the stone age."

"See the Ambassador," Sasha instructed. "Tell him to inform Washington that I am sending a special envoy. We'll use the General Secretary's plane."

He looked at George Afigbo's cable again, remembering the raucous, hustling city where they had met, and the vipers' nest on East 67th Street, and the sanctuary he had found, for a time, with Elaine. All that belonged to a different age, a world before the flood.

Elaine had been held for three days in a private room in a clinic outside Moscow. It was a pleasant room, with a view across the silver birches. But there were bars on the window, and her door was kept locked, and the only person who came to see her was a woman about her own age who introduced herself as Amalia. She had a broad, friendly peasant's face, and she wore a gray military uniform instead of a nurse's white. Elaine couldn't even go to the bathroom without her. Twice a day Amalia accompanied her on brief walks in the gardens. She was chatty enough, on subjects like when the first snows were expected. She even pointed out a hunting lodge among the trees and said, "That used to belong to Stalin." But she closed up tight whenever Elaine asked, "What am I doing here? Am I a prisoner? Please tell me what's happening."

Then Colonel Orlov arrived, with a Chaika limousine and a motorcycle escort, and asked her to get her things together as quickly as possible. There wasn't much to pack, although they had brought her clothes from the hotel. She bundled up in a thick sweater under her coat, but the wind still sawed through to the bone as she crossed the courtyard to the waiting car. When they crossed the Moskva River, she saw that ice had already started to form along the banks. She studied the familiar skyline of Moscow and realized that something was missing. Where was the great red star atop the onion domes of the Kremlin?

"That's not all that has changed," Orlov said enigmatically. He was not much more forthcoming than Amalia.

She recognized the yellow hulk of General Staff headquarters from her drive with Guy Harrison. She caught a passing glimpse of the statue of Gogol, and found it unsettling. She remembered reading an account of the writer's final decline into madness. Gogol had succumbed to the influence of a monk who preached black reaction and told him that his books were a sin against God. He had ended by burning the manuscript of his last masterpiece. The story had shocked her. Russia, she thought, was a country of violent excess, even in atonement.

She heard gunshots from the direction of the river, and looked at her escort. He seemed to be fighting to stay awake.

There was a barricade and a machine gun post at the end of Frunze Street, and the officer in charge called someone on his field telephone before letting them drive through. As soon as the Chaika stopped, Orlov jerked into action. He rushed her up the steps, between massive columns, into a lobby that was swarming with men in uniform. All of them were armed, and they all seemed to be moving at a half-run, the heels of their polished boots clattering against the floor. There was something else that was odd, but she couldn't place it until Orlov had cleared a path for her and propelled her into a reserved elevator. There were no flags, no emblems, no photographs, as if the walls had been swept clean.

A sergeant in battledress watched them, unsmiling, as they rode up to the fifth floor. He was cradling a kalashnikov.

They emerged into a waiting area that was as bustling as the lobby below. Couriers raced back and forth, and several men in generals' uniforms were arguing with an impassive major about their rights to an immediate audience with someone.

Orlov took her arm and steered her around the crowd. "Tell the Chairman she's here," he called to the major, who abandoned his desk and vanished through a great padded leather door.

Elaine was conscious that all the eyes in the room had been turned on her. There was a buzz of speculation, some of it obscene. Elaine's command of colloquial Russian was not sufficient to catch all the nuances, but she caught the general drift, and turned her back on the men. Orlov growled something, and the voices fell silent.

The major came back, followed by a plump-faced man about Sasha's age who smiled at her and said, "He's waiting for you."

Seeing her hesitate in front of the door, he nudged her gently forward.

She was reaching for the handle when the door was flung back and Sasha was standing in front of her. He seemed enormously tall, even in that huge room with its high ceilings, and he had lost weight, so that there were shadows under his cheekbones. He was pale, as if he had been living in that room, with the drapes closed, since he had turned on his heel and left her in the parking lot near the Visotny Dom.

Her throat felt constricted. She could barely utter the two syllables of his name.

He reached behind her and swung the door shut. It blotted out the noise of the outer office, and for a moment all she could hear was her own breathing and the low hum of some electrical device.

She met his eyes, and they frightened her the way they had done at their first, unlikely encounter in Bloomingdale's. There was the same intensity, the same mixture of puzzlement and recognition. He scanned her face as if he was trying to make sure who she was.

They moved closer together, not in a sudden rush, but as if compelled by a magnetic force. When he put his hands on her upper arms, it was not clear whether it was to draw her closer or to hold them apart. But even through the thickness of her floppy sweater, she felt his touch as an electric charge, and her whole body quivered.

We are the same, she told herself. *The world has changed, but not us.*

He leaned over her, and her lips parted. She felt his breath on her cheek, the firmness of his body as they came together; she smelled woodsmoke and old leather. Then he pulled back with the sudden, curving motion of a pine tree whipsawed by the wind.

"Sit with me," he said, leading the way to a pair of armchairs flanking a tall window covered by heavy red drapes.

He could hardly bear to look at her. In her sweater and slacks, with her hair grown out of the geometric planes she had once favored and tumbling down to her shoulders, she was Tanya as well as Elaine. She was everything that meant happiness and peace.

He gripped the armrests of his chair as if he meant to drive his fingers through the fabric.

"What has happened, Sasha?" she asked, breaking the silence. "What's happened to *you?* I heard them call you Chairman."

"There are eight of us," he said absently, as if the subject had nothing to do with him. "We call ourselves the Military Revolutionary Committee. I don't suppose Orlov told you very much."

"He might as well have been mute."

"Do your remember the story of the French Revolution? Louis XVI was roused by his valet and he demanded to know what the disturbance was. Is it a revolt? And the valet replied, No, sire, it is a revolution."

"You mean, you've made a revolution?"

"We have begun," he said with renewed passion. "We can no more turn back than a bullet can return to the barrel of a gun. We have to succeed, to give meaning to the lives that have already been broken."

She saw again the man with the kind eyes who had been tortured because he tried to help her.

"Feliks was your friend, wasn't he?"

She told him how Nikolsky had died with his head in her hands, and she watched Sasha turn away, closer to tears than she had ever seen him. She went over and sat on the arm of his chair, stroking his hair lightly with her hand. There was more gray in it than before. She wanted to hold him, to comfort him. He still wouldn't look at her.

"Sasha," she murmured. "I love you. It's the only thing I've had to hold on to."

He put his arms around her then, and pulled her down so that her head was resting against his chest. She could hear his heart beating, too quickly.

"Tell me what you want of me," she said. "I'll do anything if you just hold me. I've been so cold without you, Sasha." She began to nuzzle his neck, to trace lines down his chest with her fingers, and felt his body beginning to respond, and for a wild, exquisite moment she thought, *We don't have to hide anymore, not even here.*

Then she felt him tense and disengage.

"Sasha, what's wrong?" she said anxiously. *It's because of Feliks,* she thought. *Because he died trying to save me. Because it wouldn't have happened if I had been able to keep away from you.*

"Don't blame yourself for anything," he said, as if reading her thoughts. "We can only go forward, not back. And you have to go back to New York."

She felt an overpowering sense of vertigo, of spinning downward from a great height, like the bleak ziggurat of her recurring dream.

She managed to say, "I don't understand."

He enclosed her hands with his. He said, "I can only be happy with you. But my destiny is not to be happy."

"Haven't we earned the right to be happy?"

"My destiny is something else. It is here, in the service of my people, and it will consume all of my energy. To make them free, I must reject any hope of freedom for myself. There is no place for us, no time. If we tried to pretend it was otherwise, I would end by destroying you."

"It's not fair," she protested. "You deny me any power of choice."

"Neither of us has the power to choose," he said simply. "Orlov will take you to the airport."

"Sasha." She looked into his smoky eyes, and knew she couldn't fight him. In place of the bitter words she had framed, she said, "Kiss me." His mouth sought hers, and she was falling again. She clutched at his neck, drawing him tighter, until she couldn't breathe. His warmth seemed to spread to every part of her body.

He said, "You take my heart with you."

He watched her rearrange her clothes, walk stiffly to the door, and pause before turning the handle. She looked back at him over her shoulder for barely more than a heartbeat, and he had to force himself not to call out to her.

The door swung open, and the Chief of Staff's office was invaded by the racket from outside before it closed behind her.

Sasha recited in Russian the last lines of Vissotsky's ballad about the wolves:

> Today, I am not the same as yesterday—
> hunted, hunted—
> and the huntsmen are left with empty hands.

He buried his face in his hands.

4 Guy Harrison roamed the streets of Moscow and saw them change. He was limping a bit, more from his gout than the episode on the road to the airport. The neon lights on the huge billboard in Mayakovsky Square, across from the cinema, no longer flashed out party slogans. The placards of Lenin had come down. The statue of Dzerzhinsky, in the square named after him, had been torn from its plinth. Churches that had been closed since Stalin's time, or even earlier, were open again, and there were lines of people out in the street waiting to attend service, the way there had once been in front of Lenin's mausoleum. The Metropolitan of the Orthodox Church inside Russia, a man who was widely believed to have worked hand in hand with the Fifth Directorate of the KGB, had retreated to a seminary. Underground priests had come out of hiding.

There was a fair amount of looting going on, even though the military authorities had threatened summary execution. The favorite targets were the abandoned apartments of the former Party elite. Squatters had moved in to some of the famous buildings on Kutuzovsky Prospekt. Street peddlers offered souvenirs of the former regime: only "five dollars American" for a genuine Order of the Red Banner, fifty for a cigarette case with Askyerov's initials. Harrison invested in the cigarette case, after some haggling. The initials might not be authentic, but the gold plating looked real enough.

Pravda and *Izvestia* and all the other Soviet publications had been suspended. In their place, the new authorities put out a fairly drab newssheet entitled *Rodina,* or "Motherland," which mostly confined itself to reprinting government decrees and listing charges of fraud and corruption that were being brought against former officials. The day Sasha had Elaine brought to him at Gogol Boulevard, *Rodina* carried a group portrait of the members of the Military Revolutionary Committee. Sasha was sitting in the front row, along with Zaytsev, Vlassov, and Leybutin. Guy Harrison thought they looked rather awkward, like schoolboys being forced to pose for a class photograph.

Various luminaries of the defunct Writers' Union were on the phone to Harrison day and night imploring him to find jobs for them in the West. A former editor who used to look down his nose at everyone turned up on Harrison's doorstep with his bags already packed, insisting that Guy should arrange to spirit him out of the country so that his literary skills would not be lost to mankind. Remembering how Erinshteyn had used to preach that exile was too good for people like Solzhenitsyn and Lev Kopelev, Harrison suggested that he should apply to the Bulgarian Embassy, where several *apparatchiki* were reputed to have claimed asylum.

Harrison went to lunch at one of his favorite spots, the Uzbek restaurant where he had gone with Elaine. The place seemed to be in complete disarray. But he could at least get a drink. He sipped it and wondered what had become of her. She probably knew more about what was going on than any of them. While he was sitting there, a large, boisterous Russian came in and greeted him as an old friend.

"Kozlov, Yevgeny Kozlov," he introduced himself, pumping Harrison's hand.

Someone else who wants an exit visa, Harrison thought. Then the name clicked. "You're the new head of television," he said.

"Just so, just so. I was just thinking about you."

"My dear chap. I'm flattered."

"Are you still writing for the London papers?"

"And New York. When your blessed junta chooses to let me file." The first reports by Western correspondents based in Moscow were beginning to trickle out. But the authorities insisted that everything had to be screened by a military censor.

"Things will get easier," Kozlov assured him. "Be sure to watch the TV news tonight. I think you're going to enjoy it."

5 It was dusk when the General Secretary's Ilyushin jet, escorted by the brace of F-15 fighters that had joined it along the coast of Newfoundland, made a slightly jerky landing at Andrews Air Force Base.

Washington was enjoying the dying days of an Indian summer; men went about in seersucker suits, their jackets slung from their shoulders. But the Secretary of State stood formal and correct in his pinstripe as he waited for the special envoy from Moscow to disembark. Admiral Lutz, the Chief of the Joint Chiefs of Staff, stood beside him in full dress uniform. There was a Marine honor guard lined up along the tarmac. Given the new complexion of the Russian leadership, the Administration had decided not to skimp on the military decorum.

The steps were rolled up, and a man in the uniform of a Russian airborne officer descended briskly, followed by two men who were obviously bodyguards.

Then a girl appeared at the top of the steps, fragile and beautiful, her dark hair streaming in the wind. She made an attempt to flatten it back into place before she started to walk down. She had an attaché case in her hand.

"She looks American," Admiral Lutz observed.

"Must be the interpreter," the Secretary of State commented.

She had reached the foot of the steps. She stood there, looking at the American delegation, while they looked at her. Kolya Vlassov, slightly uncomfortable in a civilian suit, followed her down the steps, with a couple of aides in uniform at his heels.

"I'm just a passenger," Elaine said to the State Department functionary who intercepted her. She started walking briskly away from the reception line.

A man went running after her.

"Elaine, wait. I have to talk to you."

She didn't slow her pace as Luke Gladden came abreast of her.

"General Vlassov speaks very good English," she said. "I'm sure he can answer all your questions."

"Elaine, are you okay? We didn't know what the hell had happened to you."

"Yes." She mumbled something into the wind as she quickened her stride.

"What did you say?" Gladden shouted after her.

"I said you could call it hell."

She let the glass door to the VIP lounge slam shut in his face.

An hour after Kolya Vlassov left the Oval Office, the President of the United States, acting in his capacity as Commander-in-Chief, ordered his armed forces to stand down. He nominated Admiral Lutz to head a special commission that would leave for Moscow as soon as possible to negotiate on the basis of the Russian government's proposals. There were already confirmed reports of mass rioting in Berlin and a rebellion in the western provinces of Cuba. A CIA intercept suggested that the Rumanian leader was preparing to flee to Switzerland with his family on a special plane. The Chinese Ambassador to the United Nations warned his American colleague that the Russians were mounting "a crude imperialist provocation" and that Peking would take drastic, but unspecified, action if Washington entered into new strategic accords with Moscow.

Admiral Lutz sniffed the morning air at Andrews Air Force Base before boarding his plane and said, "Good hunting weather."

The men of Leybutin's Anti-Corruption Command raided a lavish penthouse apartment not far from the Visotny Dom that had been the Moscow home for a famous American capitalist who had been doing business with the Soviet leadership for half a century. He lived in a style worthy of the Tsars, courtesy of a grateful Soviet government. He bestowed some of the art treasures he had been permitted to export from Moscow on kings and heads of state abroad to buy entrée to their banquets and receptions. Those in the West who had followed his fortunes with suspicion said that he was the prototype of the kind of businessman Lenin expected to "sell the rope" with which he would be hanged. Leybutin, dazzled and disgusted by the treasures that he found in the penthouse, saw a different pattern of light and shade as his investigators showed him the evidence of fantastic kickbacks that had been paid to members of the Soviet government. It was of no interest to him what this entrepreneur's loyalties may have been, if he had any beyond self-interest to begin with. What mattered was that, for Russia, he had acted like a malignant distemper.

Kozlov invited Guy Harrison to attend the filming. General Leybutin was going to be there in person, to make a brief statement.

Leybutin arrived late and angry, and hurled his briefcase with such force at a Louis XV chair that its gilded arm cracked ominously.

Kozlov rushed up to him. "What's wrong?"

All Harrison could make out to begin with was a long string of curses. "I should have squashed him on the spot, that greasy slug!"

It gradually became clear that Leybutin was complaining about the Deputy Trade Minister, Askyerov's Armenian. He had eluded arrest for the first couple of days after the coup, but the anti-corruption squads had tracked him down to one of his lairs, the dacha of an over-the-hill girl-friend, the widow of a Ministry of Interior official who had died under mysterious circumstances. It turned out that the Armenian and his lady friend were at the center of a very lucrative racket, smuggling vast quanti-ties of roubles to Kabul, where they could be sold for hard currency in the bazaar. The dollars and pounds sterling and Deutschmarks, in turn, could be used to buy up black market goods, from scotch whisky to video cam-eras, for resale in Moscow. Askyerov, the godfather of the whole opera-tion, was taking the biggest cut.

When Leybutin, who had been wounded in Afghanistan and watched several of his friends die there, heard the details of this smuggling ring, he was ready to kill the Armenian on the spot. When the Armenian tried to bribe his way out of his difficulties by offering Leybutin "one million American," the general went berserk. He seemed to be trying to tear the man limb from limb, and would probably have succeeded if his men hadn't managed to restrain him.

Leybutin obviously needed time to recover. Kozlov left him alone and wandered over to where Guy Harrison was standing idly inspecting the American millionaire's collection of Fabergé eggs.

"What will they do to the little bugger?" Harrison asked without look-ing up.

"The Armenian? Oh, he'll probably be shot," Kozlov said casually. "They'll put him up in front of a military court, because the case now involves war crimes. But they'll want him as a witness first, to deal with Askyerov and the others."

"What else have you got on the menu?" Harrison had watched Kozlov's first show, a guided tour of Askyerov's various residencies.

"Well, for tomorrow," Kozlov smirked, "I think we'll do the vice ring that supplied Bolshoi dancers and underage girls to a number of illustrious gentlemen of the Central Committee. The public can't get enough of it."

Harrison thought the same might apply to his editors. For a change, he had no trouble getting the military censor's approval for his story.

Sasha had personal business to settle in Moscow. He drove to the apartment building on Peschanaya Street where he had grown up. He had wanted to go alone but Zaytsev, who was in charge of security, had insisted that the rules applied to all eight members of the junta, under all circumstances: they were to travel with a minimum escort of four men, all of them drawn from Spetsnaz. There had been an incident just that morning, the first of its kind in Moscow. Someone had fired from a window at Leybutin's car. The sniper had once been an agent for the Third Directorate of the KGB. He seemed to be unhinged, and was almost certainly acting alone. But there were too few of them, as Zaytsev pointed out, to take risks.

So the children came running to look as he stepped out of his car, flanked by his guards.

He made them wait outside when he entered Number 14. It was strange that his mother had remained in the same place all this time. Thanks to his influence, she had got possession of the whole apartment years before. There were no longer noisy neighbors jostling for space in the kitchen. In what had once been the family room, nothing seemed to be altered. There was babushka's antique Singer, gathering dust. There were the snapshots of his father, and a newer photograph of himself, taken the day he first put on his major-general's uniform.

"Have you been all right?" he asked his mother. "Is there anything you need?"

Their conversation was stilted, but it had always been that. Her requests were banal, even ridiculous when addressed to the most powerful man in the country. She had been trying to get a new refrigerator. Could he help?

It was all so familiar, so predictable. But he sensed something out of place. The way she kept trying to shunt him away from a particular door —the one leading to what had once been that drunk Fufkov's room.

"Is there someone here?" he asked suddenly. And she jumped.

"No!" She said it too loud, and too quickly.

He gripped the door handle and turned.

"Please, Sasha." She put her hand on his sleeve.

"Who is it?"

She wouldn't say, so he threw the door open. There, on the far side of the room, crouched in the corner like an animal at bay, was Krisov. He hadn't changed much. His hair was sparser perhaps, his features more pinched, the eyes small and red like a ferret's. There he was: the once so self-important Party functionary who had deformed Nina's life. And she was still siding with him.

"He thinks you're going to shoot him, Sasha," his mother pleaded. "Please don't hurt him."

Sasha laughed, then fell silent, remembering Krisov's intervention at his grandmother's funeral.

"What's going to become of him?" his mother was asking.

"You know our policy." Sasha addressed this to Krisov. "Did you have any profession?"

"I worked all my life for the Party."

"What was your father's profession?"

"He was a plumber."

"All right. There are schools for plumbers. You'll report to this office"— he scribbled the address and a brief note—"by ten in the morning. As you told me yourself, Citizen Krisov, there is no place for parasites in our society."

His next call was on Professor Levin, long since retired from the university, who had found himself a couple of rooms near the Arbat. This time, Sasha broke the rules and went without an escort. It was painful enough to revive the memories of Tanya, and his first discoveries of the truth about his father and his country, without spectators.

Levin was nervous at first, then hostile, but his sense of history prevailed, and soon he was drawing a complicated analogy between the arrest of the Central Committee and the way Lenin's chekists had seized the entire leadership of the rival Social-Revolutionaries when they had assembled in the Moscow Opera Hall to indict the Bolsheviks.

He paused to roll himself another of his terrible homemade cigarettes, and Sasha said, "None of this might have happened except for you. And Tanya."

He trembled as he said it, reliving the scene of Tanya's arrest, and the horror of her suicide in the labor camp. Out of her suffering, his purpose —his whole being—had been tempered.

But the professor was shaking his head, and wheezing as if his lungs were about to give out.

"If Tanya were here," he said at last, "she'd probably still be cranking out *samizdat*. Against you."

"I don't think so. I think this is what she would want. If not, then"—he stumbled, but picked himself up again—"I've failed everyone. Is that what you think, Arkady Borisovich?"

"Don't ask an old man. Maybe you're right. It's not for me to say. Maybe Tanya would have sided with you. I can't pull up my roots. I'm a Marxist, Sasha. For all that I've seen, I don't blame the idea, I blame its interpreters." He started coughing, and Sasha was alarmed by the purplish flush that spread across his cheeks.

"Can I get you something? Water, perhaps?"

"No, no. You'll have to excuse me, Sasha. I'm not what I was. On days like this, I feel the chill of the Perm region in my marrow. Do you really believe you can win without the camps? Without terror?"

"We'll try."

"First the philosophers, then the terror," Levin mused. "But you're no philosopher, are you, Sasha?"

"You should know. You taught me history."

"Perhaps that's what will save you. The study of men struggling, and falling, and climbing back. Yes, perhaps you're right. Tanya would have been with you. She cared more about people than abstractions."

"I've come to you with a proposal, Arkady Borisovich."

"Can't you see I'm done for? What proposal?"

"For three quarters of a century we've lived with lies, to the point that they came to seem more real than truth. Even today, there are lies that I still don't recognize, they're so deeply ingrained. It's the same for you. How much more so for ordinary Russians! We have a lot of digging to do before we get to the bedrock. I intend to appoint a commission to write the definitive history of our country since 1917. All the archives will be thrown open. Think of it—the minutes of the Politburo, the dossiers of the KGB! I want you to chair the commission."

Levin mumbled something about his age, about his ideological objections to the Military Revolutionary Committee. But he accepted in the end, as Sasha knew he would. No one who had dedicated his life to history could turn down the chance of a first look at the papers that had been meant to remain sealed forever.

The Marshal prowled his splendid apartment in the Visotny Dom, and drank a great deal more Akhtamar brandy than any doctor would have countenanced. General Luzhin, still his friend and admirer, though firmly committed to Sasha's Committee, would come round some evenings to play chess. "It's their turn," he would try to explain to Zotov. "Our generation had its chance. Now it's up to the boys. Don't forget, most of the Bolsheviks were under forty." At first, the Marshal would get violently angry. Once he actually chased Luzhin out of the apartment and into the hall, where two of the tough soldiers who stood guard day and night came to his rescue. But as time passed, and the number of decrees from the junta increased, and the TV news every night added to the discomfiture of the former elite, Zotov began to concede, grudgingly, that his son-in-law appeared to know what he was doing.

Twice a week he traveled, in the company of his deferential jailers, to the state guesthouse where Lydia and his grandson were living. Once he found Petya playing the Russian version of King of the Castle. He had just pushed an older boy off the top of a mound in the garden and was chanting, "I'm Tsar of the Hill!"

He scrambled down when he saw his grandfather. The Marshal bent down to receive his embrace.

"Is it true what the others say?" he said to the Marshal.

"What do they say?"

"They say my father is the new Tsar."

"Don't ever let me hear you talk that way!" Lydia shouted at him, and hurried toward the child as if she meant to spank him.

Marshal Zotov saw the boy squinting up at him, puzzled, trying to understand.

"Let him be," he ordered his daughter.

He tousled the boy's hair and said, "There'll be no more Tsars, Petrushka. But you should be proud of your father. Because of him, Russia will never be the way it was before."

It was too early to tell, with any degree of certainty, whether Sasha and his comrades would remain masters of Russia for long. As the old order fell into ruin, spontaneous uprisings and demonstrations erupted all over the country, despite the new government's appeals for calm. Some of the people who took to the streets were supporters of the junta. Some were workers demanding immediate pay increases and the recognition of independent trade unions. There were ethnic clashes that pitted European Russians against Central Asians. Slavophile extremists were beating up Jews. There was a lot of random looting and brigandage, and in Kiev and Sverdlovsk the military authorities shot some of those who were caught red-handed.

Some of the surviving Party functionaries in Azerbaijan and Central Asia were plotting secession. Spokesmen for the Moslem Brotherhood, whose existence inside the borders of the former Soviet Union had never been suspected, surfaced overnight with a similar, but conflicting proposal: that the Moslem peoples of the southern republics should break away and rejoin the greater community of Islam.

There was trouble within the army itself. Since it had been revealed that the coup was not the work of the Chief of Staff but of a circle of younger officers, some regional commanders had cut communications with Gogol Boulevard. In the Far East, the District Commander tore up the order from Moscow that relieved him of his duties and set up private radio links with other disaffected generals. But when he issued orders for the forces under his command to prepare for a military assault on Moscow "to restore the legitimate socialist regime," he was shot by his own adjutant.

The Military Revolutionary Committee was supreme in Moscow, and seemed to have overwhelming support throughout European Russia. But there were fears that the stage had been set for the emergence of regional warlords, as in the civil war that had wracked the country after the Bolshevik coup, and for a long purgatory of starvation and fratricidal killing.

There was only one certainty. A man who had been a lifelong enigma to most of those around him had succeeded at what few before him dreamed possible: he had brought down the Soviet system, without war.

6 It was more than two weeks after the coup. Snow was falling from a sky like a coal scuttle, and the news from the southern republics had not improved.

The black Zil sailed along, in the middle of a little convoy, until the driver braked in front of the wrought iron gates of the old cemetery of Vagagankovskoye, where Vissotsky had been laid to rest a few years before. Only one man had been buried there since. The escort cars hovered at a respectful distance while two men in army greatcoats got out of the limousine. One was tall and athletic. The other was of less than middling height, but might have been hewn from the trunk of an oak. They both looked as if they had been up all night.

They walked together to the new grave, next to Vissotsky's, just inside the gate. They stepped within the metal grille that had been put up around it in the old-fashioned way. There was a simple bench, where they sat down, side by side. There were petals on the snow, blown roses, that must have been brought from a place warmer than this.

The shorter man pulled a bottle of Armenian brandy out of his pocket, **P08** and a couple of metal tumblers. He extracted the cork with his teeth and filled the glasses. Both men tossed off the drink.

The tall man took the bottle and refilled the glasses.

"Pomyanem," he intoned as he poured brandy into the grave. "Let's remember him."

For a moment, they sat in a silence that was absolute except for the feathery sound of snow falling through the branches of the firs.

Then the tall man stood up and said to his companion, as the friend they had buried might have done: "Fedya, why are you fucking a cow? *Nalivay!"*

ABOUT THE AUTHOR

ROBERT MOSS is the co-author of *The Spike* and *Monimbó*, and the author of *Death Beam*, all international best-sellers. He is a prize-winning journalist and former Editor of *Foreign Report*, the influential intelligence bulletin of *The Economist*. He has written for many American publications, including *Parade*, *The New York Times Magazine*, *The New Republic*, *Commentary*, and *National Review*. Born in Australia in 1946, he is a former Lecturer in History at the Australian National University and currently a visiting lecturer at a number of universities and NATO military academies, including the Royal College of Defence Studies. A recognized authority on espionage and terrorism, Moss was the first to reveal the Bulgarian involvement in the attempt to assassinate Pope John Paul II, in testimony to the U.S. Senate in June 1981. He has covered wars and revolutions all over the world and is the author, amongst other non-fiction books, of *Urban Guerrillas*, a pioneering study of terrorist techniques. He has interviewed many of the most important Soviet Bloc intelligence defectors. He divides his time between New York, London, and field research for his books.

A taste of freedom and power, a thirst for revenge, and love affairs old and new are the volatile elements that spark a new Russian revolution in this dazzling novel by Robert Moss, coauthor of the best-sellers *The Spike* and *Monimbo* and author of *Death Beam*.

Alexander Preobrazhensky—Sasha—is a man who loves his country but hates his government. Haunted by the legacy of his father, who was killed for trying to expose Soviet brutality in Prussia during World War II, Sasha grows up driven to avenge his death. Then Sasha's first love, the proud and innocent Tanya, is taken from him by the same government that took his father, and Sasha's hatred of the Soviet system deepens.

You fight power with power, and Sasha becomes single-minded in his pursuit of it. He lives for it. He marries for it. And he becomes the youngest general ever in the Soviet army. His secret desire for revenge never wanes—yet he still has no clear plan.

Assigned to a diplomatic mission in New York City, Sasha experiences his first exhilarating sense of freedom. He also meets Elaine, the beautiful American woman who teaches him that love is an emotion even more powerful than hate. Later he fights in Afghanistan and is sickened to realize that the "workers' paradise" is little more than a living hell except for the privileged few. He meets others, others who are dissatisfied, who want—demand—change.

Soon Sasha's plan begins to take shape. Russia—not to mention the world—will never be the same again.

Stunningly written and brimming with suspense, *Moscow Rules* is an unusual portrait of the world behind the Iron Curtain and staggering testimony that people and their emotions are more powerful than any system.